The Last Dance In Delta

There is never a good war, or a bad peace. – Benjamin Franklin

Hal Shearon McBride, Jr.

McBride, Hal (1937-)

The Last Dance in Delta

1. Post-Traumatic Stress Disorder (PTSD); 2. World War I; 3. World War II; 4. Oklahoma; 5. Baseball; 6. South Padre Island Texas; 6. Chateau Thierry; 7. Belleau Wood; 8. Peleliu; 9. Okinawa; 10. Pavuvu; 11. Small City Life; 12. Marriage; 13. Parenting; 14. First Marine Division

This book is a work of fiction. Any resemblance to actual events or persons, living or dead, is entirely coincidental.

"The Last Dance in Delta," by Hal Shearon McBride, Jr. ISBN 978-1-63868-060-4 (softcover); 978-1-63868-061-1 (eBook.)

Published 2022 by Virtualbookworm.com Publishing Inc., P.O. Box 9949, College Station, TX 77842, US. ©2022, Hal Shearon McBride, Jr All rights reserved. No part of this publication may be reproduced, stored in a retrieval system, or transmitted in any form or by any means, electronic, mechanical, recording or otherwise, without the prior written permission of Hal Shearon McBride, Jr

DEDICATIONS

**FOR
My Wife
BILLIE JEAN MCBRIDE
For a lifetime of encouraging belief**

**And
My Mother
FOLLIE BELLE MCBRIDE
I was a Fifth Grader when she first believed**

Special Recognition
Victoria Isabella Cuaderes McKenzie

Acknowledgments
Jon E. Conard
Emily Ann Tichenor
David William Walker

OTHER BOOKS BY THE AUTHOR

To Bear Witness: A Memoir (2009)

Who Be Dragons (2010)

Billie and the Boys: A Memoir (2011)

Gatewood: Tales from the Life and Times of Charles B. Gatewood (2015)

Just Thinkin': An Inaugural Collection of Columns (2018)

Table of Contents

CHAPTER 1: The Crossing 1
CHAPTER 2: The Summer of 1917 5
CHAPTER 3: Honeymooning at Kinta's Cabin 20
CHAPTER 4: By Train and Ship and Truck 40
CHAPTER 5: At the Bridges 54
CHAPTER 6: Into the Hands of an Angel 63
CHAPTER 7: The Homeward Crossing 69
CHAPTER 8: Home in Oklahoma 73
CHAPTER 9: Yep Baseball 78
CHAPTER 10: Sunday, July 8, 1923 84
CHAPTER 11: A Distress Signal 90
CHAPTER 12: July 1925 92
Chapter 13: The Atwater-Kent, Model 55 100
CHAPTER 14: A Roaring Good Time 103
CHAPTER 15: The Boy Needs a Glove 108
CHAPTER 16: The Fist Fight 114
CHAPTER 17: A Flathead V-8 121
CHAPTER 18: The Fairest of the Fair 125
CHAPTER 19: December 7, 1941 139
CHAPTER 20: The Last School Dance 145
CHAPTER 21: As You Were 159
CHAPTER 22: Examining the Unexaminable 183
CHAPTER 23: It's Just a Thought 191
CHAPTER 24: Committed to Paper 197
CHAPTER 25: A Dance with the Past 208

CHAPTER 26: Life on the Road 215
CHAPTER 27: Yet Another Lesson 221
CHAPTER 28: Spring of 1967 225
CHAPTER 29: Come '68 231
CHAPTER 30: New Year's Eve 1968 238
CHAPTER 31: New Year's Day 1969 253
CHAPTER 32: A Storm of Opportunity 259
CHAPTER 33: Life on the Island 269
CHAPTER 34: My Oldest Friend 274
CHAPTER 35: A Night at the Wannie 279
CHAPTER 36: The Mating Game 287
CHAPTER 37: It's a Fine Time for a Dance 290

CHAPTER 1:
The Crossing

FAMILY HISTORIES ARE MOST OFTEN a collection of loosely connected stories. Such chronicles begin where they begin. They conclude where they conclude. That is as it should be.

Sixteen-year-old John Joseph "JJ" Kelly left his family on their impoverished farm just east of the settlement of Kells in County Meath, Ireland. Their absentee landlord had again raised the rents and Britain continued its starvation policy in Ireland.

He made his way thru Dun Laoghaire to the sea port of Dublin. There, unable to find a vessel headed to America, he signed on with a ship sailing to the West Indies. Young Kelly was then able to secure a job on a sugar boat headed to Mobile Bay.

JJ Kelly, caught unawares of the raging civil war, along with two other Irishmen aboard, found himself conscripted by the Third Alabama Cavalry. After seeing a deserter summarily executed on his second day with the Third Alabama, JJ concluded his short-term interest was best served by siding with the farmers who surrounded him.

He fought with the Third at Gettysburg and Chickamauga and was moving into position in Natchez as the war was grinding to a close.

During his third week in Natchez, his squad ambushed a Union patrol probing for weak locations in the Confederate line. At this time in the war, a dead Union soldier was the best available rearmament depot for a Confederate soldier.

Here JJ found a musette bag with twenty-eight rounds of .36 caliber shells for his Leech and Rigdon long barreled revolver complete with brass trigger guard and butt plate and his breech loading Springfield. He evaluated his gambling winnings from over two years in the army of the Confederate States of America, saddled his horse, a self-awarded gift from the CSA, shook hands with General Hood, and headed across the Mississippi River into Arkansas.

Skirting settlements, he trailed the path of the Arkansas River until he neared Fort Smith. Having no desire for any encounter with the Union army, he took a direct western path rejoining the Arkansas River near its confluence with the Poteau River.

Now clearly in Indian Territory, he remained on the south banks of the Arkansas River until he reached Tamaha Landing.

After a run of good fortune in a dice game on the dock, he replenished his cash stores. Then, he improved his diet in the cafes of Tamaha Landing. Except for one stormy night, he slept outside. He would later tell of renting a room, drying his clothes and sleeping on the floor rather than risk becoming accustom to an off-ground mattress.

Reluctant to press his luck and remain near the Arkansas too long, he left Tamaha after two weeks. He followed the wagon ruts south until he again intersected the Poteau River. Then, angling to the west-southwest, he crossed the Winding Stair Mountains before wandering onto what he hoped was an available site to farm in the foothills of the Kiamichi Mountains not far from McAlester's Store, some fifty miles north of the tiny Choctaw settlement of Delta.

On a spring day at McAlester's Store, JJ met and fell in love with Kinta LaFave, the daughter of a prominent Choctaw businessman, rancher and politician. Young Kinta, fifteen years old with skin colored like chicory coffee filled with cream, was possessed of the round supple body common to her tribe, raven black hair and ample bosoms.

Although quite deliciously agreeable, Kinta was far removed from the slender, red-haired, creamy skinned, freckled chested Irish girl of his dreams. He discovered the reality of her pleased him in a fashion a dream never could.

Conversely, this exotic stranger with the oddest of accents, a Gaelic infused southern drawl was the material of her dreams.

They fell irretrievably in love. JJ Kelly and Kinta LaFave married within the year.

Under the tutelage of his father-in-law, Ernest LaFave, JJ learned the natural ways of the land and the unnatural ways of the business world in the Choctaw Nation.

Some three years later, again with the guidance and encouragement of Kinta's father coupled with a tribal grant of 320 acres of superior river bottom land and two sections of forest, JJ and Kinta moved south into the emerging community of Delta where they established Kelly Land, Lumber and Mercantile.

Prosperity came quickly to the energetic, outspoken and principled Irishman and his straightforward, unambiguous Choctaw wife. The couple built a two-story, four-bedroom home at the end of Apple Street on the outskirts of Delta. At the time, the outskirts of Delta were only six blocks from the center of downtown.

There at the end of Apple Street, in their large front bedroom and with the guidance of a Choctaw midwife, Kinta gave birth to their two sons, John Charles in the fall of 1870 and Earnest Joseph in 1878.

In a twinge of nostalgia for his family and Ireland, JJ began to seek his family. His best efforts were unsuccessful. However, his efforts did result in the Irish Counsel guiding a number of Irish immigrants seeking a chance to him and to Delta. Within a matter of years, the combined Irish and Scottish residents came to rival the Choctaw citizens living in the Delta area.

JJ built a church and imported a priest.

In John Charles, no longer a boy, JJ had his serious son, a studious and sturdy young man, who hung on his father's every word. He considered his father to be the oracle of all things business. John Charles absorbed all the knowledge the oracle shared. By his twentieth birthday, he was fully involved in the Kelly businesses.

In June of 1891, John Charles Kelly married Betty Finn Folsom. The town folk considered her to have caught the most eligible bachelor in the county.

Earnest Joseph Kelly came easy to saddle life and had an adventurous streak wide enough to provide his parents with many sleepless nights. In 1898, following an incident involving a railroad foreman's young wife, Earnest left Delta and joined Teddy Roosevelt's Rough Riders.

Local lore had him at the forefront of the charge up San Juan Hill. Finding military life to his liking, he chose to remain in the service. Ultimately, he succumbed to disease while fighting in the ensuing Philippine-American War. He never returned to Delta.

Upon being told of her youngest son's death, Kinta withdrew to a cabin on the Mountain Fork Creek at the confluence of a native oak forest and a stand of loblolly pine. She and JJ had acquired the cabin after it was abandoned by a Choctaw farmer and his family in the lean years following the panic in 1893. JJ found the man and offered him a scrap of money. The farmer accepted and moved further west.

JJ thought he had purchased the acreage because it had water and timber and it was cheap. It was Kinta who pointed out the "bones" of the cabin were exceptionally sound. It was constructed of timber harvested from the site. It had a native stone hearth and fireplace that covered three-quarters of one wall.

Kinta looked at the cabin and saw all the qualities of Choctaw craftsmanship.

JJ looked again and observed the previous owner should have built cabins rather than trying to farm. Kinta agreed.

Kinta found a place to grieve and start her recovery. JJ visited regularly until they rediscovered each other. Grief slackened. Love deepened.

CHAPTER 2:
The Summer of 1917

ON SATURDAY, JUNE 2, 1917, after their high school graduation on the previous night, Elizabeth Anne McCrary and Robert Peter Kelly were married in St. Joseph's Church in Delta, Oklahoma.

Bob's father, John Charles Kelly now commonly known as Charles, would feint his displeasure at the cost of having the family's favorite priest, Fr. Aaron Brewster, travel from his present assignment in St. Louis to Delta to perform the ceremony. In truth, this vailed complaint allowed Charles to blow his own horn, toting his ever-increasing financial prosperity. He enjoyed stretching the truth a bit while clamoring about the high price of acquiring a daughter-in-law.

The truth was Charles Kelly adored his new daughter-in-law to be. Her father, Dub McCrary, was a major landholder in the county and the owner of the Bank of Delta. Charles deemed Dub might be the only soul in Delta who could justifiably look down his nose at him.

Elizabeth brought both the community standing and the personal persona Charles thought improved the already commanding Kelly position in Delta.

And he was simply quite fond of her.

Further, Charles coveted her daddy's land. It didn't match the existing Kelly family holdings but it was high-quality farm land.

Charles Kelly saw the marriage as quite advantageous to him.

Papa Charles was quite aware that he saved significantly on the cost of the honeymoon. Bob's enlistment in the Marine Corp followed by Bob and Elizabeth's decision to marry before he left limited the variety of available options. The bride and groom's timeline made a costly honeymoon involving travel impractical to impossible.

When presented the honeymoon dilemma, Charles, never one to look a gift horse in the mouth, promptly suggested the use of the Kelly family fishing cabin on the Mountain Fork Creek. He proposed that with a quick remodel and a deep cleaning the cabin could be made into a proper honeymoon location.

Plus, there was already a very romantic family legend associated with the cabin that involved his father and mother finding their way back to each other after the death of his brother, Earnest.

Importantly, Elizabeth, already a nature buff and a fan of clean clear fast-moving water, approved. She was a devotee of John Muir. She had begun to read his books about the time adolescence invaded her consciousness. She openly wept when she learned of his death just a few years ago.

Being aware that over the years his wife, Betty, had been mortified by her husband's selective frugality, Charles believed this to be a fine occasion to at least appear as if he were opening his checkbook. He was aware his wife would be most embarrassed if here, at the time when her youngest son was about to marry a girl of whom she quite approved, he was seen to be even remotely chintzy. Charles knew the path down which his best interest lay.

After due consideration, Charles assigned his best craftsman and in a burst of wisdom, he placed the preparation of the honeymoon cabin in the capable and proficient hands of the children's mothers.

The mothers accepted. The opportunity to be in charge of one last component of their child's life gave each woman a sense of empowerment.

On the appointed day, Betty Kelly gathered up Bonnie McCrary, the mother of the bride, and the mothers took charge of the long overdue cleaning and re-outfitting of the Kelly family fishing cabin on the Mountain Fork Creek. Although the cabin was used, year-round, by the Kelly men and their guest as a base for fishing and hunting excursions, it had been unoccupied since a pre-Thanksgiving turkey hunt.

Betty and Bonnie were the first ladies to venture into the depths of this male bastion in years.

Quoting the story, he had heard from his mother, Kinta, since he was a boy, Charles had assured Betty that the cabin had excellent bones. Betty promptly concluded he was correct.

The cabin appeared sound. Even the split wood shingle roof appeared sturdy and intact. The polished raw wood floor revealed no stains that would suggest a leaky roof.

The view of the Mountain Fork Creek from the porch was spectacular.

Betty Kelly was rather tall for her time, standing about five feet and six inches. Although the padding of late middle age had embraced her core, her clothed silhouette remained striking.

Embracing the view, she placed her hands on her hips, thumbs and shoulders back, breathed deeply and halfway sighed, "My goodness Bonnie, this could make a girl take up fishing."

Bonnie glimpsed her daughter's future mother-in-law. The morning sun backlit her hair. The sunlight seemed to glide and bounce through her sandy tresses creating an aura around her head.

Bonnie thought some folks are just blessed.

Bonnie wasn't envious, she was admiring. Smiling to herself, she thought the woman was blessed with a waist and a bust folks noticed. It was the shape she aspired to when she was a girl.

Betty Kelly was surely a fine-looking woman.

Bonnie was short but not small. As to size, she felt fluffy. Her fashion choices suggested a matron of a greater age. In her efforts to conceal, she revealed. While quite generous in her assessment of others, she was hypercritical of the woman she saw each morning in the mirror.

Betty stood on the porch mesmerized by the Mountain Fork Creek. She wore a full apron. Today, a sweaty lock of hair tumbled over her forehead. She felt full. Her world seemed in order.

"What do you believe the men would think of a girls' fishing trip?"

"Well, I don't want to think about the condition of my house if I ever left it longer than overnight," Betty said with a falsetto alarm in her voice.

Bonnie laughed and answered, "Well, it would – My goodness, Betty, it has been forever since I have spent a night away from Mr. McCrary."

"Nor have I from Mr. Kelly." Betty stopped, smiled, then asked, "Did that come out right?"

Neither chose to share their unspoken wishes.

With the assistance of Tillman Johnson, a long-time employee of the Kelly's general store, Tillman's wife and their two teenage daughters, the mothers directed an intense scrubbing and cleaning of the cabin.

The cleaner cabin was then stocked with a wagon load of new essentials.

Sulfur was spread around the cabin in hope that all sorts of creepy-crawly creatures would be discouraged from intruding on the honeymoon.

The ladies, mothers and mothers-in-law to be, tired but quite pleased with the outcome of their efforts stood on the porch and gazed toward the Mountain Fork.

"Bonnie, I think the children will like this a lot."

When Bonnie didn't respond, Betty turned to see her staring at the doorway. She appeared lost in her own thoughts.

"Bonnie?"

Bonnie started. Her answer was not responsive. Rather she gave voice to her thoughts.

"Do you think your Bob will carry my Elizabeth over this threshold?"

"I don't know, I suppose. It is traditional. Has Elizabeth asked something?"

"Not of me." There was a hitch in Bonnie's speech, "At least not to me. Perhaps of her sisters." Following a broader pause, she said, "Not to me."

"Well, maybe the two of you will talk before --." Betty's sentence trailed and was left unfinished. She believed intrusive inquiries should be cautiously measured.

"They only have a few more days to be children," Bonnie pensively observed. She sighed and continued, "They just don't stay little very long."

She expected no answer and got none.

Delta was not so large that everyone didn't know everyone else. A community intimate enough that everyone felt they had a valid interest in everyone else's business.

Truth be told, if from nothing other than their parish activities, Betty Kelly and Bonnie McCrary knew each other well. Just not so well that Betty was comfortable prying into a mother-daughter affair days before a wedding.

The fact that Tillman Johnson and his family were completing the delivery and set up of a new bed frame and tick mattress, a wedding bed, amplified her sense of discomfort.

"Bonnie, I think I stomped on a line. Forgive me?"

Bonnie waved her off.

Betty was grateful that Tillman Johnson and his deep throaty voice inserted itself.

Striving to obtain her attention, Johnson said, "Mus Betty."

Betty replied, "Yes, Johnson."

Betty felt Tillman Johnson capable. He was a fixture at all the Kelly enterprises. He possessed the subtle knack for getting things done.

The purple black hue of his skin and his imposing physical presence were so striking it was impossible not to take initial notice.

Betty knew husband relied on Tillman Johnson and trusted him.

"Mus Betty." His bass voice fit his physical presence.

"Yes."

"Yes, Ma'am, Mr. Charles sent this box here along with this here note. The wife and girls be cooking the meat and fixings for a nighttime dinner. Ya and Miss Bonnie be lettin' me know how ya'd want ya beef steak. Appears a filet of sorts."

Stretching the sleeve of his denim shirt from under the strap of his Big Smith overalls, he wiped the sweat from his forehead.

He handed her a small cardboard box topped with a package wrapped in white butcher paper.

"And Ma'am, Mr. Charles says there be a note inside ya box."

"Thank you, Johnson."

Betty watched him move back toward the rough camp he and his family had cut into a grove of elm and willow beside the creek. Her husband had marveled at the feats of strength he had seen Johnson accomplish in the course of his work. Watching him move, clad in overalls and a home-stitched faded denim shirt, a shirt likely constructed from the remnants of a previous pair of overalls. A shirt now drenched in perspiration.

She looked at the bottle and briefly wished Charles had sent wine. Not that she liked wine better than the whiskey because she didn't. She was unsure about the preferences of her companion.

She briefly considered it, took a firm grasp on the bottle and moved on.

"Bonnie, Bonnie Lady, look what my Charles sent us!" Betty extended her hand displaying a pint bottle of Ancient Age.

Somehow believing she needed to provide Bonnie with some further clarification, she said, "A good bottled-in-bond whiskey and some fine local soda water."

Setting the bottle of Ancient Age on the table, she reached back into the box and extended two ten-ounce crystal rocks glasses.

"Oh, I like your Charles even more now. I was fearful I'd have to go with my nighttime toddy."

Betty looked at Bonnie and considered how much more she now liked Bob's mother-in-law to be.

"Well, I think we might just move your toddy time up a bit." Betty felt her upper body relax, exhaling as if punctuated with an explanation point. She thought what silliness.

Bonnie began in a sing-song voice, "Oh, Me-O-My-O, I do hope the ladies of the Delta Temperance League are not lurking in the bushes."

Betty looked at her and thought, "Lordy woman, how did I not know this about you."

Bonnie, an amused smile forming on her face, asked, "And just what does his note say?"

"He wrote 'Bonded spirits for bonding with new family. Enjoy.'" Betty smiled and added, "My Charles fancies himself clever."

Her feet stirred. She was pleased with her husband.

"Don't they all," Bonnie observed. "Husbands I mean."

They laughed. New roles and new relationships can feel awkward. But they don't have to.

Lifting an unnoticed fruit jar from the box, Betty announced, "And a taste of Miss Florence's dandy vinegar salad dressing."

Bonnie blurted, "Oh, I know her secret."

Not waiting to be asked, using her best secretive voice so the trees could not speak of her betrayal of Miss Florence's secret ingredient, she whispered, "A splash of Tabasco."

Matilda Johnson served a dinner of small beef steak filets, fish filets fresh from the Mountain Fork, mud-caked potatoes baked in the coals of the cook fire, parboiled poke salad and a remarkable green salad composed of an assortment of native greens and wild onions that Matilda had gathered from the banks along the Mountain Fork drizzled with Miss Florence's dressing.

"That was delicious! How on God's green earth did she cook those potatoes?" A fine cook in her own right, Bonnie knew good cooking when she encountered it.

"I don't know about the potatoes, but I do know I will never be able to taste Miss Florence's dressing again and not smell Tabasco sauce."

Both laughed.

Matilda wanted to share her recipe for mud-baking potatoes. However, protocol commanded that she wait until asked. So, she went about clearing the table. Feeling invisible, she left the mothers to their own devices and to the devices of demon whiskey. The pending marriage of their children weighted heavily on their minds.

Betty Kelly said, "First time I have taken a sip without my husband present in – well, I can't recall the last time I did." This sin felt fun, she placed a hand over her mouth to smother her giggle.

Bonnie McCrary smiled in agreement. Then, she said, "Me either. And I'm uncertain Mr. McCrary would approve."

Night sounds from the Mountain Fork Creek and its banks attempted to soften the mood. They briefly succeeded but the seriousness soon returned.

"Bonnie, you know we think the world and all of Elizabeth." It was more a statement than a question.

Bonnie nodded and said, "We couldn't have picked a more ideal husband for our daughter."

"I don't believe a mother can ever get ready to send her son off to war, it is so far away. It feels unnatural." Betty suppressed her tears and continued, "They will hardly be married."

"I've tried to talk to Elizabeth. She just says Bob would be going off to war anyway and she would be left alone. She told me she wanted the two weeks as Bob's wife rather than being the girl friend he left behind. He would be her Bob."

Betty could only muster, "Well."

She thought, forming the words but not speaking them, "Her Bob, my Bob. Damn changes are so hard."

Betty was uncertain as to exactly when ownership of her son had changed hands but she knew as certainly as she knew the sun would rise in the morning that it had. Her tears came.

She tried to smile to quash her tears. She couldn't.

Finally, tapping down the tears with her sleeve, she said, "Darn it Bonnie, I am thrilled he is marrying Elizabeth. She is a treasure and I know it. But it hurts terribly and I don't know why."

Searching to change the subject, Betty, her voice more forceful than she intended, exclaimed, "What on earth did you tell Elizabeth about married life?"

The words were no more than out of her mouth when she wished she could retrieve them. Or at least soften them. Charles had an expression for what she had done, "Your mouth just overloaded your rear end."

As Betty was praying the words hadn't been heard, Bonnie was answering, "Do you mean about wedding days or wedding nights, the honeymoon talk? Or the nitty gritty of a marriage?"

Bonnie's face flushed, then became somber as she continued, "Oh, Lord, I've said nothing. I've just wormed around it. And she has hinted."

Her speech quickened revealing her heart, "I'm at such a loss. My Mam only told me that Mr. McCrary would know what to do."

She took a deep breath and moved on, "He didn't. Not really. Oh, God, this is so embarrassing."

She took another drink of Ancient Age.

The women quieted. The sounds of the creek became more soothing. As the water raced over unforgiving stones that created the rapids, dusk deepened. The stream's melody softened. Without effort, its essence inhaled them.

Betty strove for a reassuring breath. She feared she had overstepped her bounds. She wouldn't have been concerned but she didn't know where the boundaries were. Marital relations, while perhaps a mental preoccupation, were just never the topic of conversation. Not even between spouses.

She took a small sip and then another. She liked the bite of the dark amber liquid. As she sipped, she saw through the glass Bonnie was taking a much larger drink.

Whiskey talk? Maybe.

"Elizabeth is my adventurous child. I always expected to open a door and find her smoking a cigar. But I was never concerned about her and boys. She sat her cap for Bob so young, in about the Eighth Grade. She never seemed to consider another boy."

Having no idea what that meant or how to respond, Betty laughed and said, "She is such a sweet girl."

Bonnie continues, "My Elizabeth was adventuresome but I never worried Bob would get her in trouble. They just have too much common sense between them."

Betty smiled. She took the bottle and poured two more fingers into Bonnie's glass. "I think we could both do with another sip."

"Or three." Bonnie matched Betty's smile.

Bonnie swirled the glass, watching the amber liquid circle the glass.

"Betty, if you had my daughter's ear, you could tell her anything, what would you tell her – woman to woman? What would it be?

Betty hesitated, then chose a most straight forward answer, "I'd tell her don't expect it to be tidy because it isn't." She stopped, swallowed a chuckle and then added, "Bring a towel."

"Oh my, you're just awful!" Her laugh started at her belly and worked its way up. "I'll pack one."

Laughter overwhelmed both women.

"I do regret I didn't spend more time explaining the facts to her when she matured." Bonnie became pensive. "When her monthly came, she talked with her sisters."

Momentarily, Bonnie added, "Just how do you tell a daughter about dabbling?"

"Dabbling?"

"Yes, you know, dabbling." Bonnie made a gesture involving the fingers of both hands that clarified the nature of her question.

Betty had no ready answer.

After a moment she said, "I was really lucky to have Maw Kinta around when my dabbling days began. She was such a neat lady."

The darkness deepened around the mothers, then encircled them. Nights on the Mountain Fork didn't descent suddenly like the dropping of a curtain, rather they seemed to melt along the hillside. The light softened to the shade of the hills. Then, it was dark.

"Bob did come to me once after some big-mouth at school felt it necessary to explain relations to him. He came storming in the back door madder than an old wet hen and told me what he had heard." Thinking ahead to the completion of her story, Betty was suppressing a giggle.

"Then he gave me his sternest stare and asked, "You wouldn't let Daddy do that to you, would you?"

Bonnie laughed, spewing out her partially swallowed drink.

"Oh, whatever did you say?"

"I told him it wasn't something he need to worry about. He said, well, good and went outside to play."

The women's uncontainable giggles broke over the Mountain Fork Creek.

Betty noticed that her feet were getting puggy, an uncomfortable sensation that seemed to attack her now and again as she tired. She adjusted her seat in the chair and then stretched the arches of her feet.

Finally, she crossed her legs beneath her skirts, grateful she had worn a house dress and very few foundations.

Bonnie asked, "Is there such a thing as a mother-son talk? I just know you are going to tell him something."

"I'm going to tell him a good wife is the finest gift God can give a man. I don't remember when I first heard that but I've lived long enough to know how true it is."

Betty continued, "With that said, I don't know what his father might have told him. I'm fearful of Charles' marital insights."

She thought, "Oh, if you only knew." But she left the words unspoken.

"I suppose I should tell Elizabeth that a wife and mother must be the moral center of home," Bonnie pondered her statement and then added, "She's faithful to our church's teaching. I just know she will be a good mother. She will raise our grandchildren in the church."

"About that, I have no doubts."

"Oh, right now I have more doubts than Thomas."

Betty started for the door, then abruptly stopped. She turned and looked back toward the creek.

"What?" asked Bonnie.

"My Daddy believed you must always say good night to running water," Betty answered. "So, I did."

"And just what did the creek say?"

"It said tell Bonnie not to forget the whiskey."

As Betty was pulling her final brush strokes through her hair, Bonnie knocked on the ornate wooden dressing screen custom built for the room. Acknowledged, she then peeked around the corner.

"Your hair is lovely. So, red. Your curls fall perfectly." Bonnie took a breath and finished, "Well, your hair is just perfect."

Bonnie's breath revealed a recent fortifying sip of Ancient Age. Her flushed cheeks confirmed the revelation.

Betty, very proud of her hair, had a persistent awareness of other women's hair. She said, "Thank you. A bit ago, under the lamplight, your hair had an extraordinary luster."

Completing the brush stroke, she sought confirmation of her assumption, "What do you use?"

Bonnie, pleased for the acknowledgement said, "Oh, now a new concoction that Mildred mixed in her shop. She gave me the recipe. I have it at the house. I know White Vaseline, a little powdered orris root, a touch of bergamot oil – well, I have the recipe written down at home."

"I just love the citrus scent of the bergamot," Betty said.

Bonnie hesitated. There was a brief silence.

With an anxiety provoked stammer, Bonnie continued, "Betty – I – Er – I have talked to Elizabeth about avoiding getting pregnant – right now. Bob will be gone – She wouldn't listen to me."

Betty's first impulse was to make some statement affirming the teachings of their church in the matter of birth control. But she just couldn't. Bonnie was clearly too distressed for such a commentary.

Bonnie blurted, "Do you think Bob would talk Dr. McMann – at his pharmacy – about some – some – barriers." Her vocabulary failing, she attempted a hesitant clarification,, "Rubbers." She flushed. She couldn't believe she knew the word much less said it.

Betty believed most wives knew more about such things than they would admit but she was almost surprised that Bonnie would acknowledge she even knew the good Dr. McMann's inventory included such items. Bonnie was just too Catholic. Yet, here she was suggesting her daughter be a party to such sin.

As Betty tried to organize a response, tears burst from Bonnie's eyes like oil gushing from one of Tom Slick's wells. A lace hankie, too delicate for the task, dapped at her eyes.

After a couple of sputtering breaths, Bonnie confessed, "I tried to talk with Elizabeth about this but she bluntly told me that her plans for children were none of my business."

Again, the tears flowed.

She continued between the sobs, "It is more of my business than she will know until she has a daughter of her own."

"Oh, Sweet Mary Mother of God, don't fret yourself so."

"I can't help it. What if the Daughters of Isabella discovered I harbored such a thought?"

"Now, the Daughters haven't arrived in Delta yet. And frankly I don't think our Knights will ever perceive the need for an auxiliary."

Between sobs and sighs, Bonnie continued, "The thought of Elizabeth being with child when her husband is so very far from her, a whole world away. The best of confinements is isolating."

"Betty, expecting a child is so hard. My last time I was just enormous. And I had three teenage daughters. When I did go out, I felt like everyone was staring. My girls felt it too. My eldest, Mary Constance, she would never say it but I know she was thinking you and Daddy have been doing it. She called me a hypocrite."

Bonnie paused, sobbed a silent sob and continued, "All my girls were thinking it. Heck, I was thinking it."

"Oh, my Bonnie, all of us know what it is like to be looked at." A long-repressed thought jumped into Betty's consciousness and was given voice, "Sweet Mary, do you remember that old man, holier-than-thou, Donald Smithson? I felt his lecherous gaze every Sunday."

Betty tried to find a stopping place, couldn't and so she moved on, "I was young and I prayed to Holy Mary to erase the evil thoughts from his mind and if that didn't work, to strike him blind."

Bonnie swallowed and her face relaxed. Her Little Billy was four now and the absolute light of her life. She now told herself that his conception was predestined. Barriers would have made no difference.

"Bonnie, I'll take care of it. Bob will have – some barriers. Just don't fret about it."

"Oh, Betty." Bonnie's uncomplicated thanks required no more words.

In a final spasm of doubt, Bonnie asked, "You do understand?"

Betty nodded. Betty more than understood, she commonly sinned herself. She sinned and conceived no more. She sinned and asked for forgiveness.

Betty didn't tell Bonnie that she would see her Charles shared his supply of condoms he kept carefully concealed in the back of his underwear drawer. The how didn't seem so critical as that it was done.

Betty thought I could have reassured her by telling her that my Charles would have no use for a rubber, he called them rubbers, if he didn't.

Betty did feel it was her sin. On those evenings, she would say, "You'll need yours tonight."

She thought, "I guess I call them yours."

Continuing, she thought, "Some nights I just need to feel safe." She smiled. "Nights I go secret sinning with Charles."

Betty liked this secret.

She laid down her brush. She looked thoughtfully into the mirror.

She intensified her gaze, then talking directly to her reflection, she said, "Rubber, rubber, rubber."

She laughed.

Bonnie poked her head around the screen and looked questioningly.

Betty waved her off and said, "Marriage requires such interesting compromises of a woman."

Bonnie nodded her understanding.

The cabin's one large room was lit by three oil lamps burning brightly with the new wicks and mantles. The fireplace with its large native stone hearth tossed a flickering light out into the room.

Beside each chair was a sturdy end table. Two books and two magazines were placed on each table.

Bonnie was nestled deep into a chair, a magazine in her lap.

As she sat, Betty said, "Do you think they will have any trouble discerning whose seat is whose? Or does the one with the Photoplays speak for itself?"

Bonnie laughed and said, "Well, Elizabeth does like the Life Magazines, too."

"I did think <u>O Pioneers</u> by one chair and the new Zane Grey book by the other might give them a hint."

Wedding plans now aside, with night sounds trickling in through the windows, the women read with only the occasional interruption.

"Do you want this other Photoplay?"

"I just can't wait for <u>Romance in the Redwoods</u>, the new Mary Pickford movie."

"I want to see <u>The Immigrant</u> too. I have read Charlie Chaplin is just super good."

"Yes, me too. I just adore the Little Tramp."

"Bonnie, it's bedtime for me. Please read as late as you want. Charles will often lay beside me and read late into the night. It truly doesn't bother me."

"Thank you, I'll not be long."

"Did you see the Victrola by the bed? It was Charles idea. He thought the kids would like to dance to the new version of The Missouri Waltz."

"Oh, the Elise Baker one. I like it."

"Just when I didn't think he had a romantic bone in his body, he pulls something like this. He went to the trouble of getting a Victor Talking Machine, Tabletop Model 109. You have no idea how many times I've hear that. He is quite proud of it."

"As long as it isn't playing Over There!"

The Mothers laughed.

CHAPTER 3:
Honeymooning at Kinta's Cabin

THE CLATTER OF THE MODEL T MOTOR coupled with the racket arising from cans tied to its bumper provided an ideal juxtaposition to the pastoral setting of the honeymooners' cabin. The dust rose from the ruts as the wheels passed along them.

At first, the couple was lost in nervous chatter. The bride scooted over on the bench seat, nestling next to the groom. Her thoughts wafted back to their wedding.

Her wedding gown was divine and white. The soft fabric had flowed nicely over her body. The gown poured over her shoulders, its back a deep V cleavage dropping to the small of her back, before spilling into a train that formed a circle behind her. Exquisite embroidered areas went from the train to waist. The ruffled details on the short and gracefully sinuous sleeves were just perfect.

She had chosen a white lace chapel cap to cover her head. The thought sent her hand to her head, checking to see that the delicate pink cloche hat she wore was still securely in place.

It was a gown she intended to store so that her eldest daughter might wear it. She deemed it perfect, timeless.

Her husband, dressed in the morning coat she insisted he wear, had been dashing standing beside her in the receiving line at the reception.

Suddenly, as the ruts ended, the groom made a quick left turn, out of the ruts and bounced into the recently mowed grassy area that served as parking. He laughed as the major portion of the following dust settled away from them. Although she felt somewhat surprised and in disarray, the bride joined him.

The trailing dust settled past them.

"Well, my love, we are here. At the end of the road."

The jubilant groom was quite pleased with himself. He leaned over and kissed his bride. They lingered, delighting in the moment.

He got out of the car, walked to her door and then with great flourish, he opened it. She placed her hand on his extended arm and like a princess, she left her Ford carriage. She smiled.

Bob Kelly and Elizabeth McCrary, now Kelly, were married. The wedding was as she had dreamed it. She had basked in family, friends, flowers and fine food. Youth abounded and was served.

Bob paused at the door. It was his intention to kiss his bride and then carry her over the cabin threshold. Most unexpectedly, his feelings overwhelmed him, leaving him voiceless.

Gazing at Elizabeth, Bob shook his head in disbelieve. He cradled her face and tried to organize his thoughts. He looked at her.

"What?" She asked. She looked puzzled.

"It is like I'm seeing you – for the first time."

"Oh, you silver-tongued devil." Elizabeth had been holding this line for a long time. Now, she chose to use it. She was pleased.

"Elizabeth, I looked at you and –." He shook his head and tried again, "I was enthralled, maybe. I don't know. I don't know, it's all so new."

She put a finger to her lips and shushed him. She understood enough.

As she looked at him, she remembered exactly how much she adored his Irish blue eyes, eyes flecked with a golden brown. She watched as his contemplative look begin to transform his expression. She closed her eyes.

The tips of his fingers caressed the curl at her temples. His palms now formed a cradle beneath the line of her jaw. His hands were not soft, nor were they rough or calloused. She had held his hands. They had touched her. She thought she knew them so well.

Elizabeth said, "I feel so safe, so utterly completely safe."

She chastised herself, saying to herself, "You, Elizabeth the wizard of words, the insatiable reader and all you can say is safe."

Against any reason, it was how she felt. She felt secure and protected.

Bob moved her toward him and he kissed her, a lingering and unhurried kiss.

"Elizabeth Kelly, I love you."

He picked her up and nudged the door with his shoulder. It didn't budge. He pushed again, a little firmer. The door remained unmoved.

Bob, now red-faced, glared at the door. Elizabeth successfully stifled a laugh.

Trying to give her voice it's most seductive quality, she suggested, "Maybe you should unlock it."

Elizabeth broke into a full girlish giggle as Bob's face further flushed.

Without a word, he sat her on her feet, unlatched the door and pushed. The door glided open. Again, he lifted his bride and with her in his arms stepped over the threshold. He walked directly to the bed and unceremoniously dropped her on to it.

She bounced once. Her dress tail flew toward her waist.

She looked up, hair and clothing in disarray, and said, "I didn't latch the door." She laughed.

With the bumpy landing, Elizabeth instinctively straightened her dress. She caught Bob's glance. His expression betrayed his hesitancy, his indecision.

Aware of his attention, she slowly completed adjusting her clothing, and then sat upright on the side of the bed and said, "Tonight."

"Tonight." A relieved pause. "It is time to uncork this bottle of Champagne."

He stepped onto the porch, leaned against the rail and reassured himself. "Tonight."

The Champagne cork sailed toward the Mountain Fork. He would later tell tales of the cork landing in the creek and floating away. It didn't.

The crystal-clear waters arising from several mountain springs sped over the Mountain Fork's rocky bed gave rise to pleasing opus. The newlyweds, quite exhausted from their wedding day, sat quietly listening to the sounds as evening fell. The chatters and calls of the nocturnal animals, eager to begin their nighttime prowl, provided a staccato counterpoint to the calming melodies of the waters.

Elizabeth allowed the evening to engulf her. She searched her mind for a fitting literary-style descriptor for her thoughts about the creek. So pleasing and intricate, yet try as she might, she could detect no recurring pattern to this natural union of notes and rhythms.

Most music captivated her. These sounds surrounded her, soothed her, caressed her and held her dear.

She was unsure where the soft throaty sounds her new husband made in the chair next to her fit into the overall performance. She was certain they fit. She was pleased. She smiled. In this moment, life seemed splendid.

Elizabeth began to organize these recollections. She vowed that what she would tell her daughter about this day would not be the same barren recollections her mother had professed to retain.

"My husband." She mulled the two words.

Elizabeth hadn't gotten her head around this change yet. She was trying. She knew she had been rehearsing this role for a number of years now. She had been writing "Mrs. Bob Kelly" and "Elizabeth Kelly" on tablet paper and in text book margins since she was in the Eighth Grade.

Bob stirred, then dozed again. Silently, Elizabeth checked him and then slipped back into her thoughts.

Eighth Grade. She was certain she had never not known Bob Kelly. They had been childhood friends and neighborhood playmates. Come springtime of their Eighth-grade year at Delta Junior High School, their relationship changed. That step forward from which one seemingly cannot retreat.

Bob and Elizabeth were attending a "girl-boy" party. It was one of those living room events that young girls' mothers were prone to organizing.

A game of spin-the-bottle was being played. The genie of the bottle would pick a couple to take a stroll around the block. Though good plotting and a small degree of good fortune, the bottle selected Bob and Elizabeth.

A hoot rose as they stood up. Elizabeth appeared confident and Bob, though quite uncertain, refused to appear otherwise. He held the door open for Elizabeth. They left.

Though fledgling, this adventurous twosome was holding hands as they walked. They counted the expansion joints in the sidewalk aloud. Their arms swung out, extended as if dancing. Their joined hands appeared to be guided by the rhythm of some internal metronome.

Then, unexpectedly, Elizabeth clasped his hand tightly and stopped. Bob, caught unawares, half stumbled forward over his tangled feet. Her face was barely visible through the dim street lamp.

Her exploratory gaze caught him and held him in a state of puzzlement. She was making a final examination of her yet unspoken proposal. Bob stood silent and indecisive.

As Elizabeth stood back lit by the street lamp, Bob realized that somehow, while he wasn't looking, his childhood friend had emerged from a cocoon into something so exquisite that he could only stare.

It seemed she was still a girl, still a friend but she wasn't. Bob was unsure. He found himself hung on the crossroads of uncertainty.

Then, in the faint light he saw her face. She was looking at him, approvingly looking at him. He thought, "Thank God."

She fought back her insecurities, stretching for the enigmatic smile she had been rehearsing for several months now, her eyes met his. She couldn't look away.

Now holding his right hand between both of hers, her slender fingers relaxed, easing their grasp. She guided their fingers until they interlocked.

Elizabeth felt confident, she felt eager.

Having expended only seconds of actual time, her smile widened becoming a mixture of the playful smile he knew well and the new, more resolute smile with which he wasn't yet familiar.

With a starting jerk, she pulled him across the lawn, steering him toward the privacy of the enclosed back porch of the long vacant Thompson home. The fatigued steps were rickety, creaking under their feet.

Eyes adjusting to the darkness of the porch, she leaned against the wall, holding Bob at arm's length. She wondered if he was seeing what she wanted him to see.

She breathed deeply and discovered Bob standing ever so close. She rested their hands on her hips.

Kissing. During their childhood, they had practiced kissing on several occasions, rehearsals so to speak. What happened next was not. This kiss was tangible and it was memorable. Elizabeth and Bob no longer felt as children.

Their head leaned forward into an ever so tender touching of their lips. Hovering, hesitant, soft and slow, they began. Lips touched, lingered, transposed, repositioned and then breathlessly parted. The emotions were exhilarating.

"Well?" Elizabeth asked. She couldn't believe her question, that she had spoken what was in her mind. For seconds, she waited.

"Holy Mary, Mother of God!" Bob said. He was flabbergasted.

In the darkness, hardly visible, Elizabeth smiled. She could not know she would cherish the experience for a lifetime, still she believed.

Elizabeth began to laugh, soft and genuine, uncomplicated. She suppressed a girlish giggle. The butterflies in her stomach were calming.

The initiative became Bob's. It had been her intent to grasp him first but before she could move, his arms closed around her, hesitantly inching her closer.

Suddenly breathless, Elizabeth felt a brace of fear that melted into an implausible sense of well-being. She felt his heart thumping, matching the pace of her own. The embrace tightened.

The Last Dance in Delta

She felt her newly acquired and discovered bust against his chest. She withdrew. Then, she didn't.

Ambiguous, inexplicable, she felt proper yet wicked. Unfamiliar sensations flowed over her. Scary and exhilarating.

Her bosoms, these miracles whose presence horrified her and yet she was convinced of their boundless potential, whatever they were. She wished they were more. She didn't' want large, just more. She had recently had a prayerful discussion with the Virgin Mary on this topic.

Still, she noted breasts felt differently when pressed against Bob. She doubted he was even aware. In Miss Riley's English class, she learned the word ambivalence. She now knew the emotion.

They kissed. They lingered. They kissed again.

She sensed the weight of his hand as it wandered, looking for a comfortable spot on her back. There were pleasant sensations. Unsettled, she inhaled and found his scent. Captivating.

She felt Bob wobble. He spread his fingers searching for stability. She steadied him. She held him closely, her head now nestled on his chest. She dreamed that he smelled the pristine fragrance of her hair.

She thought, "Oh, my this is nice."

It was nice. It was just all so new.

Again, she sensed his tentativeness. His fingers grasp at the fabric of her dress. She felt him release and again secure himself. He touched places. If Elizabeth minded, she didn't tell him. She was again ambivalent.

She sensed his anxiety. She hoped it was more astonishment than dread.

Bob was struggling with boundaries. He knew they existed but he was uncertain as to their location. His limited knowledge made him cautious. His amorous pursuit made him bump against the borders.

Intense curiosity constrained by sheer terror.

At any sense of her discomfort, he immediately withdrew. It was not always what she wanted.

Elizabeth felt a power, unfamiliar and enormously scintillating.

They kissed again, more unhurried, lingering, both unwilling to release the embrace. So, they clung to each other hoping they were doing it right.

Breathless, Elizabeth said, "We have to go."

Uncertain and knowing leaving was the last thing he wanted to do, Bob replied, "Okay."

His hand dropped into hers. They retraced their steps down the steps. At the base of the steps, Bob stopped. He drew Elizabeth near and kissed her again. An unhurried, reassuring and quite comfortable kiss, the kiss of a very young couple in the throes of a beginning.

After walking the block back to the party, they stopped on the sidewalk just off the dimly lit porch. Elizabeth adjusted her dress, then brushed it straight. She flicked a twig from his shoulder. She surveyed him more closely.

"Oh!"

Although partially concealed by the pleat of his pants, her eyes scrutinized a potentially problematic protrusion. Her sisters had warned about such occurrences.

She placed her thumbs in his belt loops and jerked Bob's pants. It took two tugs to make the proper adjustment, aligning the fly and fluffing the pleats. The pants settled into a more efficient concealment.

Her jostling returned his focus to porch and party.

"There." She stepped back quite pleased with herself.

Bob blushed a brilliant red.

Elizabeth tried not to smile but she did. She was so pleased with her initial visit into Wonderland.

Giving his hand an affectionate squeeze, Elizabeth stepped to the door, paused and waited for him to open it for her. He understood and performed his social obligation with a flourish and enthusiasm.

She twirled past him into the room.

In relief, he inhaled only to catch her scents lingering on the night air. He inhaled deeply as boyhood moved over.

Inside the living room, Elizabeth glanced back toward Bob. She smiled her most mysterious smile. Telltale hints covered his face suggesting much while concealing little.

Elizabeth hoped every girl in the room was insanely jealous. She was so full of herself she was bursting. She felt luxurious.

Densely covered with dogwoods and redbuds, the hillside across the creek rose steeply away from the water's edge. They sat; the bride snuggled into the arms of her groom.

"Bob, did you see the Jonquils?"

"I did. They are beautiful. I was a bit surprised but spring was rather late this year."

"They so perfectly line the walk down to the creek." Her sigh was wistful, then she asked, "I can see a sitting area under the large oak, might have a great view of the creek from there. And well shaded."

"My grandpa J.J. bought it from a farmer who didn't make during the recession." Bob contemplated the well-ordered border of radiant yellow blooms.

"Jonquils tell me a woman once lived here, tried to make a home of this cabin. The line appears so natural, like they belong here."

"Remember the Johnson and Musser Seed Catalog?"

"Yes, of course. My mother has bought bulbs and seeds for years from them."

"I believe every family in the county has. Of course, that was before Kelly Mercantile opened a seed department," Bob chuckled.

"Of course," came Elizabeth's condescending retort. She went on, "The flowers say a woman was here. She lived, she loved and cared for a family. A crumb of prettiness into a hard life. She was putting down roots. Something that came back each year. Reminders."

"Men don't tend to plant things their family can't eat."

Elizabeth swatted his leg and rejoined, "Life has to have some pretty in it or it isn't really life." She thought and added, "Pretty is the difference in life and survival."

"You know, the mistletoe is a sturdy little turkey buzzard but I think the jonquil should have been our state flower."

Elizabeth answered "This November we will have been a state ten whole years. It just doesn't seem possible."

"The Jonquils tell you that."

"Yes." Elizabeth snuggled next to him and said, "I'll plant Jonquils all around our home."

His arm now comfortably settled around her, Bob held her close.

The face in the mirror was hers. Young, rather girlish for a woman who felt so mature. She examined her hair with a deep ambivalence. Her coal black Irish hair, deep curls corkscrewing from her head. Wonderful hair for a girl but what about for a woman? She extended a tight curl and released it. She pondered her question.

Oh my, Elizabeth McCrary, now Kelly, had questions. My Sacramental Vows of Marriage. Mrs. Elizabeth Marie Kelly, Elizabeth Marie Kelly, Mrs. Robert Kelly.

She sat before the mirror behind the dressing screen. She smiled at her own silliness. She stood and repositioned her day dress so that it covered her undergarments. She felt uneasy.

Speaking to herself, she thought, "Why on God's earth?"

Answering herself, she replied, "Mother's clothes line." She smiled. "Hang the sheets on the outside toward the street. Then, men's clothes, then our personals in the middle and Ladies' clothes nearest the house. are to be hung on the line closest to the house." She could hear her mother's voice and tone. Her smile widened. She recalled the day, to her mother's great dismay, she unthinkingly took the sheets down first with the thought of making her bed before tossing fresh washed cloths onto it for folding.

Her smile broke into laughter.

The present level of her modesty surprised her.

Elizabeth straightened her gown and then unleased a questioning stare into the mirror. She had insisted on a defined decolletage in her gown. Trying it on for her mother and sisters had produced a modicum of discomfort. Tonight, she was quite pleased with her selection.

She raised the tail of her gown, pulled the draw-string and stepped out of her drawers. She picked them up and folded them neatly and placed them under her dress.

The Last Dance in Delta

The new, almost blushing bride drew a deep breath and smiled at the girl in the mirror. She felt solid. She remembered how she had scandalized her sisters with her refusal to wear sleeping drawers. She saw no need to disrupt her sleeping habits just because she was married. Still, she paused.

She reached into her toiletry kit and retrieved a small glass jar with a blue lid. Her eldest, and her married, sister Mary Constance had offered her tiny bits of advice, more disconcerting than comforting.

She hesitated, reading the lid, Chesbrough Blue Star Vaseline. Her thoughts careered through her mind.

Elizabeth sighed, then placed a foot upon the vanity stool and secured a small spot of the gel on her finger. As she applied, she heard her mother's voice, "How many times have I told you, don't touch." She smiled.

Slightly oily, the gel clung to her fingertip. Avoiding contact with her gown, she wiped her finger with the damp wash cloth draped over the basin. More than absorb, the oil seemed to smear.

She straightened herself. Now, she felt wicked. She liked the feeling. A bemusement.

Stepping into the corner of the room, Elizabeth began to lower the wick to extinguish the dressing table lamp. The mural caught her eye. Suddenly intent, she stared at the dressing screen. She hadn't looked closely at the mural painted on the wooden screen until now. An owl, a woodpecker and a cross-shaped shamrock with the blend of a squaw's moccasins with a bow painted on a white cloud set on a blue sky. She stepped back and examined it more closely.

"Bob, have you seen the mural on this screen?"

"No."

"Come look."

Elizabeth asked, "Isn't that just extraordinary?"

"Half a bow and half a woman's moccasin, painted as if they are one."

"Does it have a meaning?" Elizabeth questioned.

"I know the owl and woodpecker are Choctaw symbols. Grandma Kinta told me a lot of stories about them, about the symbols but I just quite remember. I'd say the Shamrock cross and the bow are personal, just for us. I don't know." He thought and then concluded, "Whoever painted it had quite a gift."

"Oh, no doubt," Elizabeth added. She continued, "It is lovely. And it has special meaning."

Bob nodded, then said, "Mrs. Kelly, let's go to bed."

"Robert Kelly! What are you doing?"

Bob, now quite frustrated with the uncooperative wrapper, didn't know now to answer. Stammering, he said, "I'm trying to unwrap this stupid --."

Several descriptive words chased through his mind, none of which he was yet comfortable speaking to his bride. Finally, he held the unyielding condom wrapper up for Elizabeth to see.

"Don't you dare!" Her voice took on an authoritarian quality that Bob had not previously heard. She sat up in the bed, both feet under her.

"What?" Bob exclaimed. "

"The church has teachings about such things."

"I know."

"Bob, you getting ready to go away, far away to a very ugly place." She continued, "I'm not going to take a chance of angering the Lord at us before you do."

Bob sat on the edge of the bed, speechless.

Giving herself a brief moment, Elizabeth continued, "Bob." She let his name settle for emphasis, then continued, "This is not open to discussion. If God wants me expecting and in confinement while you are away, then it is God's will."

She looked at him and finished, "Now put that awful thing away."

Bob shrugged his shoulders and tossed the unopened package into his suitcase near the window.

"Elizabeth, I didn't mean to distress you."

"I know and I'm not distress." After a brief thought, she said, "You didn't go to the pharmacy to buy those things did you. Everyone in Delta will know."

"I didn't."

"Where? How?"

"Does it really matter?"

"No. As long as it wasn't the pharmacy."

"My father gave them to me."

"Oh," Elizabeth answered. This was not the answer she expected. She gathered herself, refocusing to the matter at hand.

"My sweet Elizabeth, if you're talking about them knowing what we're likely to be doing here in a bit, I think they might have already guessed."

Elizabeth had no ready answer.

She relaxed back into the pillow, made a fluffing adjustment and resettled. With her hand, she patted the empty space beside her.

Still sitting on the edge of their bed, Bob felt tentative. He rolled his shoulders. The tension in his neck refused to leave.

Watching the muscles in his back move, she felt unsettled, uncertain as what she should be feeling. Disconcerted. She stirred and wished Bob would settle in beside her.

Elizabeth again pondered Mary Constance's frantic last-minute guidance. "Hope he knows and pray he hurries."

Despite her doubts, Elizabeth felt a palliative quietening. She was reassuringly happy.

Bob turned his head and shoulders toward her and asked, "Mrs. Kelly, may I have this dance?"

Elizabeth bopped him on the head.

They laughed and rolled toward each other and met in the middle of the bed.

They honeymooned in eastern Oklahoma in the late Spring. Twice during their honeymoon nighttime thunderstorms rolled over the mountains and into the valley. While storms are commonplace during an Oklahoma springtime, these storms were memorable.

Vibrating claps of thunder would awaken them. Seeming to follow some preordained sequence large lightning bolts cracked through the opaque darkness of the predawn sky followed by the anticipated thunder. Their surroundings seemed to pulsate, then peacefully resettled.

Bob shared the well-worn weather-watcher's tale that stated if one counted the space between the lightening and the resulting thunder, you could determine the distance in miles to the lightning strike.

Awakened by the sounds of the storm, the newlyweds snuggled. The fresh scent of the just washed air bore a smell of newness. The rain-cooled air carried a fragrance the honeymooners deemed to be ideal. The wind driven rain added a material presence. A contented warmth embraced them as they snuggled beneath the blankets.

Elizabeth whispered of a soft, delicate bouquet. Bob tried to describe a more basic musk. Both tried.

The rain-sweetened air embraced them both like a toasty comforter on a February night. They discovered an opulent warmth in the cabin on the creek bank. They enjoyed each other's physical presence.

"How long do you think it will rain?"

"A lifetime."

Bob, clad in sleeping shorts and a sleeveless undershirt, sprang from beneath the blanket and announced his intention to bathe. He grabbed the bar of soap from beside the wash basin on the night stand and seized a nearby towel.

"Woman, I'm headed for God's bathtub."

Elizabeth chuckled at the specimen of masculine foolishness now framed in the cabin doorway. Woman, she thought, mulling his words, last week you were a girl.

"Oh, Lord God, this water is cold!" Bob spoke, speaking to no one but himself.

He wasn't exaggerating. The air temperature was warming but the creek water not far from its spring-fed headwaters remained seasonally chilly. Chilly but still the body was capable of quickly adjusting.

He had finished washing his hair and was scrubbing his way toward his waist when he heard Elizabeth on the rocks behind him. He turned. Elizabeth, her robe draped over her swimsuit was inching her way down the rock and gravel bank.

She laid her towel on the bank beside his and started to untie her robe, then suddenly she stopped. She realized Bob was looking her way.

"Bob Kelly, you keep your eyes forward until I'm in the water."

"It's okay. We are an old married couple now."

"Well, we're not that old a married couple. So, you just keep your eyes downstream."

Bob laughed and did.

Elizabeth laid robe aside. She smoothed her traditional short sleeve, knee length navy swimming suit with a small white ruffle about the waist. She stretched the matching bathing cap and pulled it on.

Now, she began to ease her way into the water.

Hardly shin deep, she halted, shivered and with a voice that reflected a degree of concern over what she had committed herself to said, "Oh my, it is cold"

"Give your body a chance to get used to it." Suspecting her need for reassurance, Bob added, "Then, it is just outstanding."

Seeing her face covered with indecision, he continued, "Just flop down in it. It'll be fine."

Encouraged but dismissive of Bob's last guidance. Elizabeth continued to cautiously ease her way deeper into the nippy stream. Seeming to stop with each step and with her elbows crossing inward, she drew her shoulders toward her ears and shivered. Appearing to move on tiptoes, she timorously made her way toward her husband.

Bob said, "You're just prolonging the misery."

Bob rose from the waters and dove toward her. Submerged he snatched her legs from under her, leaving her draped across his shoulder. He ran, more stumbled, toward deeper water until he fell sending them both splashing into the Mountain Fork.

Bobbing in chest deep water and obviously pleased with himself, he shouted his justification for his action, "Best to get all wet at once."

He extended his arms toward Elizabeth.

With displeasure in her voice and fire in her eyes, she yelled, "Don't you touch me, you – you – you, T.R.!"

"T.R. – Teddy Roosevelt?" Her reference to the former President left him slack jawed. "Teddy Roosevelt?"

In a poor behavioral choice for the moment, Bob began to laugh.

"Bob Kelly, don't you know all the nasty words my father has said about President Roosevelt!" She stopped, reset and continued, "At the breakfast table – as he read the Delta paper."

"No, I don't but I have a feeling you're getting ready to tell me."

Elizabeth told him.

With the realization that the water was no longer biting at her skin, Elizabeth's displeasure diminished.

Thinking he had detected a change, Bob asked, "Am I still a T.R.?"

"Oh, you are still a large T.R."

With a better-timed laugh, Bob said, "Come sit in this pool with me. It's wonderful."

In a turn back toward the flirtatious, she said, "How do I know I will be safe sitting next to you?"

"Well, Lady, I don't know what cold water does to a woman but a gentleman shrivels up like a prune," Bob said as he feinted standing up on the pool of water.

"Bob Kelly, you sit down. That is an awful thing to do to a lady."

"I just wanted you to know where I stood on this matter of your safety."

"Bob, husband or not, you sit down."

Still laughing, Bob extended both arms and flopped backward into the water, feigning a backstroke, righted himself in waist deep water and began to apply the soap.

She stood in the water, made her decision and sank down until the water brushed her chin.

She looked at her lathering husband and noticed the hair under his arms. Her sisters had been teasing her unmercifully over recent weeks about marrying a boy so young he would not even have hair under his arms. She was secretly pleased he did. Although it really didn't matter. She smiled.

"Here Sweet Elizabeth." He extended the bar of soap toward her.

He added, "Look. This store soap will float right to you."

The Last Dance in Delta

She reached in an effort to secure the bobbing bar from the water. She missed. Bob splashed by her and retrieved it.

Elizabeth leaned toward him and kissed his cheek.

"I love you, Bob Kelly."

"I love you too. Now, are you going to take this bar of soap or do you want me to lather you up."

"You T.R., just hand me the soap."

Bob looked at Elizabeth. His face softened. He shook his head somewhat in disbelief.

"What?"

"Elizabeth, you are just splendid. I've truly never seen anyone so beautiful. I had no idea."

Bob paused a bit hoping he hadn't said something wrong. He hadn't.

They swam and they bathed in the deeper water of the Mountain Fork Creek. They laughed.

Gloriously exhausted, they splashed from the creek and comfortably dried off on the large, flat sun-warmed stones. With a rubbing motion, Bob attacked his body with his towel. Elizabeth used her towel to delicately pat the water from her skin. Each watched the other and noted the difference.

The towel draped over her shoulders, she covered her shape until she placed her arms into the sleeves of her robe. She slipped into her robe.

With her back to him, she seemed to make some magical moves with her arms, then bent at the waist, stood on one leg, then hopped once and deposited her bathing suit on the rocks.

Bob's jaw dropped. Elizabeth, with her back to her husband, completed drying.

"Is Houdini in your blood line?" Bob exclaimed. "That was just dang incredible."

Clutching her robe closed and acting as if he had made no comment, Elizabeth said, "I'm heating up the coffee. Would you enjoy some?"

She reached behind herself to find the waist tie from the robe. It slipped from her hand. The robe bloused.

Bob acted as if he didn't notice. He did. She knew he did. She felt it would be impossible not to be pleased by his interest.

"The coffee sounds good."

Bob extended his hand. Elizabeth took it. They walked back to the cabin.

Bob leaned near and observed, "You smell good."

Elizabeth's hip bumped him.

The Mountain Fork saw no more of them on that morning.

Elizabeth had brought several changes of wardrobe for dinners. She decided not to wear them just now. Not that the dinners weren't lovely, they were. Matilda Johnson and her eldest son, Tendall seemed to mystically appear each day in the late afternoon, fully equipped to prepare their evening meal. Over the years, Matilda had prepared meals in the home of both the bride and the groom. She knew them well. Even now, on their honeymoon, she called them her children. She was mostly right.

The table covering was crafted from a red and white checked oilcloth spread over an oblong wooden table on the stone patio. The seating for this occasion was two high back, cane bottom wooden chairs. For the evening meal, the table was covered with a cloth table cloth and matching napkins. The table was set with the McCrary family silver and China. There were fresh cut flowers on the table each evening. Elizabeth couldn't explain the sensation but she felt the flowers framed her perfectly as she and Bob talked over their dinner or when they sipped the unaccustomed wine at meal's end.

She knew her husband was looking at her and she was just fine with it.

Mr. and Mrs. Bob Kelly conceded it was possible better meals might be served in some distant and exotic honeymoon location but they doubted it.

Friday night brought a dinner of fried fish direct from the Mountain Fork Creek with potatoes and hush puppies. Matilda cooked over an open camp fire in two cast iron skillets. The food came directly from the pan to their plates.

The Kelly's ate at the table while Matilda and Tendall sat by the cookfire. Close enough for the first casual conversation since their wedding.

The flow of conversation was easy and familiar and welcome. The Johnson's knew McCrary and Kelly families well.

"Miss Elizabeth, come now let me show ya Tendall brought"

The ladies stepped inside the cabin. Matilda spoke, "Now Tendall put a twenty-five-pound block of ice in the box. Brought another dozens of eggs, jug of milk and a fresh loaf of white bread, baked this morning."

"Matilda, thank you. I so appreciate what your family has done for Bob and me."

The acknowledgement visibly pleased Matilda.

As they passed beyond the line of sight from the patio, Matilda continued, "Miss Elizabeth, your Momma feared that with you honeymoonin' and all, well, it could stir your monthlies to arrive a bit early. She sends you some of your cloths."

Elizabeth shook her head in moderate disbelief and said, "Matilda, please thank my mother for me. Assure her I am doing just fine."

"I told her looked to me as you was honeymoonin' just fine." Matilda's smile was broad and most understanding.

Elizabeth was uncertain exactly how to answer. She was grateful Matilda hadn't confused her sore thighs from hiking up and down the banks of the Mountain Fork with, well, with honeymoonin'.

Her voice now inundated with maternal feelings, Matilda said, "If there is anything you be needing, you just tell Matilda."

Elizabeth acknowledged the genuine kindness of the offer. Elizabeth now felt she and Bob were learning and that such things as were now floating through her mind were theirs to learn.

The nights past, Elizabeth became increasingly comfortable and adventurous in her wifely skin. She slowly ventured forth on a voyage of personal discovery.

She knew some things from girl talk. Deductive reasoning was taking her more places.

The lamps were put out and darkness engulfed the cabin.

As the nights had passed, Bob felt an increasing confidence, a self-confidence with his gentleness. Elizabeth allowed him those minutes of familiar foreplay before righting herself in a fashion that gave Bob few choices. He could rise and break their embrace. He didn't want to do that. Or he could allow her to lead this dance and find himself flat of his back. He balked, relented and found himself prone.

She was upright, over his hips, when a wave of uncertainty stuck. On their previous nights, she had laid almost motionless on her back, then she would unfold herself so that he knew she was available. In her fantasies, she had envisioned this gesture as being like a bud on an Oklahoma climbing rose opening itself to be passively warmed by the morning sun.

It wasn't too late to simply revert to that passive position. It seemed a safe choice. Still, she chose the unfamiliar path. She placed her palms on his chest and settled. His muscles felt solid. Her fingertips toyed with his wiry hair.

The motion of her gown randomly brushed against her body. She knew the feeling and she liked it.

She became aware of his movement beneath her. She smiled at the resolve he was demonstrating. She allowed this frantic search to continue several minutes.

Her voice surprisingly husky, her intent seductive, she said, "Be still."

In a few moments, unfamiliar with passivity, his hand was reaching upward, groping. She realized she would need to teach him to be more accepting.

She shepherded his hand. He found her breast. She exhaled and involuntarily moaned.

She gathered herself, determined, then repeated her words, "Be still."

Bob allowed her to lead this dance. For the first time, she matched his urgency and resolve. For Elizabeth the outcome was unexpected. As for Bob, he hoped he hadn't hurt her.

As with all good things, Elizabeth and Bob's honeymoon ended. The rest of their life began.

CHAPTER 4:
By Train and Ship and Truck

TWO WEEKS AFTER HIS MARRIAGE to Elizabeth McCrary, Bob Kelly boarded a Katy train and left his bride. He looked at the station sign proclaiming Delta, Oklahoma that now hung above Elizabeth's head. He saw symmetry but no humor, maybe only the darkest of comedies. He was leaving both.

He was uncertain as to what he expected but leaving Elizabeth standing on the station platform was far more difficult than he had ever anticipated. If he could have jumped from the train into her arms, he would have done it.

The war in Europe did not seem as important to him as it had when he enlisted. At this moment he would conceive nothing as significant as just one more day with his wife.

He regretted his decision but knew there was no way to now escape its consequences.

Standing of the platform at Delta Station, Elizabeth wore her most courageous face. She waved him a smiling farewell. As sight of the train began to fade, she felt light-headed, unstable. Her world wobbled.

Her mother, Bonnie McCrary, attune to her daughter's circumstance, saw her quiver and quickly moved to her side. As Elizabeth's unsteadiness became tangible, Bonnie stabilized her daughter and then guided her to a station bench. They watched as the smoke of the train rose from behind the tree line.

The women gave no voice to the matter until the smoke disappeared from sight.

Elizabeth, taking her mother's hand, said, "Thank you, Momma."

Elizabeth's eyes locked on the spot where she thought she had last seen the smoke. She clung to a flawed but flowery fantasy that Bob would come racing back down the tracks into her arms. But her husband and the train carrying him had disappeared. She felt empty, just empty.

Supported by her mother's arm, Elizabeth walked the sidewalk from the station to her parent's home.

Bonnie secretly cursed her husband, Dub, for not being there. What good was being one of the few families with a car if it wasn't there when you needed it? It was so hard to see her daughter hurt so deeply. Yet, she knew Elizabeth would have it no other way.

As if cued by the shutting of the door, Elizabeth found herself awash in tears. Her mother held her tightly.

The townsfolk of Delta had long believed Bob was the most blessed of the Kelly boys. It was Bob who was ordained to ascend to the family throne. It had always been there for all to see. Bob was the one with the fine future.

Most expected he would return home from the war a hero and ready to assume the mantle of Kelly leadership in Delta.

Despite the overwhelming anxiety he was currently battling, even Bob was confident he had a fine future in front of him.

Boot camp at Parris Island left Bob believing he was prepared to charge into combat and defeat the enemy. He believed in himself. But he was heartsick for Elizabeth.

While the news provided the recruits was limited, they heard of each German sinking of a passenger ship and the resulting death of innocents. With this selective presentation of the news, the recruits were increasingly convinced of the righteousness and the necessity of this war.

The news of the flu pandemic that raged across the United States concerned him. He feared for Elizabeth. She wrote him reassuring letters telling him that the flu had not hit Delta. Bob had doubts.

Boot camp conditioned Bob and taught him many skills for combat. It mentally sharpened him. Still, combat remained an abstraction.

Bob was not prepared for an ocean voyage. The Atlantic crossing repeatedly reinforced his growing sense of time and distance, how far away this war was from the Ouachita Mountains and the fertile foothills and river bottom land that cradled Delta.

Bob found sleep at best challenging. He had to sleep in a hammock that he split time with another Marine. Hammocks crammed and packed in a space so poorly ventilated that every foul smell emitted by man and boat hung in the still air. The non-existent ventilation made the air seem an obscene insult to a man's lungs.

When these vulgar olfactory sensations were coupled with the swaying and tossing of the ship, nausea was the inevitable outcome. These were nauseating and disheartening times for a flat land boy from a land-locked town.

Convinced only fresh air would help bring him restful sleep, Bob picked up his coat and life jacket and made his way onto the deck. He hoped to leave behind him the incredibly diverse assortment of fetid smells. He hadn't previously known that such a collection of unpleasant smells could be secreted from the human body.

Bob began to conclude some stenches were simply irremovable. He was convinced these blasphemous smells would linger in his lungs and on his gear until they could be cleansed by the salt water air.

He gained some optimism because the piney scent of the astringent in the mop water and the pungent smell of tobacco did attempt to conceal the dastardly odors. Then, upon failing, at least made them slightly more palatable. Even this was temporary.

With the first deep inhale of fresh salt air, he coughed. It wasn't that the salt water air had a smell, it didn't. The absence of a noxious stimulus is positive.

He took three steps and coughed again. The cough seemed to come from some place deep in his chest. He looked for a place to spit. Finding none, he made do.

Bob steadied himself, no small feat, placing the steel bulkhead to his back. Once fixed, he tried to focus on the horizon. Dusk was falling.

Through the shadows of nightfall, the fog and the mist, bobbing in and out of sight, he could just make out the forms of their escort. A dark grey shield against U-Boats in an ashen world.

For a moment, he remembered a fishing cork darting behind a small wave as it bobbed along the wind bumped surface of the larger pond on his family land back in Delta.

The memory was an ambivalent reminder. It drew him back into Elizabeth's embrace while reminding him of how far from home he was. With each roll and pitch of the deck, he knew it wasn't home that lay before him, it was France and a war and an unknown enemy.

A voice from his unconscious bellowed "Trust your training."

The cold breeze nipped at his essence. How far away from wife and home he was struck him. An awareness that there are circumstances just too grim to grasp fractured its way into his consciousness.

Mercifully, the concept of his own death continued to lay just beyond his awareness. His cognizance of the uncertainty that lay before him was stern enough.

Doubts increasingly nagged him. Could he do what was expected of him? Thinking back to the recruiting poster that seduced him, he thought, "Maybe I should have left it to the Marines."

Again, from the recesses of his mind, Bob heard a vaguely familiar voice instructing, "Trust your training! Trust your training!"

He tried to shake Delta from his mind. He moved. He shuffled his feet. He again steadied himself against the bulkhead, then he moved on.

Bob wobbled, just avoiding two Ensigns hurrying somewhere. One tossed him a glare but both hurried along their path.

Naval Officers. He knew when he walked up the gang plank to board the SS H. R. Malloy, he was pleased to spy a Lieutenant Commander. Bob had heard troubling tales of troop ships under civilian command. Although he expected most of these alleged happenings contained substantial exaggerations, he was relieved to see the Navy in full command.

Finding a vacant space on deck, he sat down and stared into the night. He started to put on his coat but stopped. He looked at the patch sewn on the sleeve; a dark blue anchor set in a red field with a V on the anchor. The patch of the 5th Marine Machine Gun Battalion of the American Expeditionary Forces, the AEF. Bob took pride in what he believed the patch said about him. He could never articulate the thought but it did comfort him.

His finger traced the patch. Again, he heard the voice, "Trust your training!"

He rolled up the coat and placed it behind his head.

Bob had just settled down when lights out was sounded. He watched the lights go out around him. His view of the escort vessels grew hazier.

Darkness descended and with it his mind drew to the sulking U-boats. Horrible thoughts of water flooding over him, capturing him below the decks had wrecked his sleep for weeks.

Bob knew he was not alone in his fear. He was recognizing how isolating fear could be. Predictably, the close proximity of war begot anxiety. Anxiety begot night terrors.

Fear induced sleep disturbances were common among the men, symptomatic of the intensity of their fears.

These men – men – a few months ago they were boys. They were still boys. Boys who were now Marines.

Back on Parris Island, Bob had overheard a gnarly old Sergeant remark to a fellow NCO, "Don't worry, when the killin' begins, it'll grow'em up in a hurry."

Bob thought on the words. His colon stirred; his stomach soured. Unseeing, he looked deeper into the dark.

Coleridge's lines of "Water, water everywhere" rattled around in his mind. Miss Garland, his high school English teacher, adamantly believed memorizing poetry was the key to a successful life. It was just a short time ago that Bob was fearful of not pleasing Miss Garland. Now it was reciting words she had demanded he commit to memory that provided a needed distraction. Bob knew this stern but gentle woman, conservative in dress with high expectations of her pupils, had no inkling reciting her cherished poetry would ease the anxiety of a man – a boy – headed to war.

As he thought about it, he considered she would be pleased. She saw poetry as having an application in every human condition. War was certainly a human condition. Bob thought of Miss Garland. He mustered a rare smile.

He was grateful for the words stored in his mind. The words eased his feelings and drew him back to a gentler time.

Peculiar how fear is so relative. How comforting even, a hint of the familiar can be.

Nonetheless, his doubts nagged him. His sleep remained ragged.

For some Marines, their fear became so intense that they urinated during their sleep. A fierce fight erupted when one man's stress relief dripped onto the man sleeping below him. To become a victim of such an event can erode the confidence of the bravest of men. Bob did not want to become either man.

Mostly Bob waited. He concluded there is something extraordinarily lonely about waiting. Waiting not by choice but by fact of existence.

Fear was isolating. It couldn't be shared.

His entire world seemed to be one breath from flying apart. He drew his coat tighter. He prayed the Rosary. Both helped. He closed his eyes and thought of Elizabeth. It helped more.

Bob made an oath to himself. "If I ever get back to Delta, I will never again set foot in a boat larger than a john-boat."

If I get back! If – the unanticipated ambiguity anguished him.

The ship tossed beneath him. Salt water sprayed him. Bob had doubts.

The solid soil of France underfoot was not an immediate remedy. Bob sensed the land to be oscillating beneath his feet. Logic dictated stability. But instability Bob sensed seemed quite real. He took hold of the rope railing that bordered the temporary board walkway and let it guide him to a post. He steadied himself and looked to the beach.

The beach overflowed, ordered yet chaotic. It was filled with men headed to war and those who were assisting them in getting there. For whatever reason he saw it as the movement between an ant hill and a sliver of honey-soaked bread. There was an identifiable directional movement, from disembarking to exiting the beach, with a knotted mass of men in-between.

On his Sergeant's command, Bob Kelly placed the sea breeze to his back and moved inland.

"Sonny, you got to do this before you can go home."

Bob overheard the words spoken by an unknown Sergeant to a demoralized young Marine, his head clutched between his knees. Bob took the words to head and heart.

At this point, Bob knew all roads home led through France.

Through eighteen cruel days in early June of 1918, the 5th Marine Machine Gun Battalion sloshed and fought their way through Belleau Wood near the Marne River. Corporal Robert Kelly acquitted himself well enough to become Sergeant Kelly.

Bob scoffed at his new rank. In his mind, attrition had as much to do with his advancement as merit. During their eighteen days in Belleau Wood over half of his battalion had been killed or wounded.

Combat coats the lens of the eye, clouding and distorting the visual perception. This refractory misrepresentation garbles a man's perception to the extent that mud and death and destruction become unremarkable segments of the landscape.

Wife and family and home were seductive memories, exotic places that if he allowed himself to linger to long would get him killed. His focus was on the next minute, the next hour and no further than the next day.

Home was now a fuzzy, almost non-existent memory lodged in the rear of his mind. He no longer expected to go home.

It was in their letters that each an indelible respite from their reality. A reality redefined.

It had been misting rain in Delta since early morning, a cooling early summer rain. Elizabeth looked out the front window, drew a very deep breath and slowly released it. She gathered her navy-blue rain slicker, shook it and looked at the white and yellow flowers that bordered its tail and the tips of its sleeves. She thought of jonquils. She wondered about the jonquils at the Kelly cabin, her honeymoon cabin. As soon as Bob was home, they would go check on them. She shook the coat again and deemed it acceptable and slipped it on. She took her umbrella from the stand by the door.

Elizabeth called, "Mother, I'm going to Saint Josephs."

Bonnie answered with a directive, "Make it home for supper."

She didn't intend to speak to her daughter as a child. Elizabeth certainly was no longer a child. Elizabeth was a worried, heartsick and lonesome young wife. Her mother had tried to ease her daughter's loneliness. She prayed for yards and felt she received inches. Still, Bonnie was most grateful.

Elizabeth stopped at the base of St. Joseph's eight steps and studied the church, not yet thirty years old yet its essence seemed so much older. It had been constructed of dark grey formed concrete stones. The moisture of the day darkened the walls. The rivulets flowing down it sides gave he illusion the walls were weeping. The marble steps were showing the beginnings of wear lending the appearance of strength to the structure.

The grey walls merged with the grey sky making the dark streams of water appear even darker. However, the suggested sadness just never materialized. Not so long ago, she and Bob had been married here. It had been a joyous place.

She reached into her purse and retrieved a scarf. She covered her head.

At the top of the steps, she paused and looked at the acknowledgement stones, reached out and touched the Kelly stone and then the McCrary stone. She searched for the words to describe her feelings. They eluded her.

Then, she spoke with some unknown voice, "I'm not praying for me, I'm praying for Bob Kelly."

She spoke to some unknown, unseen gatekeeper. She didn't know why, she didn't know if she said it aloud, she simply did.

She turned and faced the massive doors, then moved in front of the north door, it was always unlocked, and pulled.

The sanctuary was dim, but not dark. With no effort, her hand found the Holy Water. Her damp fingertips touched her forehead as she began the Sign of the Cross. She remembered her Baptism. She made her way to what her father enjoyed calling the Family Pew. She genuflected, again made the Sign of the Cross and slid into the pew.

She eased the kneeler down but still there was an echo as the metal screw that secured the rubber grommet struck marble. She knelt, adjusted the hem of her dress beneath her knees and settled.

Elizabeth prayed. Time passed. Her knees tired.

She lifted her head and looked at the Great Crucifix mounted behind the Alter and found a blessing. She said a prayer of thanks.

She heard footsteps echo on the marble floor. The steps stopped beside her. She looked up. With his hand, her father motioned her to make room for him. She did.

Given his advancing arthritis and a rainy day, kneeling was uncomfortable for Dub McCrary. Still, he edged in beside his daughter, shared her kneeler and offered a prayer. He prayed for his wife, for his daughter and her husband.

His prayers completed, he placed his arm around her shoulder and hugged her.

"Daughter, let's go to supper."

Elizabeth nodded.

She halted before descending the stairs to the sidewalk. She removed the scarf and folded it into a side pocket of her purse.

As she was tying on her rain scarf, she looked at her father and said, "I know Bob will be fine now."

Dub looked at this daughter and thought he caught a glint of confidence in her eyes. He said, "Struck a deal with God, did you?"

Elizabeth didn't answer.

They walked home to supper. In peace.

It began to rain harder as they stepped up on to the porch.

In late June, Bob Kelly's unit moved away from the Marne River.

The 5th was placed in reserve in a small town on the outskirts of Paris. From Bob's perspective, no one spoke English. Yet, the town and the townsfolk gave the resting Marines a sense of symmetry and tranquilly. The Marines discovered a routine that was agreeable, predictable and oddly familiar. A blend that possessed innumerable restorative properties.

Bob was surprised to find that such ordinary village life existed within just a few hours of the dreadfulness of the war. The smell of fresh bread wafted its way along the narrow stone streets supporting the impression of tranquilly. Beyond mere illusion was the reality that warm bread could be brought, shared and eaten. Bob had forgotten how profoundly sensuous the smell and taste of hot bread could be.

The sound of women's voices bargaining in the market had a soothing property to it. The sound was reassuring. Restored recollections of wives, mothers, and girlfriends raced to occupy the heads of the men. Nothing whispered home in a soldier's ear like the sounds of women going about the routine tasks of daily life.

While never able to accept the illusion as fact, Bob did begin to feel more safe and secure. At brief intervals, he could visualize his survival. It was at these times he would write a flood of letters to Elizabeth. He wrote flowery descriptions of the village hoping to reassure her of his safety.

Call it women's intuition, Elizabeth saw beneath the veneer of words. Bob's final letter of this series was only a brief hurried note. She sensed the brevity of the communication indicated a hurried departure, leaving the safety of the French village and back into harm's way.

Elizabeth refolded the most recent note, returned it to its envelope and placed it in the quilted letter box on her bedside table. She picked up her purse and checked for a headscarf.

The Last Dance in Delta

She found one. She looked at it and set it aside. She opened her dresser drawer and selected a solid soft blue headscarf, one that Bob had given her saying that it made her eyes snap. She loved him saying so.

She closed the drawer of the dresser her Grandmother McCrary had left her. She took a finger and traced an outline concealed in the grain of the oak. Elizabeth valued her ancestry.

She walked to St. Joseph's Church.

Saint-Maur-des-Fosses is a quaint and agreeable town that lays to the southeast of Paris along a loop in the Marne River. As June was closing in 1918, Sergeant Bob Kelly and the 5th Marine Machine Gun Battalion waited.

The expectant anticipation of an inevitable return to combat weighted heavily on their minds. It permeated their very souls, combat veterans and newly arrived replacements alike. Similar but distinct.

Each in his own fashion, every man was preparing for the inescapable return to the front. Bob systematically reviewed his equipment.

Thoughts of survival invaded his consciousness. He now understood even fantasies of immortality were dangerous and unreliable. He could not allow himself even momentarily to be distracted by such an extravagant illusion.

He broke down, lubricated and polished his trench shotgun, a Winchester Model 1897, twelve-gauge pump with a shortened twenty-inch barrel. Bob reasoned it to be the most serviceable and lethal weapon a Marine in a machine gun emplacement could possess, especially in close quarters of a compromised trench.

The trench pump carried nine shells, double-aught buckshot. When in an emplacement, he kept one shell chambered. Eight in the magazine.

His m1917 bayonet, a seventeen-inch-long blade, would be scabbarded but at the ready. Holstered was a Smith & Wesson snub nose revolver, a gift from the Delta Police Department that had arrived just before his departure from the United States.

Thoughts of Elizabeth besieged his conscious awareness. He attempted to quash his vision. He failed.

His back welcomed the sun-warmed stones. He nestled against the stone fence. He thanked God as the warmth eased the tension that dwelled between his shoulders. His muscles loosened. The tightness fled. He dwelled in the words of his wife.

In Delta, Oklahoma, Elizabeth Kelly knelt in St. Joseph's Church. Her knees settled into the leather of the meagerly cushioned and well-worn kneeler. A true world away yet a distance transfigured by the transcendent invocations of a wife, a Marine stirred from beside a stone fence and moved toward a waiting truck.

She arranged her dress so that her bare knees contacted the wear softened leather. The leather of the kneeler greeted her knees and she felt hope. It was a greeting exchanged between reliable old friends. Her dress settled.

She made the Sign of the Cross and recited the prayer. She gathered her hands between her chin and began her prayers.

She prayed the Hail Mary, first in Latin and then in English so that all in harm's way could feel the blessing. The Hail Mary was always her first prayer and her next to last prayer each day. Initially, she did it without complete understanding. Over time, as she contemplated her prayers, she came to consider them as an appropriate acknowledgement of God's power while acknowledging God's proximity.

On the thick rainy summer morning of July 18, 1918, Sergeant Robert Kelly and the 5th marched back into the valley of the Marne River near the town of Chateau Thierry tasked with blunting another German counter-offensive.

Heading for a position that overlooked a complex of bridges spanning the Marne, it had taken them hours, driving over the ruts and potholes of dirt roads, to reach their positions. A pouring rain storm had turned the road into a sea of mud. The water filled the holes making the road appear level. The driver would blast head-long into sizable holes. The truck had careened along going up and down while sliding sideways.

The Marines were tossed and bruised. A bone jarring collision with the bottom of a large hole brought curses from the rear of the truck.

While righting himself after such a collision of bone and wooden seat and speaking to no one in particular, Sergeant Kelly said, "Beats the Hell out of walking in this slop!"

"Fuck you!" came a reply from the dark.

A bolt of lightning lit the ominous sky. The clap of thunder that followed was impressive.

A Yankee voice from mid-truck chimed in, "I think God damn spoke! And he's damn loud."

Most of the Marines laughed. All of them knew a rough truck ride was considerably better than sloshing along thru the unrelenting mud, wading in soaked boots and wet socks.

Either way they arrived at the front too soon for the combat veterans. Not soon enough for the raw replacements.

The German counter-attack was in full thrust and gaining momentum. The Hun was regaining ground that the AEF had bled and died for in Belleau Wood. The French army was beating a hasty retreat in an effort to escape across the bridge complex. Their orders were to mine the bridges and then to destroy them before the German tanks and artillery could cross even if it meant trapping some the French rear guard on the German side of the river.

Securing the bridges in tact was as important to the Germans as demolishing the bridges was to the Allies.

The 5th was positioned in existing trenches and firing pits overlooking the Marne and the eastern approaches to the bridges. Giving up on his search for a dry place to sit, Sergeant Bob Kelly covered himself with his poncho, then ate two French biscuits he had pocketed from the previous evening's hurried meal.

He could hear the distant roar of a pitched battle. He turned abruptly and pushed any thought of home from his mind.

Elizabeth knew Bob's note must have been hurriedly composed. Her intuition told her it was born from a strong need to share his feelings with her, an effort to reach out to her.

Dearest Elizabeth,

My husband part wishes to forever protect you from any and all ugliness. The exhausted soldier part of me wants to share my concerns with you. I do not know what news of this war reaches you in Delta but it is important for me to tell you that at this time I am safe, resting in charming French village. My nights are filled with dreams of you and that restores my very soul. I must attempt to convey to you the great pleasure I find on the pages of your letters. It is on those sheets I find hope. My Love it is your words that now sustain my soul.

I must go now.
I remain your loving husband,
Bob

Elizabeth refolded the tissue thin paper, careful to follow the existing creases. She replaced it in the upper left-hand drawer of her desk, tenderly covering it with a pin cushion.

Elizabeth never felt more alone than when late in the evening and dressed for bed, she sat down at her writing desk to write Bob. Once she had thought that the ritual of taking the eyedropper from drawer, unscrewing the lid from the ink bottle and refilling her Swan fountain pen might become comforting but it hadn't. Her pen did seem to fit her hand and that was helpful.

She would hesitate and gaze at the blank sheet of paper, trying to determine a beginning. Not her salutation, but the first paragraph. After the date, she always wrote, "My Darling Husband," It fit, it was how she wanted to greet him.

Tonight, a film of tears slipped across her eyes. Her vision blurred, she opened a drawer and withdrew a handkerchief.

She dabbed away her tears, then blew her nose.

As she began to write, she felt connected to her husband. She felt so very lonely. She tried to conceal her fear.

She poised the pen.
July 18, 1918
   "My Darling Husband"

CHAPTER 5:
At the Bridges

GUNNERY SERGEANT MARCO GIUSEPPE RICCI was reared on Lexington Street in the Little Italy neighborhood of Chicago. His father had fled the blinding poverty of rural Italy. In jest, his father would tell him the soil was bad but it didn't matter because he didn't own any of it.

His father, Salvatore, labored for eight years on various construction projects until he turned the needle work that his grandmother had taught him into a career. At first it allowed him to secure a job, then marry a co-worker's daughter, Donna, and begin a family. Salvatore believed God had truly blessed him.

Gunnery Sergeant Marco Ricci, now a veteran of twenty-one years in the Marine Corps, had enlisted in the Corps at sixteen. He fought in Banana Wars. Now, he fought in France.

The United States Marine Corps was his life.

He silently stepped behind Sergeant Bob Kelly and asked, "Kelly, this the closest pit to that tree line?"

He caught Bob unawares. Startled, Bob turned and looked at his Gunnery Sergeant. He greatly admired Sergeant Ricci. Bob saw a Marine's Marine; he saw the Gunny's heroism in Belleau Wood that he didn't believe any human possessed.

Gunny stood stiff and straight as he gazed over the field toward the tree line. Bob thought at times that Gunny's spine must be Marine issue. It seemed Gunny's head could turn a full 360 degrees without moving his shoulders.

"Yes, Gunny."

Gunnery Sergeant Ricci's gunmetal grey eyes had way of penetrating while scanning a man. Bob didn't understand it but he accepted it as fact. It was a gaze that froze Bob.

If Gunny has something to say, you'd best listen.

Without making a visible gesture, Ricci's eyes guided Bob vision, "You see the tree line breaking up from the river bank?"

Some three hundred yards from Bob's position, a dense tree line composed of white elm and beech gave a boundary to a creek that fell sharply down toward the Marne. Smatterings of hackberry and a yellow flowering gorse feathered out toward cleared land.

"Do you see where the gorse suggests there once was a decent pathway leading to the river?"

"Yes, Sir."

"Well, it once was."

The Gunnery Sergeant continued, "Not going to be long and the fighting will be down there on the bridge, your machine guns will convince the Hun the fires of Hell have been loosed on him. He'll want to do something about it."

Gunnery Sergeant Ricci checked Sergeant Kelly to be certain his message was received and understood. It was.

Ricci went on, "The Hun knows this place. I'm betting he will come right up the far side of the creek, up that old cart path and try to take you out of this fight."

Continuing, he instructed, "The Hun wants to come pouring out of the trees and surprise you. When he tries that shit, you'll be ready to blow his balls off and hand'em to him."

Ricci paused, assessed Kelly and added, "Cowboy, I want that Hun officer to feel like a steer in a Chicago stockyard."

Bob nodded and the slightest smile cracked his face. He understood and the idea appealed to him.

Gunny took a step away, turned with an afterthought and said, "Might consider setting some limit stakes."

"Yes Sir."

Gunny left as unnoticed as he had arrived.

In the short time remaining to him, Bob briefed his men. He felt an unusual sense of calm. It made no sense at all.

The Last Dance in Delta

He had two Marines from East Texas under his command. Both men had been avid squirrel hunters as boys and now, still under 21, were superior marksman. At first, he wasn't certain exactly how he was going to use their special skill, but he knew he was.

Then, the dog robber came in with dynamite and strong loads for the squirrel hunters Enfield rifles. Seeing the available hardware, dynamite could be planted, marksmen could hit it and for all the world it would look like fire from small cannons.

He did have available two 60 MM mortars but nothing else. He only needed the German officers to believe he had trained all the major artillery on the tree line for a few minutes.

The sounds of the struggle continued to move toward them. The louder and closer, the drier Bob's mouth became. He took two substantial swigs of water hoping to mute the dryness. It didn't help.

The fight moved closer.

They waited.

The German Army appearing as an irresistible wave of grey, slowly and steadily engulfing the French rear guard.

Bob had been iffy about the quality of the French soldier, poilus. His mind changed as he watched through the lens of his binoculars. The positions ebbed and flowed. The withdrawing French were extracting a considerable price from the advancing Germans.

Bob could never account for the random associations that passed through his mind while waiting for combat. Nonetheless, they did.

This morning he again thought of the advice his aging grandfather gave. "Price of land can be high depending on where it sits." "Location, location, location."

The engaged armies spilled over the approaches of the bridges. The withdrawing French were reluctantly yielding ground to the advancing German forces, buying their countrymen additional time to complete rigging the bridge.

The signal flares flashed all along the Marine lines. The charging German soldiers were met by withering wall of machine gun fire. The 5th and 6th poured every round humanly possible in the advancing Hun. Although released in short bursts, the recoil and vibration of the weapon made the fire more pointed than aimed.

Given a clear field of fire, the gunners raked and raked across the bridge complex. As the fighting on the bridge became hand to hand, the fierce and unrelenting machine gun fire caused the enemy to pause.

The order was given to sustain the fire on the bridge no matter who was in the field of fire.

Machine gun bullets once unleased were indiscriminate, tearing into Hun and Poilus alike, not caring what color cloth a man wore. They lay together, equally dead, equally wounded. The wounded continued to try to kill each other. The dead were dead.

In the confusion of the melee, Bob became mentally fragmented. He always sought to place such memories into neat compartments. Now, these memories resisted, refusing to be kept.

A runner from Battalion slid into the firing pit next to Lieutenant Dawson Thomas. Bob was uncertain when the Lieutenant had arrived but he was now commanding.

The thrashing of Lieutenant Thomas' arms told Bob no good news had arrived. The Lieutenant rolled out of his pit and dove in beside Bob.

Gasping for breath, his speech sputtering, Lieutenant Thomas shouted, "Sergeant Kelly!"

Then, he realized the sergeant was squatted next to him.

He gathered himself and spoke, "Sergeant, the God-damn Hun bastards are crossing the river headed for that creek."

Agitated, he pointed to the tree line Gunny had pointed out earlier in the day. Bob briefly thought of telling Lieutenant Thomas the Gunny's earlier observations. He offered a modified presentation.

"Sir. Gunny Ricci was by earlier and helped me with a defense plan since my platoon was last on the line. Might be just what we need Sir."

After hearing the plan, Dawson Thomas approved the idea. An idea that was quickly becoming his.

"I'll pass it back to battalion Sergeant. Carry on."

Then, he added, "Kelly, when you have the Hun bastards fully engaged, I'm going to send Kinney on a loop and try to seal the base of the creek so they can't escape."

Bob nodded his understanding and said, "Yes Sir."

Bob didn't share that he was avid in his belief that the Hun was not going to be in any mood to retreat on this day.

He realized Lieutenant Thomas was staying and sending a runner back to battalion. The Lieutenant moved up a notch in Bob's hierarchy.

The Germans warily exited the cover of the dense vegetation along the creek that had provided them with superior concealment during their approach. The Marines patiently held their fire until Lieutenant Thomas felt the Hun was fully committed to the open ground. Caught exposed on open terrain, the Germans had been unable to spread their ranks before an incredibly lethal cascade of fire cut into them.

Sharpshooters hit the raiders leading the charge sending them spilling in front of the men following them. The pathway out was narrowed.

A thought passed. Bob saw them as falling like grass before the blade of scythe in a bar ditch near Delta. He would later wonder where on earth he found such a bucolic reference in midst of such ferocity.

The dynamite blew convincing the Germans they were zeroed in by Allied artillery. They weren't but they believed they were so they acted as if they were.

The 60 MM mortars begin to drop in.

As they attempted to regroup the machine guns cut deeper into their numbers. The Germans had planned on surprise being to their advantage. On this day surprise was a fickle lady who turned on them.

The German attempt to breakout and silence the machine guns was thwarted. The attackers withdrew and fled back into the creek. They went hurling down the creek bed back toward the Marne River.

Sergeant Kelly's men had just pulled a deep breath when the sound of fire came from Sergeant Kinney's downstream position. The Hun hadn't yet escaped.

Then, from near the river, came the distinctive staccato bark of two German MG-8 machine guns.

The German commander, while anticipating the need for an effective recovery of his men, had never expected a full-blown retreat.

Bob heard someone scream, "Get your gloves!"

It was him.

Corporal Austin Dennis was dumbfounded, confused. Then, he saw Sergeant Kelly hurriedly putting on his asbestos gloves. Cradling the barrel of the machine gun in his arms while blessing the man who thought of the fire-proof fabric that made the gloves, Bob hurled himself down the slope toward the fight. Ammunition belts dug into his back and flapped against his legs.

Sergeant Kelly's gun crew quickly responded. Corporal Albert Thompson, carrying the tripod was just underway went an indistinguishable bullet dropped him. He fell to his knees and collapsed face forward down the hill.

The gravity of the situation registered on Corporal Dennis. He was out of his pit and on the move. His gun crew as now alongside him stride for stride.

Sergeant Kelly found a downhill sprint while carrying a blazing hot machine barrel can become a delicate dash. He felt the forward tilt of his body robbing him of stability. As he overran his base, his balance was lost and he felt the inevitable fall forward over take him.

He hugged the blistering barrel closer and leaned into the fall. He rolled down the hillside.

Gathering himself, he rose to a knee and then to his feet. His breath burned and agony radiated from his ribs. He pushed, fell forward and moved forward on fours toward the fight. Mysteriously upright, he tried to run.

Corporal Dennis' reputation for being poorly coordinated was merited. But he was now lumbering alongside Bob.

Bob felt his ankle shatter and felt a stabbing pain take his foot from under him. Struggling to sustain balance, he hopped on his right foot a few paces before falling into the levy that now guided the creek as it widened and approached the Marne River.

"Damn Kelly, don't ya know where ya nose goes your ass will follow."

Bob lacked the breath to answer.

Bob scooted and scrunched his way up the embankment, shoving his machine gun until it topped the levy. The mud soothed his burning bicep where the scalding barrel of his machine gun had burned away his shirt, branding him and leaving his bicep smoldering.

He thought the fat was bone. He vomited. The smell invaded his nostrils and he vomited again.

The air swished as a bullet passed, then another kicked up the dirt beside him. He brought himself back into the fight, placed his tripod-less weapon on the top of the levy, and began to squeeze off bursts in the general direction of the creek that now lay below his position.

"Dennis, the gun boat."

Kelly and Dennis adjusted their aim toward the German gun boat which had been laying down a base of fire under which the raiding party struggled to escape.

Lifted with the asbestos glove, Bob entrenched his machine gun. His fire raked across the deck of the gun boat. The Germans tried to turn their fire toward him. Dennis joined in and cleared the deck.

The guide ropes anchoring the gun boat in place were cut. Unable to start its motors, the current of the Marne began to carry the boat away.

Unbeknownst to the machine gun crews, Lieutenant Thomas had led his rifle company out of the pits, down the slope and was now bringing heavy rifle fire to bare on the beleaguer Hun.

As fast as Kelly and Dennis had engaged the German raiders, the fight was done. Abandoned on the river bank, eighteen German soldiers seemed to be trying to surrender against the orders of their commanding officer.

The outraged German officer shot at his men. Marines, at the combat ready, opened fire.

Few Marines, if any, were in the mood for taking prisoners this day. Few prisoners were taken.

Bob attempted to stand. He couldn't. He fell back on a knee. He saw the stream, the water raced but couldn't filter the blood. Men, some in death throes, others dead, all covered by mud. Mud everywhere. The water seemed unable to wash any of it away.

Bob sank on both knees. Shaken, his vision blurred. An emotional concussion.

The bridge blew sending stones and bodies sailing, landing where they might.

A baseball sized stone landed only a few yards from Bob. He thought how beautiful. He focused. It wasn't a stone. He retched.

Marines moved around him. Men accustomed to the earth-shaking artillery barrages laid down by the enemy were not overly distracted by the intense vibration underfoot. As they predicted, it too passed.

Flying stones and body parts drew slight attention beyond their time.

Again, Bob tried to right himself. Using his trench gun to stabilize himself, he stood. He looked at the shotgun and didn't know how he came to be holding it. He saw his bloody boot and realized his twisted ankle wasn't a twisted ankle. He could see bone poking through the blood. He cursed. Disoriented, focus kept eluding him.

He felt alone. He sank into the ground.

"Corpsman!"

He only knew the voice wasn't his.

Bob Kelly collapsed.

"Holy Mother of God! You have burnt the living hell out of yourself."

Bob saw the thin stream of smoke rising from his smoldering shirt. The gloves didn't help when you embraced your machine gun next to your body. His shirt had burnt away leaving exposed skin. Skin now crisp. The reek of his burnt flesh fouled his nostrils. He winced.

"Corpsman!"

Again, the voice wasn't his.

Bob heard the Gunny Ricci's voice. He didn't know when he arrived.

"You a sorry son-of-a-bitch, but you a hell of a Marine!" Gunny's voice carried a genuine excitement and exaltation.

"Corpsman! Corpsman!"

Gunny stood to allow the Corpsman access to Bob.

Bob didn't hear the report of the sniper's Mauser. He did catch a glimpse of Gunny's head when the bullet struck it.

Merciful unconsciousness arrived. Bob surrendered to it.

CHAPTER 6:
Into the Hands of an Angel

SERGEANT BOB KELLY WOKE IN A HOSPITAL to the east of Paris. The earthy smell of fresh mown grass filled his lungs. Associations of home raced through his awareness. He coughed. Pain racked his body.

He tried to stir further. The constraints of his bandages felt heavy, refusing to allow him to move. He strained against their bulk. An indescribable pain in his chest challenged him to take another deep breath.

"Sister, Sister! The gentleman is awake." The young Novice called out. The unconcealed excitement in her voice exposed the great pleasure she felt to the Yank waking.

Sister Maria Therese, her floor length habit swirling over what many would have considered quite delicate ankles, glided toward him. She had a look on her face that was most excited, suggesting just a touch of self-satisfaction.

At his bedside, she smiled and spoke, despite a very French accent, with the unfaltering English she had been polishing since the war began.

"Sergeant Kelly, I presume." Sister's voice softened as she continued.

Bob tried to conceal the throbbing agony that tore through every inch of his being. He mustered the focus to produce a hesitant smile and said, "Sister, my mother said angels wore black."

Sister Maria Therese's smile widened. She replied, "Only one of many things about which your MaMa was correct."

The manner in which she pronounced MaMa, two distinct syllables, gave Bob a decidedly positive push. Over the coming weeks Bob would discover Sister Mary Therese to be rigid, inflexible and intolerant of any absence of effort. She was demanding and altogether quite adorable.

But today with MaMa on her lips, she was his Angel of Mercy, a vision lending him hope.

The slender, smallish woman, barely reaching five feet in height, in a single fluid movement reached down and flipped his sheets back down to his waist. Her sharp features came into focus as she bent forward to more closely examine his burns.

"You have made an angry looking mess – en colere – you have made of yourself," she said more in observation than from any desire to communicate a literal fact. "But with Holy Mary's help, you and me, we heal it and young wife will think you – va-voom."

Sister gently stroked his hand and smiled a most disarming smile, then intently looked at his injuries as if surveying them for the first time.

"Sister, anything leaking?"

Pressing her thumb and first finger together, indicating only a small amount, without losing focus, said, "Un peu."

Then, as she gained awareness, she clarified, "A little. I will give a – personage." She searched her English, found the word and added it, "Character."

She added, "But it might first be ugly to become lovely. Droite?"

She paused, her intensity lightened, she smiled and said, "Engrais avant recolte"

She leaned nearer to his ear and whispered, "Crap before crop."

She saw his eyes soften and felt his chest relax under her hand. She patted his chest and nodded her head. Then, returned to tending his wounds.

Sister's eyes dissected every centimeter of his wounds. Then, using alcohol bathed tweezers, she began to remove selected slips of skin. To the areas of skin judged adequately healed she applied a lotion she had concocted, some blend of silver, sulfa and a cream that makes a woman's skin softer than that of an infant.

"Doux comme les fesses d'un bebe."

The Novice assisting Sister giggled. Bob caught the word that sounded like baby and surmised the meaning.

Sister carried on a quite charming tete-a-tete, partly in English and partly in French. Her repartee always included reassurances about how his wife would view what she called the character marks of a man.

The young Novice said, "La virilite brite."

"Oui." Then, Sister interpretated for Bob. "She says you are a shining man."

Bob was appreciative but unconvinced.

Sister explained to the Novice that Bob's body was going to heal with or without his consent. She believed his mind to be quite another matter.

Sister Maria Therese took the Novice's hand forcing her timid pupil to make full eye contact and spoke in English for Bob to hear, "Share your light!"

Then, she reinforced it with the Novice, "Paragez votre Lumiere."

"Sceur, je ne connais pas ma Lumiere."

Sister Maria Therese's hand embraced the Novice's cheeks, she smiled and nodded an affirmative nod and said, "Ah, Mon enfant." She kissed her cheek and left.

Bob felt powerless, his psyche continued to float on some nonsensical, illogical and irrational path. His night terrors intensified. Sleep was elusive. Reason was repositioned then lost. Life was disturbing fluid. Bob was emotionally adrift, floating without direction or purpose.

The Novice, the girl was there beside his bed when he first awakened from his long sleep, now seemed to be always at his bedside. No matter when the terrors aroused him from an erratic unreliable sleep, she seemed nearby.

He was clearly her charge.

The Last Dance in Delta

She would quickly take his hand and place it securely in hers. Her grip was sturdy. Her voice became soothing, exuding the optimism of her youth. He trembled.

Bob's situation embarrassed him. His helplessness and his incapacitating fear humbled him. He sought refuge from the horrifying intrusions. He found none.

The Novice would almost intuitively awaken as her patient's terrors would commence. She would take his hand and place it firmly and reassuringly in hers. While her own faith might ebb and flow as if a channel tide, she offered all she had to give, every ounce of strength she could muster. She gave freely of herself.

The young Novice, hardly a woman, stared at the broken warrior as he wept uncontrollably.

She began to sing Berceuse de Brahms, her own beloved lullaby from her childhood.

"Bonnie nuit, cher tresr, Fermetes yeux, et dors, Laisse ta tete, s'envoler. Au creux de ton oreilier, Unbeau reve passera, Et tu l'attraperan. Un beau reve passera, Et tu le relendras."

(Good night, dear treasure, Close your eyes and sleep. Let your head fly away in the hollow of your pillow. A beautiful dream will pass, and you will catch it. A beautiful dream will pass and you will remember it.)

Bob, feeling debased by his condition, his helplessness, his devastating fear, pressed his head into her elbow, hiding his face in the blousing fabric of her tunic and clutching her hand for dear life.

Bob felt as a small child seeking the shelter of his mother's bed, hiding from the disabling thunder of the storm. Seeking refuge, he pressed harder into the Novice's covering. He attempted to hide from the horrifying sights and sounds churning in his mind. He sobbed.

The corners of the Novice's eyes wept, blurring her vision. Somehow, Bob felt the tears he could not see.

Her blouse draped over his head, smothering his sobs and providing a shelter from a cruel and violent world that swirled in his mind.

The questioning Novice looked up into the eyes of Sister Maria Therese.

Sister said, "I told you his burns will heal faster than wounds to his mind. It seems, you, my child, possess the ointment that might heal a warrior's very soul."

The Novice cradled the broken Marine as he now cried uncontrollably. She carefully adjusted her soft cotton tunic concealing his head. He was as a child. Though she was little more, she placed her hand under his head, supporting him and drawing him to her. The feel of his hair in her hand pleased her. She drew him nearer and helped him find her.

The Novice nursed the warrior toward health.

In the moments between darkness and the light, the questioning Novice gazed into Sister Maria Therese's eyes. They held. The Novice looked for wisdom, for approval. She saw understanding and reverence.

Sister said, "Sometime we must begin again to be reborn. Your soldier is worthy of the fight."

Sister Maria Therese genuinely believed she had glimpsed life and salvation in a depth that even she could not understand. She knew that the hand of God had reached out and touched her Novice. Her love for the Blessed Mother deepened.

Sister tried to explain to herself. She felt God had allowed her to glimpse redemption, a rebirth and salvation.

Her face shown in a light best seen by God.

She smiled from somewhere deep in her soul and it reflected in her face.

Now not healed but healing, as mornings came, Bob began to find tangible comfort in his Catholic faith. Each morning, shortly after daybreak, Sister Maria Therese brought communion to him and the other Catholic soldiers in her care.

"The Body of Christ."

"Amen."

"May the Lord heal you and see you safely to your home."

Bob wondered about the technical propriety of her procedure but he never wondered long.

"Now, today, today we retrain your mind yet more"! Sister's directive left no doubt as to her intentions. Then, with the same flourish that accompanied her arrival, she left.

Bob had returned to the beginning to begin again.

CHAPTER 7:
The Homeward Crossing

IMPROVED BUT NOT YET HEALED, Bob Kelly made his homeward crossing aboard a hospital ship. He spent his days in a deck chair under a blanket and his nights in an actual bed.

A bed in a ward. Not luxurious but adequate. A ward that wasn't filled with the stench that comes from confining anxious men in a restricted space.

He took his meals and found them increasingly palatable. He enjoyed them but by the next day, he couldn't remember them.

Mostly he read. He found the selection in ship's library to be dated but remarkably satisfactory. Perhaps unchanged from the days when the ship was an ocean liner.

He found the spine had not been cracked on a copy of Booker T. Washington's Up from Slavery, so he cracked it. He re-read Jack London's The Sea Wolf and Call of the Wild for an unknown number of times. His continuing nighttime traumas sent him on an unsuccessful search for Sigmund Freud's The Interruption of Dreams.

His night time disturbances, terrifying nightmares, provided him with constant reminders that his battles were not yet done. He knew he had fights yet to fight but he did not feel unarmed.

He hated their erraticism, their violent unpredictability.

Bob Kelly told himself he knew two things. One, he was going home to Elizabeth. Second, he had seen enough killing for a lifetime.

The Last Dance in Delta

He promised himself that if peace existed in this world, he was going to find it. Once found, he was not going to leave it.

As the crossing seemed to extend itself and the North Atlantic became cold and bouncy, Bob's mind attempted to broaden his considerations. Intellectualizations he hoped would ease his conscience.

He started to think of Columbus and his crews. He found his current predicament to be lacking any comparable sense of adventure. He didn't mind.

Falling back on his discussions with Mr. Frazier, his high school history teacher, he began to grasp the hardships the sailors must have experienced. He wondered how those men endured the daily grind aboard the vessel. It was just their job.

Unable to find a substantial tie to Columbus' men, Bob approached a conversation with a Sergeant from North Carolina, another wounded Marine. Bob's logic dictated that a Carolina man might be more acquainted with the ways of the sea than an Oklahoma boy. Bob cautiously shared his mental escape.

The Carolina man was a solid listener. His observations were precise so long as the topic wasn't sex.

"Well, Sergeant, I'm bettin' old Columbus' boys, sailing around here on them old rickety boats, weren't gettin' any either."

"You and I have something to look forward to when we get home. I'm not certain Columbus' crew could even cling to such hopeful thoughts,"

Bob accepted that Carolina's needs might be less complex than his. With each passing day Bob became more aware that he was going to make it home. Only now did he allow himself the luxury of thinking about a life with Elizabeth.

So many of the thoughts now radiating through his mind were carried on Elizabeth's voice. He could hear her.

He missed her fragrance. He missed her sounds as she moved about. The softness of her hands, her slender fingers melted between his. He loved holding her hand.

He wondered if his recollections were accurate. He didn't know why he doubted but he did. They were too perfect.

As the miles floated by, Bob's yearning for Elizabeth increased. Only now was he able to admit to himself how horribly he had missed her.

To keep himself from obsessing about Elizabeth, Bob abandoned Columbus and began considering the Pilgrim's crossing. His admiration for them grew by the day as he tried to understand how difficult their voyage must have been.

How bad did it have to be to make leaving home and hearth in search of something in this "new world" seem like a sane thing to do? How challenging must Ireland have been for his grandfather, JJ Kelly, to make a crossing to America?

He became rather somber as he realized his logic had led him to consider his grandmother Kinta's family migration to eastern Oklahoma. The Choctaws had been forcibly removed from their homes in southern Mississippi to Indian Territory. It saddened him beyond what he could manage today, so he sat these thoughts back to consider on another day.

He was healing.

With the Pilgrims, he hypothesized these men were not just risking their lives but the lives of their wives and children. He struggled to identify the circumstances under which he would knowingly put Elizabeth's life in harm's way. He could not think of a single situation that would merit such a risk.

Carolina thought and asked, "Do you think they were getting' any on the Mayflower?"

"Sweet Jesus man, do you have a one-track mind?"

"Maybe."

"Well, I feel sorry for your wife."

Carolina became subdued. His voice softened and became filled with concern. He asked, "Do ya think a woman will make love with a one-legged man?"

Bob felt an unexpected surge of both compassion and doubt. Carolina's reaction surprised him and made him uncomfortable.

Still, he answered, "Of course." He hoped his personal lack of conviction with his answer wasn't bleeding through.

Wanting to avoid any undue display of sympathy, Bob added, "She has to, she married you."

Bob laughed but it was quite uneasy. His reply had only added to his discomfort and done nothing to ease what was now a clear and deep concern to Carolina.

Deciding to just keep stroking forward, Bob continued, "Carolina, I don't know what the hell I mean. I'm sure she can't wait to bed you again."

The Carolina man with the single leg was finding Bob's uncertainty strangely comforting.

"Ya think it's my middle leg she's interested in?"

Bob bypassed the easy retort that his middle leg was no longer his middle leg and replied, "Well, I can tell you for certain it isn't your romantic inclinations that attracts the lady."

Carolina laughed.

Bob shared more of his thoughts on the morality of the Pilgrims. The Carolina Marine dozed off to sleep.

Bob had awakened his own apprehensions. He thought of Elizabeth. He was profoundly ambivalent.

He doubted.

This long, measured boat ride to America allowed him to cast aside his wishes of self-harm. In the salt water air, he examined peace. By the end of the crossing, Bob still had not reached an agreement with himself.

He thought maybe peace was only the absence of war.

Bob wanted peace.

He had doubts.

CHAPTER 8:
Home in Oklahoma

Chronologically, Bob Kelly had not been away from Delta long. He had left Delta a boy, recently married and believing himself to be a man. He was returning home knowing better.

Somewhere in France, along about the time unrestrained inhumanity was tearing at his soul, that illusion was destroyed.

It seemed that before he just was. Now, he felt only the raw vestiges of who he once was had survived to return to home and hearth. A tattered ill-defined remanent.

He was with Elizabeth. She was his wife. Now, he wasn't returning to a comfortable, well-established and familiar lifestyle. It was all new when he left and it was still new now.

Man and woman together. Wife, husband, marriage. These concepts were still so new to him.

Despite the lines being blurred and ill-defined, Bob and Elizabeth Kelly loved each other. They were committed to the creation of an environment in which that love might flourish.

It was simply harder than they ever imagined.

Each direction he turned his ideas about himself were being challenged. The responsibilities of a husband in America at the close of World War I were clearly defined. As the authoritarian man of the house, he was to provide for and guide his family, to be the bread-winner.

He stretched himself in earnest but erratic efforts to conform to these definitions. They continued to elude him.

The Last Dance in Delta

"Son, its easy. You get up and come to work. How hard can it be?" His father didn't grasp his youngest son's uncertainty. To him, while the path of manhood might be confining, it was quite clear.

Bob's brother, John Charles Kelly, Jr., had stayed home, remained uninvolved in the war except for reaping the enormous profits that had been generated. Junior had also married his high-school sweetheart and followed the well-blazed trail his father and his grandfather had left.

For John, Jr., life was well-defined. Be it marriage, business or religion, John, Jr. understood the rules and he followed them. Life was both simple and rewarding.

Junior had graduated from Delta High School in its tenth graduating class, the only boy in a class of five. He established himself in the blossoming family farming and retail businesses and then, married the town beauty, Claire-Marie O'Brien.

Parenthood quickly descended on Junior and Claire-Marie.

Bob knew he wasn't Junior. He felt ill fit for his brother's life. It wasn't that he disliked the businesses, to the contrary, he quite enjoyed the dry goods business. The property and the newly evolving concept of investment piqued his curiosity. In that world he was rather prospering.

All uncertainties aside, what was becoming increasingly clear to Bob was that he would be expected to come to work in the family businesses.

Why not, he had a wife to support.

Bob had changed and he knew it. He needed to think. But what is the quality of a confused man's thinking? He was unsure. He wobbled a bit.

Delta was changing yet it was unchanged.

Bricking the main street and putting up a few additional electric street lamps was still being discussed. His father and brother were considering constructing a new feed store with a concrete loading dock but hadn't committed to the actual construction yet.

Bob thought to himself, "Delta is the same." He shook his head, smiling at his own naiveness, and thought more, "Of course it is, I wasn't gone that long."

Another part of him responded, "Only a lifetime."

Physically, Bob had a limp in his left leg. He believed his shattered ankle to be the least of his injuries. Bob told himself he was confident, confident but concerned.

War will make a man lie to himself.

Deep in the night, when sleep should be a man's friend, Bob was haunted by his own thoughts. Memories poured out from between the cracks, fractures left unguarded by sleep. Some he knew, some he didn't. All were chilling. He thrashed.

Bob believed any man who had done and seen what he believed he had done and seen would be forever changed. To believe otherwise would provide a fundamental challenge to his core logic.

Fortunately, Bob was comfortable with the religious and moral concepts of forgiveness. He granted himself a degree of absolution.

Fear. Bob's fear brought tangible change. It disrupted his sleep. It eroded his confidence, leaving his self-concept in a schizophrenic state of disarray. He knew something was amiss.

He could put forth a public persona that radiated assurance, faith in himself. But it was a façade, a protective pretense.

He judged nothing as predictable, nothing as reliable, nothing was established. Doubt creeped into his very essence. Doubt is disruptive.

Elizabeth. Elizabeth was his exception, his rock. Elizabeth was the one person in his life he totally and completely trusted.

It was with Elizabeth he could give voice to his doubts. He told her everything. He varnished nothing although he knew there had to be times that she wished he would.

He had stepped off the train and onto the platform of Delta Station and the girl ran and leaped into his arms. Her raw joy was unabashed.

The Last Dance in Delta

Then, the woman had fallen softly against him, seeking the assurances she so desperately needed. He had held her, unwilling to turn loose until his father cleared his throat.

Life was given an initial affirmation. Despite all of the ragged ends he knew were dangling, he found authentication in Elizabeth's arms. And she in his.

Again, John Charles Kelly, Sr. cleared his throat. Betty Kelly and Bonnie McCrary had looked at each other. Their eyes smiled. They liked their children very much.

From reading between the lines of his letters, Elizabeth sensed some of her husband's misgivings. She had known Bob since their infancy, unable to remember life without him. She had been most relieved to find that the inherent kindness remained engrained in the man, that it had not been destroyed. Maybe only scorched around the fringes.

She could not quantify it but she knew it.

She shared her apprehensions with no one. They were hers and hers alone. She knew the coming days and months and years would require every inch of resolve she possessed. She acknowledged these and accepted them.

Elizabeth steeled herself. She believed whatever might be required, she was capable of providing.

Elizabeth found words of comfort and guidance in a letter she received from Sister Maria Therese. She had cared for Bob in France when his wounds were fresh. Sister had marked his initial path toward recovery.

Elizabeth Kelly loved her husband. She would not put their life on hold for one day beyond what was unequivocally required.

Against this poignant milieu, Bob and Elizabeth Kelly allowed their lives to begin anew.

As for Delta, its citizens were in desperate need to believe in their hometown hero. The County Tribune had published tales of Bob's valor. The editor, absence facts, created a legend. Bob had been glorified, made into a revered warrior. Idealized by all except Bob. Bob heard the stories. He knew the truth. He judged himself neither heroic nor commendable.

Bob Kelly had merely survived. Others did not. He was uneasy. He felt an inevitable reckoning awaited him.

He had had his twenty-five days at Belleau Wood. Days filled with trenches and waiting and terrifying nights. Sudden eruptions of fighting, earthshaking rolling artillery barrages, combat that was hand to hand, face to face and eye to eye. Mustard gas. Dear God, mustard gas.

Repeated curtains of mustard gas. Gas made all fashions of retaliatory brutality feel justified, even morally acceptable.

Justifications. They were only veneers and veneers wear thinner with time.

He prayed for the memories to leave him. They didn't. Rather they slinked away into the cavernous crevices of his mind. From there, in the dead quiet of darkness, they could seep out to torment him.

Belleau Wood. Back to Belleau Wood. Bob could recall and acknowledge only detached bits. Reality was bent and distorted. He was left with a kaleidoscope and its gyrating shards of colored glass.

Yet, during his awaking hours sanity held sway. He could even begin to think of tomorrows. He anticipated success and believed success lay on the path marked by the concrete, the unemotional and the analytical. It had to.

Their house sat on the southern edge of the Kelly farm and just beyond the northern limits of Delta. She knew her husband could tell her the exact acreage. She only knew it was large and well-watered. And it was Kelly family land.

Mid-autumn came, the ground cooled and Elizabeth planted Jonquil bulbs.

And Bob did come home.

CHAPTER 9:
Yep Baseball

THE SPRING OF 1921 CAME. Jonquils bloomed along the walks of Bob and Elizabeth Kelly's home. The brilliant yellow blooms suggested promise. Hope could be found even when confidence lagged.

They had discovered a recovery process such as Bob's demanded measurement in tiny fragments. Elizabeth sought promise through conception. A conception that had not come despite her finest efforts since Bob's return.

She had come to refer to the arrival of her monthly as "the disappointment". As spring progressed into summer, she was several times convinced conception must have occurred. She felt it deep in her psyche. Then, when reality would force her to go to her drawer to retrieve her sanitary belt and napkins, disillusionment moved toward depression.

Bob knew but he didn't know. At times he was simply lost, self-absorbed and locked in an indistinct and imprecise struggle with his own terrors. He walked a lot.

Bob felt there must be something he could do. This woman, one he increasingly believed he knew, ultimately left him befuddled, just muddling along.

But who do you ask? Bob didn't know, so he prayed that she would teach him. He feared she might be uttering the same prayer. He hoped not because right now he could not find himself.

"Me thinks thee seeks thy arse with both hands, but it eludes thee." Elizabeth paraphrased Shakespeare to describe his circumstances. It pleased them both.

Still, he tried. Elizabeth tried harder. In their passionate pursuit of a child, they were finding each other.

Came a late summer day that Elizabeth's period arrived. Bob put his arm around her and she suggested he might want to take a walk. Bob decided to take a longer walk than ordinary.

In the course of the walk, Bob came upon two young boys playing baseball in a vacant lot. Bob had a thought. In fact, he had two thoughts.

Town baseball teams had long dotted the Oklahoma landscape.

Such teams were comprised of young men, decent baseball players all, who during the week were farmers and ranchers, carpenters and house painters, coal miners and strip miners, store clerks and store owners, and occasionally a man of the cloth.

Come the weekend, they were hometown heroes.

Bob thought Delta needed such a team. Local boys needed local heroes. Second, boys need a place to play baseball.

In February of 1922, Bob sat on his porch drinking his after-dinner coffee and reading the Sporting News that had arrived that day. The Sporting News was baseball's bible. Published weekly in St. Louis, all of the statistical details of previous week baseball action could be found between its pages. Even above the Wall Street Journal, Bob loved The Sporting News. He poured through its pages, committing much to memory.

The '21 season was in the books and '22 was just around the corner. Pitchers and catchers would report soon.

His St. Louis Cardinals had finished third and he felt they were on the verge of something big. Branch Rickey, the manager, Bob believed had them on the right path. Rogers Hornsby had hit .397 and had driven in 176 runs. Urban Shocker had led the league in wins with 27 was in the fold for another season.

The St. Louis Browns, the St. Louis entry in the fledging American League, had also finished third in '21. George Sisler

The Last Dance in Delta

was promising, his .371 had him nipping at Ty Cobb's flannels all season.

Although new, the American League had star power. Babe Ruth with the Yankees hit 56 homeruns and drove in 121 runs during the 1921 season.

And the league now had the unabashed support of The Sporting News, in fact, they hyped the new league, exactly twenty years old in 1921.

After their loss to the Giants in the World Series, writers saw the New York Yankees as the team of the future. Bob was iffy being always prone to believe that role belonged to the Cardinals.

"Baseball."

Elizabeth stared and sought context for his sudden enthusiasm. Bob was clearly keen about something.

"Bob?"

"Elizabeth, Sweet, I'm going to town for a few minutes."

"Do you expect to be long?"

"Baseball."

Elizabeth shook her head. She had rarely seen her husband so animated about something seemingly so mysterious.

She shouted as he stepped on the porch, "Baseball?"

"Yep. Baseball."

Bob put in an appearance at the Kelly Companies offices over the First State Bank of Delta, the McCrary bank. The brick building with massive marble columns at the bank entry was the only enterprise in which the McCrary's and the Kelly's held an equal interest.

Seeing his father-in-law at his desk in the bank, Bob tapped on the window, then waved to Dub McCrary.

Dub smiled and waved back.

Bob topped the stairs.

"Good morning, Maylene."

Maylene Woodard was his father's secretary and office manager. After her sophomore year in high-school she was considered the finest student in the secretarial training program. Now, some twenty years, twenty pounds and three children later, she remained quite attractive. She had the olive skin of a woman who had significant Choctaw blood and the raven black hair of her ancestors.

"Mornin' Mister Bob. Here to see your Daddy?"

"My father and my brother, please." She looked indecisive, so he added, "Just need a minute."

Looking up from his desk, Charles Kelly saw Bob.

"Well, Son, what merits you paying a visit to the office?"

"Baseball!" Excitement made an unwelcome push into Bob's voice.

His father smiled and shook his head. He was just happy to see his youngest enthused about something. Bob was more than enthused.

In the pages of The Sporting News and their promotion of the new American league, Bob found a passion he thought had long passed. In the Kelly Company office, the Delta Shamrocks Amateur Baseball Team and Red River Baseball Association was conceived and birthed.

Elizabeth spoke directly, "Bob, you know my daddy's quite the baseball fan. He isn't going to like it if you don't include him. At least in the money part."

"Well crud, you're right. I just wasn't thinking."

After a visit with his son-in-law, Dub McCrary and the First State Bank of Delta made a sizeable investment in the Delta Shamrocks Amateur Baseball Team.

William "Bill" O'Brien, the Head Teller at First Bank, was also a County Commissioner. The questions about the fledgling team using of the county facility disappeared. County equipment roared into action and baseball field at the County Fairgrounds, out of use for a number of years, was revitalized.

Prisoners from the County Jail enjoyed three days in the sun as they removed loose stones and otherwise weeded the field after the road graders passes, leveling the infield.

Dub and Bob bumped into each other, arriving at the same to time to survey the progress.

Dub observed, "Well, I see Cooter has got a sledge and is trying to unearth a boulder size rock." He laughed.

Bob laughed. They watched Cooter, a five-foot, ten-inch mountain of muscle with a propensity toward bar brawls, trying to break up a sizable stone just outside the foul line at third base.

"Who do you think is stronger, Tillman or Cooter?"

Bob shook his head and said, "I truly don't know but if they ever decide to find out I don't want to miss it."

Dub continued, "Nor would I."

Bob concluded, "I've seen Tillman move the impossible at the store."

As sledgehammer once again rung against the stone. Dub shook his head in a blend of admiration and amazement and said, "It would be a sight to behold now wouldn't it."

Both men knew such a contest between a black man and white man would never happen.

His voice softening to a whisper, Dub told his son-in-law, "My money would be on the darkie."

Bob flinched ever so slightly. Though keeping his own counsel, Bob agreed but he thought it would be a heck of a fight.

First State Bank of Delta's sponsorship added community prestige to the forming organization. Additionally, Dub McCrary was a baseball fan.

His financial and moral support were vital to the emergence of the Delta Shamrocks as a first-class amateur baseball team.

The Red River Baseball Association gave the Shamrocks a solid league in which to compete.

In their inaugural season, the Shamrocks played pickup games against whoever was available. Opponents that first season were largely teams from sizable rural crossroads with a school and a community identity. None were very distant from Delta.

A somewhat invigorated Bob visited every community within a reasonable distance, attending Lions Club luncheons, VFW forums and Elks Club dinners trying to organize an adequate number of like-minded young businessmen to form a regional baseball league.

The summer of 1923 the fledging four town league, none more than sixty miles removed from the other, with a twenty-four-game schedule of Sunday doubleheaders played during the months of June, July and August.

Bob Kelly, now 24 years old, was the catcher and by default the manager of the Shamrocks.

Her managerial and bookkeeping skills on full display, Elizabeth Kelly became the General Manager and a baseball fan.

The Delta Shamrocks were a community service.

Bob and Elizabeth built a baseball field for the boys.

CHAPTER 10:
Sunday, July 8, 1923

THE MCINTOSH IRONMEN were in town for a doubleheader. Their ace, a tall and burly man pushing thirty years old and showing the beginnings of a middle age paunch, had hung out in the lower echelons of professional baseball for a number of years before returning home to work the family farm. Elmer Bloodworth was scheduled to pitch the second game of the double header. Because of reputation as a quality pitcher and as somewhat short-tempered, Bloodworth always drew a crowd.

Bob spread the news that Les Earl, a forty plus-year-old left-handed round mound of slow breaking stuff who rarely missed the plate and was a local favorite, would pitch opposing Bloodworth.

The standard league admission was fifteen cents for adults and children under 12 were free. Players families free. The gate was on the honor system. A two-pound coffee can was placed on a table at both entrances to fairgrounds. Fans came in, placed their money in the cans and made their change if necessary. It was a true honor system and Bob knew baseball fans to be honorable.

Also, Elizabeth had confirmed that most of the money was and would be made at the concession stand.

First of the two seven inning games started at 2:00 PM. This allowed adequate time for all to attend Sunday Morning Church services. Sunday dinners cooked and served.

The second game, the Bloodworth-Earl matchup would begin 30 minutes after the first game. Following a Shamrocks victory in the first game, the second game began on schedule.

Bob hit a ringing single in the first inning, driving in Bud Wigginton from second base. Bloodworth pointed at him and smiled.

In the fourth, Bob hit a screamer that kicked up chalk behind third base before scooting into the corner. Bob stood on second base with a stand-up double. Bud's brother, Pete, then drove him home.

As Bob crossed the plate, Bloodworth who gave up runs begrudgingly glared at Bob. This time, Bob smiled. Bloodworth frothed. He also now trailed in the game 3-1.

Les Earl found something on this afternoon that he hadn't seen in a goodly number of summers. After five innings, he had walked no one and struck out seven.

Hitting second in the top of the sixth, Bloodworth, before setting himself in the batter's box, yelled out to Earl, "You don't dare throw me one of your watermelons."

He stepped in and tapped the plate with his bat. On his first pitch, Earl broke off one of the big, soft roundhouse curves only a lefty can throw. It dropped in for a called first strike.

He worked the second pitch just off the plate, outside. Bloodworth moved up in the box, ready to hit a slow breaking pitch.

Bob flashed the sign and Earl threw all the fast ball he had left. It jammed the right-handed hitting Bloodworth who swung and made feeble contact down on the handle. The foul ball dribbled toward the visitor's dugout.

"Damn watermelons." Bob smiled and added, "Bettin' you can't hit it twice."

"Up yours Kelly,'

"Play ball!"

This time the roundhouse fooled Bloodworth. He stood as the soft curve broke in toward Bloodworth and caught the paint.

The umpire's right arm shot up and he loudly declared, "That's three!" He turned and walked toward the screen and his water jug.

Bob held the ball up and mused, "Watermelon."

By the bottom of the sixth inning, Johnson Bloodworth was full on seething angry.

The top of the Shamrocks order was scheduled up. Tommy Hern led the inning off with a walk from the fuming Bloodworth, ball four coming on a pitch Bloodworth thought was in the strike zone.

Bud Wigginton swung late but got his second hit of the day by scuffing a soft looper that dropped in front of a hesitant right fielder. Hern, having to watch the ball down, eased into second.

With runners on first and second and no one out, Bob stood ready to step into the box. Turning to exchange a word with the umpire, his back was turned to Bloodworth.

Bob Kelly never saw the baseball Johnson Bloodworth threw at him. The ball struck square in the back of his skull. Blood spurted from his split scalp. He staggered once, half-turned and fell forward.

He landed face first in the dirt and clay around home plate. He moaned and rolled to his side.

He tried to right himself and then he did.

"God damn it, Coach stay down."

Bob gathered himself, on one knee and balancing his right side with his bat. He tasted dirt. He spit, unsuccessfully. The metallic coopery taste of his blood mixed with the gritty clay of the batter's box.

He tried to get up and failed. He pressed and came back to his knees. He reached up and with a dirty hand tried to wipe the gritty mixture from the corner of his mouth.

Uncertain, he wobbled, then steadied himself. He gripped his bat in the right hand and pressed it into the ground.

He pushed away the hands that tried to assist him.

"Here bite on this!" The owner of this excited voice shoved the corner of wet towel into Bob's mouth. The touch of water helped right him.

Bob felt an unreasoned rage climb into his psyche, confused, all rational thought left.

The still enraged Bloodworth was virtually standing over him, pointing an accusatory finger at him.

He saw the Hun standing over him. He saw the pistol at the ready.

Bob gripped his rifle and swung. The rifle cracked into the shin of the German officer. The German fell into the mud of the trench writhing with pain.

Bob swung his rifle again, striking the Hun in the square across the shoulders driving him face first into the mud. Another of the Hun tried to wrench him away. Bob's free elbow caught him square in the face.

A five-gallon water cooler constructed of corrugated metal and still containing considerable water as well as a good-sized chunk of floating ice sat on the end of the Shamrocks bench.

How Elizabeth, tears of pain and anger flowing down her face, found the where-with-all to pick up the jug and to carry it toward the belligerent men remains a mystery.

But, she did and players parted like the Red Sea before her advance. Joe O'Connor, a mountain of a third baseman and the only remaining blacksmith in Delta, took the water jug from her, lifted it high and dumped it squarely over Bob. The rather large remnants of the ice block struck Bob in the shoulder before falling squarely into Bloodworth's face.

"Damn you, Bob Kelly, stop!"

Elizabeth began to impulsively bark each word in a repetitive distinct staccato clip, "Stop! Stop! Stop!"

Sobs joined her tears as her fists were reigning blows on his shoulders. She screamed, "Just stop!"

Her arms locked around his neck.

Bob's confusion seeped from his eyes. He heard his wife. How? Not here in harm's way? He stopped. Visions vacillated. The Hun was Bloodworth, Bloodworth was the Hun. There was no Hun, there was no Bloodworth. Yet, there was both.

A strange man sat with his broken nose spurting blood and completely befuddled.

Bob looked and saw his wife. Rage left.

Bob's head hurt.

He reached up for O'Connor's arm. Joe pulled him upright. Unsteady, he viewed the carnage around him.

The Last Dance in Delta

His eyes must have reflected his confusion because Joe thumped him on the shoulder and said, "You won."

Bob looked at Elizabeth. He started to form a sentence then fumbled it. He looked at her. His disorientation dismayed her.

Struggling for a grip and then catching a glimpse of the Model T, Bob said, "Looks like you'll have to drive me home."

She assisted him to the car and into his seat. Then, scandalously she got into the driver's seat, revealing her lower thighs as she hiked her dress high enough as to not impede her access to the pedals. She started the Model T.

She called to her brother-in-law, "Junior, find Doctor Fulton and have him come to the house."

She arranged her dress. Satisfied, Elizabeth Kelly drove her husband home.

Within hours the entire town of Delta knew Bob Kelly had been teaching his wife, Elizabeth, to drive. It was just shameful.

Bob's night terrors didn't miraculously leave him but they now grew better. Elizabeth and Bob's nights often passed more comfortably.

"Did you hear about my Daddy?"

Bob's head hurt too bad to shake a vigorous negative answer.

"He tried to convince Sheriff Kennedy to arrest Bloodworth."

Bob found a chuckle and asked, "And?"

"Well, Daddy was convincing the good sheriff that it was assault if not assault with a weapon."

"This is a time I might agree with your Daddy cause it damn sure felt like a weapon."

"Oh, you T.R., you don't know what it felt like."

"Well, you're obviously no F.N.!"

"F.N.?"

"Florence Nightingale."

Elizabeth drew a pillow back but stopped short of throwing it, fearful she might hit him. She smiled.

She walked to the couch, bent down and kissed his forehead, a lingering full-on forehead kiss.

"Florence doesn't share your bed."

Days later, Bonnie McCrary reminded Betty Kelly, "I told you that Elizabeth was the one I feared I would catch smoking a cigar. Who knew about cars?"

The mothers laughed.

"I heard she hiked her dress like a flapper."

"How funny, I just love our Elizabeth."

The mothers tried to suppress a girlish giggle. They couldn't.

CHAPTER 11:
A Distress Signal

IT WAS THE FRIDAY AFTER THANKSGIVING and it was a breathtakingly pleasant day. Bob had taken Tom McCrary, Elizabeth's cousin from Oklahoma City, flyfishing up at Blue Hole.

Elizabeth, morning coffee in hand, stepped on the front porch and mused about yesterday. Thanksgiving had been a pleasant celebration at the Clan McCrary. Her family dinners, holiday or not, were by any standard quite formal. Even she found them stiff. She was pleased with the fashion in which her husband had adapted to her family's gatherings.

Kelly holidays were boisterous, McCrary holidays were not.

He offered no critique of her family. Well, other than occasionally offering an observation of her father's investment strategy.

"I behave myself because I want your folks to believe you married well."

"I did marry well," she paused. "Just not as well as you," Elizabeth sparred.

She smiled and moved off the porch, walking toward the newly poured front sidewalk. She visualized a sidewalk planting of additional jonquil bulbs next week.

Back on the porch, she nestled into the porch swing. A throbbing pain struck her lower abdomen, an uncomfortable cramp. Her time of denial was now brief. Her disappointment was not.

Two days ago, she sat with her sister-in-law, Claire-Marie, and held her hand as she sobbed until her soul cracked because she was pregnant with her fourth child. She did not know how she was going to tell Junior.

"Well, I'd sure find something to tell Junior alright."

Yesterday, Claire-Marie had wept because she was expecting. Today, Elizabeth wept because she wasn't.

Elizabeth stood. She screamed at the air. "It's not right!"

No one heard. So, she repeated it several times. Still, no one heard.

"Fuck! FUCK! – Fuck."

Her face flushed. She couldn't believe her outburst. It wasn't even her word yet she screamed it. And still, no one heard.

She made the Sign of the Cross.

She adjusted her apron and straightened her dress. Reassembled, she went to her dresser drawer to gather her essentials.

CHAPTER 12:
July 1925

AUGUSTUS "GUS" ROBERT KELLY was born on Tuesday, July 21, 1925. In the midst of a hot, humid Oklahoma July, his mother, Claire-Marie Kelly, began serious labor shortly after midnight. Her labor with Gus, her fourth child and third son, was relatively short. At 1:01 PM according to the ticking, noisy old mechanical clock on the wall of the middle bedroom and following a solar eclipse, the baby boy was born. He was youngest and last of the four children born of her marriage to Charles Andrew Kelly, Jr.

Had this newest child been a girl, her mother-in-law, Betty Kelly was intent on naming her Aoife with the intention of using the traditional Gaelic pronunciation EE-fa. The name meant both beautiful and radiant.

Claire-Marie wanted a girl. Gus was another boy. She was bitterly disappointed.

James Fulton, M.D., paused in his completion of the required forms. He yawned. He had spent a long night with a very ill child living in the San Bois bottoms before arriving at the Kelly home. Now he looked over the top of his half-glasses at Claire-Marie. The joy he saw in the faces of so many mothers wasn't there.

Doctor Fulton, now in his mid-sixties, stretched. This smallish man, now balding with an expanding waistline, found some relief from his chronic rheumatism.

He took his watch from his vest pocket and mentally thought his way through his afternoon.

"Have you and Junior decided on a name for the lad?"

"Augustus Robert Kelly."

She sighed.

He adjusted his glasses. He considered how grateful he was for bifocals. Then, he recorded the name.

Claire-Marie edged the soft receiving blanket back from her son's face. She studied him.

"What do you plan on calling him?" the good doctor asked. At this time in his career, the doctor had little actual curiosity about a child's name but he needed to explore the mother's affect.

"Gus."

The smiles and enthusiasm he often saw in even the most exhausted of new mothers still did not emerge. He made a note.

She didn't say that she had an ample number of Charles in her life, her husband, his father and her eldest son. It was even her middle son's middle name. So, Augustus for Shakespeare and Robert for his uncle, Bob.

Clare-Marie became aware she was tired, she wanted to sleep. She made a slight adjustment expecting to increase her comfort only to discover she was quite tender. Then, the infant Gus' empty mouth began to suckle. She sighed in acknowledgment and exhaustion, she brought him to her chest, she felt her breast let down.

Again, she sighed and helped him better latch on. She felt tears forming.

There was an ever so soft tap on the bedroom door. It cracked open. Her sister-in-law, Elizabeth Kelly, edged her head inside the doorway.

"May I?"

Dr. Fulton, assuming the question was directed toward him, responded, "Of course, come admire this healthy baby boy."

Dr. Fulton again stretched and straightened his back, seeking even a modicum of relief. He then began to debate between lunch or a brief nap on his office couch.

He snapped his black bag shut, again congratulated the new mother and left the room.

Elizabeth was one of Claire-Marie's favorite people. She did want to share a smile with her, just not right now. She arranged the corner of the blanket so that the infant's head and her breast was covered. She didn't know why this sudden burst of modesty overtook her. She and Elizabeth had often talked while her older children nursed.

Elizabeth wanted to comfort her sister-in-law but every option seemed awkward. She intuitively felt some reassurance was needed. She was just wavering as to where to begin. She leaned forward, her hand hesitantly hovering before coming to rest on Claire-Marie's arm. Then, she saw the tears, a visible trickle inching its way down on Clare-Marie's cheek. Using her thumb, Elizabeth touched the tears, spreading the moist drops against the salty sweat that moistened Claire-Marie's face.

Elizabeth came to be happy with her sister-in-law, but she knew immediately these were not tears of joy being shed. She shrank back into the chair. The leather squeaked. Elizabeth's hand indecisively stroked the arm of the chair.

For moments, neither woman spoke. Then, Gus released his suction grip on his mother's nipple. His head wobbled, unsteady, then settled contentedly against his mother's chest.

Elizabeth leaned forward hopefully. She said, "Here, let me take him."

"Oh, God yes, please do."

Childbirth had exhausted her. Caring for her three older children had exhausted her. Taking care of her husband and his needs had exhausted her. Physically, mentally and emotionally Claire-Marie was exhausted.

"I'm just plain tuckered."

She adjusted herself on the bed, made a sound of discomfort, then said, "Oh, Sweet Mary, I'm so sore, help me."

Elizabeth laid the infant in his bassinet and helped its mother adjust herself on the bed.

The amount of blood troubled her. She wished Kinta was there. Claire-Marie slept.

Dr. Fulton stepped over the shallow ditch and into the street. He noted the splotches of dried mud freckling the car's black finish. Maybe Ford will add a color so. But every color will show Oklahoma mud.

He lifted the seat. He picked up the dip stick and checked the amount of gasoline in the tank. He judged he had enough gasoline for at least another fifty miles.

The doctor replaced the seat and went to the other side to get in. Settled, he reflected a mental concession and reached for his bag. He withdrew a nondescript bottle, unscrewed the cap and downed a gulp.

He examined the label. He chuckled realizing it made no difference what the label read, he called it all Lydia Pinkham's magic elixir. It was a lovely blend of vegetable oils, alcohol and cocaine. A magical concoction that eased the pain of his rheumatism.

He leaned back into the seat, really just a padded buggy seat, and admired his Ford with its Inline 4-cylinder engine with a spark ignition. Today, he was most grateful for the electric starter Mr. Ford had equipped his cars with some five years ago.

Dr. Fulton just didn't feel he had another crank left in him, not on a scalding hot day.

He drove downtown.

On the day of Gus Kelly's birth, miles to the east in Tennessee, John Scopes was found guilty of violating the Butler Act which prohibited the teaching of evolution in the Tennessee Public Schools. He was fined one hundred dollars. William Jennings Bryan, a special prosecutor, offered to pay the fine. The American Civil Liberties Union attorney representing Scopes, Clarence Darrow, declined and appealed.

Although he remained uncertain about Darrow's socialistic bent, Bob was an admirer of Clarence Darrow. He unsuccessfully lobbied his brother and sister-in-law to name the newborn, should it be a boy, Darrow. Darrow something Kelly. His effort was soundly rebuffed.

On the day of Gus' birth, his Uncle Bob was more attentive to the trial than he was to the arrival of his newest nephew. He had followed the trial with considerable interest. He grabbed the headlines from WKY Radio broadcasting from its studio in the basement of the Hutchens Hotel in downtown Oklahoma City. A few days later, he would relish the details from the St. Louis

The Last Dance in Delta

Post-Dispatch which arrived regularly in his mail box at the Delta Post Office.

The Post-Dispatch arrived as rapidly as Bob felt he needed his news.

As with many in 1925, Bob was riveted to the stock market. However, he saw more gamble and less security than his peers. He found the idea of purchasing anything on a margin unacceptable while feeling stocks to be doubly so.

The investment of Kelly monies had become Bob's bailiwick. Despite the goading of his brother, The Kelly Companies bought no stock on the margin.

After his return from the war, Bob had carved out areas of the family businesses that allowed him reasonable personal isolation and was in the process of forging them into quite profitable arms of the Kelly enterprises.

Bob cautiously followed the stock market. He saw it as much riskier than did his peers. He believed in Mark Twain's insight, "Buy land, they ain't making anymore." Perhaps, his most useful observation of France during his time there was noting how expensive the land was and he concluded he knew why.

Bob judged Twain to be wise beyond wit.

Bob looked at the United States, now with forty-eight states, and reasoned that between birthrate and immigration our population was growing while our land size wasn't.

"Look Junior, you take any decade and land is going to be worth more at the end of it than it was at the beginning of it."

"If I buy a John Deere, I'll sell it and make a profit."

"But I don't buy two John Deere. I don't need two. A lot of money can be made from these little wads we don't need to spend today. It is going to be what we do with these bits of extra money."

Bob Kelly was becoming very good at growing these little bits of money into very big bits.

Bob was slowing starting to fancy himself a farmer and rancher. But it was from his desk in the downtown offices of The Kelly Companies that others came to view him as head of land acquisition and investments. In barely seven years, Bob created an invaluable position for himself in which his tendency toward social isolation was an asset.

The Delta Shamrocks continued to flourish. They were becoming a community asset. Bob was baseball's primary advocate in Delta.

Elizabeth and Bob Kelly remained powerless to conceive. As is often the case in a small rural community, there was considerable and diverse conjecture. The hypotheses ranged from straight forward speculation about Elizabeth's infertility to the belief that Bob had sustained an injury of a quite personal nature during the war that he was unwilling to disclose.

Aware, Elizabeth had mused that in the creation of such myths the wife was somehow flawed while the otherwise perfect husband sustained an unavoidable injury. Her summary conclusion was that some things are simply as they are.

At bridge club, Doctor Fulton's wife, Mabel, swore that the doctor didn't know. When pushed, Mabel was tempted to tell a particular nosey-netty that she didn't know about Elizabeth Kelly's pregnancy concerns but she did know about an anomaly in the nosey-netty's nether regions.

Of course, she had no such knowledge. But she alone knew her husband would never share such information about a patient with her. She liked leading the other ladies to believe that he would and if it was adequately juicy, he regularly did. And she hoped her husband never discovered her deception.

The new born Gus' mother, Claire-Marie, remained perpetually exhausted. Elizabeth's maternal assistance was appreciated and increasingly utilized.

By the summer of 1927, Elizabeth Kelly's home was fully equipped to provide comprehensive care for young Gus.

Elizabeth had time in abundance for the lad. Bob teased her that she doted on the boy. At that point, she would, with a smile, make an old Gaelic gesture suggesting he should rather piss off.

Bob was having greater difficulty in finding a role for himself. He was observant. He became accomplished at observing and remarking on his wife's swiftly developing maternal talents. Basically, Bob felt useless.

In a backroom conversation at Kelly Mercantile, Tillman Johnson allowed, "Mr. Bob, ain't nothin' more useless than a daddy when a woman's mothering."

"So, what does a guy do?"

"Ya stand back and wait till she needs ya."

At this point, Bob didn't think Elizabeth was going to need him again. When Baby Gus wasn't with her, Elizabeth fretted.

When, while at their home, young Gus broke out with a bad case of chicken pox. Oatmeal baths, calamine lotion continually dabbed on with a soft flannel cloth, doses of aspirin carefully measured to infant strength were administered.

Dr. Fulton said it would take five to seven days to resolve itself.

Elizabeth's fretting became an insidious worry that refused to release its grip. Her perpetual activity left her exhausted.

Bob was needed. He wasn't the first team but his effort wasn't lacking.

"It's just awful that a little one is sick like this."

"Yes, it is."

After six days only a few angry crusts remained. Gus seemed quite happy.

Bob Kelly pushed back from the dinner table, adjusting his chair. Gus was toddling across the floor.

Bob scrutinized the boy, then said to Elizabeth, "Your nephew walks like a drunk sailor."

Gus took a hard seat on the floor. He grabbed a ball with both hands and threw it in Bob's direction.

Bob reached up and caught the rubber ball just when it looked as if it would sail over his head.

"Dang! The boy has an arm on him"

Bob rolled the ball to Gus. Gus gathered it in and fired it back in his direction. Bob reached to make the catch. The wobbling Gus applauded his uncle's efforts.

Bob looked at the boy and felt something stir. He didn't recognize it. He liked it. And Bob liked Gus.

Catch is a universal bonding game.

Bob and Gus found common ground. They both like to throw a ball. And catch a ball.

Elizabeth smiled. She felt a calm, a relief like a person feels when a tint of equilibrium is gained.

Gus flopped on his butt.

Chapter 13:
The Atwater-Kent, Model 55

July 1929

"MORNING, MAYLENE. HOW'S THE FAMILY?"

"Doing well, Mister Bob."

"I hear your eldest has been boxing for the VFW. You should be proud of him."

"Oh, yes, we are. We hope he can fight in those Golden Gloves in Muskogee in August."

"That is a good event that has really caught on. Let me know if he gets in."

"Oh, I certainly will."

"My brother in his cave?"

"Yes sir. Just go right on back."

"Brother, Atwater-Kent had a new radio available, a Model 55."

Junior's general disinterest reflected in his eyes.

He continued, "The Kiel Company out of Milwaukee is building hand-crafted cabinets for them."

He did his best to make Junior believe that was a tidbit with which he should be quite impressed. The fact was Bob had never heard of the Kiel Company of Milwaukee but he knew it would only take a well-placed article in Delta's only newspaper and every literate soul in the county would know who the Kiel Company was.

Junior started to quiz his younger brother a bit, but thought better of it. He simply asked, "How much?"

Bob continued as if he hadn't heard his brother's inquiry. "It has the highest quality vacuum tubes. It is a technical marvel for me and piece of stunning hand-crafted parlor furniture for Elizabeth."

"Bob, how much?"

"Retail is $175 unloaded right here on our dock."

"Well, Jesus Bob! Why don't you just bring the entertainers right here to the Lyric?"

"Well, I've researched --."

Junior gave a derisive snort and concluded, "Oh, I know you have researched the living hell right out of it."

Bob smiled. He resumed his pitch, "Now, Brother, you are going to want one too. Claire-Marie would absolutely love it."

Bob paused, then went on, "Think about this. If you unleased some of that charm of yours, I'll just bet you could get us an exclusive dealership for Atwater-Kent radios in our part of the state. Then, the model 55 would only cost us $105.00"

"Researched it did you?"

"Some."

"You got the telephone number I need to call?"

"Left it on your desk."

"Oh, Bob. You still thinking it is good move for us to get out of Homestake Mining? You got us out of a ton of stuff over the past two years. Couldn't we make more staying put?"

"Maybe, but we like cash for now."

"Oh, we do, do we?"

"Yes. we do. Later, Brother."

On his way to The Delta Café, Bob thought, "I like it and investments are my part of this business."

Over the past seven years, as he increased the Kelly Company's positions in cash, cattle and the distressed land he might purchase, his family had questioned him. He resented it but never expressed his resentment. He thought they had never questioned him as the investment profits had poured into the family coffers.

Bob Kelly, Kelly Companies, had still never purchased a single share of stock on the margins.

Bob started to sit down on a stool at the counter.

The Last Dance in Delta

"Bob come join us."

Bob's father-in-law, Dub McCrary hailed him from a booth where he sat with two other local merchants. In the Delta Café, the afternoon coffee always had a rather steely flavor or maybe as Elizabeth contented, it was just scorched. But it was always hot.

Bob liked his father-in-law. Bob would joke with Elizabeth that her father was far to proper to ever be a Kelly. Elizabeth knew her dad valued and enjoyed life's formalities and often tried to impose them on Delta's small city social circles.

Bob came to be more accepting of these as he came to realize Dub sincerely valued these stiffnesses and conventions.

"What is going on with the Kelly Companies?"

"Just trying to tie up a distributorship."

Bob didn't include the concept of exclusive distributorships.

CHAPTER 14:
A Roaring Good Time

THE 1920'S WERE PROSPEROUS TIMES for those who could tolerate the jeopardy. These were times of times of affluence, consumption and excess.

In the rural towns of America, like Delta, success was defined in several different fashions. As with their metropolitan counterparts, it was always ostentatious. Delta's affluent drove Ford's but the youth fantasied of the Dusey, Duesenberg's supercharged straight eight Model J, that long vehicle with the spare mounted behind the left front wheel with its elegant trunk attachment. with its two-passenger cabin.

Car dealerships in Delta went from one to four. Specialty clothing shops emerged. There were now three banks but the Kelly Companies remained loyal to Dub McCrary.

Some families gathered, pooled their money and constructed the Delta Country Club complete with a nine-hole golf course, two tennis courts, a ball room and a dining room. While not Tulsa Country Club, it was rather nice. They built the clubhouse from native stone and the dance floor in the ballroom was made of wood hewn from the hardwood forest near Delta.

Celebrated on the Saturday night between Christmas and New Year's Day, the Years End Ball at the Country Club was the highpoint of the winter social season. Gowns and their accessories had been in the planning and construction stages since the previous year's celebration. Consistent with the times, it celebrated the successes of the previous year and not some prayful hope for better time in the New Year.

Although it was not the intent at its selection, it was an expedient date for those who would seek absolution on New Year's Day.

Prosperities children now tended to move away from the restrictive accountability they believed dwelled in their family homes and in Delta-sized communities. They sought a libertarian autonomy coupled prosperity in the cities. They found decent paying jobs that didn't involve the unrelenting, bone-breaking labor of the farm. Further, they found city reared spouses and they settled in the city.

Parents died. A few returned to the land, but most didn't. Bob offered a fair price and purchased their land including the mineral rights. Land that would soon be discovered have oil and natural gas beneath it as well as coal that could be strip mined.

As the decade evolved, The Kelly Companies became increasingly committed to providing high quality employment to the county.

Just to the north of Delta, a negro community, Johnstown, named for Tillman Johnson's grandfather, also flourished. It was a quieter more agrarian prosperity. In Oklahoma in the 1920's, understated prosperity was the safer sort for negro communities.

Johnstown had an exception.

For years, utilizing the pure water from several natural springs, corn grown on their farms and aged in new barrels made of oak harvested from forested Kelly land, Johnstown residents had distilled a remarkable 100 proof Bourbon concoction.

Now, some of the uninformed called it whiskey. Tillman Johnson insisted that the Johnstown creation met the standards of corn and aging in new oak barrels to be considered Bourbon. So, Bourbon it was.

With the onset of Prohibition, Tillman found a great unfilled demand tapping at his door. Tillman, being a law-abiding man, had no desire to undertake a criminal enterprise. It just rather evolved.

At Prohibition's advent, Oklahoma had a number of thriving and affluent all-black communities. He forecast a dwindling, then nonexistent, supply of good quality bourbon in their part of Oklahoma. He believed the Johnstown still had a natural in if not a moral obligation to the all-negro towns such as Johnstown, Boley, Taft, Rentiesville, Lima, Lewisville and Vernon. Further, there were substantial black communities contained within the cities of Muskogee and McAlester.

Eager entrepreneurs soon sought distributorships.

The Johnstown community bourbon business expanded. The original still, now some forty years old, could not manage the demand. Tillman needed a bigger and better still.

Tillman evaluated the options and decided on a business discussion with Bob Kelly. A meeting soon convened on the Bob's front porch.

Bob had misgivings about involving the family enterprises in an illegal enterprise but he was interested in helping Tillman and the Johnstown community. So was Elizabeth.

In fact, Elizabeth within the year had unsuccessfully attempted to convince the County School Board they should undertake building and operating a school in Johnstown which was now larger than any other rural community sustaining a one or two room school. Current education in Johnstown was judged "informal yet effective".

Beyond that Bob struggled seeing making good sipping bourbon as illegal.

He explained to Tillman that the Kelly Companies couldn't finance an illegal enterprise such as a whiskey still.

"A Bourbon still."

"Right, sorry Tillman. I do know better."

Tillman smiled as if to say I know you do.

"Tillman, I'll tell you what I'll do. There are few men I'd even consider a pure cash transaction with, but you are one." Bob rubbed a baseball he had retrieved from a basket next to his chair, then continued, "I'll make you a loan, just me to you."

Bob studied Tillman and adjusted his offer, "No, I'll make a cash investment in your bottling and barrel-making company. Not a loan, you'd owe me nothing."

Bob had come home from the war to an inheritance. He decided to use it for the good.

Tillman looked earnest and Bob went on, "Get whatever still you want for your Bourbon. I also want a second still. You're going to try to grow some barley and learn how to malt it."

Tillman's sudden excitement overwhelmed him and he blurted out, "You wantin' to make scotch whiskey!"

"Well, single malt whiskey. The Delta bottoms aren't Scotland but they'll have to do."

"Mr. Bob, the fun 'ill be in the tryin'."

The two products were distinguishable by a simple label one reading TJK Single Malt Whiskey and one reading TJK Bourbon. A dandy and safe distillery that provided spirits during Prohibition and then cash money jobs during the Depression.

Johnstown constructed a fine four room school of native stone and lumber secured from surrounding land. Some noted the construction resembled Delta Country Club.

A brass plaque hung over the doorway to the Lower Grade School room that read Elizabeth McCrary Kelly Room. The similar plaque over the Upper Grade School room read Matilda Raymond Johnson.

The ladies were greatly pleased.

Bob knew the Single Malt wasn't the finest ever made, but it wasn't bad. Tillman's Bourbon was the finest.

On Monday, October 28, 1929, the roar went silence. The stock market collapsed. Still most folks in Delta had no concept as to what had happened. A few, Dub McCrary and few professional men, physicians and attorneys lost considerable monies.

Kelly Companies bought half the McCrary bank. It saved the bank and saved Dub from ruin. The new owner of five percent of the bank was one Tillman A. Johnson.

Times changed. People needed a drink.

The afternoon coffee club at the Delta Café continued.

Very young Gus Kelly took a late afternoon fishing excursion down to the pond with his Uncle Bob, Gus had his line on the bank playing with it more than his uncle believed he should.

Bob looked at the boy who was now once again checking his hook and said, "Now Gus, I want you to think about this, how many bites are you going to get if your hook is in your hand?"

Gus thought. When the answer came to him, he just shook his head. Then, he smiled.

Bob was never one to belabor a point but he was prone to summarization. "You've got to keep your hook in the water if you want to catch a fish."

Gus rolled his cane pole and sent the hook into the water. He sat down and said, "Come on fish."

Gus later learned his Uncle Bob applied that philosophy to any number of things. "You just have to try again. Or try something else. It is all in the trying."

CHAPTER 15:
The Boy Needs a Glove

BOB WAKENED EARLY ON THE MORNING of Monday, October 28, 1929 and went fishing. On Monday, November 4, 1929, Bob again awakened early and went fishing. The New York Stock Exchange had lost one-half its value. Bob and The Kelly Companies had not.

He had given his best investment advice several years earlier. He had been opposed to buying into the New York Stock Market with borrowed money. None was purchased by Bob nor the Kelly Companies.

Lake Placid hosted the 1932 Winter Games and few in Delta noticed.

March 1, 1932, Charles Lindberg, Jr. was kidnapped from the family home in New Jersey. Ten weeks later, on May 12, the boy's body was discovered not far from the family home. Now, in some senses New Jersey seemed a great distance away. Aunt Elizabeth learned about irrational associations and concerns.

Gus Kelly's mother decided to enroll him in school a year early. Such enrollments of a five-year-old into the first grade were not common, but neither were they rare. So, having just turned seven, Gus was completing the second grade.

His mother, Claire-Marie Kelly, had argued he was so bright he needed to be allowed to begin his formal education. Gus was more a creative child than an early budding scholar. He was curious and felt compelled to discover how all things worked.

His Aunt Elizabeth, who still provided most of his daycare, was concerned. His Uncle Bob knew that regular games of catch and conversation would cure anything with a boy.

"Catch!"

Bob and his seven-year-old nephew enjoyed playing catch. In the beginning, any available ball would do. Elizabeth urged rubber balls of any size. She judged rubber ball safer for both boy and man.

Having the two most significant males in her life playing together in her yard greatly pleased her.

Many afternoons this summer, Elizabeth would pick Gus up under the guise of giving his mother a break. Bob would finish up as early as possible and come home to join them. Gus and Bob would play baseball or go fishing.

Elizabeth rocked on the porch and watched the endless games of catch. Acting as a public address announcer, she would offer a running commentary on their games.

After dark, Bob would crack open the sporting news and each day in its time, he read the summaries of previous weeks Cardinals games to Gus. He would embellish the narrative to describe Sportsman's Park and the game action so that it sounded like a live descriptor.

Gus learned to read box scores.

A colorful character by the name of Dizzy Dean had joined the defending World Champion Cardinals. Dean added a colorful dimension to Bob's descriptions.

Recently, following a Shamrocks practice, Bob had brought home a few baseballs. He now sat on the steps of the porch and rolled ground balls to Gus.

With his nephew seeming to gain arm strength by the hour, Bob began using his glove to catch the ball.

Logic struck Gus. "Uncle Bob, I want a baseball glove!"

"Well, let me see what I can do."

"I could field better with a glove."

"What kind of glove?"

"One like yours."

Bob's soul smiled. He was an uncle on a mission.

Bob had a most subtle excitement to his pace as he climbed the stairs towards the Kelly Offices.

Bob entered the landing with questions running through his mind faster than he could process them. Exhilaration did that to him. With no acknowledgement beyond a head bob to Maylene, he walked straight into his brother's office.

"Junior, who do you consider the best leather smith in this area?"

"Marvel Blevins, no doubt. I think his name is Marvel," Junior said, then expanding said, "Anyway, got himself a shop out in Keota. Understand he makes a fine pair of boots if that is what you have in mind."

"It's not." Bob was pensive. "You remember that pitcher for the Cardinals who was always talking about having webbing in his glove?"

"Somewhat."

"Bill Doak. Seemed like a good thought to me, a strap, straps, straps woven into a web between the thumb and the first finger." Bob said. He continued, "Gus is wanting a baseball glove."

Junior's look showed only puzzlement.

Bob asked, "Do you know how hard it is to buy a baseball glove for a boy?"

"I confess I don't. But I fear you're getting ready to tell me."

"Hard! Damn near impossible."

"So?"

"Let's see if we can make a boy a baseball glove."

Bob stopped by the warehouse.

He went to the wrapping table and tore a sheet of brown wrapping paper from the roll. With a wax pencil, he started to sketch the glove he had in mind.

"Anybody know much about Marvel Blevins?"

"Got a shoe shop over in Keota."

"Does great work if you can catch him sober. His daddy died in that mine explosion over at McCurtain a few years ago."

"He's got a right cute momma. A widow woman now."

"I hear she'll put out at times, if you're interested."

Bob ignored the remark and said, "Is his work so good it's worth putting up with a drunk for?"

"Not in my mind. He'll drink on the job."

"I'll tell you who else does a job with leather, the guy who hit you in the head with a baseball."

"Bloodworth?" Despite himself, Bob felt agitated.

"Well, not him, he's got a boy. Thomas. Thomas Bloodworth. I hear the boy has a true talent."

"You know how to get in touch with him?"

"I'll try."

"Do. Ask him to call me."

Bob had sketched a webbing composed of woven strips of rawhide about the size of a shoelace. Thomas Bloodworth created a webbing of wider strips of leather and attached between the thumb and first finger.

After flexing the glove for a short time, Thomas attached each of the four fingers together with a rawhide lace.

With visible pride, he displayed the glove for Bob's approval.

Bob looked at the glove, flexed it.

"Thomas, can you make me one of those? A man's glove."

"Yes, I can."

Bob looked at the boy. Physically he was his father's son. Long straight legs, narrow at the waist, broad at the shoulders with the straight black Seminole hair. A handsome young man, maybe twenty years old.

The boy hesitated. Shifted his feet.

"Is there something else?"

"May I have a tryout with the Shamrocks?"

Two weeks and four gloves later, Bob formed Kelly Baseball Equipment Company. Thomas Bloodworth was hired as the company's first employee.

It was mid-morning in the Kelly Companies shop. Tillman and Bob sat on the hand-crafted bench and sipped coffee.

Tillman observed, "You know for the time being we won't be needin' so many barrel staves?"

"Likely not."

"Don't really want to lay nobody off right away."

"I'm sure."

"Well, I was thinkin', we have fine wood, we have got good men trained like we want'em, block and trims is special good," Tillman tried to measure his friend's interest. So far Bob was nodding.

"Well, I was thinkin', it seems an easy adjustment from staves to baseball bats." Tillman's considerable anticipation, shoved his words, "It wouldn't take much of a tune up, I don't think. And you're already selling baseball gloves."

Bob mused, "Seems to me it will take more skill to mill a bat than a barrel stave. But daddy's will buy bats for their boys."

"Yes sir, they will."

"Tillman, something else that has been on my mind. Let's hire a couple of young guys – apprentices."

"Old hand might see Buck as after his job. Think?"

"Maybe. We should give them a raise and a title for doing the training job. Wait. Think about this. The apprentices will be kids of people we already have on the job somewhere? What do you think?"

"I think the sawmill is goin' be around for a while and it takes folks trained to the job."

"Think on it."

"I think milling baseball bats will take more skill and more men than cutting barrel staves."

"Never met a boy didn't want a baseball bat."

Junior had been listening and watching.

He said, "Brother, I have a meeting with those Sanditen brothers in Holdenville next week. Seems that Oklahoma Tire and Supply idea of theirs is catching on. I'd like to show'em a few of these."

The Kelly Baseball Equipment Company grew. The KK logo burned into each bat and glove would become the hallmark of quality in gloves and bats. Even in the depths of the Great Depression, boys wanted baseball gear.

Late that afternoon, Gus and Bob played catch in the front yard. That evening, Bob and Elizabeth sat in front of the radio and laughed as the junk rattled from Fibber McGee's closet. Gus leaned against Bob's leg and slammed a ball into his brand-new glove.

As for the Delta Shamrocks, they are playing well. A number of boys now pounded a fist into their glove and hoped to catch a foul ball.

Bob pointed out to Junior, "Baseball team is never going to make any big profit, but we're all going to profit from it."

Junior smiled.

Gus said, "Uncle Bob, this is my friend, Mary Helen Ellsworth. She'd like to play catch with us."

Mary Helen, dressed in a striped tee shirt and overalls, banged her fist into her mitt and got into a fielding position. Reluctantly Bob rolled the ball her way. She fielded it and fired it back toward him. She handed Gus back his glove.

"Well, okay. Then, let's do this."

"Girl, can you swing a bat?"

"Yes sir, I can." And she did.

Come spring she joined the daily work up games on Bob's field.

Elizabeth said, "It is nice to see Mary Helen playing with the boys."

Bob responded, "She can play until she grows boobs."

Elizabeth swatted him with the magazine she was reading and said, "You are just awful."

Bob shrugged.

Elizabeth thought, "You're right." She didn't say it.

CHAPTER 16:
The Fist Fight

Fall of 1939

GUS AND MARY HELEN WERE SOPHOMORES at Delta High School when Gus had his first true fist fight. It came after Mary Helen, her eyes filled with tears, confided in him that John Thomas "JT" Boggs, her present flame, had proceeded beyond the point with which she was comfortable.

Under the lace bark elms that bordered the Ellsworth and Kelly home property line, the friends sat. Mary Helen talked and Gus listened. While not a new pattern of communication for the them, they were more intense.

As the conclusion of the story approached, Mary Helen spoke through her sobs, making emphasis by firmly grasping Gus' arm. She talked and began to feel better. She talked and Gus's anger rose.

She told him of her efforts, "First I tried to be cute, but I said please don't." Intense weeping. Then, I said stop."

"Gus, he touched me anyway." Her sobs became a full blown, soul wrenching lamentation.

"Oh, Gussie, he found I was --." She frantically searched for a word, an expression that she didn't find so uncomfortable she couldn't tolerate it. "I was excited down -- ."

She made an identifying motion and said, "I horribly embarrassed myself." Sob. "He laughed at me. He laughed at me." Sob. "Then, he stopped."

She collapsed into his chest. She wept. Gus sat still and held her, patting her shoulder as one might comfort a small child. He pulled her closer to him and reassured her.

Finally, she sat up, leaned over and kissed her friend on the cheek.

"Oh my, Gussie, you are such special friend. My special friend. I don't know what I would do without you."

Gus held her close. He struggled for something to say, didn't find it so he said what had first entered his empathic mind, "I love you."

Mary Helen's tears returned. She got herself up and she ran toward her house.

Gus mulled the situation most of the following day. He knew of no one with whom he was willing to seek counsel. He thought of his Uncle Bob or Aunt Elizabeth. And he believed he knew their thoughts on such matters. After considerable consternation, he decided to do what he believed was the right thing.

The next evening, Gus sought JT. He found him shooting snooker at the pool hall. Gus went in and sat down until JT completed the rack and then approached him.

They talked. JT tried to dismiss him. Gus took a position between JT and the snooker table.

JT glared. Gus glared back and felt his outrage again growing.

JT backed up a step, extended his cue and tapped Gus on the shoulder, leaving a small round smudge of blue chalk.

Gus swatted the cue away.

JT turned, laid the cue on the table, rolled it as if considering something, turned and pushed his curly hair off his forehead. His face took on the expression of "Alright, you've bothered me enough now."

"Across the street boy." JT intended the term boy to be derogatory. Gus took it that way. Never speaking, they agreed to step across the street and down the block into a vacant lot that at times had been used to settle such disputes.

JT was two years older and physically more imposing that Gus. He stood a good six feet, two inches and showed the muscular results of summers of physical labor. JT tried to posture this to greater advantage. Although he didn't tower over Gus, he did stand taller and broader, more a man and boy comparison between the pair.

Gus was wiry and he was growing taller.

A small group started to form, some interested parties, others just curious.

Gus suggested an apology be extended to Mary Helen. JT responded with several disparaging remarks toward Mary Helen.

"You're just mad because I found out that she's a slut before you did," JT asserted. His friends snickered. JT felt embolden.

He stepped toward Gus, then hissed under his breath, saying, "She tell you she got so slickered up for me she wet herself?" JT laughed.

JT turning back toward his supporters and said, "Just flat out pissed herself." He laughed.

It was now obvious to Gus that no apology was forthcoming.

Gus took a step to his right, surveyed the variables and decided to follow his Uncle Bob's advice for such occasions. "If the fight is inevitable, get in the first punch."

Leading with his left foot, he launched a straight right hand over a right step, striking JT square in the nose. Gus knew he had broken JT's nose from the splattering sound and the spurt of blood. Gus then prepared to defend himself against the licking he believed was coming.

Surprised and disoriented, JT tried to throw a punch only to walk into Gus' half-hearted and defensive right hand. It staggered him. Gus recognized his unexpected advantage, closed ground, loaded up and delivered his right hand with every ounce of strength he could muster striking JT dead middle just below the ribs.

JT grunted as he expelled air and fell to his knees. He gasps for breath.

"Kick him! Kick him!" Gus didn't recognize the voice.

JT covered his head with his hands and tucked in.

Gus had no intention of kicking him. He did intend to hit him if he tried to stand.

"You try to stand and I'll knock your fucking head off,"

Addled, JT was determined to stand.

JT made it to his knees, his breath still not coming easily. He tried to stand but collapsed back to his knees. He made a demeaning remark about Gus throwing the first punch.

Gus moved closer, bent slightly and said loud enough for most to hear, "One of us had to."

The gathering laughed.

Gus went home. His hand hurt.

"Damn you, Gus Kelly! I only wanted your kind ear. I needed you to listen to me. I don't need you to fix everything for me," her push of speech left her breathless. She took a deep breath and continued, her words still running over each other, "I needed you to be my friend!"

Confused and befuddled, Gus said, 'I was being your friend."

"No! No, you weren't! You were being Gus Kelly, boy hero!" She banged his chest with her fist and asserted, "I just hate you."

Tears exploded over her face. She slumped down, her back resting against the trunk of a lace bark elm. Mary Helen sobbed. Gus stood silently, at a loss for words.

"Gussie, I didn't need a protector." Her voice was softening.

Gus knew she was right. But he also was discovering a truth about himself. So, he just blurted it out, "I don't care. I'll always be your protector." He strove for emphasis, "Always have been, always will be!"

He now prepared himself for the verbal blast he was certain was coming. For the second time this night, he misread the pending response.

She said, "I am so embarrassed. Everybody thinks – that I teased him."

Mary Helen wanted to tell him that JT discovered she was as excited as he was, that her body responded in an involuntary way just like his did. What he had discovered with his touch terrified her. She didn't know he didn't know quite what to make of his discovery.

She sighed. She knew she couldn't take her best friend any further, some intimate secrets just weren't meant to be shared nor fully understood.

So, she concluded by saying, "Boys and girls are the same just really different."

She thought it to herself and then said, "I don't know what the hell I mean."

Gus laughed and stretched out on the grass.

Mary Helen patted the ground beside her and said, "Gussie, my Gussie, sit here."

He sat down beside her. She laid her head against his shoulder. He placed his arm around her and secured her, then he felt her snuggle close.

After a moment, Gus asked, "Well, what do we do now?" He asked because he certainly didn't know.

They sat quietly until a feeling of tranquility appeared. It seemed neither wanted to break the spell, so neither spoke. Both liked the moment immensely.

"Gussie, do you ever think about touching me?"

"Ah, geez."

In the dark he couldn't see her face to know how serious her question was.

"Well?"

Gus felt a moment of resignation followed by acquiescence. In this moment that seemed to ask for mutual trust between the closest of friends, Gus decided to follow the risky path of complete honesty.

"Yes, you know I do. But I don't do it."

"Some wait for an invitation, others don't."

"I suppose." He felt he knew but he wasn't committing.

"Gussie?" She hesitated, then went on, "If I ask you, would you?"

"Oh, Sweet Jesus, Mary Helen!"

Gus didn't know it but tonight there were no right answers.

Mary Helen snuggled closer to him, adopted her most feminine voice and said, "Let's go steady."

"Sweet Jesus!"

"Is that yes?"

"Yes."

Mary Helen kissed Gus. It was a familiar kiss yet utterly unfamiliar. Life again seemed so splendidly innocent.

The early fall evening had the feel of spring. This happens now and again in eastern Oklahoma. The air was warm and humid, not July humid but nonetheless damp. The air carried a smell that Bob always associated with fresh mown fields. After supper coffee was a treat Bob and Elizabeth regularly enjoyed. Neither knew why but unlike the mugs of coffee they drank in the early morning hours, the remains of the day were always served in a nice cup in a matching saucer.

They drank their coffee and talked. They spoke of what pleased them before going into the living room and turning on the radio. Tonight, they came to the porch later than ordinary.

Gus had come out late in the afternoon after he finished at the store. He and his Uncle Bob went fishing down on the lower Mountain Fork Creek, which sliced through the northern edge of Bob's land, some six miles of the homeplace.

They talked too long to catch many fish.

"Did Gus say anything about his altercation with JT?"

"He did." Bob teasingly paused.

Elizabeth looked over the top of her newly acquired and not yet adjusted to glasses. No further words were required.

"It seems by his account, that JT got a bit fresh with Mary Helen, she told Gus and he felt compelled to do something about it."

"That sounds a little overly simplistic." It was clear she expected greater clarity and more details.

"Well, the truth is Gus didn't say much more than that but if I fill in the blanks, it happened about like this. Well, first, as we have talked before, kids these days, these Depression kids just do some courting things that our generation wouldn't have even thought about."

Elizabeth acknowledged their previous observation as well as reiterating her expectation that he would proceed without further encouragement from her.

"I think Old JT must have moved into unfamiliar territory for both of them, think he touched her drawers and found them, let's say damp. I'm betting he thought she'd wet herself and it spooked him. Now, his spooking spooked her."

Elizabeth just shook her head. Bob did have a way with words.

Bob stopped, thought and concluded, "I think the kiddies scared each other half to death." Again pausing, he said, "Think they would have been a lot better off if they'd just charged on ahead."

Elizabeth said, "Like you said, kids today are a lot more risqué."

"Seems to me they get to know each other a whole lot better, quicker."

"You are just awful."

"Yes I am."

Bob stood and stretched and then continued, "*Calling All Cars* is coming on in about 5 minutes. I want to be settled when the police siren sounds."

Elizabeth smiled. Bob gathered the cups and saucers.

"Give those to me and you go fix the chairs."

Bob angled their comfortable chairs in front of the radio.

"Why do we, why does everybody, sit looking at the radio to listen to it?"

Junior tilted his chair, leaned back and rested his feet on the window sill. He looked out across Broadway Avenue, enjoying watching the cars move along. He thought about the city council meeting last night when Greg Abbott had complained about cars parking all day in front of his medical office. Dr. Abbott was proposing parking meters like Oklahoma City had gotten a couple of years ago. Junior allowed he had some sympathy for the good doctor's plight but Delta was Oklahoma City.

He spotted his brother Bob coming out of the café and heading toward the office. Just the man he wanted to see.

"Bob, I have a franchise thought I want to talk about."

Bob nodded, stepped into Junior's office and sat down.

CHAPTER 17:
A Flathead V-8

FOR SEVERAL WEEKS, A MAROON 1941 MERCURY flathead V-8 convertible had been sitting front and center in the showroom window at Delta Ford. The dealership was located next to Skinny McDaniel's Grocery and the convertible promptly caught Elizabeth's eye. She brought it to her husband's attention.

Today, leather-bound western style checkbook visibly in hand, Bob strolled into the Delta Ford Dealership, searched out the owner, Stew O'Brien and began a negotiation for the purchase of the automobile with all its accessories. Bob made what he knew to be a fair offer. Stew declined and countered.

"Stew, you know I'm not a big haggler. I've made you a fair offer."

"Now Bob, I can't do that. Why I'd be almost taking a loss."

Bob held his tongue, knew better but said no more. Appearing rather stoic, Bob rose from his chair, folded the leather-bound checkbook, and placed it in an inside pocket of his red windbreaker. He extended his hand.

Stew, anticipating further negotiation, was perplexed.

Bob reached out and took Stew's hand. He sustained his grip until he had finished saying, "You know, I'm sorry you couldn't take my offer. You'd have made money and I'd had a vehicle I liked."

Bob left.

Bob angled his 1937 Ford pickup in to space in front of the dry goods store located next to the stairway leading to the second-floor offices of The Kelly Companies.

The Kelly Companies were the only occupant of the second floor. A receptionist at her desk greeted Bob and stepped into the open floor.

"Good morning, Mister Bob."

"Morning, Connie."

Constance "Connie" Doyle, Delta High School, Class of 1939 and the daughter of the town optometrist, was the newest of The Kelly Companies staff of eight ladies whose desks were arranged over the length of second floor corridor.

Connie was a smallish girl with something of a boyish bent, as boyish as one can be while wearing a stylish dress. Using McCall's Patterns her mother, Martha, churned out fashionable garments of her daughter. Everyone liked Connie. She was fresh and youthful.

"May I get you some coffee."

"Please."

"Your office or Mr. John Charles?"

"My brother's please."

"Morning, Maylene."

"Good morning, Mr. Bob."

Bob thought how he found Maylene's presence to be reassuring. Her title was now office manager and she did manage the office. Her pleasing personality allowed her to run the office in a rather directive fashion without offending many.

Of average height, she had physically matured into a woman of strength. Her posture brought her upright. Now fortyish, she possessed an ample bosom with a balancing behind. Most found her appealing.

Bob stepped to the open office door and tapped on the facing.

"Good morning, Brother. What brings you into the office on a lovely fishing day?"

"Now, Junior you know I can't just fish my life away."

Junior laughed.

Bob asked, "Given any consideration as whether you wanted in on the Godfrey place?"

"You vouched for the price, so I'm fine with it," Junior replied.

"Good. I've already bought it. I'll just have Maylene make all the account transfers."

Junior laughed and said, "How much did we pay for it?"

"$1750."

Bob walked over and sat down at an empty desk and picked the telephone up from its cradle.

"Operator."

Bob recognized Edna Thompson's voice. She was exactly the operator he wanted. She was a very good operator and noted for her nosiness.

"Good morning, Edna. Can you do me a favor?"

"Well, morning Bob. What do you need?"

"Would you get me the telephone number for that Fred Jones Mercury place up in Oklahoma City?"

"Bob, I've got to finish checking in and I'll call you right back with it. Is that okay?"

"Of course."

Bob smiled and rocked back in his chair. He was visibly pleased with himself. Today the dregs of the morning coffee tasted just fine. Maxwell House surely was good to the last drop.

Junior's curiosity was now tweaked. He asked, "Alright, what are you up to?"

"I hope I'm buying that Maroon Mercury Convertible that Elizabeth and I have been coveting."

Junior grinned.

The phone rang.

Rather than buzzing, Connie called out, "Mr. Bob, this is Mr. O'Brien down at the Ford place."

"Thank you, Connie. I'll take it down here."

Connie put him through. Bob picked up the phone up from its cradle and answered it.

"Bob, this is Stew down at the Ford place. I've been thinking and I decided I am going to take you up on your offer."

Bob didn't respond.

Nervously, Stew leaped further in, "Your offer on that Mercury Convertible on the showroom floor – the one we were talking about this morning."

"Stew, that is good. Truth is I was fixing to call the Jones place in Oklahoma City but I prefer doing business here in Delta. I'll bring you a check buy right after lunch."

Bob paused and then yielded to his better nature saying, "Listen Stew, I don't need that till Saturday. Let it sit in your showroom for a few more days. Might stir a little more interest."

Stew sighed and answered, "That would be just great. Do you mind if I pass it around that you've bought the car? That will stir some more interest."

"Don't mind a bit."

"That is good of you, just great. Bob, I gotta tell you I'm really happy we could work this out."

Bob restated, "Like buying local." Then, he hung up.

Junior was smiling. He said, "You are just one crafty devil." Junior laughed, "No, you are one sneaky little shit."

Bob smiled but said nothing. He got up, put the coffee cup in the lunch room sink and moved toward the door.

He stopped. "Maylene, Edna over at Central will be calling here in a minute with a phone number. Take it and write it down, tell her I said thank you, and then toss it in the trash can."

Maylene acknowledged his instructions, then added, "And add that to the list of things I know nothing about."

"Yes"

As he went down the steps he thought, "Maylene knows where all the bodies are buried." He laughed.

He thought he'd go over to Ruth's Café and buy local, an open-faced chili-cheese burger. He liked open-faced chili-cheese burgers. Ruth just piled the chili on.

CHAPTER 18:
The Fairest of the Fair

IN THE FALL OF 1941, there were three Oklahoma State Fairs. One was in Oklahoma City; one was in Tulsa and one in Muskogee. The Muskogee State Fair was the closest to Delta. It was the fair in which all of Delta High School's FFA Chapter entered their projects.

It possessed a midway filled with attractions that where otherwise unavailable in the rural eastern parts of Oklahoma. Each year during the September run of the Muskogee State Fair, Delta students loaded onto a school bus and went to the fair.

During the afternoon hours, the Delta high school students dutifully attended the show barns and event centers. They signed the roster sheets which a teacher held at each site.

As late September daylight began to wane, the sounds of the gasoline driven generators that powered the carnival midway tantalizingly stirred adolescent minds. The lights of the Ferris wheel, spinning vertically, danced through the dusky sky as the Tilt-A-Whirl karts, erratically skimming along horizonal with the asphalt surface, pirouetted to their own music. The clanking sounds of a hurriedly assembled Roller Coaster spurred the adrenaline and lured the adolescents toward the midway.

Like a hoard of migrating ants with one voyager or another bouncing out of line to explore the games of skill along the perimeter, the teenagers paraded in from the vast semi-mown parking areas to the midway. Excitement emanated from them.

The sounds, the smells, the lights and they are young. The still innocent Class of 1942.

Gus smiled when he saw Mary Helen Ellsworth on the midway. Mary Helen was his closest and most intimate friend. Gus couldn't remember not knowing her. They shared the deepest and most private secrets of childhood. At times, adolescence had wedged them apart. At other times adolescence had shoved them snuggly together.

Sometimes they had dated, sometimes they hadn't. They were currently in a time neither were dating, each other or otherwise.

Gus and Mary Helen could be a very comfortable fit.

Gus paused and looked at his friend. The waves in her coal black hair spoke to time and effort. He knew his Wildroot and a part in the middle was much the easier. At five feet, five inches, she was taller than her peers and she was rounding into her mother's form which was considerably better than otherwise. Mary Helen had a figure.

As she turned into a brighter light, Gus noticed the bright red lipstick. He liked that look on her. Her mother didn't.

Mary Helen was fun. Gus smiled broadly as he thought of his friend's boundless energy and curiosity. Adolescence had provided no limits to confine it.

Even as high school seniors they were still playmates.

Still and all, Gus had fished, played baseball with the boys and periodically checked his armpits for hair. Mary Helen held tea parties and pushed her baby dolls in a carriage while learning of lipstick and practiced her smile in a hand mirror.

Both valued their traditional gender roles and worked at first acquiring them and then at polishing them.

Mary Helen's mother was stern with her about how a young lady should behave. There were no ifs, ands or buts. However, Mary Helen had already encountered sensations and emotions that gave rise to questions that her mother's conventions did not answer. Her mother had stoically delivered a sanitized explanation of the birds and the bees.

Mary Helen had a nose for duplicity.

Mary Helen had watched her two older sisters as they made their way through puberty and adolescence. She guessed what they were giggling about was neither bird nor bee. She was certain it was exciting and stimulating. She couldn't wait.

From her sisters she learned femininity was fun. She learned the manipulative value of her femininity. She had repeatedly tested these powers on Gus as they emerged.

She came to believe that little boys would jump through hoops for what she had. She was now beginning to understand what she had and she was glad she had it.

Gus was her friend. She relied on him to help her confirm her suspicions about boys in a completely safe environment. It was on these gender differences that the two often compared notes. They now trusted each other implicitly.

With an impish chuckle, Mary Helen asked, "Has your dad had the talk with you?"

Gus shook his head no. He was absolutely convinced there would be no additional conversation with his father concerning sex. It seemed his father's curriculum for sexual instruction involved birds and bees and an illustrated book. Nothing else should be required.

His father's explanation was that it was considerably more than he had gotten from his father. Gus believed him.

His Uncle Bob had been more helpful.

"Do you mind that your parents screw?"

Mary Helen both ask her question and experimented with the stronger word. She was coming to believe people were just too polite when discussing sex.

"Oh, Sweet Jesus, Mary Helen! I don't even like to think about it."

He gave a shaking motion with his shoulders and added, "Gives me the shivers."

"Well, if they didn't think about doing it, you wouldn't be bouncing around on this earth." She paused, "Oh, they had to be more than just thinking about it now, didn't they?"

"Ah, Geez! Enough already!"

He knew Mary Helen enjoyed making him uncomfortable. She knew he knew.

The Last Dance in Delta

Any young man could easily fall under the influence of the sounds and smells of a carnival midway. Little could enthrall an adolescent male like the outside pitch for the strip show. The performers would come out and take a seat on the most elevated stage on the midway. No one's view was obstructed.

The barker, a blend between a blue comic and a salesman, assured the assembled crowd that for a quarter you could watch as these exotic dancing ladies removed most of their clothing.

The guys watched and poked each other in the ribs with their elbows. Knowing a flock of girls were hovering nearby, watching from the darken edges, the boys tried to look interested but not too interested. A classmate pulled out a cigarette and tried on his best Bogart imitation. Gus chuckled.

The barker drew his attention back to the stage.

"Miss Sue, please treat this fine gathering to one final stroll before ya go back to freshen up for ya performance."

He twirled his cane and gave a theatrical wink to the crowd.

Gus was uncomfortable. The crowd mulled and moved, interested but undecided.

As Miss Sue took a brief runway walk, the other girls made their way behind her, each playfully removing her robe as she passed and dropping it to the stage as she eased behind the tent flap. Still wearing her glittering robe now loosely draped, Sue finished with a mischievous flourish.

Perhaps trying to avoid staring, Gus looked closer at the robes as they fell onto the stack. They were worn, frayed.

A drum sounded. Gus jumped. The tent flap opened and an arm appeared holding Miss Sue's robe aloft. The robe twirled and then was allowed to drop to the stage. Miss Sue's face appeared and she blew a kiss to the assemblage.

The eager crowd hooted its approval.

A voice filled with electronic static crackled above the troop, "The price of admission is twenty-five cents!"

Gus jumped. The firmness of the hand on his arm startled him.

"Dang, Mary Helen. Scared the living toot out of me."

"You were just too busy looking at those naked women." She paused, perhaps giving a final evaluation of the circumstances.

She pressed a dollar bill into his hand and with a firm directive quality to her voice she said, "You're taking me in to see the strip show."

"Oh, sweet Jesus, Mary and Joseph!" He had heard that tone in her voice before. He could tell her no but he knew that would be a waste of air. There were times he was just no match for her. This was one of those times.

"Gus, you take me or I'll take myself."

Gus hoped if he didn't say anything she would change her mind. On the other-hand he knew better. He'd always known better.

His voice sounded firm yet resigned, "Well crud! You'd just do that wouldn't you?"

Gus already knew the answer to the question.

Mary Helen knew Gus. She was familiar with his anxious but interested expression. She knew Gus was selectively adventurous, but she knew she could depend on him to join her in her quests. Her protective knight. Her Quixote in his tin hat.

Gus stepped up beside her and took her hand.

They scrutinized the ticket seller and waited for the line to shorten, watched with some relief as the group of four giggling young women stepped up to purchase tickets, then stepped hurriedly up to the window of the ticket booth. The ticket seller, a grizzled, wiry, slight old man who looked as if he had had his battles in his life and lost most of them, now he just looked exhausted.

His Uncle Bob once remarked about such a man, "He chose to fight life and life kicked his ass."

Sighting the couple, the ticket seller's expression changed. An ever so slight spark lit behind his eyes. Gus was now in the protective mode he adopted when he felt responsible for Mary Helen. Despite twinges of pity, he concluded the man simply looked lecherous.

Gus stuck out a dollar bill and said, "Two please sir."

He worked to keep his voice deep.

"Well now, ain't ya the proper little prick," the seller said, his voice saturated with cynicism. "Ya twenty-one."

The Last Dance in Delta

Gus responded without hesitation, "Old enough to take my wife to this show."

Having reversed her Delta High School class ring that she had just received the previous spring, Mary Helen displayed her hand. In the dim light it looked for all the world like a wedding band.

Gus' response to the challenge of the craggy faced man in the booth pleased Mary Helen no end. A derisive smile cracked the old man's face as he laid out two tickets on the counter and pushed them toward Gus.

"Sir, my change?"

The grainy woman taking tickets at the entry flap laughed. The ticket seller cut a pointed glance in her direction, then pushed two quarters across the counter.

Gus picked up their tickets and then the quarters. Mary Helen took his arm. They marched in lockstep toward the flap. Several classmates had watched their performance from the shadows. Gus sensed their judgmental glances. He knew a couple couldn't wait to blabber this tale all over Delta.

From somewhere in that group of teenagers huddled at the edge of the light, a singular female voice rose, "You go M. H., you go!"

In the fashion a body's backside smiles, Mary Helen smiled.

Gus handed their tickets to the woman at the entry. Gus then held the tent flap open as if it were a door for Mary Helen. No grand gesture, just habit.

The woman ticket taker took note and said, "Ya pay Ronnie no mind. Life just runnin' short on him now adays." Behind the husky voice stood a short blocky fortyish woman, her rusty hair parted as if she still aspired to being a flapper of the twenties.

Addressing Mary Helen, she said, "Little lady, you and ya boyfriend, ya husband, ya want to sit on the front bench over there on the far side. Just in front of them Miss Prisses."

She motioned toward the four college age girls already seated. One girl was smoking a cigarette with a haughty aplomb.

"Ticket man be coming by after first part of the show. You'll see. Give'im these." She placed two green tickets, faded from reuse, in Mary Helen's hand.

The ticket taker's eyes gave hint to some almost lost satisfaction their circumstances brought to mind. She was enjoying the moment.

Mary Helen closed her hand, secured the two worn tickets, smiled and nodded. Gus wondered if just by looking the woman could tell Mary Helen was the worldly one of the pair. Maybe there is some secret, knowing communication between women of all ages and stations.

The seating was rows of wooden benches that resembled those in front of the bus station, the domino hall and any number of other places in Delta where men gather and sat, whittling away the Great Depression. The benches were arranged in a semi-circle around a wooden stage. The ground between the benches was now worn to bare dirt by the shuffling of feet. Gus knew because he was looking straight down.

"Don't tell me you're not a tad bit curious." Mary Helen's elbow found his ribcage. She grinned.

He knew that, as always, she was taking some pleasure in his discomfort. He tilted and slightly lifted his head. Looking into her eyes, all he could think was of a Laurel and Hardy line, so he said it.

"Another fine mess you've gotten us into!"

She muffled her giggle.

Gus would have been more comfortable if they would have darkened the room like say in a movie theatre. Gus began to sneak a look around the tent. Gratefully he spied no familiar faces. He relaxed a little.

Mary Helen on the other hand seemed calm, like this was old hat to her. Gus knew better.

He was about to say something when she said, "Put your arm around me."

He did. She snuggled to him and smiled, "I want to feel claimed right now."

He stifled a full laugh. Mary Helen felt the need to have a protective male by her, now that was something new. Gus found this unexpectedly exposed need to be filled with potential for future teasing. Nonetheless, he clasped her next to him.

The Last Dance in Delta

There they sat on a wooden bench in a tent on the midway at the Muskogee State Fair, once again partners in crime, off on another quest.

The lights dimmed.

From somewhere just off stage, a Victrola begin to play a rendition of the *Puttin' on the Ritz*. A woman slid from behind the stage curtain. Her robe was loose, the fabric shimmered, clinging to her. She swayed onto the lighted stage, keeping reasonable rhythm with the music. To Gus' amazement, the tent hushed.

It was not an artistic dance performance but no one expected one. This was not a gathering of artistic performance critics.

Mary Helen elbowed him and said, "Nice legs."

Realizing she was serious Gus brought his eyes up from the ground. He agreed. The woman tried to appear light-hearted but it was obvious she too had unwisely challenged life to a duel.

Three minutes later the dancer posed before them, now clad only with pasties on her breasts and wearing what Gus assumed to be a G-string. He had over-heard talk of such at the pool hall. The dancer struck a final pose. The audience clapped.

Gus gave the woman an A for effort. Mary Helen was prone to a more critical view. While mostly it came back to legs, hips and breasts, she observed the woman's hair styling needed some attention. Gus hadn't noticed.

Two more dancers performed similar routines to different music. Gus gave positive reviews to a young small breasted girl.

"Gussie, you're just feeling sorry for her lack of titties," Mary Helen tweaked him. Ever the critic, she had yet to see anyone that impressed her. It was the whole performance that seemed to enthrall her. She included the audience as part of the entertainment.

During an unintended glimpse, Gus saw Mary Helen's finger outlining her breast. Mary Helen was unabashed and said, "Just checking."

In a half whisper, Gus responded, "You got'em all whipped."

"Oh, Gussie, now I know why I like you so much," she paused and then finished, "Not that you'd know. Mine were flat as flapjacks the last time you saw them."

Giving an exaggerated look, he said, "Well, things – and boobs have changed."

Their faces broke with large, adoring smiles as they remembered other times and other places.

The next performance was a full figured, heavy breasted woman's jiggling act performed to Bing Crosby's *Brother Can You Spare a Dime*. This quickly became a crowd favorite. And the crowd became noisy bordering on unruly.

The narrator promptly stepped out and assumed control.

He made an unpopular announcement. He said, "Ladies and gentlemen, that concludes our regular show. A ticket to remain for our premier show is fifty cents."

He allowed the moans and grinches to fade, then said, "I guarantee you that those of you who remain will be pleased with your choice. There are beautiful girls you have not seen who are a part of the premier show only. You will not be disappointed."

He walked across the stage, stopped and added, "And to answer the question on most of your minds – You will see everything you hope to see. If you choose to see our premier show, just keep your seats, please have your fifty cents ready and Ronnie will come by, collect your money and give you a green ticket." He pointed to the grisly ticket taker standing in the corner and then continued, "Those of you who are leaving us now, please make your way out the side flap of the tent which is now being held open for you. We hope you enjoyed our show and thank you for your attendance."

A general grumbling moved around the tent as decisions were made.

The departing crowd groused all the way out.

Most chose to shell out the additional coins and remain. The giggling group of women who Mary Helen and Gus now knew were coeds, sorority girls, at a nearby college were remaining. Mary Helen retrieved the two green tickets from her purse and surrendered them.

She gave Gus a big smile and reassuring pat on the knee.

Gus wasn't comfortable enough to return the pat.

The lights again dimmed.

The Last Dance in Delta

The initial dancer attempted to fulfill the Barker's promises. She teased with the curtain before abruptly dropping it. She sashayed across the stage to the notes of Crosby's *The Way You Look Tonight*. The song assisted the presentation of innocence the woman wished to project.

Up to this point, Gus' primary focus had been upon his own shuffling feet punctuated by sideways glances at the performers. Now his quick, slightly embarrassed sideways glances were at Mary Helen. They now sat hip to hip with Gus' arm snug around her shoulder.

She leaned in on Gus' ear and said, "This one is a dandy little tease, seems real."

"What I'm seeing looks awfully real to me."

Gus' ribs again paid the price for his mouth.

It hit Gus that for Mary Helen there was something academic about this experience. For him it was certainly an educational experience. Authenticity? The bouncing breast looked quite real to a seventeen-year-old boy.

Mary Helen whispered, "It's okay to look."

There was less wardrobe involved in the premier second act. Nonetheless, it took Gus a moment to realize the pasties were gone.

Now selling a third act, the barker repeated his pitch, promising that in the third and final act all would be revealed.

"Staying only cost you an additional fifty cents."

With considerable bluster, the sorority girls declared their intention to remain.

Gus and Mary Helen's eyes met, his questioning and hers assertive. Gus pulled his wallet and removed a dollar bill. He checked although counting the three remaining dollars wasn't difficult, the last three of his hard-earned fair dollars. She reached out and he handed her the dollar bill. This was her quest. He was just along for the ride.

After an opening foursome to the sounds of *Back in the Saddle Again,* the quartet dispassionately removed the three small dots of fabric that covered their essentials. To Gus' disappointment the young woman he had considered attractive was not among the group.

Still, these were the first near nude women Gus had seen. He had seen Trevor O'Quinn's alleged French post cards but he didn't count those.

Gus had moved from protective disinterest to a generalized curiosity. Mary Helen remained intellectually interested and comparatively curious.

The completely disrobed women stood near the front of the stage, scarcely moving. Some of the men now edged toward the stage. A rope barrier stopped their advance. Gus hadn't noticed the rope boundary earlier. He assumed he must have been looking at his feet or at the performers.

In a loud voice, one of the men protested, "Taint nothing but her bush!"

Emboldened another chimed in, "Didn't pay no fifty cents to look at no fuzz!"

Another man, fat and dirty were the descriptors that flooded into Gus' mind, stepped to the rope and seized the rope with both hands and tersely screamed, "Want see ya cunt!"

A single word dragged them all across a boundary. For the first time Mary Helen flinched. Then, she cringed. In a virtually reflexive motion, Gus tightened his arms around her and pulled her to him. She tightened her arm around his waist and moved closer to him.

One of the men started to step over the rope. Gus didn't know where it came from but an arm swinging a small colorful club struck the man square across the shoulders. He spun in anger only to feel the club drive into his solar plexus. He doubled up and hit the ground writhing in pain.

"Get him up and sit him down." The cold steel in the barker's eyes and the sternness of his voice left the man's friends with no doubt as to their best course of action.

Gus felt a chill up his spine. The voice seemed sinister. Without any tangible justification, Gus would have sworn if the barker had swung again, he would have split the man's skull apart.

The wine-colored rope dangled in front of the stage. A waving empty delineation of space.

The Last Dance in Delta

One of the sorority girls retched, then vomited. Another burst into tears and dashed for the flap. One of her companions reached out but missed her sobbing friend. The fleeing young woman became tangled in her own feet, stumbling forward. Her pursuing friend lifted her to her feet, she staggered and heaved again. They all hustled to the attended exit flap. The vomiting one appeared to be gasping for air as the tent flap fell behind her.

Gus saw a small man with a broom and a bucket spread the same red sawdust floor sweep, same as he used to sweep the store, over the spots of vomit.

The older lady, the ticket taker, bent over picked up a thrown shoe, examined it and then opened the flap and tossed it into the night.

A weak, sobbing and broken sound came from the dark, "Thank you." The old woman laughed.

There was a loud banging tap. All eyes turned to the stage.

The stage lights went up a bit. The one dancer who remained on the stage seemed to be arranging what appeared to Gus to be plumply stuffed ottoman. A buzz ran through the crowd, a crowd that seemed to be mesmerized by her movement. Her hips swayed rhythmically to the music.

She sat on the ottoman, extending into toe point first one leg and then the other.

"She is the prettiest of them all," Mary Helen whispered.

Gus nodded his agreement.

In a soft circular motion, she rotating her hips, slowly positioning herself for display. She posed as if for an artist was about to sketch her as the ultimate revealed woman. She left little to the imagination.

Gus struggled to look so he looked away. Yet he didn't want to turn his head. In trying to distract himself, he noticed the woman's eyes. Unemotional, almost unseeing hollow eyes. He couldn't possibly know it yet but he would soon see this dispassionate look in the bars and brothels that service Camp Pendleton.

The customers now gratified and satisfied began to applaud and whistle enthusiastically.

The older lady from the front entrance, their pseudo-guide on their venture, stood nearby. Moments prior to the program's conclusion she stepped next to them.

"I'll tell ya when ta get up and go." Her words carried both consideration and pragmatism.

The men left. Some grousing to each other and nervously laughing. Some now hurried, the fear of being seen visible on their faces, their eyes darting around the crowd.

Over near the stage, awkward words seemed to be exchanged between the barker and a few men who hung back.

Their guide now held the flap open and said, "Okay Sweeties, now would be ya time."

Gus said, "Thank you very much."

His thank you was quite genuine. Mary Helen smiled and gave an accepting nod. The woman was pleased.

She now caught Mary Helen's gaze toward the stage and explained, "Those'll be stayin' for some extra entertainment." She allowed those words to settle.

Then the world-worn old woman broadened her smile. She motioned to Gus and said to Mary Helen. "Ya can take him behind this flap if ya of a mind. Be private 'nuff. If'en you don't he'll be humping ya leg all the way back to the farm."

Gus sputtered. Mary Helen laughed.

Detecting the hesitancy on the faces of both youngsters, she added, "Be standin' right here. Yawl not be bothered."

Without cracking a smile, Mary Helen responded, "Oh, he'll not go without, just not now."

The guide flashed a knowing smile. She watched their exit.

Now outside and taking in a deep breath of evening air, Mary Helen spoke first, "Gussie, I know that embarrassed you but you hung right in there. And I thank you."

He exaggerated a Tarzan-style chest thump of his chest.

"Johnny Weissmuller should stand down." Gus felt quite adolescent but couldn't withdraw his gesture.

She giggled, "You're so funny."

She took his arm and they walked out onto the midway. She truly adored this boy.

The Last Dance in Delta

She stopped, looked up at Gus and said, "Oh, you'll be going without tonight."

"Figured as much."

Later, as the school bus drove through the deep dark of the night, Mary Helen dozed on Gus' shoulder beneath the warmth of his Delta letterman's blanket. Gus liked his world.

Mary Helen stirred. She snuggled closer.

In a voice that rose from near his ribs, "Gussie, I think we should start dating again. What do you think?"

Without pause, he replied, "I would like that."

"Me too."

That night, snuggled tightly in his arms, Mary Helen slept the sleep of the angels.

Her world seemed quite perfect.

CHAPTER 19:
December 7, 1941

ON SUNDAY, DECEMBER 7, 1941, at 7:55 AM Hawaii time, the Empire of Japan launched a surprise attack on the United States Naval Base at Pearl Harbor, Hawaii.

Under the pressure of the attack, a quick dispatch was sent by Admiral H. E. Kimmel to all Navy commands. It read:
Air raid on Pearl Harbor x This is not a drill.

It was an unusually warm December day in Delta. So warm in fact that several Delta families were utilizing the picnic tables at the City Lake. A spirited game of horseshoes was underway in the pits. The swings and merry-go-round installed the previous summer had children draped from them. A cluster of young mothers milled about talking as they watched over their children.

Trying to steal a warm day in December, Bob and Elizabeth Kelly had brought a large picnic basket to the lake. Their nephew, Gus Kelly and his girlfriend, Mary Helen Ellsworth, had come with them. The fried chicken, potato salad, deviled eggs, Jello salad with canned peaches and pears, biscuits and apple cobbler had been eaten. Leftovers had been neatly wrapped.

"No flies. No ants." This Elizabeth thought to herself was a splendid benefit to a December picnic.

Gus and Mary Helen were stretched out on a quilt, deliberating the animal shapes that could be observed in the high cumulus clouds floating overhead. Bob and Elizabeth lingered at the picnic table and gazed out over the lake. The late afternoon sun comes early in December.

Bob remarked on the high quality of work the CCC boys had done in creating the Park and its stone pathways.

Elizabeth agreed, then offered, "I like Mary Helen. She just seems like a such a nice girl."

"Yes, me too. She is funny and I like funny," Bob paused and then continued, "God, Elizabeth that was just a wonderful picnic. You outdid yourself."

"It really was good, wasn't it?"

They relaxed back against the table. He patted her hand and briefly held it. Bob liked his world.

"Bob! Something is wrong!"

Suddenly she bolted upright, erect, she pointed down at the water's edge. Several young people who had earlier been fishing were now engaged in what appeared to be hyper-agitated conversation.

Bob stood and started to walk to the young men. He had yet to take a step toward the lake's edge when he saw Junior's Ford Deluxe Coupe kicking up dust as it angled into the campgrounds.

Spotting Bob and Elizabeth's Mercury convertible, he slanted across the grass and stopped just short of their car.

Extraordinarily excited, breathless although he hadn't really exerted himself, anxiety now pushed his speech.

"Brother, the God damned Japs bombed Pearl Harbor."

Bob tightened his lips and shook his head. With a sigh, his shoulders dropped. "Well, damn."

Elizabeth released a long, protracted, "No. Oh, no." Then, she thought, "Where in the hell is Pearl Harbor?"

She looked for Gus and found him standing near her. She didn't know where the thought came from but it flooded her conscious awareness, "Please God, no."

She fought back tears.

Bob placed his arm around her and drew her close to him. They both felt sad. They both felt angry. They felt at a loss for direction. They looked at the lake.

Bob took Elizabeth's hand and they walked toward the Mercury. Elizabeth was simply following her husband's lead. Bob popped the trunk.

Junior hailed him from a few paces behind, "What are you doing?"

"Brother, I'm pouring my wife a drink and then I'm going to have a big snort myself. You?"

"Oh, what the Hell, yes, pour me one." Junior was thoughtful and then added, "I didn't know Elizabeth drank the hard stuff."

"She didn't until this afternoon."

Gus and Mary Helen, drawn to the activity, were now standing near Elizabeth, their hands tightly clasped. Elizabeth looked, then stared at the young couple. Her mind scrambled.

She looked at the handsome boy she and Bob so adored. Mary Helen sat next to him, gripping his hand for dear life.

A tingling chill of pure horror raced along Elizabeth's spine. She looked at the young couple and her vision brought her to near panic. The word war rang in her head.

Her head in her hands, she sat on the picnic bench and tried not to cry. She thought her head would explode.

Gus saw his aunt, released Mary Helen's hand with a gentle departing pat and moved to a seat beside his aunt.

"Are you okay?" Gus felt silly asking the question. He could clearly see that she wasn't okay but he didn't know what else to ask.

Elizabeth nodded in the affirmative. Her answer belied the fact.

She patted Gus' knee. She wondered if she could send another boy, another boy she dearly loved, off to war.

Gus had no doubt about his eventual enlistment. He adhered to a common wisdom among the young men of Delta. He wasn't going to wait to be drafted and fold in to some infantry outfit to fight beside another draftee.

His admirable peers were at the recruitment offices the next day. The despicable ones said they would wait and be drafted.

The Last Dance in Delta

War had been talked in the halls and the secretive smoke hole of Delta High School for several years. In large part fueled by adolescent bluster. But it was war with Germany.

Some recent films, <u>The Fighting 69th</u> with James Cagney and Charlie Chaplin's <u>The Great Dictator</u>, set a positive stage for the war experience. Gary Cooper's film, <u>Sergeant York</u>, perceived as a true accounting of the experiences of Alvin York in World War I powered more than a few testosterone-fueled patriotic surges.

Bob, against his better judgement, agreed to attend a showing of <u>Sergeant York</u> at the Ritz Theatre, Delta's only theatre. He got up and left during the first combat scene.

Gus later heard that his Uncle Bob went home and broke a baseball bat hitting the trunk of the huge ash tree in his front yard. Gus viewed this act with great admiration.

That was not Bob's intent.

Bob had felt war in the breeze for several years. He regularly prayed that it might pass them by.

He listened to Edward R. Murrow's broadcast from London. Murrow said, "This is London" and placed a heavy emphasis on the "This". Bob's antenna sprang up. He listened intently as did much of America.

On occasion, Bob heard bombs in the background. He wondered if Murrow was truly on a roof top as he was purported to be. The genuineness with which Murrow closed, "Good night and good luck" and the terse manner in which "good luck" slipped from his lips convinced Bob of the man's authenticity.

For a few minutes each night, Edward R. Murrow delivered the war and London's anguish home to Delta. Bob believed and shared with Elizabeth his belief that, intentional or otherwise, Murrow was helping prepare America for the inevitability of another war. A war to which no one could not long remain indifferent and unresponsive.

Bob felt in 1940 when the Selective Service Act of 1940 was passed establishing the first peacetime draft a war was in the making.

Regardless, he got to watch Gus complete his football career at Delta High School. He was hopeful that Gus could make the Shamrocks roster this spring.

War with Japan wasn't at the top of Bob's mind. He thought Europe and Hitler and Nazi Germany were the primary threats to the United States. Recently Italy's fascist state under Benito Mussolini seemed primed for war. But Japan. He just didn't see that coming.

On days that immediately followed the bombing of Pearl Harbor the Kelly family, like so many other Americans, stayed within earshot of their radios. They heard President Franklin D. Roosevelt label December 7, 1941 as a day that would live in infamy. The Kelly clan believed him to be correct. How could anyone possibly forget?

At this early time there was a sense of helplessness, the task ahead seemed so overwhelming.

They soon heard that Germany and Italy had declared war on the United States. The world was again at war, a larger wider war.

Bob thought about the battle that had been raging in Great Britain. He wondered if our country had the stomach for such a relentless, brutal and destructive war, a war waged against civilians as well as against soldiers.

He was happy for the ocean that separated the United States from Europe. He knew an ocean also separated us from Japan but Japan seemed so unknown, so distant and so very far away.

Bob wanted to help but felt helpless. He knew he was beyond enlistment age although he would periodically in his fantasies give it fleeting consideration. He accepted that men in their fantasy life perceived themselves as more competent that they were.

Since the reinstatement of the draft, a spattering of young men from Delta had been drafted. Bob had no doubts that after the attack this would change. Many of Delta's young men would be drafted. Many more would volunteer.

The Last Dance in Delta

Bob found a way to serve. He volunteered to serve on the local draft board. By February he was head of the Green County draft board.

He walked Delta's neighborhoods. He saw the ever-increasing number of blue star Service Flags displayed in the windows. They served as a constant reminder of Delta's commitment to serving America.

The first Gold Star Service Flag sobered him as little else had since he had returned to Delta from fighting his generation's war.

He stood on the sidewalk and emotionally examined the placard in the window. He had known William Hiram since he was a small child. He knew how proud his father was when he became a fighter pilot in the Army Air Corp. He died trying to get his plane in the air at Hickam Field on December 7.

"What a fine young man. Man!" Bob released a breath and shook his head as if trying to grasp an idea, then said aloud but to no one, "Man. Hell, he couldn't buy a beer at the pool hall."

He started to look around to see if anyone had heard him, then he just didn't care. No one had.

Japan invaded China on July 7, 1937. Bob hadn't identified the threat. In retrospect, he supposed that conflict just seemed too far away, physically and emotionally. When Nazi Germany invaded Poland on September 1, 1939, he became somber. Denial was no longer successful. Still and all, he chastised himself for failing to understand the Japanese threat.

For years, Bob had been able to sustain the belief that his generation had fought the war to end all wars. This illusion provided him with some degree of comfort. Somewhere in the early-1930's he began to question his belief.

December 7, 1941 was a shock. What others claimed to have anticipated, Bob found quite unexpected. There was another world war. Bob was disillusioned.

CHAPTER 20:
The Last School Dance

1942 WAS AN IRREGULAR SCHOOL YEAR. Delta High School Graduation had been advanced to Thursday before Prom on Friday to accommodate the military enlistments of a large number of male students. This was ultimately a wise move by Delta's Board of Education. Delta's young men entered the United States Army as high school graduates. Most from the surrounding communities did not.

In the Spring of 1942, Gus borrowed his uncle's Mercury convertible, washed and polished every inch, and drove next door to the Ellsworth home. He walked up the front steps. Tradition-bound, James Ellsworth opened the door to allow his daughter's suitor, her Senior Prom date, entrance.

Beside her mother, Mary Helen stepped through the dining room doors. There she was. This girl, this woman, he felt he had known all his life was beyond stunningly beautiful. She was perfect.

Gus was stood motionless. He just didn't know quite what to say or think.

Perhaps it was the tiniest of ruffles about the boundaries, the manner in which the rose-pink gown rose from the bodice erasing all doubt as to the existence of her bust. Or it could have been the manner in which the gown flowed from her waist almost to the floor. Her hair was flung up in a fashion he had never seen before.

Gus found himself presented with a transformation of the female psyche into a tangible presentation of femininity for

The Last Dance in Delta

which he simply was not prepared. He was expressively trapped in some abyss between boyhood and manhood.

He stammered, "Sweet Jesus, Mary Helen."

The corsage fell from his hand. He said something as he retrieved it. He hoped he mumbled an apology for his use of the Lord's name. He wasn't certain.

Mary Helen and her mother were ecstatic. Her father perhaps not so much.

Gus tried to pin the shoulder corsage of four perfect red roses on the dress and yet avoid touching the exposed skin, an impossible task. Mrs. Ellsworth aided him, only to press his fingers firmer against her daughter's skin, but they proficiently completed the task.

She reached on the fireplace mantle and retrieved her Brownie box camera.

"Stand right here. By the fireplace."

Gus stood beside Mary Helen.

"Gussie, put your arm around her."

He did. It seemed the gown never covered anywhere he ordinarily touched. Logic told him it did, but mercy.

He did not know what mothers felt at moments such as this but he knew Mrs. Ellsworth was excited. He saw exchanges between mother and daughter that eluded him.

They hurried down the sidewalk to the Mercury, top down. Gus opened the door for Mary Helen, he watched his friend and wondered when she stopped wobbling on her high heel shoes and began to move as if they were extensions of her legs. He told himself he couldn't have missed it, he had been right there, next door.

As he settled in behind the driver's seat, she said, "Gus, drive slow. I don't want my hair messed before we get to the dance."

"You know we have to back up to my parents so Mother and Aunt Elizabeth can see you and take their photographs."

"Oh, I know but I'm also ridden a mile or two with you."

The Kelly women made over her. There was much too make over. Bob's mother, Claire-Marie, didn't know quite how to express her emotions. Her son dressed in the compulsory slacks, starched white shirt and colorful tie. Still, she looked at him and saw a boy nudging his way into manhood. A look of innocence. The girl on his arm, a girl she had known since hours after her birth, was clearly now a young woman.

Taking Brownie photographs allows a closer examination of another, an aunt can stare with being obvious. Elizabeth scrutinized the girl, the woman, she thought might soon be her favorite nephew's wife.

Mary Helen's gown fell delicately from her pleasingly rounded hips, there was a lush tone to her flawless skin as it raced across her shoulders and down her arms, her cleavage exposing the promise of perfection and framing a jeweled drop of three linear diamonds. She stood poised in her heels. Her upswept hair still somehow accenting her face, presenting both face and hair in the most stunning fashion.

Somewhere, seemingly unobserved, Mary Helen Ellsworth had become a beautiful woman.

Junior looked at the three women and saw cumulative beauty. Then, he thought, "Girls really do get there first."

He reached behind the picture frame and picked up his glass with a whiff of Four Roses remaining. He drained the glass and put the glass back behind the frame.

Gus parked his Uncle Bob's dandy convertible near the entry to the recently constructed WPA gym, now the traditional site of the Delta High School Senior Prom. He walked around the car to open her door and assist her out. As he was doing so, she took out her compact mirror and checked to be certain her lipstick hadn't smudged in the light kiss they exchanged outside the Kelly house.

Very few couples arrived by car as Gus and Mary Helen had. Most had walked hand and hand along Delta's sidewalks to their Prom. A fine procession of lovely girls in picturesque home-sewn gowns. The gowns fit and design was largely dependent upon the skill of a family's number one seamstress. Boys, many in their first pair of adult pants that were not blue denim, were proud if uneasy. A starched white dress shirt and a father's or Uncle's most colorful tie. Most wore Khaki pants purchased from the Kelly Dry Goods Store.

The girls were striking, the boys were doing the very best they could.

Mary Helen looked up and admired her date. How long had it been since she first taught him to dance? Eighth grade she thought. She had taken him to the hallway and over the floor furnace she taught him to box step. It had not been that long ago and yet felt forever ago.

They had been the forever friends who went to the Muskogee State Fair, returned a dating couple and became lovers.

Now, they arrived at their Senior Prom. In truth, Mary Helen made an entrance. Gus escorted her.

The Mix-n-Match Service of Delta High School was more than successful this prom season. Of the forty-two members of the Class of 1942, all were in attendance.

In the weeks leading up to the Prom, these Seniors, male and female, listened to their radios and heard ten thousand American soldiers had surrendered as Corregidor fell to the Japanese. The news seemed fill with word of desert battles across North Africa which at best would be classified as standoffs. Those seemed to be fought between Germany and England. The German Air Force continued to pound England with nightly bombing raids.

The Prom may have looked the same but it was distinctly different. This year over half of the male graduates had already enlisted in the service. To Mary Helen's great distress, Gus was among the enlistees.

Mary Helen have voiced her strong objections to Gus' enlistment in the Marine Corps. Their pre-enlistment arguments had been filled with vitriol. She believed she has used almost every tool in her feminine toolbox, every tool she was willing to use, to dissuade him. Gus enlisted and their quarrels ceased.

Mary Helen felt Gus had made his decision and now she must make hers.

Mary Helen could have sulked but she chose to act otherwise. She considered consulting Gus' Aunt Elizabeth but decided better of it.

Gus had acted in a fashion consistent with his moral compass and sense of patriotism. Mary Helen knew that he could have acted in no other way but it didn't lessen her distress.

Gus enlisted in the Marines. He never considered any other branch of service. His Uncle Bob had been a Marine and that was that.

Most years the hot topics would have been who was leaving to try to find jobs in Oklahoma City or Tulsa or who was getting married later in June. This year it was who has enlisted and who hasn't. A couple of the mechanically gifted boys were headed to Tulsa in hopes of securing employment at Douglas Aircraft. Employment that was vital to the national defense and provided a draft exempt status.

Then, the dance band, imported from Muskogee courtesy of the First Bank of Delta, brought a hush to the room. This was a big deal at Delta High School.

There on the basketball floor, under yards of crepe paper streamers, the lights dimmed and the Prom dance began. Four large pedestal fans tilted so that their breezes gently stirred the crepe paper streamers giving the appearance of constant movement. Side lights cast their glow upward through the undulating ribbons of paper, enriching the shadowy illusion.

The band, The Dark Knights, had set up in the broad-based permanent wooden seating. Right on cue, they opened with their rendition of Glenn Miller's *Moonlight Serenade*. A soft dance that enticed even the shyest of couples onto the floor. In an unfathomable transformation, youthful silhouettes exotically moved and swayed, figures soaring through the dark, inexplicably guided by the poignant melody.

Gus extended his hand, palm up. Mary Helen took it. In two short steps they found the dance floor. Gus leaned forward and kissed her cheek. In the hazy shadow half-light, he mouthed, "Mary Helen, you are beautiful."

Her face radiated joy. It was dance now or explode in happiness. She subtly stepped back with her right foot, Gus took the hint and the lead.

By the end of the first set, they had danced a rumba and a fox trot, waltzed to a melody that resembled Strauss' Blue Danube, and even tried to shag before stepping from the floor as the notes of the first set faded.

They stopped by the refreshment table, decided on a bottle of ice-cold Coca-Cola rather than the bubbling effervescence of the fruit punch. Hands now chilled and dripping, they weaved their way up toward the space they had reserved at the top of the wide permanent wooden bleachers.

Gus flipped droplets of icy water onto the back of Mary Helen's neck. She shivered. He laughed. She called him an asshole. He laughed louder.

"How could such words come from the mouth of such a beauty?"

Mary Helen leaned forward, bussed his cheek as she moved her mouth toward his ear. She whispered, "My sweet Gussie, go fuck yourself."

Gus roared, held her close, then spontaneously patted her behind. Neither of them knew quite what to make of the familiarity that suggested. This was something only their parents did.

They nested on their blanket and sipped the Coca-Cola. They looked down on the now almost empty dance floor, the basketball floor, and watched the few couples still milling about.

Feeling a need for candor, Gus said, "You know you do look incredible?" A question with no expectation of an answer.

Mary Helen opened her purse and extracted the half-pint of Ancient Age Gus had stashed there. She handed the bottle to Gus who poured a splash into the now half empty Coke bottles. Although the Coca-Cola helped, she wasn't fond of the taste. She liked the fizzy feeling it gave her.

Her father, who fancied himself a connoisseur of such elixirs, attempted to explain to her that bourbon was a form of whiskey that contained more than half corn mash. Tennessee Whiskey and Kentucky Bourbon. She had listened but candidly she only knew that even though prohibition was no longer the law of the law, Oklahoma remained a dry state. So, a good liquor was whatever the bootlegger had in stock.

She took a sip, felt the sting. Again, she concluded that she was iffy on the taste but she appreciated the sensations it brought.

"Makes me think of what Will Rogers said about us, Oklahomans will vote dry as long as they can stagger to the polls."

"Well, he is one of us so he can say it."

They clinked their Coke bottles and took a sip.

Someone slipped a copy of Blind Willie Johnson's *Dark Was the Night* on the victrola. This blend of Blues and Gospel somehow fit Delta, Oklahoma in the spring of 1942. The revelers paused and listened, held each other close and hoped against hope.

Artie Shaw's *Stardust* followed. It's lyrics further tempered the mood.

And now that purple dusk of twilight time
Steals across the meadows of my heart
High up in the sky the little stars do climb
Always reminding me that we're apart
You wonder down the lane and far away
Leaving me a song that will not die
Love is the stardust of yesterday
The muse of years gone by.

They listened with an increasing awareness. This was group of young people that had known each other almost their entire life. The vague sense that life as they had known it was about the ripped apart, an entire world put asunder, was creeping up on them. The lyrics pulled them toward grasping the loneliness of separation, a mindfulness that some farewells are forever and irreversible.

Though I dream in vain
In my heart it will remain
My stardust melody
The memory of love's refrain.

A few couples eased toward floor. Unhurried, some seemed bound by the music while others did not.

The Last Dance in Delta

Gus and Mary Helen stood on the plank seating and swayed with the sounds, scarcely moving. They held each other close.

Gus placed his fingers to her cheeks, tilted her head and kissed her. Mary Helen melted into him.

The music ended. The Victrola made its prickly sounds as it continued its round and round movement, the needle floated along bouncing up and down. Then, someone lifted it away.

The band returned. The gym darkened more deeply than before. The crepe paper streamers still moved under the direction of the fans.

The dances were more paced. Hands found exposed skin. Touch that was not their father's intention but what their mother's well knew and even hoped for their daughters.

Gus and Mary Helen continued to dance in their high corner, taking an occasional glimpse toward their classmates down on the gym floor. Each couple searching, sensing an unfamiliar need to secure something lasting, to create a memory. Without understanding why, the Class of 1942 sensed the need for a keepsake, a reminiscence that might carry them through some long lonely nights looming just over the horizon.

Mothers told their daughters precautionary tales. No one knew what to tell their sons.

A few fathers had been in World War I. They chose to suppress their memories.

The formal dance adjourned at twelve midnight. School was done. The week after Delta's enlisted sons would begin to board buses headed away. For some away in a forever sense that none of them could quite yet grasp.

St. Joseph's mothers had prepared a breakfast feast for all parishioners and their dates. All attended. A room was provided for the young ladies to refresh themselves and to change into something more comfortable.

They left the Church Hall, prom-wear all safely hung on clothes rack for later pickup. The revelers were wonderfully full of food and life.

Mary Helen flopped into the passenger's seat and scooted toward the middle as Gus walked around to the driver's side.

She put her hand on his knee, started giggling and said, "You have to hear this." She hesitated, adding, "You can't tell a soul."

Gus couldn't help laughing as he said, "Okay."

"Eileen's mother insisted she had to leave her girdle on under her comfortable dress." She was trying to stifle her giggle. "Her mother's going to check when she gets home."

"It's okay, Billy Joe's not one to back off a challenge."

They laughed.

"Gussie, let's go to our place."

Gus turned the convertible into the rutted lane that led from the section line road onto the acres behind Bob and Elizabeth Kelly's home place. It was lined with large, perhaps overgrown, native cedars where the path had been cut among a grove of native cedars. The grasses between the ruts had grown enough that they scratched along the bottom of the car. He stopped and backed into a space he and Mary Helen had stopped any number of times during their dating years.

Gus' Uncle Bob had joked, "Gus, I think you're about to claim squatter's rights on my north forty."

His uncle still knew how to embarrass him.

Gus checked his position and turned off the motor.

He stretched, arms reaching skyward, looked toward Mary Helen and said, "God, what night!"

Mary Helen trapped his arms and kissed him. His arms fell around her. impetuous

"Scoot this way." He eased toward the middle. Then, they kissed. Then, she kissed him again. Prolonged, exciting and empowering kisses, memorable kisses running over each other, forming a mass.

He kissed her neck and nuzzled her clavicle. He undid the fastener at the top and then unbuttoned the top buttons in the row descending down her back. He fumbled with the strapless bra, an unfamiliar garment for him. Impetuous and excited Mary Helen deftly unfastened it and adjusted the front to allow him easier access.

If there was any awkwardness to the motions, they went unnoticed. Surfaces were reexplored. Familiar yet each time fingers travelled the pathways between her breast Gus found sensations yet undiscovered, a fresh, spontaneously emitted utterance, a murmur to a breathy sigh. He took such sounds as positive acknowledgments of his efforts and interest.

His hand found her leg. Her hose was a new and unexpected impediment, feeling grainy beneath his fingers. He preferred the silken skin with which he was better acquainted. Now faced with a quandary, Gus hesitantly advanced his hand.

Mary Helen stiffened then swiftly withdrew her objections. She relaxed into the seatback allowing her hips to ease forward, her knees parted. Gus had no doubt he had been encouraged to proceed.

Mary Helen looked at the sky, the clouds seemed a bright white and appeared hustle along across the sky while backlighting the undulating cedars as they gently waved in the late evening breeze. She tried to impose order where none existed.

She loved his touch, unskilled compared to that of her own familiar fingers but enthusiastic. Gus's caress was just beyond her control, seemingly unable to stay focused to task as she might have wished but quite delicious. Delicious was the descriptor that kept repetitively running through her mind.

Then, his motions became firmer taking on a precise elegance. The conclusion caught her by surprise. She found her hand upon his frantically guiding him. All illusion of control was lost. Pulsations racked her. Her release scandalized her. The sensations were startling, so incredible. She couldn't explain it but she felt luxurious. It made no sense. Each previous experience had been subtle, controlled. This wasn't.

Gus struggled to help. He was unsure as what had just happened. Bewilderment reigned.

Despite the moments of confusion that followed both considered challenging luck and life but they didn't. Still, there was an urgency to the night. They kissed. Gus caressed her.

Strangely, Mary Helen thought of her mother. They had a ritual. Any night she left the house for a date, her mother would say, "Don't let him touch your whee-whee.

Upon her return, her mother would ask, "You didn't let him, did you?"

In the morning, not for the first time, Mary Helen would lie to her mother about this matter. Before she had told tiny lies, this one was going to be a whopper.

She put her hand on his cheeks and kissed him, long and firm. Then she noticed him.

Sliding to his side, she released his zipper and said, "Here, let me help you with that."

The witching hour had approached. Prom evening was almost done. The drive back to their homes was reinvigorating. With the top down the convertible created a late spring wind that cascaded through their hair. All else that might have lingered now blew away.

Gus parked in front of the Ellsworth home. He turned off the ignition and leaned back into his seat.

"What an incredible evening. Miss Mary Helen, I do love you."

Mary Helen said, "Gussie, we have to talk."

She was solemn and serious.

"Well MH, that sure breaks a mood."

"Don't Gussie. I can't tease right now. I just can't."

Now her tone stopped him cold in his tracks. He nodded. She couldn't see him but she knew.

"You've enlisted. You're going in the Marines. You're going away, away for a long time, away to the war, a war that's a world away." Her speech pushed her words one on top of the other.

Gus was still. Sensing no response was forthcoming, she drew a deep breath and went on.

"Gussie, I'm not your Aunt Elizabeth. Oh, God there are times I wish I was. I wish I had her character. I have heard stories of how she waited for your Uncle Bob. Her prayers. I do admire her greatly. Hell, everyone admires her." Mary Helen's voice became even more measured, almost dispassionate. "I'm not her. I can't be her. I don't want to be her."

She paused and looked at Gus. She felt her eyes soften, then moisten, but she did not flinch. Perhaps she was trying to preserve the essence of him. No matter how well thought out her words, this was still complicated.

This hesitation was about the only element of these moments she hadn't mentally rehearsed.

She regrouped and begin again, "I am not your Aunt Elizabeth. Gussie, I'm not going to be waiting for you to come home from your stupid war. I know you'll change, even your Uncle Bob changed and I'll change while you're gone."

Gus started to speak but she schussed him.

"You could have chosen me!"

She looked, trying to gage the impact of her words. She recognized an anger she didn't know she possessed. She went on, "You might never have had to leave. You might not have gotten drafted."

"Mary Helen, you know I love you." That was all he had.

"Oh, Gussie, I love you." She stopped. She stared at him. She felt the hurt to her very soul. Then, she finished her say. "You chose the fucking war over me!"

Now she cried.

"I just can't Gussie, I just can't."

Oddly, she patted her eyes. His smell exploded from her handkerchief. She wanted him terribly. She thought we should have done it tonight. First times are once in a lifetime. She knew it was a first she wanted to share with him. But she couldn't. And he wouldn't. And they hadn't.

"Gussie, I've dreamed of moving from my parent's home into my husband's home. It has always been my only dream. You know that."

Gus scuffled in his seat. He fought to keep his tears away. He failed. In the effort, a nervous perspiration coated his upper lip. He felt rickety and hated himself for it.

Her voice increased by an octave. "Say something damn you."

His voice softened. It didn't weaken. In fact, it in its softness it gained strength.

"I've already told you that I love you. Mary Helen, that's all I've got." Gus tried to find more words but couldn't. "That's all I've got." Again, a pause. "It is just all I've got."

"I think I'll always love you, Gussie, but love has nothing to do with it."

"Who the hell told you that?"

"My sisters." She snapped, then wavered. "And my mother. That love has nothing to do with a happy life."

He could not have been left more flabbergasted.

Before anything else could be said, Mary Helen reached to open her car door.

"NO! You'll not do that. I am opening your car door, walking you to your front door and kissing you good night."

He now had her hand firmly grasped and was looking her as squarely in the eye as a man can in the dark of night.

"We will talk about this tomorrow in the full light of day."

Mary Helen did respond but she did remain in her seat.

Gus opened the car door and held her arm as she got out. He kept his hand at her elbow as they walked up the sidewalk, stepped up onto the porch and stopped at the door.

He turned her toward him, lifted her face and kissed her. He looked at her in the light of the porch and said, "When I picked you up tonight, I thought you were the most beautiful woman I had ever seen. Now, I know you are."

He paced his words, "You are beautiful. I do love you." With both hands on her shoulders, he finished, "Good night sweet lady. We will talk about this tomorrow. Well, later today."

She didn't laugh. She didn't smile.

"Goodbye, Gussie. What glorious times we had."

Gus eased the Mercury into his own drive. He collapsed forward and folded his head onto the steering wheel. He stifled a sob. Straightened himself, unbuttoned the inside jacket pocket and withdrew a ring case from his jacket pocket. He opened it and looked at the yellow gold band with its three emerald-cut stones. He wished the stones had been larger.

His Uncle Bob had told him no man ever thought the stones in an engagement ring were large enough. His Aunt Elizabeth assured him it that each girl thought every stone in her ring were quite large enough.

The Last Dance in Delta

Well, he could still ask her on her porch. Just not tonight. Tomorrow rather than tonight. Things might be different in the light of day.

The small box felt heavy in his pocket.

Gus walked across the lawn that separated the Kelly home from the Ellsworth home. He now had a plan. He felt the small box in his pocket.

He bounded up the steps onto the porch and rang the doorbell.

"Well, good morning. I hear you had a lovely time at the Prom." Mrs. Ellsworth was rather surprised to see Gus at her door.

"Good morning, Mrs. Ellsworth. Yes, Ma'am, it was wonderful." Gus said, then ask, "May I speak with Mary Helen?"

Mrs. Ellsworth was unable to conceal her surprise. She gathered herself and said, "Why Gus, she left on the early bus to Muskogee. She is going to catch the train there and going to spend some time in St. Louis with my parents."

Gus couldn't conceal that he was caught completely unawares. The ring box dropped from his hand, bouncing on the wooden porch. He shook his head as if to clear it. He reached to retrieve the box.

She stared at the box, transfixed, "Oh, Gus, I am so sorry."

Gus slid the box into his pocket.

She saw the dumbfounded expression on the face of this young man she had known since he was an infant. She burst into tears.

On Wednesday, July 1, 1942, Bob boarded a Rock Island Railroad train headed west toward Camp Pendleton.

CHAPTER 21:
As You Were

Sunday, July 5, 1942

AUGUSTUS ROBERT KELLY saw the Pacific Ocean for the first time. He rode a bus through the gates into Camp Pendleton.

He was fed and vaccinated, issued dog-tags, an identification card, and a service record book. He was given a haircut and he was clothed.

He was introduced to his Drill Instructor. After brief deliberation, his Drill Instructor determined that he was in fact a boot and not a shower shoe but it was a close call.

He was happy his name was Kelly. The Drill Instructor was of Irish lineage and proud of it. His Drill Instructor enjoyed creating unflattering names, labels, for the recruits whose names he judged unpronounceable.

Having grown up hunting with his Uncle Bob, Gus found considerable success as well as refuge on the rifle range.

Despite the intense conditioning, the unrelenting demands of the Drill Instructor and the always looming specter of war, Gus was finding tangible measures of progress to be quite gratifying.

Saturday, August 2, 1942.

James Ellsworth impatiently waited for his daughter, Mary Helen, at the railroad depot in Muskogee. He was disappointed in her behavior as it concerned the young Kelly boy. Still, he had missed her and would ultimately be happy to see her.

The Rock Island diesel rolled to a stop beneath the large awning that extended over the track. Red Caps, at the ready, jumped into action and placed the stairs beneath the exits from the eight passenger cars.

Mary Helen stepped onto the train station's platform, saw her father and forced a smile that for all the world appeared natural. James took his daughter's arm from the gloved hand of a Red Cap. His daughter securely off the train, he tipped the man a dime.

"Thank you, Sir."

They sat on a bench under the awning waiting for the luggage cart to arrive with her suitcases. First both looked down, studying the brick floor of the platform, but her father's question about the health of her aunt in St. Louis eased an otherwise awkward beginning. By the time they heard the iron rimmed wheels of the baggage cart being pushed along the dock by a Red Cap, they were talking more freely.

James Ellsworth secured his daughter's bags. tipped this Red Cap another dime, then carried the bags to his car.

By the time they had crossed the viaduct into downtown Muskogee, he had decided he wanted to take his daughter for an early dinner, before the church crowds hit, at the cafeteria near the large Katz Drug Store in the heart of downtown.

He was happy to have her home. She seemed preoccupied.

25 October, 1942

Augustus Robert Kelly completed Marine Corps boot camp. Gus was proud. He was confident. He believed his training had prepared him for survival in combat. He was quite full of himself.

Mary Helen wrote him no letters. He didn't know why he expected her to, but he did.

November 2, 1942

After declining several potential courters, Mary Helen Ellsworth was invited to a dance the upcoming Saturday, November 7, 1942 by James Thomas "JT" Boggs. They had previously dated. It was this relationship that ended in a fist fight between JT and Gus Kelly. Mary Helen judged the poor result to be as much from her inexperience as from JT's ingenuousness.

The dance date rekindled their relationship. JT was involved in his father in the Delta Chevrolet dealership and professed his intent to live his life in Delta. He met the essential boxes on Mary Helen's check list.

17 July, 1943
PFC Augustus Robert Kelly, USMC, walked off the gangplank in Melbourne, Australia and into the ranks of the First Marine Division. The First Division had arrived in Melbourne exhausted and depleted from the Battle for Guadalcanal.

Reasonably replenished, the First Division was now fully engaged in preparations for the next deployment.

Wednesday, December 22, 1943
In a wedding that was the highlight of the holiday season, Mary Helen Ellsworth was married to John Thomas Boggs. The newlyweds planned, following a brief honeymoon in Dallas, to make their home in Delta. They had refurbished one of her father's rental houses to live in until they could design and construct their home.

Mrs. John (Violet) Crandall, Delta's finest seamstress, sewed her wedding gown from a pattern she had gotten from Neiman-Marcus in Dallas. The French Lace elements enthralled her, she felt delightfully perfect as the dress travelled along the curves of her body, a body trapped between the soft pillows of womanhood and the firm, crisp angles of adolescent. Before the mirror in her gown, she felt flawless yet inexplicably unconvincing.

But the French Lace. It was French Lace.

Her long nightgown with matching robe, she felt she looked like Ingrid Bergman in *Casablanca*. She loved the subtle seductiveness of Bergman playing Ilsa Lund, torn between her passionate love for the dashing and heroic patriot, Rick Blaine, and the security and safety offered by her husband, Victor Laslo.

She identified with Ilsa and being loved by two men. She sought self-justification. It came and went.

Looking at the image in the mirror, she could only see her mother. She had wanted red, her mother encouraged pink, she bought black.

The Last Dance in Delta

She had a 1943 bridal shower. Through a collective gathering of ration stamps and the prudent use of the acquired materials, the cakes and punch were quite tasty. Readily available War Bonds were the most common and the most patriotic gift.

The families were made every effort to accumulate a collection of used appliances and second-hand furniture. The war effort was peeling off every chunk of metal available.

The home was skimpy furnished but Mary Helen knew better than to complain.

She had enjoyed more the intimate personal shower her friends hosted. There were no gifts beyond the collective purchase of a twenty-five-dollar War Bond which cost eighteen dollars and seventy-five cents.

The girls secreted in a fifth of Old Crow which was mixed into bottles of ice-cold Coca-Cola or Seven-Up. Ribald stories were told, often exaggerated by the married girls among their number.

"I don't know for certain but I've been told" stories, stories which often placed well-known Delta couples in the role of protagonists, produced scarlet red cheeks and uproarious laughter.

Mary Helen found herself avowing, "Oh, I'm not doing that."

Strangely, she felt she should hear a voice saying, "Oh, sweet Jesus, Mary Helen."

It wasn't the wedding of her dreams, but it was acceptable.

Before catching the train, the next morning, the couple was going to spend their wedding night in the Charles Hotel in downtown Delta.

Outside the door of their hotel room, JT took her hands in his, leaned in and kissed her. She felt the prickle of whiskey on her lips. He lifted her, wobbled and carried her across the threshold into hotel room.

She moved, hinting for him to set her down.

He carried her straight across the room and unceremoniously dumped her onto the bed. Her hands thrashed to suppress the bottom of her dress.

Trying to straighten herself and move across the bed, she was glad she had decided on a superfluous dress change after the reception. Her mother had somewhat insisted on it, stating she would be grateful for a bladder break at that point in time. Mary Helen admitted her mother had been right.

JT grabbed. His hand caught her by her neckline. The fabric gave.

"Let's be getting' the dress off."

Mary Helen was startled. She didn't see it coming.

JT sat on the bed and leaned over her. She pushed him back and said, "Wait, just wait a minute!"

She tried to scoot toward the edge of the bed. "We're going to, but slow down."

His hand pressed her shoulders into the bed. She was startled, surprised, now a touch troubled her. This wasn't in her plan.

JT persisted. The smell of whiskey emanated from him. Confused and angry, he glared at her.

"No!" She screamed. She had lost control.

She felt cornered, helpless. Helplessness terrified her. She detected perspiration on her upper lip. Her tongue wiped it. Salty. Wet.

He released one of her shoulders in an attempt to grab the bottom of her dress. This gave her the freedom to roll away from him. She did.

She braced up on all fours, facing him. She was furious. She screamed, "NO! Stop!" She glared at him like a cornered animal. She was now afraid. And Mary Helen wasn't ever afraid.

Despite her heighted awareness, she didn't see his open hand flash toward her face. His open hand crashed into her cheek. The hit took her sideways, buckling her arms and knees.

She was now pinned to the bed. She was angry, injured and confused.

He held her fast to the bed,

"Isn't this how Gus did you?" There was anger and desperation in his voice.

She was startled. She screamed, "What? What!"

The Last Dance in Delta

His hands were hurting her shoulders. She tried to squirm free. He released her shoulder, hit her again, then pressed harder against her shoulder.

His knee tried to separate her legs. He failed.

JT rose to his knees, locked onto her eyes and hissed, "You try anything and I'll really hit you next time."

Then, his voice taunted her, "By God, I'm going to fuck you." He hit her again.

Mary Helen gathered herself and made every effort to soften her voice. "JT, please let me go to the bathroom. I don't want us to make a baby."

"No need, I've got a rubber right here." He retrieved his billfold and displayed the small square packet.

"Hurry." She feinted and stalled.

"Now, don't you fight me on this." Despite his words, everything said he did want her fighting him.

Mary Helen lifted the hem of her dress to her waist, then again said, "Just please hurry."

Seeing her as subdued, JT hopped to the side of the bed, took off his pants but leaving on his boxers. JT bit open the wrapper and tossed it aside. He was a little embarrassed as Mary Helen watched him put on the condom.

He got on the bed. She smiled and seemed to coyly pull the crotch of her panties aside for him. Her intent was to mesmerize him. He slapped her again.

JT. fumbling with her panties, never saw Mary Helen lift the iron lamp from the bedside table. She swung it with all the force she could muster. The lamp crashed violently into his head. He crumpled forward.

She was breathing heavily in both fear and raw stone-cold anger.

He was semi-conscious, moaning and sprawled on the bed. She lifted the lamp and swung again. She missed his head, striking him full in the shoulder. Frustrated, she drew back again and aimed for his groin. This time, her aim was spot on. The condom provided him no protection from her final blow.

She picked the telephone up. When Central answered, she said, "Ethyl, ring Bob Kelly. Hurry!"

Bob answered on the second ring.

"Uncle Bob, I need your help. Now!"

"Mary Helen, what the Hell's happened? Everything okay?"

"No. God damn it, no." Mary Helen stifled a sob and said, "Come to the hotel and get me."

"Be right there. I'll meet you in the lobby."

"Just pull up front, I'll come out."

"Don't you leave!"

"I won't."

Even in the dim light of the street lamp and the hotel awning, it only took Bob Kelly one look at Mary Helen's discolored and swelling face and he was out of the car. He opened the trunk, shuffled through the tool box and brought out his castration pliers.

Bob charged into the lobby. He pointed the pliers at the night clerk and so terrified the poor man that he simply blurted out the room number.

Bob dashed up the staircase and banged open the door. Then, shoved it open.

JT's hair was matted with blood and he was still struggling with the pain rising from his scrotum. Bob screamed something as he swung the pliers just short of contact.

Realizing JT's condition, Bob pulled up and began to tap JT's crotch with the gruesome but efficient looking pliers.

He yanked at JT's boxers, continued to thumping, his voice rang as steely cold as his pale blue eyes.

"Boy, you understand me good. Mary Helen's going to annul you out of her life. You bother her, just once, even a hello, and I'll neuter you, you son of a bitch!"

JT moaned in obvious pain.

Bob needed something to hit. He swung the long pliers, breaking the water pitcher on the table, spraying glass shards across JT and the bed.

"Nothing lower that hitting a woman."

"You listen good now. I don't want Mary Helen to ever look up on the street and see your sorry ass. You understand?"

In a most ill-advised move, JT feeling some act of resistance was necessary to preserve his manhood, extended the middle finger of his right hand. JT saw the business end of the extended pliers move and protectively raised his left hand to deflect the blow. The castration pliers broke his left arm just above the wrist.

Bob laid the long metal castration device on JT's upper thigh and advised, "Don't you ever think about letting me see you in Delta again."

For final emphasis as a teacher might use a pointer, Bob banged the metal pliers into JT's thigh.

"You understand me?"

Scowling JT nodded.

As an afterthought, Bob added, "See if the Army will take a sorry sack of shit like you."

JT's response was unsatisfactory.

Bob lifted the pliers. JT cowered and shrank, saying, "Yes sir. I understand."

"Boy, if you think I'm not thinking about turning you into a steer, you'd better think again."

Bob returned to car. He patted Mary Helen's hand and said, "It'll all be alright."

Bob drove Mary Helen home and walked her to the door. He rang the doorbell.

Her parents opened the door. Her mother cried, her father faunched.

James Ellsworth nodded to Bob Kelly.

"James, I took the liberty of calling Dr. Sam from the hotel lobby. He should be here in a moment. She can tell you what happened."

Bob turned to Mary Helen, paused, placed his arm around her and hugged her. "And Sweet, you tell them everything. Do you hear me?"

Her tears raced from her swollen eyes over her increasingly discolored cheeks, she nodded and said, "I will."

She looked at Bob, then said, "Uncle Bob."

He turned toward her.

"Thank you."

Bob Kelly smiled, then brushed her cheek with the back of his hand.

He left. He felt a fresh flush of youth. He felt a flash of usefulness in the midst of a world war he was too old to fight.

Bob began to organize how he would explain this saga to Elizabeth. From her feminine insights, she would have questions he had not thought to ask.

"Oh well," he thought, "On some things she'll have to accept my conjecture."

Doctor Fulton was no longer the elderly gentleman who birthed and cared for so many Delta residents. Doctor Fulton now referred to his eldest son, Samuel Ray. Originally, he was called Dr. Sam to delineate him from his father. The label stuck.

A sign hanging from the fixed awning extending from the east wall of the store front office still declared Fulton Clinic. Dr. Sam would joke now and again that he wasn't certain what a clinic was but his father found great pleasure in using the self-assigned designation. Since his father's death, he hadn't felt the need to change the sign.

Sam Fulton was the first from the county to graduate from the University of Oklahoma School of Medicine. He was pleased with himself and Delta was proud of this native son.

James Fulton, pushing seventy at the time, was returning from delivering a little girl to Bill and Melita Thomas in Lona Valley. The gravel road coming back into Delta over the mountain had two sharp curves, one at the top just before the road began its steep descent down to Polecat Creek. A second at the bottom of the decline as the road straighten to move toward the bridge crossing the creek.

Telltale marks in the gravel suggested the Ford skidded on the top turn, spewing gravel across the leafy base of the post oak forest. The vehicle appeared to have picked up speed as it moved down the steep roadbed. There was no indication Dr. Fulton made any effort to make the final curve but rather continued on a path through the elms and cottonwoods before coming to rest with its front wheels submerged.

While quite damaging, the wreck didn't appear to the casual eye to be of adequate force to have been lethal. Yet, Doctor James Fulton was found slumped over the wheel and quite dead. A bottle of Lydia Pinkham's Elixir was found unbroken in his inside suit coat pocket.

Bill Thomas recalled Dr. Fulton's last comment was, "Mr. Thomas, right now, I'm just plain tired."

Sherriff Ethan Finn, the first to arrive at the site, was said to have straightened the scene up a bit.

After doing a slow visual survey, Dr. Sam observed, "Mary Helen, you look a lot better than when last I saw you."

"I feel much better."

He checked her shoulder and felt several muscle protuberances. He applied pressure to them and she winced.

"Please unbutton the top couple of buttons on your blouse so I can get a better look."

She nodded. She unbuttoned and shrugged the blouse, baring her shoulders.

She tried to convince herself any embarrassment was unfounded. So far, she was unsuccessful. She flinched when his fingers pressed into the muscle of her shoulder.

"An elastic bandage would help support this, but – well, the war effort has all the elastic bandages in existence. I'll support your shoulder with regular tape. After two days, you can take it off and see how it goes."

"How long before the bruises leave?"

"Before long, but not all at the same time. Just be patient young lady, you took a real thumping."

And he thought, "And you gave out better than you got." He thought it but didn't say it.

Doctor Sam Fulton stirred, making motions she associated with his leaving.

"Didn't my mother tell you what else I wanted?"

"I rather you requested it for yourself."

Mary Helen thought "fucking doctors." She took a breath, considered backing out before she bluntly declared, "For me, my mother and my Church, I want you to confirm that I did not consummate a marriage with JT. That I've never consummated anything with anybody."

Dr. Sam smiled at the young woman he had known since she had the chicken pox when she was three. He had always liked this girl, now this young woman.

"With all those bruises, you'll have no difficulty getting an annulment from the State of Oklahoma. I do suppose such a confirmation would go a long way toward getting an annulment from your Church."

"Just please, just get on with it." She was embarrassed, annoyed and more than a little unhappy with herself for feeling she had to provide proof of the continuing existence of her virginity.

At some level below awareness, a baseless emotion slipped into her consciousness, "God damn you Gussie, where are you when I need you."

Mrs. Evelyn Hightower, Doctor Sam's R.N. and her mother's friend since high school, stepped into the room. She handed Mary Helen a gown and said, "Undress and slip into this."

Mary Helen wanted to cry but she didn't.

"Well, Mary Helen, everything is as God made it." He formalized himself and concluded, "Your hymen is intact."

"I know."

"So?"

"So, tell my mother." An unintended acidity slipped in and she continued, "And tell your wife."

Evelyn Hightower, standing stiff backed and functionally blending into the wall, thought surely that directive included her.

Doctor Sam's expression said, "Kathryn has done nothing to deserve that." Mary Helen saw his face. She realized she had unduly tweaked him.

"Doctor Sam, I'm sorry. Truly. This whole thing has left me wound up," she felt her tension ease. She now went on, "I wanted you to tell you wife and tell her it would be a good deed if she spread it around bridge club. There is a nosy netty or two already spreading stories that just aren't true."

Facing the wall, washing his hands, he said, "I can tell you somebody gave the man a mountain size concussion."

Laughing to himself, he wanted badly to add, "And a horrible pair of black and blue softball size testicles." He didn't. He felt a touch guilty about enjoying his private laugh. But not much.

"Mary Helen, young lady, you will be fine."

Dr. Sam left the room. Evelyn Hightower, on his heels, shot a long-suffering motherly look in Mary Helen's direction.

Mary Helen wanted to flip her off but refrained.

Now alone in the room, Mary Helen thought, "Physically." She sighed and again thought, "Gussie, Gussie, where the hell are you?"

She put on her underwear and skirt, tossed the gown on the examining table, yanked at her panties, straightening them beneath her skirt, tucked in her blouse and left.

She stopped on the sidewalk and thought, "God damn, I hate doctors."

The sign gave a soft squeaking sound as the suspension chain rubbed against the screw eye. In the confines of her mind, she flipped the clinic off.

Tuesday, December 28, 1943

John Thomas Boggs was inducted into the United States Army.

Wednesday, March 8, 1944

Junior and Bob Kelly sold a twenty-five percent interest in the First National Bank of Delta to the Clarence Finnegan family of Tulsa, in exchange for stock in Finnegan Oil and Gas. It was agreed that Clarence Finnegan's youngest son, Tate Michael Finnegan, a thirty-two-year-old Princeton graduate would be the president of the bank.

Young Finnegan stood five feet, ten inches tall, was slender and reasonably good looking. His hair was darkened by a daily dab of Wildroot Cream Oil and combed with a straight-line part.

In Delta, it was his dapper dress right down to the two-tone shoes that marked him.

He was said to be intelligent, articulate, a skilled if not an overly ambitious banker and an excellent golfer. All who knew him agreed he was a kind and gentle man.

His age and a slight difference in the length of his legs excused him from the draft.

He moved to Delta, purchased the historic two-story Calhoun home on North Main Street and immediately begin to renovate the home. In the interim, he took up residence in the Delta Hotel and availed himself of its dining room.

Tuesday, July 4, 1944

As he completed his winning round in the Independence Day Classic at the Delta Country Club, Tate Finnegan saw Mary Helen Ellsworth standing in the shade of the large ash tree just up the hill from the eighteenth green. She was stunning.

The die was cast.

13 September, 1944

The First Marine Division, men hardened by Guadalcanal and inexperienced replacements not long out of boot camp, waited as the Navy shelled and bombed Peleliu, six square miles of island blanketed in oppressive sweltering heat.

Gus Kelly was a replacement. He saw the bluster of many of his peers and wondered what it obscured. He watched the shelling and observed that no one could survive it. Yet, he understood that they would.

The veterans became somber, most seeming to be lost in their thoughts. Conversation became pragmatic checks and reviews of their equipment. M1 Carbines were readied and re-readied. Oil and rifle cleaner was used then packed. Knives, especially the new ones with their deeply grooved handle, were sharpened with spit and whit stone. Musset bags were checked and rechecked.

Gus was concerned. The subdued expressions of the veterans suggested an intimate knowledge he did not possess.

The Last Dance in Delta

George Thomas, a fellow Oklahoman from Tulsa who he met in boot camp, sat next to him and leaned into the bulkhead and asked, "What do you think Gus?"

Gus gave something of an Irish snort and answered, "Shit G, I'm afraid to think."

Confession being good for the soul, Corporal Thomas said, "I just want to go."

"Yeah."

"Do you think anybody could live thru that?" George motioned toward the flames leaping from the island.

"I hope not."

"Damn, I just want to get off this fuckin' ship."

A voice from near them said, "Boot, ain't nobody shootin' at ya on this fuckin' ship."

Gus and George went quiet.

15 September, 1944

"Hands on the vertical, boots on the horizonal!"

With that chanted reminder the amphibious assault on Peleliu began. The First Marine Division spilled over the sides of the troop ships and covered the rope nets like harried ants headed back to the nest.

The LVT, the alligator, carrying Gus and George powered past the LSI which lay one thousand yards off shore pouring covering fire onto the island before bringing the second wave in for landing.

Gus couldn't make spit. He opened a stick of Juicy Fruit and offered George a stick. George accepted. The immediate rush flavor helped some. Salt water splashed up and over the sides of Alligator.

Gus focused on a veteran of Guadalcanal, a Marine he watched during the Australian training.

The unknown was terrifying.

The Gator scaped bottom, the first sounds of steel scraping on sand was like electricity. The tracks spun, engaged and dug in, moving the vehicle onto the beach and toward the tree line. Every nerve sprung to attention.

The Guadalcanal vet went over the side, Gus followed him, and George came off behind Gus.

After two steps, Gus stumbled and went head first into the beach. He kept his rifle clear of the sand. His Juicy Fruit got gritty. He chewed it anyway.

He looked back at the body he had stumbled over, a body partly embedded in the sand by the tracks of the Gator.

Gus gagged but did not vomit. He tasted the acid and tried to spit it out and almost lost his Juicy Fruit. He kept chewing his gum.

"Off the beach! Get off the beach!"

"Assemble in the tree line!" "First Squad! On me!"

A coconut fell. It struck the ground next to George's head just grazing his helmet. He rolled away, assault knife in hand, screaming, "Lookout! Lookout!"

The Gunny, trying to keep calm, laughed and said, "Watch out! The coconut is trying kill itself falling on 'Old Lookout's' head."

The nickname stuck. George Thomas was "Lookout" for the duration.

By nightfall, they had moved inland on this narrow volcanic island, two miles wide and six miles long. It had an airstrip and mountains that rose from a dense jungle floor and were pocked with caves.

An airfield military intelligence viewed a vital to an ultimate attack on Okinawa and the mainland of Japan.

Gus was thirsty. Everyone was thirsty. Some water barrels hadn't arrived, all the rest were contaminated by a toxic, foul-smelling gasoline that wasn't properly cleaned from the cans before they were refilled with fresh water.

"Just who the hell thought used oil drums was a good way to haul fresh water?"

The choral response was, "Marine Intelligence!"

Gus spoke up, "Old Choctaw said if you're thirsty put a pebble in your mouth."

"Does it help?"

"Does if you can drink rocks."

"Fuck you, Kelly."

Gus was unsure where he found any sense of humor.

"Alright! Talkin' about it just makes it worse." When Gunny spoke, they all listened.

The next morning two natural waterholes were found. Both had been poisoned.

17 September, 1944

The First Marine Division crossed and secured the airfield on Peleliu. At days end, Gus believed he had survived the most horrific day of his life. Over fifty percent of his regiment were killed or wounded that day.

Flights of fresh water arrived.

Gus Kelly sat in the bombed-out shell of the command building in the airport complex. He sipped fresh water. He couldn't think of words to describe the luxury. He smoked his first Lucky Strike.

The unbearable heat remained unbroken.

27 September, 1944

"Alright Marines, Chesty is going up on Bloody Nose Ridge and burn the fuckin' monkeys out of their caves. We've been selected to go with him."

29 September, 1944

Gus saw a man burn alive. Gus gagged and turned away. An officer killed the man with a single shot from his sidearm.

02 October, 1944

Gus saw three men burn alive. The flamethrower routed three of the enemy out of a cave on Bloody Nose Ridge. They were covered in burning diesel from the flamethrower.

Gus and Lookout sat on a boulder overlooking the mouth of the cave. He did not vomit. No one raised a rifle.

After five days on Bloody Nose Ridge and fully one-half of the company wounded or killed, the flamethrower was your best friend.

Gus and Lookout could not know the stench would cling to their immortal souls for a lifetime.

Monday, October 9, 1944

The St. Louis Cardinals defeated the St. Louis Browns 3 to 1 to win the 1944 World Series in six games. All six games were played in Sportsman's Park, a facility that served as home field for both teams.

Gus missed the "Streetcar Series." He would have loved it.

18 December, 1944

Corporal John Thomas Boggs was killed in action in the Ardennes region of Belgium. Corporal Boggs was driving his truck in a desperate effort to bring ammunition into the undersupplied men preparing to defend the crossroads town of Bastogne. Driving his truck at high rate of speed, Corporal Boggs failed to complete a turn and his truck careened down a steep slope before exploding at the base of the grade.

26 December, 1944

The First Marine Division departed Peleliu. Rumors spread that a return to Melbourne was at hand. The news sat well with the Marines.

01 January, 1945

The First Marines Division disembarked on Pavuvu. Pavuvu was in no fashion Melbourne. Pavuvu was an abandoned coconut plantation. The neat, orderly rows of trees were the only neat, orderly elements to the island.

For years unharvested coconuts had fallen to the ground and rotted there. Pyramidal tents with ten cots each had been hastily erected on this vile surface.

Pavuvu was populated with two enormous creatures, rats and land crabs. Both species seemed to conjointly rule the island, the rats scamping down the tent ropes and the land crabs finding their favorite haunts in boots and beds.

Relentless yet intermittent rains kept everything soaked.

The Marines ate what they less than lovingly called B rations, heated C rations. The entertainment was limited to a large outdoor theatre where the best and worst of Hollywood were played each night. Alcohol for enlisted Marines was limited to three beers each evening. Barter was commonplace.

In a single memorable evening, Bob Hope and his troupe, through great effort on Bob Hope's part, performed at the theatre. Some years later, when Hope was the guest of honor at the Annual Pro-Am at Southern Hills Country Club in Tulsa, Gus went out of his way to meet and thank Hope.

Gus staked himself out by the bridge that brings a player across the creek from twelve fairway to twelve green. Gus made a poster board sign, folded it and placed it in his pants at the small of his back and then held it up as Hope crossed the bridge. The sign said, "I saw you on Pavuvu." Bob Hope was stopped. They talked. Over thirty years had lapsed but neither man had forgotten their experiences on Pavuvu.

Preparation for the next invasion kept the young Marines from injuring each other. And kept them focused forward toward something they all believed was next.

Gus was certain Pavuvu had no redeeming virtues but the fact no one was shooting at him. That and Bob Hope.

They didn't yet know the next island's name and they couldn't have pronounced it if they had. They knew it was there and waiting for them.

Gus wrote a number of letters to his Uncle Bob and Aunt Elizabeth, the first letters he had written to them since he shipped out.

Pavuvu was God awful but it wasn't Peleliu.

Monday, January 1, 1945

Mary Helen Ellsworth and Tate Michael Finnegan attended the Gala New Year's Ball at the Delta Country Club.

The dinner was the finest that rationing would allow. Beyond a case of decent Canadian gin, whiskey was Canadian Club, Four

Roses or Ancient Age, the beef was provided by the Kelly Ranch, scalloped potatoes, a variety of canned vegetables and sweet tea. The tea was sweet only because almost every member's kitchen had contributed a smidgeon of sugar.

Tate had arranged for a fine western swing band from Tulsa. "Not cheap but worth every dime."

Mary Helen and Tate danced.

Elizabeth nudged Bob and said, "I think Mary Helen has set her cap for him."

The band leader stepped forward and made an announcement, "I want you folks to hear a new waltz tune my friend John Bond has come up with. Here it is the *Oklahoma Waltz*."

Tate stood, extended his hand and said with an exaggerated drawl, "Darlin', let's dance."

The late-night sounds embraced them. Each movement seemed easy. They touched, blotting out all the distance between them. For the moment, Mary Helen felt as if she were the starlet in her own movie. She made her decision.

"Tate, let's go."

Tate met her gaze. Kept it for a moment. He nodded and said, "Lets".

It caused quite a stir the next morning when Mary Helen accompanied Tate down the staircase, through the lobby and into the dining room for the Delta Hotel New Year's Day brunch. It was a jaw-dropper.

A couple of ladies openly stared. One leaned into the other and said, "Well, there will be no more speculating about the state of her celebrated hymen."

That afternoon, Mary Helen began to organize her wedding to Tate Finnegan. The next day, she took over the refurbishing of the Calhoun house on North Main Street.

01 January, 1945

In the early morning hours, after consuming a volume of celebratory drinks of underground gin, Gus, Lookout and several of their comrades commandeered a flamethrower and lit up hundreds of rats and land crabs.

Later, Gus and Lookout attended a Mass in Celebration of the New Year.

Saturday, February 9, 1945

Before a small gathering of their families, Mary Helen Ellsworth and Tate Michael Finnegan were married in St. Joseph's Church in Delta.

Saturday, March 10, 1945

The St. Louis Cardinals reported to their Spring Training camp in Cairo, Illinois only to find the site flooded. The Cardinals announced that Spring Training would be conducted in Sportsman's Park in St. Louis this season.

01 April, 1945

At dawn, the First Marine Division landed on the beaches of Okinawa. By night fall, they had fought their way inland. As on Peleliu, the Marines found the Japs dug in deep and holed up in elaborate systems of tunnels and caves.

"Ace, get your ass over here."

Axel Lewandowski, Ace for ease of both tongue and communication, came skidding in behind a felled palm tree.

Ace was a replacement who joined the squad on Pavuvu. He was saved from far worse nicknames because he was from Gunny's hometown of Chicago.

"Captain needs a runner, you're the lucky bastard."

06 April, 1945

"Shit, the God damn Nips creeped into Mule's foxhole last night and slit his throat. From fuckin' ear to ear."

Mule wasn't the first and he certainly wasn't the last. The men now dug their foxholes for three, trusting one man to always be awake.

06 April, 1945

That afternoon, the rains began. Mud, the consistency of glue, rose over the boot tops and worked its way toward the feet, making walking a challenge. Vehicles, jeeps to tanks, bogged down and buried in the stinking, sticky paste.

08 April, 1945

The sky darked into a deep black as the storm rolled over the mountains.

"Sweet Jesus!"

Flopping like a frightened carp, Gus leaped from the foxhole he and Lookout were enlarging.

"Oh, Shit! It's a fuckin' dead Jap."

"Sweet Jesus! I dug up his God damn grave!"

"God damn! Look at the fuckin' maggots! Son of a bitch!"

"Oh Jesus, That smell! That is nasty!"

"I don't give a God damn if it's your Christ resurrected, you'll occupy that shit hole and keep the line." Gunny barked. Gunny locked on tight and roared, "Ya don't like his company, toss him out."

The three dug the body clear. As they lifted the dead Jap from the ground, the left leg snapped loose at the knee, leaving Lookout holding a boot with a foot sticking out. He dropped it into the storm water collecting at the bottom of the fox hole.

With a half turn, he slung the boot and leg toward the brush.

The trio rolled the remaining body out of the fox hole, carried it to the brush line and threw it in.

"Hill is steep, hope the son of a bitch washes down it."

The irony struck Gus and he mused, "Damn, inconsiderate of the asshole to get buried in our fox hole."

"Fuck you."

Ace extended his combat knife, displaying an enormous maggot on its point.

With clear dismay in his voice, Lookout said, "Oh my God! God Damn! Throw that son of a bitch away!"

"Sure. We got plenty more."

The wall of the former grave was working alive with the massive maggots.

"Son of bitches been eatin' better than K rations?"

"Give it a break!" Gus bunched his poncho around his neck and turned his eyes toward the line. The rain had not slackened.

The Old Gold did not eliminate the smell but it helped. He wished he had a pack of the Luckies the officers were smoking.

19 April, 1945

The rain continued. The mud deepened. The Japanese dead were being left unburied. The rain fell, the damp, heavy air reeked of death and rot, profoundly offending the nostrils. The mind must be deadened to avoid being overwhelmed. The amount of barbarity acceptable to the soul is amplified.

Gus and Lookout watched as an Okinawan family scrambled from their hut, human shields for a several Japanese soldiers. Jap fire struck the most exposed Marines. Two Thompson submachine guns returned fire. The family fell first leaving the Japs unshielded. A flamethrower lit them up.

Miraculously, a young girl, maybe four or five years old, stood erect, crying, just outside the boundary of the carnage. A kind Marine reached out to her. She blew up.

The Japanese Officer who set off the device was butchered.

Lookout stared at Gus. Gus shrugged.

A replacement from Mississippi, skin now the color of maggots, said, "God damn, like a fall hog!"

The rebel vomited.

"He'll get over it." Lookout said.

"Past caring." Gus lit an Old Gold.

06 August, 1945

The United States Army Air Force dropped an atomic bomb nicknamed Little Boy on Hiroshima, Japan.

07 August, 1945

Lookout lit an Old Gold. He sat on a sizable chunk of lava beside Gus. They passed a pint of Usher's Green Stripe back and forth between them.

"The ocean does have a sound to it."

"It does."

"Right here is the only fuckin' place that don't smell like rotten --," Lookout couldn't find the words. "Hell, everything on the God-forsaken Island smells like some kind of rot."

Gus grunted in agreement. "The smokes help."

"Why do the officers get Lucky Strikes and we can't even get Chesterfields?"

"Because they're officers."

"When I get home, I'm gonna hire me an officer on one of my daddy's rigs, just so I can boss him around."

"God damn, don't hex us!"

"Ah, this is over."

"No, it isn't. I'm bettin' we are burnin' them out of fuckin' holes a year from now." Gus became thoughtful, "On the main island."

"God damn, I hope not."

09 August, 1945

The United States Army Air Force dropped an atomic bomb nicknamed Fat Man on Nagasaki, Japan.

02 September, 1945

Aboard the USS Missouri in Tokyo Bay, the Japanese government signed the formal document agreeing to an unconditional surrender.

Wednesday, October 10, 1945

At 7:33 PM in the middle bedroom of the Finnegan home, the former Calhoun house, with Samuel Fulton, M.D. attending, Mary Helen Finnegan gave birth to the healthy seven-pound, eleven-ounce Tate Michael Finnegan, Jr.

Tate Finnegan, Sr. smoked a Roi-Tan and took a couple of sips in honor of his namesake.

Wednesday, December 26, 1945

In the deep quiet of Young Tate's nursery, Mary Helen sat down in her rocker. She unfastened the top buttons of her gown and prepared to feed her son. He muzzled and then latched on. She cradled his head and whispered, "Oh, what a sweet little guy you are."

She found she increasingly enjoyed these private moments as she nursed her son in these deep morning hours.

Young Tate had finished, full and satisfied lay sleeping against his mother's shoulder. They both enjoyed the rocking.

Finally, she got up, changed his diaper, swaddled him and laid him back in his crib. She started to leave the room, but lingered a moment. She walked back to the bay window, adjusted the rocker and sat for moment. She looked out the window into the crisp cold clear night sky.

She reflected on her son's first Christmas.

Mary Helen believed she was satisfied with her life.

A Christmas with the world again at peace.

6 February, 1947

By the time the First Marines returned to the United States all the fresh blush of victory had long left the country.

Robert Augustus Kelly, after spending the year after the war in China, periodically battling the Communist Chinese, was mustered out of the United States Marine Corps.

Gus Kelly, Axel "Ace" Lewandowski and George "Lookout" Thomas rode the train together as far as Oklahoma City. Then, Gus got off the train to make a connection to Delta. Ace and Lookout kept their seats. Lookout would exit the train in Tulsa and Ace stayed aboard until the train reached its final stop in Chicago.

Gus' uncle, Bob Kelly, and his father, Charles Kelly, met the train.

"Welcome home."

CHAPTER 22:
Examining the Unexaminable

A LADY IN THE PEW directly in front of him whispered to her husband, "Do you think he left the poor dear a note?"

Gus didn't know. His first reaction was to tell the woman to piss off. But he didn't.

He hadn't wondered much about a note. Now that he was thinking about it, he wondered if a note would actually help. He suspected there were demons that could not be explained in a note. Further, he thought it was a futile undertaking to pursue understanding in the words of a man as he contemplated taking his own life.

Gus gave a scarcely discernible shake of his head. It was a gesture more for himself than anyone else. He asked himself a question. "How do you make an illogical act appear logical?"

He further tempered his question, "In a note."

Characterologically, Gus sought order in the midst of disorder. Others had pointed out this trait to him. Gus was unclear as to whether the trait was an asset or liability.

Gus' thoughts moved to the war. He wondered how any civilized concept escaped combat, combat in the Pacific. Gus chastised himself.

Gus didn't want to think about the war. He most assuredly didn't want to think about Okinawa. Now, sitting in a pew among civilized folks, to bury a comrade, the incongruous thoughts intruded.

"Japs!" The thought intruded without context, uninvited. He tamped it down again.

"You'll never hear the shot that kills you."

Lookout had found comfort in the intonation. Gus hadn't.

Gus had unsuccessfully attempted to apply logic to Lookout's refrain.

"Lookout, think about it. The bullet travels faster than sound. So, of course, you don't hear it."

"Then, I guess if I got wounded, I maybe think I heard the shot that hit me because I did – just after it hit me."

Gus flinched as he envisioned Lookout's smile.

Lookout could find humor in a shit pile.

Feet shuffled. Kneelers raised. Everyone stood.

The casket accompanied by the Priest and his entourage came down the center aisle.

Gus thought, "Well, Buddy, you're getting buried in the Church because somebody chooses to believe you accidentally blew your brains out."

Macabre humor is a survival skill. If you can laugh at death, you might just survive all the craziness around you. Gus didn't really believe this, never did. He did believe in the psychic healing power of a good belly laugh.

Some men live and others don't.

He watched the casket wheel by and thought, "And some of us are just damn long at the dying." He reprimanded himself.

Gus couldn't remember when he first heard the axiom. Fable or fact, the hypothesis wedged in some shadowy niche of his mind and it remained lodged there. It was certainly not the only dark thought that he had tucked away in these remote crevices. Combat fills them up rather quickly. It stains the mind.

Gus believed he left considerable slices of his humanity sprinkled about those Pacific islands.

He sat in the pew. The unwelcome intrusions continued to probe his consciousness. Somber thoughts, as quickly as he became of aware of them, he pushed them aside. Then, as if possessing a resistance of their own, they shoved back.

Gus didn't remember talking much of living or dying during those nights and days. Maybe such questionable wisdom as knowing the relative speed of a bullet was intended to reassure a man. He recognized that obsessions with such trivia might serve an emotional purpose, especially when death might seem inevitable.

Damned if he knew why he should find this insight reassuring. He had only hoped not to be gut shot.

Gus did believe that by the time he had crossed the landing strip on Peleliu the odds favored his demise. He just knew he couldn't be that lucky twice.

The smell of incense brought him back to the sanctuary. The Priest's words found him.

He tightened his lips and tried to drive back the distracting, unwelcome thoughts. He shook his head.

Service complete, Gus made a hurried exit out the huge vaulted doors at the rear of the church. He emerged into the boiling, motionless air of an Oklahoma August afternoon.

He felt wobbly. His mouth tasted of bile. He pushed it down.

Gus tried to steady himself but he rather fell back. His rump made a hard landing as he leaned against the wall at the base of the steps. He scooted back against the marble light post and drew a deep breath. He lifted his shoulders trying to roll the tension from them. He realized the arm pits of his starched white shirt were soaked. He was saturated not so much by the scorching August heat as from the unanticipated strain of burying a comrade.

Gus disliked funerals. No, he hated funerals. This one was particularly unsettling.

He took another deep breath and a rush of warm air filled his lungs. He recognized the symptoms of anxiety. He didn't believe his response was due to the funeral or to death. The war had introduced him to death and had left nothing mysterious about the process.

George Thomas' death had left a lot of people confused. Most seemed lost as to why he would take his own life. He appeared to be flourishing in his father's oil business. There was serious talk about a political career in his near future. The local political gurus of his father's generation observed that this was the perfect time for a decorated war hero to run for office.

Those close to him were convinced he desired a life in public service. He seemed excited at the prospect.

Further cementing the view of the speculators, George and Jennie's marriage seemed ideal. Within the last month, Jennie had reassuringly told her youngest sister, Eileen, how wonderful she had found the mid-years of marriage to be.

Turns out George Thomas did leave a note. A note that only further bewildered her. It implied a perplexing contradiction. His words were like his intimacy, they contained a remarkable tenderness and warmth, yet was an indefinable distance.

This fundamental contradiction haunted her during the long days following his death. The thought that her love for him was not enough to keep him alive left her inconsolable. Many things she once considered so valuable, now seemed quite trivial.

Jennie had been anticipating Gus' arrival at the funeral. Using her sister's descriptions, the young woman had intercepted him as he arrived. She then guided him to an alcove off an enclosed cloister.

Jennie held hope Gus could provide insight where others had failed. He couldn't.

Jennie's eyes cut deep into him. Tears welled and she irately demanded, "It was the fucking war, wasn't it?"

Gus met her angry, injured stare. He took her hands in his, eyes fixed on hers.

Then, he shook his head and said, "I don't know, Jennie. I just don't know."

Jennie continued to bore in, "But you think something don't you?"

He was reaching to form a coherent answer but before he could, she added, "More the fucking war than anything else."

Gus didn't know why people thought they had to have a wise answer at a funeral. He knew he didn't have one, not today.

Before he could say a word, Jennie lunged toward him and clutched him. She clung to him. Her head buried into his chest. Her fingers dug in and rolled up the back of his coat, unwilling to let him go as her sorrow spilled over him. He would have given her the answer she needed to hear if he had a clue what it was.

Jennie sobbed. Gus now held her tightly until she released her grip. She stepped back. Her eyes softened. She dabbed them with a dainty hanky.

As only a woman will do, Jennie checked his attire. She brushed some makeup off the front of his charcoal grey suit coat.

Jennie mustered what piece of a smile she had left and said, "You have no idea how proud he was of you, his friend, the great western author."

Her smile deepened as she continued, "You know he was thinking about running for Governor?"

"I did."

"One of his fondest dreams was that you would come down and campaign with him for a few days."

"I don't think I'd have drawn much of a crowd for him."

Twinges of Jennie's biting wit edged back and she said, "That is what I told him." She fought to keep it near the surface.

For some reason that made no sense, it was at this point that Gus believed Jennie would make it.

Jennie started to leave the alcove, stopped and turned and asked, "Will I see you later?"

"Yes. And Jennie, I think it was the friggin' war too."

Jennie turned and was considering the friggin' part when Gus whispered to her, "I have trouble saying fucking out loud to a lady."

Jennie swung at his arm only catching a lot of coat sleeve.

As he walked toward the sanctuary, he thought Lookout married well.

Gus and Lookout had talked intermittently over the years. Both felt but never said that it was impossible to talk without the war interrupting the conversation. Both had had enough of war.

A month or so ago, George observed, "You know, maybe you and I are trying to be done with a war that isn't yet done with us."

Gus agreed, "Maybe'.

Gus knew for a fact that they shared a dark voice that invaded their nights and tauntingly whispered directly into their very essences, "We buried better men than you."

The Last Dance in Delta

In Tulsa, no one knew him as Lookout, he was George Thomas. Gus knew Lookout well but George was another matter. They were the same yet distinct.

As irrational as it was, George seemed unable to forget what Lookout had done. George had become increasingly intolerant of his alter ego. During a telephone visit about a year ago, Lookout had divulged his belief he should have died on Okinawa.

Mildly irritated at the time, Gus blurted out, "Well, you didn't!" Quickly calming he added, "And I didn't! So, we just have to go on living."

Gus puzzled over why George would take his life. Lookout he might have understood.

Lookout voiced an observation, "You know, folks look at a vet with a lost leg or arm or burned all to hell and they think they understand. It is the shittin' emotional disfigurement that they don't get."

An emotional deformity that Lookout would carry every step of the reminder of his life. The exact degree of its intensity he diligently kept concealed even from those closest to him.

Gus answered, "That's because they don't want to get it." Gus continued his search, "Because they don't want to get it, it makes them uncomfortable."

"And God forbid its contagious."

"Don't you know we all died over there on those god damn islands?" There was a strange intolerance in Lookout's voice.

After a silence, Lookout asked, "Do you think there is a vet who doesn't have it?"

Gus didn't hesitate, "Not a combat vet."

"Do you think even Chesty has it?"

"Chesty Puller, the General, the Marine's Marine."

"Oh, no doubt, but do you think he has the nightmares and the terrors."

"And feels guilt for just being alive? Yes. Yes, I think he does."

On one end of the line, George Thomas shook his head. Gus clenched his lips tight and took a breath.

"So, we just live with it?"

"Gus, Confession ever help you with the guilt for what we did."

"Strangely, yes. Let me clarify. Help, yes. Wipe it way, no."

"I know we only did what had to be done, but God bless."

"Of course, we all did. We did or we died." Gus stopped. "Or we did it and died anyway."

A Eulogist walked past. This Eulogist, a young man who appeared to be in his middle twenties or so, spoke of George as a YMCA baseball coach.

It seemed did seem that George had done little wrong in life. Lookout was another question. On Okinawa, Lookout did the necessary things to survive and help his friends survive. George was Lookout's harshest critic.

"Lookout killed himself and George died in the process."

Gus didn't know the source of this enlightened thought. It just arrived.

Perhaps it came from a confluence of memories that had spent the post-war years careening around his mind, their razor-sharp edges making gouges as they banged into the boundaries of his mind. War left nothing unscathed. Maybe a fact he was now beginning to accept.

A pain knifed through his right shoulder. He rotated it. The heat retained in the stone felt good.

God, it hurt. The right shoulder whose frailty had shortened his two-year baseball career following the war.

He hadn't classically thrown his shoulder out. He'd injured it in a brawl on the pitcher's mound after he had tossed a little chin music at an especially irritating opponent.

The injury sent him from baseball to college and to writing. He had no true regrets. But he would like to write a baseball book or two. A pain brought him back to the milling crowd.

Gus would miss his friend. Together and because of each other, they had survived Peleliu and Okinawa. Not horror or any other single adjective could describe the awfulness a Marine rifleman endured and inflicted during combat. Now as it kept them close, it kept them apart.

The Last Dance in Delta

Gus knew the sleepless, terror-filled nights that refused to allow a man to forget. He had an increasingly intimate relationship with those unruly emotions. He had thought time would make it better. It didn't.

Gus had tried to lose the memories that had accumulated in the various distorted pathways of his mind. Scotch Whiskey helped. Somewhat.

In the dark of deep night, a deformed recollection would come seeping back, escaping the murky sections of his psyche in which he had imprisoned them. Recall would shake him from his sleep, thrashing arms trying to keep the invader at bay, then a wave of nausea would come over him, then it would pass, leaving him soaked in sweat, weak kneed and disoriented.

It was a murky maze of disgust in which a man could lose himself.

The Priest was standing on the sidewalk near one of the family automobiles talking to several men. In his closing words about going in peace, Gus unexpectedly found home and hope. He found a thought, a raw boisterous ideation. Maybe, just maybe, he could write their stories.

Could he take words and give form to such wild, raw emotions? Could words and paper form a trap for such terrifying emotions? If he could do that, if he could do that, could he then manage them?

Slowly, Lookout's hearse began to move. In that somber silence, Gus spoke to him, "Well, buddy, we're going to have ourselves a damn dandy exorcism. I'm going to get us a typewriter, a bottle of good scotch whiskey and we're going to get after it. Before I decide it isn't a good idea."

The casket was leaving, he continued the thought, "Buddy, Am I ever going to need your help."

The hearse turned the corner. Gus, almost audibly said, "Thank you."

CHAPTER 23:
It's Just a Thought

THE CROWD MILLED.

Gus looked back toward the arched doors of the church. Maybe he just wanted to look away from the path of the departing hearse.

Again, he became conscious of the stagnant air and stifling humid heat. He felt wobbly. A sour taste creeped up into his mouth. He pushed it down.

Gus tried to steady himself by again leaning back into the warm stone balustrade bounding the stairs. It was still sun warmed. He was better.

The man was handsome. Taller than most and slender, his funeral suit appeared expensive and perfectly tailored. It was nonetheless the most somber of black attire. His cowboy boots polished to a high shine and his black onyx bolo tie laying stark on his starched white shirt gave a somber elegance to the man fitting the occasion.

Gus thought to himself, "The man is blend of John Wayne and Cary Grant." The man might be accustomed to less formal attire but you'd never know it.

Believing the man to be moving toward him, Gus freed himself from the warm stone and stretched his frame to its full six feet and three inches. His height coupled with his sinewy build gave him a commanding presence on most occasions. Just not today.

"Been ask to give you a ride to the cemetery."

At that flash in time Gus couldn't say that he remained undecided about going to the cemetery.

The man extended his hand to Gus in a fashion no alternative existed but to shake it. Gus considered his hands to be large. The extended hand engulfed his.

"I'm Jennie's uncle, W.K."

Gus knew he was being scanned in a fashioned that measured his manhood.

"I enjoy your westerns. You have a talent."

"I work at it, Sir."

Sir! Gus didn't know where in the Hell that came from. Then, he concluded W.K. carried himself like a man who merited being called sir.

W.K.'s hand drew Gus's attention toward a black limosine idling at the curb.

"You got anything in the works?"

"I do. I always to try to keep a book underway." Gus wasn't about to share the brainstorm that might place his existing boilerplate work on the back burner.

"Good. I believe a man should always keep something in the mill. I believe every time you drill, you're getting closer to a gusher."

Gus thought that sounded like his Uncle Bob's fishing axiom, "Can't catch a fish if your hook isn't baited and in the water."

Gus continued, "I'm a grinder."

"I used to be. Just a cattleman who fell into the oil business" W.K. allowed. He scratched his neck behind his right ear. "Don't have any use for another oil well. Not too much use any way." He smiled.

W.K.'s open hand again motioned toward a car idling at the curb.

"We will catch the end of the procession."

Settled into the car, there was a brief awkward silence and then W.K. said, "Two of my buddies killed themselves after our "war to end all wars." He waited, then added, "George and I talked about it some. The Japs seemed different from the Hun I fought."

Gus cleared his throat. Then, he said, "I think that gas would have scared the crap out of me."

Characterologically, pragmatic W.K. said, "We fight the war God gives us to fight."

"Yes Sir. I believe that too."

"Well young man, you have a Laddie pencil and a Big Chief tablet. Write about that someday."

"It's been on my mind these past few days."

"Good."

A few right words can span generations.

It doesn't matter what kind of fake grass is put over a mound of dirt near a grave site, it still looks like a pile of dirt and a grave. You know where it's going after you leave the cemetery.

Gus and W.K. stood off to the side. The rifles fired the salute. Gus closed his hand so tightly that his nails felt as if they would cut into his palm. Phantom sounds of yesterdays echoed in his ears.

Gus bit his lip. It bled.

Gus got out of the car in front of the Adams Hotel.

Gus gripped W.K.'s hand and said, "W.K., thank you for the ride."

Gus stopped, probed and said, "George was lucky to have had you as his friend."

"George was a good man."

As Gus walked toward the entrance, W.K. called out to him, "And don't forget to keep writing the westerns."

Gus nodded and waved.

With a wry grin, W.K. added, "But you might write your story first. Remember, you do have a Laddie pencil and a Big Chief tablet you know."

Facing the Adams, Gus extended his arm and waved without looking back. It was a wave that said, "I got it! I got it!"

W. K. smiled to himself and acknowledged he rather liked Gus Kelly.

The Last Dance in Delta

Gus stopped. The Adams wasn't the Mayo but it was nice. The ornate art deco architecture of the Adams Hotel fascinated him. A man turned and left the hotel desk. A steel tap on the heel of his shoe rang with authority on the marble floor.

Gus stepped up to the desk and said, "607 please."

The clerk reached into the box and slid the key attached to a plastic tab to him.

"Does the hotel have a liquor store?"

"Nope, got a bar but it's 'bring your own bottle'."

Accustomed to a client's befuddlement, the clerk explained, "Don't have liquor by the drink in Oklahoma. We haven't had package stores long."

Gus just shook his head. He thought he should come home more often.

Apologetically, the clerk said, "You're here in the Bible Belt."

Gus nodded his understanding but he was too Catholic to believe that Jesus was opposed to a good drink of whiskey.

The clerk now spoke a little quieter. "Just show the bartender your key. He'll fix you up."

Gus nodded, "Thanks."

Gus suddenly realized he needed a drink in the worst way.

Seated at the bar, it took him a few words to convince the bartender all he wanted in his double scotch was scotch. No soda, no water, no ice, no ice chips, just scotch.

Gus didn't know exactly when it began, but he knew he liked the taste of good scotch whiskey. The Usher's Green Stripe wasn't good scotch but on this day it would do.

He drank Usher's around V-J Day on Okinawa. It tasted damn fine then.

Three drinks later the remnants of the afternoon had faded into dusk. Gus found himself hungry for the first time today. W.K. had recommended a favored downtown eatery, Bishop's. It was an easy walk away.

Gus considered the house specialty, a Brown Derby. Then, he decided a New York strip, rare, was a more reliable selection. W.K. had steered him down the right path. The beef was fine and the chef knew a rare steak when he met it.

The restaurant was busy. Gus found the hustle and bustle both distracting and soothing.

He would have enjoyed an after-dinner scotch but it was dry Oklahoma. He settled for sipping on a second glass of sweet tea. The sweet tea was excellent. This was Oklahoma.

He wouldn't describe Tulsa's evening sidewalks as busy but the downtown was active with window shoppers. He began to watch the window shoppers. These shoppers seemed quite youthful, filled with fantasies of the future, dreamers. He pondered them.

Gus couldn't find common ground with their dreams and aspirations. No doubt theirs was the American Dream. Gus struggled to find life beyond the next five hundred words.

He paused and looked at his reflection in a window. He wondered about Gus Kelly. In a disquieting moment, Gus didn't recognize his reflection. He thought about abandoning the project. What a conundrum, a riddle of his own creation. He didn't want to write this story. Yet, he knew he had to write it. If he could place his hero in white hat and give him the moral high ground, the story was simple. Easy ethics.

He looked at the reflection and said, "You know the story, you write it."

He walked on.

"I can write about me and war, my war. Our war." He hesitated before agreeing with himself.

He got caught up the crowd leaving an early movie at the Rialto. Happy faces. Kids. That girl looks like Mary Helen. Nah.

His mind settled, he thought, "I need clothes if I'm staying a while."

Gus laughed to himself. "Aunt Elizabeth would be mortified if I got run over by a bus and was wearing dirty underwear."

He told himself he would get to a store soon. It took him until his third day on his last pair of boxers before he went to Renbergs.

He sought commitment. He found it.

Gus wrote. Confusion reigned supreme. He worked to exhaustion.

Tired, he attempted sleep. He would be startled awake by the smell of Okinawa, a stench that seemed forever leached into his bones. Some nights he could feel the warm droplets of blood spray across his face as a Marine exploded nearby. He could taste the blood, iron and zinc. A metallic tang invaded his palate. The iron smell of blood invaded his nose. Sensations made their way from shadowy fractures of his mind into his pre-conscious sleep before cracking through the wall of self-deception.

Every nerve in his body crackled.

Nights he jumped straight up in his bed leaving the bed soaked with sweat, the steamy dampness of Peleliu or Okinawa.

He sat upright in the bed and again wondered if Chesty Puller had night terrors.

Several times, he fell off the bed and scrambled for his foxhole. He stabbed his pillow.

His head struck the bed frame with such force he thought it was the distinctive snapping report of a Jap Arisaka, type 99, sniper rifle. He rolled deeper under the bed into his foxhole.

He spoke to no one of the night terrors. The war was fifteen years in his rearview mirror now and he feared no one would understand. Yet, since Pavuvu, he had never been without them.

No. He had spoken to his Uncle Bob on occasion. His uncle had listened then confessed to his own continuing nocturnal challenges. His were similar but distinct, equally unyielding. His visits with his uncle were enlightening and reassuring.

The only clemency he granted himself as he lay soaked in his bed was to remind himself, "Least you don't piss yourself." He knew many on Pavuvu had and maybe still did.

What began as fiction became a memoir. For the first time since he crossed the shell pocked and cratered airstrip on Peleliu, Gus felt like he was fighting back. He wrote his memoir. He took control a word at a time.

Gus laid in the bed. He was thoughtful. He was awakened by the whoosh of air as a shell from a Jap 99 passed overhead. He felt the nausea climb. He went to bathroom and threw up. He sat down and began to write.

CHAPTER 24:
Committed to Paper

TEN MONTHS CAN PASS QUICKLY when you are lost. Gus typed. As random thoughts interrupted his sleep, he recorded them in scribbled notes. His sleep was more a blend of the anesthetizing effect of scotch whiskey and the exhaustion that came from emotionally revisiting of the unforgettable. It was a time of intellectual resurrection. Winter had come and gone. One snow brought Tulsa to a grinding halt. The spring storm season had arrived in Oklahoma.

When the window of his room rattled under the pressure of the wind, Gus had stopped, got up and went to the window. Looking down he saw small branches stripped bare of their leaves being carried along on an invisible river of air. All sorts of loose paper careened off the walls of the buildings that confined their flow. Hail stones collected along the window ledge and then left.

He always returned to his typewriter. He gazed at a plate with the word Royal written on it. A line tailed off the R and underscored the rest of the word. Each time he paused to think he was staring at the trade name. He pondered the word and its placement. He drew no conclusion.

At times, he felt guilty when he left his room, leaving his contest with his recollections still unresolved. But he did leave to go to a small café down the block to sit in a school desk and have a Coney. On occasion a return to Bishop's which seemed to be

The Last Dance in Delta

open at any hour of the day or night was satisfying. He did try the Brown Derby and he liked it.

Gus made coffee all day and all night. The pot, washed, rinsed and renewed in the bathroom sink, was never dry. He again drank coffee and chewed Tums. The balance worked for him. The Adams Hotel sold Tums in its gift shop, Tums, Tom's Crackers, Planter's peanuts, Snickers and Butterfingers.

More than one morning he sat on the edge of his chair, drank fresh hot coffee and munched on the peanut butter filled crackers. A couple of mornings he thought of the Wheaties slogan, "The Breakfast of Champions".

Throughout the day, he snacked on dry Cheerios, putting his hand into the box, withdrawing a fistful, placing them on the table top and eating a few at time. By pacing his cheerio consumption, he paced his mind. The correlation puzzled him but he was certain it existed.

Then he realized how many times that phrase had been used to describe whatever rations where available in a foxhole. He just couldn't force a smile.

He sipped coffee and held the paper still in the typewriter so he could read his words. A flair pen allowed him to leave a mark on the page with little pressure. In his pencil days, he had been known to punch through the paper when he proofed lines he did not like.

It was the slow sipping of the coffee that gave him the time to contemplate his words. Gus was never quite certain at what point his coffee cup took on scotch but it did. It wasn't uncommon for him to have a glass of scotch and a cup of coffee both going at the same time. He was glad he had stopped smoking.

There was something reassuring about his white Corning Ware coffee pot setting on a hot plate. When the account he was writing disturbed him he contemplated the three blue flowers surrounded by long leaves on the side of the percolator. It retrieved him from 1944 and yanked him back into 1959.

W.K. forced a weekly reprieve upon Gus. W.K.'s car would be outside the Adams at 9:00 AM sharp to pick up Gus and deposit him at the door of Christ the King Church for a 9:30 Sunday Mass. W.K. had made it clear this was not an optional appearance for his now friend, the author holed up in the Adams Hotel. W.K. did not have the actual leverage to enforce such a directive. Still Gus felt obligated to comply.

"It is good for your soul and good for your liver."

"Well, W.K. I haven't been to Mass so often since I left my Momma's house."

"It wouldn't hurt you to go more often."

W.K.'s wife, Elaine, was a stunning and well-maintained woman in her mid-fifties. At this point each week she would scold them.

"Did you boys not learn anything from the Homily?"

They would smile then go enjoy a brunch at a lovely old red brick country club. The dining room was on the second floor affording an unexpectedly impressive view of Tulsa's prairie skyline.

W.K. was right. Gus reclaimed his faith.

The knocks on the door were persistent sounding more like a tack hammer than a fist. Gus stroked in another word, read it and scooted his chair away from the table. He glanced back at the last sentence. The knock became more determined. Gus felt a mild irritation at the intrusion.

Gus opened the door and Jennie made her entrance. Her eyes were snappier than her voice. Whatever Jennie wanted she felt she had waited long enough.

"Alright you, turd bird! You've been holed up here for I don't know how many months writing about yourself and my husband", Jennie popped. She continued rapid fire, "We don't know each other all that well but by God there is such a thing as courtesy time and Mr. Kelley you have run long past it."

Gus stared at her. Over the years he had seen a number of photographs of Jennie and their children but he had only physically seen her on her wedding day and on the day that she buried her husband.

Jennie was a small yet once slender woman. The weight of motherhood and of aging had now begin to attach itself to her. Almost in contradiction, her appearance remained quite pleasing, her legs were satisfying and her breast ample. Perhaps her waist

The Last Dance in Delta

betrayed her a touch but most could consider her shape quite pleasing. Her loose-fitting sleeveless blouse had color, not the bright colors women now seemed to find stylish but it was not somber. Her skirt was stylish, the hem breaking at mid-calf. Even with fire flashing from her eyes, she was a pretty woman. Under other circumstances Gus might have taken more immediate note.

Gus had awakened about five this morning with words to write. He got up, put on a pot of coffee and he wrote. He hadn't showered or shaved. Jennie's presence made him aware of the shortcomings in his morning routine.

"Jennie, would you like some coffee?"

"No thank you." Calmer but still curt. Nodding toward the box he had received from his publisher the previous day, she asked, "Is that it?"

"The manuscript?" Gus knew he was being evasive when there was no reason to do so. "Yes, most of it. It has some suggestions from my Publisher."

"Same people who publish your westerns?"

"No, my agent took this to Random House. They liked it."

"Good." She looked at the paper stacked inside the box. "I want to read some of it."

"Sure."

"Adams has a couple of rooms with a desk and a chair just off the Mezzanines. I can use one of them."

Seeing Gus was puzzled, Jenny added, "I asked on the way up."

Gus nodded his understanding.

She thought and said, "I'll have questions."

Gus smiled and again nodded his understanding. He picked up the box and carried it to the Mezzanine office. Jennie sat like a Nun on a mission. Truth be told Gus was glad to have her out of his room. His lack of tidiness bothered him some but not as much as having George's widow in his room did.

"I'll check on you in a bit."

Several hours later, now freshly showered and shaved; Gus came back to the Mezzanine with two cold bottles of Coke. The limited conversation was pointed.

"You didn't hold back, did you?"

Gus nodded his agreement and said, "It's all there. No sugarcoat, no whitewash. Only way I could write it." I couldn't do it any other way."

"Good."

"Oh, there were certain things I tried to avoid. But then, I just go back and add it. All the necessary truth is there."

He paused and thought. "No, all I know is there. Even the parts I don't fully understand."

"Better", Jennie said.

He left her with his words and her thoughts.

Shortly after five o'clock Gus heard a knock low on his door. As he moved toward the door as second knock sounded like a kick. He opened the door and Jennie was standing with both arms around the box. Her hands and arms full, she had knocked on the door with the toe of her shoe

Gus opened the door wide, reached out and Jennie bent forward. As she bent forward her neckline opened offering an unobstructed view of her bra and the cleavage that spilled from it. There was no way to avoid a glance. Gus looked and then he looked away.

Jennie was aware. She made no effort to adjust her clothing. She liked her breasts. It pleased her that they merited more than a glance. She liked Gus.

He turned and placed the box on the floor at the foot of the bed.

"Gus, these words are so very hard to read."

"I'm sorry. I've told my truth."

Jennie nodded, "Yes you have."

Both were silent.

"Gus, I wish I had had these words a long time ago. I'm proud of my husband's friend, I'm really proud of you". She concluded, "You're going to be proud of this."

She paused and realized Gus was having difficulty so she continued, "Some of the paragraphs so distressed me I had to stop and read them again."

The Last Dance in Delta

Tears trickled from the corners of her eyes. "Thank you, Gus. I can't imagine how difficult this was to write."

Although it made no sense, Jennie wished her husband was there, she wanted so badly to hold him. Just one more time.

"Gus, I miss him so bad. I have this terrible fear that the last word I said to him was no." Her tears washed across her cheeks.

Gus didn't know what to say. He pulled his shoulders up, then slowly released them. His Uncle Bob's Scottish shrug of helplessness.

Gus knew the words; the sentences and the paragraphs had been painful to form. The thoughts had taken him back to shadowy places. Places he really didn't want to ever resuscitate. Each thought would drag him deeper and deeper into those vile experiences. At times, he could again overhear the voices and the sounds inside his head.

Two nights ago, the belief that his socks were soaked was so pervasive that he had jumped from the chair where he had nodded off. He hopped to the bed trying to remove his socks with each bounce. He fell backward into the wall before sliding down to the floor, pinched between the wall and the bed.

He slung his arms in every direction to an effort to free himself from the swamp that was increasingly engulfing him. The deeper he sank, the more terrified he became.

As his panic subsided, he found himself sitting on the edge of the bed. In his hand he held a dry sock.

Then, nausea welled. He tasted the sour bile. He just reached the toilet before he retched.

Gus returned from his thoughts and continued, "Jennie, if had I sugar-coated it at all, some folks just wouldn't get it, others would just know I was lying. Some would try to read between the lines and create some piece of heroic fiction."

He had remembered a memoir written by another member of the First Marines. To Gus it seemed to be no more than a collection of humorous tales, worthy of a Fraternity house at almost any state university. Oh, not that the tales weren't true, they likely were. But this Marine just never got around to writing about the gut-wrenching stories of combat he had to know.

For Gus, that Marine's stories just fell far short of touching any emotionally cathartic chord. They were funny but unsatisfying.

Gus wavered seeking some more precise word. Then, he said, "I was writing the truth and I want people to have read the truth."

He shared a recollection, "My Aunt Elizabeth always said the truth can be cantankerous at times. Folks will keep trying to change the facts they find tiresome. You can't leave waffle-room when you talkin' about the truth."

He smiled and proceeded, "I always considered her to be a wise woman."

Again, Gus hesitated. He refocused his thought. Then, he reached toward her face with his fingers. He softly tilted her chin until her eyes made full contact with his.

He said, "Jennie, there was a God-awful ugliness to it all. War brings out a cruelty in us that I just don't get. We held each other together as if wrapped in a collective insanity. I was there, I felt it and I never understood it."

Gus stopped. Then, he added, "Oh, hell Jennie, war is fucking insane."

Gus drew a deep breath and continued, "I still have nightmares that terrify me." He shook his head and allowed, "I'd just like to get past being scared."

Tears formed and flowed from Jennie's eyes. Tears collected in the corners of Gus' eyes and small stream trickled down his left cheek.

His thumb tried to stem the flow from her eyes. He failed. Her tears ran like a clear stream but her crying made no sound. She didn't sob. Instead, she pulled a tissue she had hidden at her waist and dabbed his cheek. Her tears continued to appear as if emerging from some unspoiled Ozark spring.

Her mouth fashioned a smile, mostly of habit. She stretched upward on her toes and placed the softest of kisses upon his cheek. As her lips brushed against the stubble of his beard, she sensed a response. She was flustered.

Confused but completely drawn. They each regrouped, allowing the feeling to beat back the despair.

For Gus, the emotion was so profound no words could make their way from his mind into his mouth. The talented wordsmith was without words.

He hadn't held back on his pages. His emotions had spilled forth open and raw. Jennie's face told him he had effectively communicated. He had brought her to an understanding. She got how hideous yet inexplicably heroic men could be under such circumstances. How heroic and terrified her George must have been.

Gus had ripped away any veneer of civilization others might have painted on war. For the first time, Jennie grasped her husband's agony, the deep aching unhealable wounds that crept into the deepest realms of his soul under the dark of night.

Jennie felt grateful. She felt an immeasurable sadness. She could have read no more than a beginning of Gus's story, her husband's story. But it was enough for now.

Jennie found her voice first and stated, "And the parts about George – about Lookout – Gus, I don't have to imagine what it was like anymore. I know your words are the plain truth, but they are so cruel."

She inhaled, expanding her chest, and said, "Gus, I just didn't know."

Gus nodded and said, "You couldn't know." Gus sought a path and added, "Nobody talks about it."

The room quieted. Both considered their words.

"Why do I feel like I failed him?"

Gus motioned with his head that he didn't know. He decided to add, "You know you didn't."

"I know no such thing!"

Again, they were silent.

"As I wrote some voice in my head wouldn't let me tell our story any other way." Gus breathed the air in deeply and released it slowly. "If I was going to tell it I had to tell it all."

Gus shook his head and concluded, "I just – I just the God's honest story."

His words faded as he lost them. What hadn't been said, he was just going to leave unsaid.

They sat, one on each side of his typewriter. Time passed. They had talked longer than they intended. Gus began Jennie's introduction to Lookout. Jennie told Gus of George.

"Gus, thank you." She added, "I'll read it very carefully when my copy arrives." She knew she was stalling.

Finally, she asked the question that was beginning to haunt her. She now knew how deeply such apparitions occupied her husband's mind.

"How do you live knowing such horrible things?" She stumbled over her words. "Knowing what you know – what you saw – what you did – what you all did – what you all had to do." She stopped. Her thoughts sped away from her, evading her grasp.

"And knowing what I did?" Gus already knew the questions. He just didn't know the answers.

Gus pursed his lips into something of a smile, then brought his shoulders up in that shrug and shook his head in a fashion indicating that he didn't know.

"Jennie, I just manage. It feels better now but it's a long way from being gone."

Gus continued. "Putting it on paper has helped me."

Again, he hesitated. "I'm concerned I might put the war back in some Marines mind after he'd worked years to stuff it away. I just don't know. But I worry about that."

Jennie rose from her chair.

She straightened her blouse, adjusting the neckline. Her fingers toyed with the diamond drop draped around her neck, stopping just above the fabric.

"Gus, I know it was unintentional but still, well, thanks for noticing." Jennie knew she had more to say but didn't quite know how, then she said, "No one has in a long while".

She paused. She knew men regularly noticed. She stammered on, "Oh, Hell, I don't know what I mean but you do. I know you get what I mean."

It passed her mind that there was a difference in being looked at and a man actually seeing her.

Gus wasn't at all certain that he knew what she meant.

Gus was convinced there was a correct thing to say, he just did not have a clue what it was. No question what he had seen had been intriguing but he felt guilty for having extended the unavoidable glimpse.

A knowing smile cracked his face and he replied, "Trust me it was all my pleasure."

Jennie looked at him. Gus met her gaze and looked away.

She wasn't embarrassed. Maybe a tad self-conscious but not embarrassed.

Finding her voice first, she revealed, "I feel like I did when I was fourteen and darn near had to force Tommy Kyle to put his hand here." She gestured placing her hand just beneath her bust.

"Well, Tommy Kyle was one lucky young man."

Jennie laughed and Gus cackled. Their awkwardness disappeared in the wave of laughter.

"Gus, I miss George so terribly." Tears again formed in the corners of her eyes.

Gus nodded his empathy and said, "Don't know how you couldn't."

Her tears raced. "Oh God, I miss him."

Jennie looked toward Gus. Sobs still breaking her voice, she said, "It was the fucking war. I knew it was."

She let a silence settle over her and then she continued, "Do you think I'll understand why George could never let it go?"

"I don't know. I do hope so. I don't know how much I understand it."

He added, "You're welcome to read more if you like."

"Thank you. Maybe. But I had to stop when the maggots got fat. I couldn't read anymore," she faltered and then continued, "It seems like such an utterly dreadful place."

Jennie hesitated and then spoke, "Gus, I was jealous of how loyal George was to all of you. I just didn't understand it. I still don't but --. Well, I rather do. No, I don't. But it's okay now."

She paused again quite lost in her thoughts. She caught the salty taste of her tears trailing off her cheek. She dabbed her cheek dry.

"Gus". Nothing more escaped her lips.

Again, words seem to fail her. It was so much worse than dreadful but how else could she describe it. Dreadful, it sounded so naïve. Jennie no longer felt naïve.

He chilled, knowing he'd never forget the maggots in the mud of Okinawa. They couldn't dig a foxhole without uncovering a shallow Jap grave. And maggots.

He tried to nod, then gave that slight Scottish shrug of his shoulders.

"My friend George was a very lucky man."

Gus believed that was the only time he had spoken of George. He had been living with Lookout for the past many months.

Jennie took his hand, lowered her head and kissed the back of his hand.

"Thank you, Gus. You're a good guy."

In kissing his hand, she was mysteriously overwhelmed by her husband's fragrance. There was no logic to it. She embraced it.

She left.

CHAPTER 25:
A Dance with the Past

AT TIMES IT CAN BE DIFFICULT TO DELINEATE between the beginnings of a new time in life and the finality of an old life. This wasn't one of those times. Maybe this was both.

Gus was appreciative Jennie had read segments of his work and found it's insights to be quite profound. She had understandings that had long eluded her. She collected insights into the husband she had so deeply loved and then lost.

Now alone in the room, Gus poured himself a Johnnie Walker Black. He needed it. He was highly critical of his lingering partial erection. He felt quite guilty. He thought the room was a tad warm. He sighed and took off his shirt, leaving him in his sleeveless vest undershirt. He draped the shirt over his chair, then walked to the window. He stared at the one-way traffic moving along Cincinnati Avenue.

The knock at the door brought him back into the room. He wasn't expecting anyone.

He grabbed the shirt, stuck his arms into the sleeves and opened the door. He looked squarely into Jennie's resolute face.

As he was trying to adjust his shirt, Jennie reached out and turned him back into the room.

She barked, "Not a word! Not a single damn word!"

Even without her direction, Gus was certain that at this moment he could not speak.

Jennie walked to his desk, assumed that the scotch remaining in the glass was his, polished it off and poured herself another.

She wasn't accustomed to straight scotch. Its strength left her breathless but she concealed most of her reaction.

She thumped the empty glass on the desk top. She turned on the radio and moved the dial to KVOO. Chuck Berry was finishing *Johnnie be Good*. Jennie's back to him, still facing the music, her shoulders began to sway with the rhythm, engaging her hips by the closing bars.

Old Blue Eyes version of *I've Got You Under My Skin* floated out of the speaker, monoaural but satisfying.

Jennie turned. "Dance with me?"

"I can't dance like George." He deliberately introduced George and watched.

"Yes, you can. I'll help you."

They couldn't glide across commercial carpet but they danced nonetheless.

She kicked her shoes in the direction of the night stand and she followed them. She turned and faced Gus. The look from her eyes told him there would be no discussion, no reconsideration, she had come seeking some firm resolution. She knew where she was and she knew why.

Jennie was not posing yes or no questions.

Gus shook his head. As with their dancing, Jennie took the lead.

Then, changing to a nod, Gus said, "And?"

Jennie placed her right index finger to her lips. Then with a simple breath, she shushed him.

Adept fingers drew her blouse from inside her skirt, leaving it seemingly adrift below her waist. Her motion brought his eyes to her fingers as she adroitly undid the first button at the top of her blouse.

Then, seeming to change her mind, she arranged the blouse tail and reached behind her. In the silence, Gus sensed a clasp being undone. He heard a zipper slide. She stepped from her skirt and folded it, neatly placing it on the seat of the bedside chair.

She turned and contemplated the man who was enchanted by her legs as they descended from beneath her blouse. She liked her legs and to the extent his eyes could be trusted, so did he.

As her fingers now found the second button, she nodded, indicating it was time for him to start removing his shirt. His moves felt awkward, ineffective because his complete attention was on her fingers as each button slid through its slot, opening her blouse.

Gus sat in his chair and, never taking his eyes off of Jennie, removed his shoes and socks. Gus dropped his shirt, then his undershirt onto the floor. He hopped, briefly taking his eyes off of Jennie, as his feet tangled in the fabric that collected as he pushed them out of his rumbled pants legs. He added his pants to his pile.

With only his olive drab cotton boxers remaining, he stood. An odd thought of insecurity raced through his mind. Why had he chosen his Army surplus boxers this morning?

As he rose, Jennie's back was still to him. Still in her underwear, she turned toward him. There they stood, six feet apart, momentarily stymied.

She looked at Gus. She didn't want to stare but she was curious. Then, she chuckled to herself as she thought they should let a few women designers work on men's undergarments.

"Well?" Again, Gus, the great purveyor of words for western hero types was at a loss for more than one word at a time.

Again, Jennie hushed him and coyly countered, "You show me yours and I'll show you mine."

His smile was simple. He shook his head in disbelief.

A delighted smile engulfed her face.

Jennie's hands moved lithely to the mid of her back and unfastened her bra. The bra loosened its grip on her breasts allowing them and the garment to relax. Without any real design, she left it draped in that fashion for just an enticing moment.

An extraordinary gentleness and appreciation came to Gus' eyes as he watched her finish removing her bra, neatly folding it, then placing it on her stack. The irresistibleness of the act took his superego aside and gave it a sound thrashing.

His lips tightened and his head moved gently from side to side. In that moment, he was smitten

She knew she was his complete and total focus. Neither of them understood exactly how this moment came about. But in that same instant, they knew it had.

Gus' expression conveyed unadulterated admiration.

"Jennie, you are the most exquisite woman I've ever seen." Gus said it and meant it. His statement came out slowly, carefully, blanketed in honesty. The movement of his head and eyes reflected an absolute captivation.

She couldn't describe how gentle his look was as it fell across her. This time she did not shush him. She wanted to say something. But she was at a loss. It had been such a long time since she felt this way. George.

She said, "Thank you."

She felt her heart thump. She pulled back the sheets and slipped between them. Then, once discreetly covered, she smiled and raised her hips. slipped from her panties. She tucked them under her pillow.

She lifted the corner of the sheet, inviting him to join her. She heard him audibly exhale.

Jennie contained her giggle as she saw his olive drab shorts sail toward his pile. He eased into the bed beside her.

In a sudden awareness of responsibility, he muttered, "I don't have anything."

Her voice reflecting a delight at his perceived situation, Jennie replied, "You don't need anything."

"Oh, good." Both relief and anticipation.

Just at that moment, a siren blasted beneath their window and scooted out on 4th Street. Jennie and Gus laughed.

Jennie woke, not recalling when she went to sleep. She stretched. Her hands grasp the headboard of the bed. She drew a deep breath and inhaled the scent of the man lying beside her. Sensations of fullness flooded over her.

Jennie nestled back into the sheets. In that moment, she knew she was going to be alright. She had rediscovered her husband and found life in the process.

Gus met W.K. at the Tulsa Club bar.

The Last Dance in Delta

"I understand your going to be leaving us."

"Yes. It's done. It's time."

"I hate to see you go", W.K. said. In fact, W.K. was dreading his departure so badly that he had explored having an endowed chair created at the University of Tulsa to keep him in Tulsa. But he knew Gus would see through that sham in a heartbeat. W.K. had made that mistake once in his family. He wouldn't make it again.

W.K. nodded to the waiter. A bottle of Johnnie Walker Blue appeared on the table. The waiter poured three fingers neat for each man.

"We're not drinking the good stuff because you're leaving. We're hoisting these glasses because you chose to stay with us a while."

A smile of understanding covered Gus's face. He said, "I am the winner."

"Yes, you are!"

The mood was so genuine and unexpected that both men hesitated.

An afternoon rain began to fall. The two men lounged at a table by the window on the fifth floor and watched the people move on the street below.

"Elaine said Jennie told her you were the finest gentleman she knew."

Gus answered, "I think she found her husband on my pages."

Gus paused and added, "And possibly a why."

W.K. nodded and replied, "So, she found the part of her husband she never knew. Your words must have struck a chord. I'd say you did well."

Gus visibly considered W.K.'s interpretation but didn't find an acceptable response. He gave his head a movement that reflected a considered understanding.

W.K. was thoughtful and then added, "If that is past her, you know, she has her past in spot that she can move on, well, then she'll have her pick of the remaining litter in Oklahoma. I know a lot of men who will be happy to oblige her".

W.K. thought about that and then said, "Write another western soon." In just a moment he added, "You've dislodged a lot of shit that has been clinging to the walls of your mind. You've scraped it off and written it down. Now flush it away."

Gus nodded, lifted his glass and emptied it. With both gesture and word, he said, "I'm trying."

"We both know that bottle isn't going to work. I tried it when I got back from my war. Didn't work then, don't work now."

The men sat quietly looking out the window. The rain intensified and umbrellas, somber to colorful, popped open as shoppers hurried along Cincinnati Avenue. The rain was coming down in sheets. The street cleared.

Talking more than usual, W.K. said, "Gus, your story is going to be gusher for you in a whole lot of ways. My free advice is you get on with writing another story. I know in my business – well, you can't find a producer unless you got a bit in the ground."

The writer found no words. Gus knew he was going to miss this new found older friend.

W.K. was right. The memoir was a gusher. It was a gusher both financially and critically. Men and the families of the men found solace in Gus Kelley's words and in his descriptions. Many found segments of their souls that they believed to have been lost forever. Others found a path out of their own personal darkness.

Intervals of life were rediscovered and reexamined.

Once at an awards ceremony a Jesuit Priest spoke of what Gus had accomplished in biblical terms. He cited John 8:32. "Then you will know the truth and the truth will set you free."

Gus wasn't free but he was better than he had been. He had told his truth. He was unclear about setting him free but it had brought him many nights of much better sleep.

The Darkest Night had become virtually biblical to World War II combat veterans and to their families. Korean vets found considerable common ground. Gus Kelly had revisited the craters of Hell for them all. God granted him the passion and the skill to tell a story that belonged to all of them.

Gus knew the truth. He knew his truth and he knew their truth. He wrote a memoir to purge the wounds of war from his own injured soul. He wrote of the battlefields on which he had raped his own moral and ethical standards. He allowed his darkest secrets to seep from the recesses of his mind onto the paper. Page after page, there it was, the core of his psyche filleted for anyone who cared to glimpse it.

And then came along Vietnam.

CHAPTER 26:
Life on the Road

GUS HADN'T SEEN KATY ZIMMER since their high school graduation. But there she was in line at a Dallas area B. Dalton Booksellers signing for *The Darkest Night*.

Gus chuckled recalling his social and intimate ineptness. As it is with teenage boys, he had carefully thought out his first attempt at applying his rapidly accumulating sexual knowledge. His plot was a huge leap since he had never even had his hand beneath the fabric of Katy's skirt, no knees, no thighs.

Gus and Katy had been dating several months. During the early days, she had been most amenable to helping him with his fumbling efforts beneath her blouse. He was both an appreciative and apt pupil.

The night arrived. He had arranged to have a pickup truck from one of his dad's retail stores for the evening. They went to the 6:30 showing of *You Can't Take It with You*. He thought beginning a date with James Stewart and Jean Arthur had to play in his favor.

Katy leaned over, her hand on his thigh to steady herself and whispered in his ear, "Oh, James Stewart looks a lot like you."

Her hand lingered. His chest swelled. He knew he had made the right choice for evening's entertainment.

Uncle Bob's land nearest town had a nice pond. It was quite accessible by pickup truck over a rutted path. After the movie and coke at the drug store, the couple drove to the pond.

With an anxious anticipation, he chose not to linger on any of their familiar intimacy rituals. Gus began to gently probe unfamiliar territory. Katy's hand met his. He thought she was calling a halt to the evening. She wasn't. To his surprise, with a slight raise of her hips, she helped him.

She took a deep sighing breath and murmured, "So nice."

Gus didn't care much for guessing and Katy saw to it that he didn't have to.

Gus' relationship with Katy Zimmer had ended in the fall when Gus began to date Mary Helen Ellsworth – again. Still, he had fond memories of his summer with Katy.

There she was in line with three teenage girls he assumed were her daughters. He wished his first thought had not been "matronly". But it was. He knew she had carefully applied her makeup and dressed her "Sunday finest" for the event.

He saw a mature mother of three daughters advancing toward him. He recognized her. She was now wearing her mother's face and figure. He saw little of the frisky seventeen-year-old girl who had once upon a time enthralled him. In her eyes he did find suggestions of the girl he couldn't keep his hands off in the seat of his dad's store's Chevy pickup.

"Hello Gus."

"Oh my God, Katy Zimmer." "What a wonderful surprise."

"Katy Hughes now."

Gus stood. He gave her an A-frame hug which she reciprocated. He was gracious.

He spoke to those waiting in line, telling them she was a special friend and to please be understanding. Most were.

Katy's smile filled her face. He joked. He leaned over and whispered something in her ear. She swatted him and said, "Oh you're just bad."

He posed with her as her daughters took photos. They all posed together and the flapper took a photograph.

But he chuckled secretly to himself and thought that she was yet another bullet he dodged while he was in the Pacific.

Before they parted, Katy grabbed Gus in an unexpected full-frontal embrace that left little doubt as to the changes and what remained unchanged. The firm and perky breasts that so fascinated him as a boy were now soft and generous.

Her stomach pressed against him. He reached out to steady himself. As he did, she moved closer.

He smiled and thought, "Body by Playtex."

She beamed. He sought some significance in her smile but he just couldn't find it.

He sat down and wrote an inscription inside her copy of his book that read, "For Katy and a moonlit summer at the pond! Gus."

She opened the cover and read the inscription. She blushed with delight as she read the words. She bent down to give him an appreciative hug. Her cleavage embraced his head.

The exchange had given her a tad of giddiness. Pleased, Gus smiled.

He watched her walk away.

His flapper brought his attention back to the line patiently waiting their turn.

Then, she placed her hand on his arm and whispered to his ear, "Well, I think she tried to dry hump you right here and now."

She patted him, looked at the waiting line and said, "Next."

When your options are to be kind or to be unkind, be kind. Gus didn't remember where he first heard that piece of wisdom. Logic dictated it likely involved his Uncle Bob and a creek bank near Delta. Regardless, the notion had served him well on his book tours.

Gus and his flapper had drinks and dinner that evening.

The last few weeks of the tour took him to the west coast. San Francisco was his first stop of the west coast swing. It seemed that all elements of a counter-cultural movement were fermenting in San Francisco. Vietnam War protesters from nearby Berkley emerged.

Gus observed that none of the group attending a B. Dalton Booksellers signing had the appearance he associated with serious students. He assumed it must be a generational thing. Then, he thought the serious students are likely in class.

Gus was glad he wrote *The Darkest Night*. The process was therapeutic. The outcome liberating. Still, at times like these, he wished hadn't shared his view in such a public setting.

The Last Dance in Delta

Many of the Vietnam War protesters chose to view his work as a satanic glamorization of war. Gus believed that a realistic read of *The Darkest Night* could lead only to revulsion; certainly not attraction to war. But the protesters, with their incomplete vision of his work, marred the rest of his west coast tour.

Gus had looked closely and found no glamour in his words. Gus was quoted in a local newspaper as saying if they bothered to read his book they would not be confused. The Associated Press picked it up and Gus Kelley was a target for the heat-seeking missiles of the Anti-War movement. His words had unintended consequences. In successfully tamping down the horrific blaze that had seethed in his mind since the airfield on Peleliu, he had added gasoline to another fire raging just beyond his comprehension.

From his prospective the outraged and sanctimonious activists naively began to bundle all War veterans under the same blanket and wrap them with the same barbed wire. With his prizewinning novel of World War II, Gus became a lightning rod for those in the anti-war movements. Again, Gus made the miscalculation of believing his casual remarks at a Salt Lake City American Legion dinner were "off the record". They weren't.

Gus became a larger target. He found neutrality was a luxury he was not allowed. He remained irritate and passionate in his belief that the protesters had not read his book. He felt they were dependent upon out of context quotes that leader of their movement had provided them.

After that first encounter Gus never responded beyond saying, "I wrote a book of truths about a World War II combat veteran, me. No more, no less. Combat has no glamour."

Gus vowed he would never again try to justify his writing. It had to stand alone supported only by its own merits.

Gus remained offended and angry. He felt he was being pushed into defending many positions with which he did not agree.

Gus concluded that if someone was fascinated war, by the death and mutilation of young men, if they found glamour there, they needed professional assistance. Gus viewed their grasp on reality as being frail or perhaps even psychotic.

Once a protester verbally pushed the issue as Gus was trying to escort a most pleasant young lady into a fine Chicago restaurant. Gus found himself more angry than hungry. He abruptly turned to confront the protester and bumped into his date. As his date struggled for balance, Gus reached out and stabilized her. His face displayed his rage as he turned and unleashed an angry glare at the protester and yelled, "You sick son of a bitch!"

As ill luck would have it the protestors were both male and female. Gus' words, more shotgun blast than rifle shot, landed in the face of a young coed from the University of Chicago. She appeared shocked that someone she was harassing might bite back. She started sobbing and tears flowed. The Tribune reporter who was following the protestors concluded something harsher than he heard must have been said.

Gus's lady friend, startled by the outburst, gazed upon Gus in different fashion. Gus was sorry for that. He liked her.

Gus took her by the arm and stepped inside. He gathered himself as did his guest.

He said, "I'm sorry, really sorry." He shook his head conveying that he was as puzzled by his outburst as she was.

His date said, "I can't imagine what it must be like."

They drank, ate and drank a little more. They left in separate taxis.

Although it would only be a paragraph buried in the next day's coverage of the events surrounding the approaching 1968 Convention, Gus was stung. He was never fond of the self-righteous and these experiences had done nothing to change his mind.

That next evening over drinks he inquired of his favorite lady friend, Beth Inman of the Tribune, "They have the right to protest. Hell, I know that. Let them protest. I don't want them stomping all over my right to privacy in the process."

"You do believe I have a right to privacy don't you?"

Beth gazed intently into his eyes and her mouth opened into her most suggestive smile. Her eyes now locked with his, she said, "No."

She giggled, pleased with the contradiction she had proposed. Beth found a pleasure in her friend's befuddlement.

Gus sailed a bar napkin across the booth at her. It fell short. She laughed.

She held the damp napkin so that it dangled between her fingers. She quizzically looked at it and then at Gus. "My, I wonder if everything is hanging limp tonight?"

"If both of us weren't into girls I'd take you home and let you find out."

"If I wasn't into girls who lust after guys, I'd take your hand and lead you upstairs."

They enjoyed laughing together.

Gus felt better. Beth always made him feel better. She was his friend. A true friend.

She saw no point in telling him about the sign being held in the window behind him that asked, "Does Napalm Teach Democracy?" Especially since several members of the now quite diligent Chicago PD were hustling the sign bearers away. She chalked it up to as her act of kindness for the day.

CHAPTER 27:
Yet Another Lesson

CHICAGO WINTERS TEND TO DISCOURAGE outdoor activities such as golf and protest marches. Gus hypothesized the nature of the crime rate also changed. He believed that street muggings dropped unless the offender was hard up for dope. On the other hand, confined to the limited space of their dwellings, domestic violence would be on the rise. Outdoor crimes dropped and indoor crimes rose.

As for Gus, he holed up in his apartment and cranked out a western novel that he felt was a dandy. He set it in Arizona, a dry heat as opposed to a wet cold.

He stayed right in his wheelhouse and wrote of the west that excited him. His hero was moral, direct, bonded to the land and saw direct aggression as a suitable method for resolving problems. His heroines were always beautiful and buxom, courageous and virtuous, assertive beyond the traditional female role yet devoted to her family and her lineage and to her man. Villains were arrogant, argumentative and cruel, controlling others through of fear, threat and intimidation. Yet, within each of his foul characters, he felt compelled to install at least one redeeming virtue.

His fidelity to this characterological framework spoke more to Gus's fundamental nature than anything else. He needed to believe most folks had a saving grace.

The Last Dance in Delta

In the mid-1960's, as Gus was focusing on dodging anti-war protesters, an aggressive arm of the civil rights movement began to increasingly assert themselves. Gus watched had watched with great admiration as Dr. King embraced the challenges presented by these more radical individuals. This more revolutionary wing which was embracing the teachings of Elijah Mohammed moving toward control of a large segment of the Civil Rights movement. Malcom Little became Malcom X only to be killed by a blast from a sawed-off shotgun in 1965 as he was attacked by three members of Nation of Islam.

There was clearly a faction of the civil rights movement that had abandoned the "Gandhi-like" beliefs of Dr. King. Their focus had the clear flavor of a Black Supremacy movement bent upon violence.

In July of 1964, President Lyndon Johnson signed the voting rights into law. The law was designed to ensure equal enforcement of the Fourteenth and Fifteenth Amendments to the Constitution existed.

Gus was beginning to find much of the behavior by both blacks and whites contradictory and self-serving. He knew he was increasingly suspicious of the Nation of Islam. He feared their separatist beliefs would only serve to further the gap between the races.

He held the KKK in the same position of low esteem that he had regarded them since he was a small boy in Delta. Not that the Delta of his youth a pillar of tolerance, it was not. But his father and his uncle often found themselves taking positions on the polar extreme from the Klan. It can be difficult for an adolescent boy, just trying to fit in, when his family insists on taking a stance not approved by the Klan.

Gus would never forget one such circumstance in which he sided with the majority in a matter involving a baseball game. The question was should the Shamrocks play a touring baseball team from the Negro League. Bob Kelly supported the benefit game but the county commissioners who sustained governance of the fairgrounds and its baseball field opposed the affair. The majority of the community supported the commissioners., Gus fell into line with his group of young friends.

The day push came to shove, Gus gave public voice to his pseudo-opinion in ear shot of his uncle. He would never forget the disapproval and disappointment he saw on his Uncle Bob's face. His uncle's disappointment cut Gus to the quick.

Gus tried to plead his case to his Aunt Elizabeth. He found his rationalizations were as unacceptable to her as they had been to his uncle. The only difference was his aunt allowed him to present his case before chastising him.

"Augustus, there are times you will be judged by your failure to stand up for what you know is right." She shook her head disapprovingly as she spoke. "You knew better but you chose to do the wrong thing for the wrong reasons. My little man that is unacceptable. You'll need to correct it."

Correcting his poor choice was one of the more difficult things a young Gus had ever had to do.

Gus played no more baseball that summer. He learned about bailing hay with his uncle's crew. He worked with Negroes and white men he suspected hated each other. But when it came to bringing in hay, they did it without a hitch. His job involved seeing each worker had what he needed when he needed it. His job required him to focus on the needs of others.

The crew chief was a Choctaw man in his mid-thirties. The men simply called him "Chief".

Chief was strong as a bull capable of doing every job in the field. Make no mistake a slacker would be fired, fired not because of his race but because he was a slacker.

On his second day, Gus, perhaps unthinking, sat on the tailgate of the pickup. He was going to get an extra blow and a long slow sip of water from the cooler.

He found himself unceremoniously dumped to ground.

Chief stood over him glaring from beneath the brim of his sweat-stained straw. For the first time Gus looked into the eyes of a man he believed in that moment could – and would genuinely injure him.

Chief's hand grabbed him by the collar and pulled him upright. Chief took the boy's gloves from the tailgate and shoved them against Gus' chest. Gloves in his hand, Gus received a directed shove toward the bailer and the working crew.

The Last Dance in Delta

"You go buck some bails boy!"

Gus' new straw hat sailed past his head.

Gus knew his family to be kind and understanding. Over supper, Gus tried to tell the story of his mistreatment. On this evening, he found a complete absence of sympathy. In fact, he felt that they somehow already knew the story.

Come morning Gus got himself up and was waiting on the curb in front of his house when Chief's truck arrived. Gus, sore and sunburned, mounted over the side and took a seat in bed next to Sid. Sid was the only man he had known before yesterday.

"Friday and pay day will fix up what ails ya." Sid allowed.

Although not yet thirty, Chief was the only man older than Sid on the crew. Sid sensed Gus wasn't fully committed to the "pay day" philosophy.

Sid added, "Difference here is for the rest of us this might be the best job any of us will ever have. Your Uncle is a good man and fair man and pays a fair wage."

Sid stopped, leaned over the truck and unloaded a wad of tobacco from his mouth.

He continued, "Ya got a future. Still ya gotta carry ya weight out here. Ya Uncle 'spects it of ya."

Gus worked. His co-workers furthered his education.

CHAPTER 28:
Spring of 1967

BETH INMAN, A FRIEND SINCE HIS COLLEGE YEARS, was the first to read and critique the words that now poured from his typewriter. They shared the words other people had written in books, newspapers and magazines. They could speak of politics but that was an area in which they mostly agreed. Still, they could adamantly disagree but hear each other's words. Neither would ever speak of it to the other, they privately considered each other an ideal companion with one critical exception.

They both preferred partners with vaginas.

Gus telephoned Beth quite flustered.

"TB, I can't tell you how thankful I am you're in."

"Let me guess. You just heard Dr. King publicly came out against the war in Nam?"

Gus, clearly disappointed and rather irritated, said, "Yes. He says the money we are spending on fighting a war in Asia would be better spent on LBJ's Great Society programs. Helping Americans who need help."

Beth's reply was more pragmatic, "That is not going to set well with the President. If President Johnson has nothing else, he has a long memory for his friends and his enemies."

"From what I can understand those are the only two positions he allows," Gus replied.

Beth laughed, "You don't mean LBJ has an us or them posture?"

The Last Dance in Delta

"That's it!" Gus laughed and continued, "Especially when it involves the Southern Leadership Conference and the head of their organization."

Beth tried to help, "Well, when you've climbed out on a few limbs with a person you expect a certain degree of loyalty."

"Yes. At least a heads up."

"Well, Gussie, Louise is going out to one of her book clubs tonight. Why don't you cook something for us?"

"I'll do steak and potatoes if you bring the beverage."

"Done. Seven?"

"Yes."

Beth set a boundary by saying, "Now only one hour on the LBJ-MLK saga. I want to watch Gomer Pyle so I can see what the Marine Corp is really like."

"Screw you."

"In your dreams."

Their ritual complete, Beth hung up.

Gus settled back into his seat in front of his Selectric, read his previous paragraphs and slowly begin to type.

He stopped and thought. He really wanted to hear Beth's thoughts on the Nation of Islam. It wasn't a new topic for them. After brief thought, he smiled at his own seriousness. He quietly laughed at himself and thought, "The Nation of Islam isn't much concerned with the thoughts and opinions of one Gus Kelly".

With distracting thoughts now flushed from his mind, the rate of his typing picked up. He again became engrossed in the telling of his tale. White hatted law men and black hatted outlaws were clear in his mind. He settled back into 1884.

Gus remained a voracious reader. To him books, magazines and essays had always been a source of rational and well-founded information; of tolerant and tolerable opinion. But today he was often finding no answer to be acceptable. In sources he previously judged credible, he was finding divisive opinion supported by what he viewed as problematic logic.

It was at these times that Gus felt quite blessed to have his relationship with Beth. His college friend was now a prize-winning political writer at the Chicago Tribune. It was a time in life when Gus was increasingly discovering comfort in isolation and Beth drew him out.

She understood his curiosity and his need to see actual events for himself. She consulted him about her projects, he enjoyed being consulted so he readily shared his thoughts with her. Each enjoyed and needed the other.

Reading, writing and research are solitary endeavors. Since the publication of his prize-winning memoir, Gus had discovered himself judged as a war monger. Gus had developed a self-protective shell and he granted admission to a limited few.

Poked into positions he didn't endorse, Gus found himself semi-actively defending opinions and policies he didn't believe in. He did know he was progressively attracted to the non-violent approach to problem-solving rather than the pursuit of violent resolutions. Gus struggled trying to understand the violent methodology espoused by emerging offshoots of the Civil Rights movement, younger people impatient with the moderate pace of progress in the older, established elements of the movement.

The anti-war movement was persistently nipping at his tail, both at his intellectual and physical tail. Gus understood a simplistic philosophy that said "War is bad, peace is good." What he could not understand was any belief system that thought it was acceptable to emotionally abandon the young men that we, as a nation, had sent to war.

The concept of villainizing the American soldier was foreign to Gus Kelly's most fundamental moral fibers. Young men, volunteers, who were fighting on behalf of our country on the other side of the world and came home to be spat upon.

From Gus' point of view, the pain a mother might feel after she buried a son killed in Da Nang and that of a mother whose son died near him on Peleliu could be no different. A Mother's son frozen as the First Marine Division exited Chosen Reservoir or a Marine who died beside his Uncle Bob in Belleau Wood were identical.

The heartache indistinguishable, one from the other.

The Last Dance in Delta

Hearing the words spoken in Grant Park, in Lincoln Park and outside McCormick Place convinced him the only combat this group had seen was on television.

A son lost is a son lost. There is no recovery.

A soldier lost is a soldier lost. Comrades must be remembered and honored.

Gus often found himself expressing the same idea in a number of different words.

One thoughtful evening sitting in a café across the street from a park, Gus shared a thought with Beth, "You know none of us get to pick the war we fight."

He thought of W.K. and Tulsa. Gus told himself he needed to write him again soon.

"You know women fight wars differently and in different places."

"How so?"

"Think about a war against feelings of abandonment, of loss. Women don't get a gun to shoot at our enemy."

"Beth, are there folks you'd like to shoot?"

"Maybe but I have a fully loaded typewriter. And I don't have a soldier-husband nor even worse a soldier-son."

Beth became lost in her thoughts.

She returned and said, "I'm not going to bed every night wondering if someone I deeply love is safe. Hell, Gus, even if they are alive. How damn many deaths do you think a wife experiences while her husband is deployed in some fucking jungle halfway around the world?"

Gus wished Beth's sense of modern feminism didn't compel her to use the word fucking so often. Ladies just shouldn't adopt the worst of the male habits to prove whatever it was they were attempting to prove.

His thoughts returned to the wives and mothers. A puzzling emotion covered his face and he answered, "I suppose she dies every bedtime and awakes to a morning of new uncertainties."

Gus paused, then went on, "My Aunt Elizabeth talked to me about what it was like for her when Uncle Bob was away during

World War I. Lordy, she was a young bride just a few weeks out of high school."

Beth nodded her head in semi-agreement. His interest in understanding of the female psyche always caught her just a tad unprepared. She took a slow measured sip of her wine.

"Over the year I've tasted a large number of wines. Your black always taste the same."

"Yes, and I like that."

Their dinner arrived.

Not knowing when to hush, Gus commented further, "And I'll bet my T-bone taste a lot better than your fish."

She smiled and said, "It should. We're closer to a stockyard than to an ocean."

She believed she would always score the final points of an evening because her companion struggled knowing when to quit.

Beth's cab faded from view. Gus looked out at the park. He dreaded going home. He corrected himself, he liked his apartment.

But it was when he was alone that thoughts of being hunkered down in a rainstorm, covered with a poncho in a muddy foxhole on Okinawa, then laying alone, asleep, that those horrifying memories crept in on him.

Gus drank to the atomic bombs and celebrated the end of their war on Okinawa.

"Always keep ya Ka-bar where ya can grab it." Good directions until you're no longer a Marine. Until you are no longer in combat.

Gus awakened to find himself sitting in his skivvies on the edge of a rack. He was soaked and panting.

"Great Mother of God Man, are you okay?"

Gus gazed at his rack. It was shredded. His stare revealed his confusion.

The Corpsman next to him said, "I don't know what happened but I know you killed the Hell outta' your rack."

"I had a bad dream."

The Last Dance in Delta

"Bad dream my ass. Just be glad Lance Corporal here was fast on his feet or there'd be blood all over your dead rack and you'd be headed for the lockup."

The Corpsman extended his hand and dropped a pill into Gus' palm, saying, "It's a sleeper. You'll sleep the night out."

With a wry smile, he turned to the Lance Corporal, scared pale, and said, "Now you, you might want to keep a weather eye out."

"Well, shit! Thanks!"

Gus felt the guys set a guard the rest of the voyage home. He would have if he'd been them.

But Gus never slept with a Ka-bar next to his bed again.

Gus no longer knew how to predict what a night might contain. You just never know when the terrors will arrive.

Gus struggled to see through the darkness into the park. He wished every protester had to experience his nightmares and then tell him where a war ends.

He remembered coming home a hero, every soldier, sailor and marine was a hero. He couldn't imagine how he would have felt if he had come home to the type of welcome young men were now receiving.

"It is just plain sad," Gus said to no one.

He tried to appear casual as he continued his stroll toward home.

CHAPTER 29:
Come '68

IN THE EARLY SPRING OF 1968, Martin Luther King, Jr. was assassinated. Gus had come to increasingly admire Dr. King. The assassination of this advocate of passive, peaceful transition left Gus in some emotional disarray. The idea of death from a single rifle shot was becoming far too familiar.

Neither President Kennedy and Dr. King got to glare into the eyes of the man who killed them. The whole idea of a sniper seemed so cold and distant, so cowardly.

Involuntarily, Gus recalled two men in his company that were so proficient with a rifle that they became snipers by default. Both Marines had grown up squirrel hunting with a single shot .22 in their native states, Arkansas and West Virginia.

Gus became convinced that if not for these men, these snipers, fewer Marines would have made it home alive.

Snipers. They killed from a distance. The remoteness of their killing provided an emotional detachment to their war. They most often never saw the enemy they slew.

Killing a Jap with a Ka-bar as he tried to creep into your foxhole, that was another matter. It was close and it was personal. You smelled the foulness of his breath and you saw light leave his eyes. He was dead. You would carry his carcass to the brush and carry the killing for the rest of your life. Gus knew it haunted his dreams and tore apart the fabric of his sleep.

Gus thought if you want a safe, impersonal distance for killing maybe dropping bombs over Germany to create a firestorm or just dropping a single bomb on Hiroshima to create a

The Last Dance in Delta

Hellfire might just fill the bill. For certain he should have joined the Army Air Corps.

He thought about recent Vietnam film footage he'd seen and added dropping napalm anywhere to his list of depersonalized killing. Napalm troubled him. He heard its fury burned all the air from your enemy's lungs.

Napalm. They used it or something like it in the flamethrowers on Okinawa. Jap snipers shot to explode the napalm cannisters on the back of Marines assigned to flamethrowers. Gus always shuttered when he thought of it.

Gus was curious if these soldiers were plagued by the same ghastly nightmares that haunted him, robbing him of whatever tranquility he hoped sleep might bring.

Gus only had to visit his nightmares to know that he still clung to the children on Okinawa. He closed his eyes.

You slice a man to death in your foxhole.

A child explodes in a Marine's arms. Both vanish in the death stench of Okinawa.

Gus shivered. He was cold.

Gus considered these groups to be self-serving advocates of hate. He saw them as undermining the hard-earned gains of the NAACP and other such organizations.

Beth had recently concluded a serious dinner conversation on the topic by teasing him, "Ah, stop the presses! Gus Kelley, the great war monger, revealed as a pacifist."

So as not to be overheard by fellow diners, Gus mouthed, "Screw you!"

Beth replied, "In your dreams".

She did enjoy their rituals.

A smile, rare in these times, found its way to Gus' face. Beth took on a subtle self-satisfied look. Their eyes transmitted a mutual forgiveness for some transgression neither understood.

Gus Kelley and Beth Inman found considerable comfort and pleasure in the company of the other. Beth believed it was fruit of the fact that Gus was accepting of her presently fluid gender preference.

Gus could appreciate the high quality of her intellectual company. With that said, he never failed to notice she was an attractive woman. Further, he liked that come evenings end, he did not feel compelled to make a convincing attempt at seduction.

Beth would acknowledge the circumstances by saying, "I like that you know I still wear panties. I'm also happy you don't feel you have to close the evening with a frantic effort to remove them."

As a reporter, she was enamored by the facts but creative enough to intellectually manage unsupported possibilities. Their conversations were making her increasingly comfortable with Gus's hypothetical and fictional world.

Beth and Gus enjoyed "what if" conversations, each extracting the most creative of juices from the other.

Although he would acknowledge that he was aware of her femininity, as the months passed, he knew her intellect stimulated him more that her appearance. Beth and Gus were fast friends.

Friends at time in their life when a reliable friend is exactly what each of them desperately needed.

He liked her nickname, "Tribune Beth", but became more comfortable simply referring to her as "TB" and then, feeling no need to be clever, regressing to simply calling her, "Beth".

Gus had concluded that there were times in life that someone, without malintent, would place that one straw too many on our stack. He now knew that an outwardly inconsequential straw can send the stack spilling down around us in disarray. In the early fall of 1968 Gus felt he was covered in straws.

The Democratic Convention scheduled for August of 1968 had been awarded to Chicago. At the time, everyone assumed that this gathering would be a celebration on the renomination of the sitting President, Lyndon Johnson. It was further viewed "a tip of the hat" to Chicago Mayor, Richard J. Daley. Mayor Daly was considered the most powerful man in the party aside from President Johnson.

The Last Dance in Delta

Then President Johnson came on national television and announced, "I will not seek nor will I accept the nomination of my party for another term as your President".

The Vietnam War had worn him out.

Gus also thought back to the day after President Johnson signed of the voting rights act. Beth had commented, "Well, old LBJ just presented the Republicans with a solid south."

Gus didn't believe that could ever happen and said so. Gus could never believe Delta or any other part of rural Oklahoma could ever vote Republican. TB knew better.

Gus persisted, saying, "Hell, I had my driver's license before I figured out Damned and Republican were two separate words."

Nonetheless, Mayor Daley went all out to prepare the city for the Democratic Party Convention. The streets leading to the Convention site were lined with flowers. Redwood fences blocked unsightly abandoned lots from view as well as muting the smell of the stockyards.

By the time the Convention arrived, the arena resembled an armed encampment. The building was surrounded by chain link fencing and topped off with barbed wire.

Gus watched the television coverage of the Convention. The Chicago Police Department was in position and on full alert. He skeptically commented to Beth, "Chicago's Finest might not be having their finest moment".

The headline read, "800 in Guard Aid Cops with Hippie Mob". Gus found it to be more confusing than clarifying.

Gus' curiosity had reached a fevered pitch. His experience with newspapers suggested they might have a point to make. Despite seemingly unending volumes of photographs and boundless television coverage, it was the newspapers who produced the greatest volume of words.

Gus tried to appeal to his wiser self, but he ultimately knew he had to see this mess for himself.

He cinched a plain leather belt around the waist of a rather worn pair of Levi's, put on a flannel shirt that had somehow survived his relocations and a favored pair of loafers. He picked up a weathered Cubs baseball cap and prepared to head toward McCormick Place.

He had thought about making Grant Park but he had heard the crowd camped there was more than just a tad rowdy.

He tried to call Beth at her office. She wasn't in, so he left a message.

He sat on the edge of his bed. He gave a final consideration to the wisdom of his plan. He took a deep breath, exhaled and rose. He left.

The chaotic descriptions of McCormack Place had not been exaggerations. Gus wandered through the crowds, stopping to listen first to one group and then another. Gus concluded there were as many agendas as there were groups. Anti-war and Civil Rights seemed to be the over-lapping themes.

Gus tried to physically include himself into the groups, avoiding standing to the exterior boundary where a sole individual might stand out and be recognized. Gus listened to a young African-American man trying to whip-up a small cluster on the inherent evils of war. He listened intently before concluding the speaker had no concept of combat.

Some speakers spoke around carefully organized talking points. Others were just spewing the venom of their own personal dissatisfaction with life.

None seem to have an intellectual awareness nor real interest in the Presidential Nominating procedure underway inside McCormack Place. The groups of people seemed to ebb and flow like the tide. A tide that occasionally bumped against a wall of Chicago Police Officers igniting a profanity laced scuffle.

Later in the evening, over a glass of good scotch, he discussed his outing with TB. He observed, "There was a considerable shortage of good manners and civil discourse."

TB laughed, "Their behavior is crappy for sure." She paused before adding, "and they don't smell very good either. Wouldn't hurt them to just take a swim with a bar of soap."

Gus said, "I thought Cronkite and Rather were being overly dramatic, maybe playing to the audience. But I'll tell you this is not the finest hour for Chicago's finest. As Cronkite said, the police are acting like a group of thugs."

The Last Dance in Delta

The Convention nominated Hubert H. Humphrey as the Democratic Candidate for President and left town.

While their numbers were never great, some anti-war protesters periodically gathered outside Gus' Chicago apartment building. The doorman did the best he could to keep them at a respectful distance.

Gus grew weary of the presence of the demonstrators and their signs. His neighbors on occasion expressed their displeasure to Gus. He was sympathetic to their plight.

He also knew that in Viet Nam the men of the First Marine Division would be in harm's way. They would follow their orders. Some would live and some would die. Gus knew, popular or not, a war was a war. And young men died.

His intellectual curiosity did not die. He was more cautious with any expression of his inquisitiveness. He was now genuinely befuddled as to why some people could not tell one war from another.

He thought many of the protesters were at an age that they had to be aware of the draft, one way or another. They had to understand how many men – men, Hell, most were boys – had been drafted.

Gus had fought his war. He knew all about combat he cared to know. In his harsher moments, he felt he did not need lessons on morality, patriotism or combat from a draft dodger.

Gus snorted at the notion that he now sought sanctuary from protesters in the seclusion of his apartment. Even though he offered the derisive grunt, he knew there were elements of truth to the accusation. He told himself he was just still fighting his own cloistered war.

He was feeling creatively stale. He wanted to flee to a place where his creative fluids could be regenerated, an environment whose very nature would lubricate his psyche. He had always enjoyed writing his western tales. He still owed W.K. a better than average tale of the old west. His recent work had been entertaining but quite average. He wanted to pay his debt.

He regretted the time he lost trying to drink away his personal darkness. Even the most handsomely amber of Scotch Whiskey hadn't been able to shine a light into the dark fissures of his brain, those hairline fractures that concealed the explosive recollections of combat. These memories were ferocious and appalling and they wouldn't leave.

Memories, reenactments of fright, terrorized his nights. No pre-bedtime ritual would remove nor discourage them. Lord knows, he had tried an abundance of elixirs reported to relieve the pain these dark intruders brought into his nights.

Sometimes he would quietly slip into Delta for a visit with his Uncle Bob and Aunt Elizabeth. He thought sitting in a rocking chair on the porch of their prairie home with the sounds of the night creatures pouring over him might soothe his mental angst. Sometimes he went but most often he would just let the thought pass. He wasn't at all sure you could go home again beyond a short visit. He adored his Uncle Bob and Aunt Elizabeth. He liked their porch.

He considered that this approach had served his Uncle Bob well. But except for his military service Bob had never left Delta. More importantly, Bob was never alone in the evenings. Elizabeth was always by his side.

He considered it but any regression into peace did not seem a rational concept.

Gus found himself unsure of his path. He wobbled.

CHAPTER 30:
New Year's Eve 1968

SETTING ASIDE HIS MORE CONVENTIONAL LOGIC, Gus decided to host a New Year's Dinner Party for the half-dozen or so close friends he had in Chicago. In the end, the guest list was composed of woman he had been dating off and on for the past year, two couples from the university, a couple from his hometown of Delta, two Augustinians from St. Rita's High School, his parish priest and his longtime friend, Beth Inman.

Beth, who a few years ago determined she was lesbian, was currently between lovers. She remained closeted.

Gus planned the menu and cooked by telephone. He dialed his favorite neighborhood restaurant, Johnny's, and made the arrangements. The shrimp would be large and the dipping sauce rich, the filets thick and rare, the potatoes twice baked, and a salad drenched in a Roquefort dressing.

Gus considered it to be a properly masculine meal.

He left the appetizers to Johnny. The chef and the food were scheduled to arrive at five. Guests arrived at seven. Gus was happy with the plan.

By the time a week has passed and he rolled out of bed on the day of the dinner, he wished he had not called the party. It wasn't that he felt he wouldn't enjoy himself, he would. But the idea of other people traipsing across his apartment troubled him. Gus just wasn't a social animal no matter how much effort he put into creating the circumstances.

Four was a nice group, five was too many for stimulating conversation.

Mother Nature chose to spare Gus the anguish. A snow storm rolled in before dawn. By mid-day, the storm had brought the city to a standstill.

Johnny called from his establishment expressing his regrets, stating that he had less than a quarter of his employees on the premises and expected no more.

"Mr. Gus, if you want to try to make it here, I'll feed you free."

"Thanks, if I can find some snow shoes in my closet, I might try it." In a single sentence Gus's voice went from caustic to placid.

Feeling a tad ashamed of his single statement mood vacillation, he added, "Johnny, I hope a few of your reservations do make it tonight. I might just take you up on your kind offer if the snow slows down some. You're only a block and half away."

"I think the snow will continue but Johnny's will be open. You come if you can. It is possible you will have Johnny's all to yourself this evening."

Good humor found Gus and he chuckled. Maybe he was more than just a tad relieved.

Privately relieved, Gus began to dial his guests, with each postponement he promised a gathering at some future date. Gus doubted any of his invitees really believed the event would ever occur. Within the hour, all the invitees except Beth had been contacted.

About the time Gus was beginning to worry about TB, a familiar knock sounded on the door.

Gus went to the door and knocked back.

"Gus, open the God-damn door. Even the damn hallway is a freezer."

Gus laughed. He looked at the four locks he had secured just a brief time ago and wondered when did he come to believe he needed four locks on his door. He decided he'd leave that mystery to be solved another day.

Beth stood framed in the doorway. She had already removed her fur hat and was using it like a fur broom to clear the snow

The Last Dance in Delta

from her arms and front. She intermittently stomped her boots scattering packed snow across the entry hall rug.

"You my friend are a slowpoke. I cannot believe a proper host would leave a guest waiting at the door", Beth scolded him as she pushed past him into the warm living area.

"I'm sorry Lady. This evening's dinner has been cancelled due to inclement weather."

She slid from her boots, hopping twice on one foot trying to keep her balance. The snow collecting on the entry hall rug into the living area.

"Now open the bar", TB said as she made a grand gesture with her arms, again brushing Gus aside she made for the cabinet. "I hope you've got some good gin."

Shifting moods, Gus responded, "I know you TB and there is no such thing as bad gin or bad scotch."

"Ass!"

To his surprise her shoulders sagged ever so slightly betraying her mood. Something had sucked the fight from her. Gus wasn't certain he knew how to manage a TB displaying tings of capitulation.

Her eyes showed a surrender with which Gus was unfamiliar. What on earth would he do with a subdued Beth?

Gus unscrewed the cap from the Beefeaters and quietly prepared a gimlet in her preferred fashion, a little lime, some soda and a considerable quantity of gin.

He sat the glass down and extended the bottle to her.

"Screw you, Gus. I'm here because I'm too depressed to be snowed in alone."

Gus laughed. "Oh, narcissistic me, I thought you'd come over just to make my life miserable."

"Gussie, no one could make your life more a miserable mess than you can do on your own." Beth said without cracking a smile.

"Hold on a minute! Let's take a stroll in the snow to Johnny's and eat a real meal."

"Let me guess. I suppose by a real meal you mean meat and potatoes."

"You damn right." Gus smiled. "You may feel free to eat all the greens you desire. Far be it from me to criticize a meal without meat."

Taking a more serious tone, he asked, "Do you think we can walk around the corner without getting mired in a snowbank?"

"I don't know but I think we should try." Beth said, already pulling her boots on.

"Johnny says the way it has blown, if we stay close to the building the snow isn't so deep. Maybe four to six inches." Gus held the door open for her and smiled.

The power and lights were out at Johnny's Restaurant. The candle light wasn't. Their flames lit the small first floor dining area. Maybe not bright but still well-lit.

Inside with the door closed behind them, they begin to stomp. The snow scattered from their lower extremities, collecting in circles on the weather mats.

Johnny with a exaggerated sweeping motion, his hands opened palm up and extended, welcomed the wayfaring couple into his restaurant. As if exposed by his wave, Gus saw four other neighborhood couples had made their way thru the storm.

Hearty and hospitable greetings were exchanged.

Dressed in his formal New Year's Eve attire, Johnny guided them to a high-backed booth that afforded considerable privacy for the diners and muffled their conversations. Placing two individuals with a profound literary bent among walls of flickering candles was an invitation to fantasy. A room bursting with dim but dancing light hinted of times long past.

Johnny's voice intruded into their illusions and brought them back to the present. He was almost whispering as he said, "Tomas will be your server tonight. The tips will be light tonight – and his family – well, please understand I am not shunning you and your charmingly beautiful date but I am rather providing you with a belated opportunity to express your Christmas charity."

Gus responded, "Dimness of the light in here must be getting to you. It is just Beth."

Beth gave a feinted glare toward both of the men who were now smiling and looking at her.

The Last Dance in Delta

Then, she said, "Well, bull hockey!"

As she spoke, he moved his leg to dampen the effect of her toe should her shoe find its mark. The size of the table alone prevented her shoe from contacting his trouser-covered shin.

She missed. She didn't like missing.

Beth leaned toward him and, as if reading from an Ellery Queen novel, said, "In the shadowy light no one could see who planted the butter knife in the diner's chest."

Tomas made his way to the booth.

"Mr. Gus, as you can see, there is no waiting this New Year's Eve."

"So, we see. It is nice to see you, Tomas."

"As it is you. Thank you for trudging through this snowy tempest to dine with us", he continued, "After such effort it is regrettable the menu tonight will be limited to an extraordinary filet and our renowned twice-baked potatoes."

Tomas' smile revealed the enjoyment he found in telling Gus they were serving his beef tonight.

Gus nodded and smiled and said, "Dang, trudging through the snowy tempest. Now that is a fine arrangement of words."

Tomas nodded and smiled his sly grin. "I try. I try. I ordinarily reserve such quips for Miss Beth's ears."

Beth smiled broadly and did her exaggerated upper body curtsy.

Gus said, "Curses! Foiled again."

"Your type will always be thwarted by the world's Dudley Do-rights."

Gus gazed at Beth with admiration and then acknowledged, "Beth, I am genuinely pleased you showed up at my door this snowy night."

Again. bringing focus to her graceful arms, Beth performed her upper torso genuflection.

"That, my dear lady, is elegant", Gus acknowledged the gesture with veneration. Beyond most all things, Gus enjoyed Beth's company.

Tomas appeared and extended a bottle of wine through the candlelight. "Mr. Johnny says this Cabernet will be perfect with your beef."

In his formal and professional fashion, Tomas removed the cork and poured a taste for Gus. Gus' approval was evident before a word was spoken.

"Excellent recommendation."

With that Tomas poured Beth's glass and then finished his pour for Gus.

Beth brought the wine to her lips in the delicate fashion only a woman can master. Style aside, she visibly enjoyed her first taste.

Beth said, "Gus you did well." She paused and finished, "For a gentleman of back-country breeding."

Beth giveth and Beth taketh away.

Gus recognized his opportunity. He said, "I'm sure you usually do the selecting and get the first sip. Ah, the seduction dance knows no gender."

With a gentle move of her hand toward her lips, she flipped him off so subtly he almost missed it.

Ultimately, the dinner was superior, unhurried and professionally paced. Despite her disingenuous protest, Beth was as much a meat and potatoes person as Gus was.

Beth and Gus abandoned any battle of wits and words knowing there would never be no clear winner. The conversation became delicious.

Their dialog moved to more personal matters. The role of their parents in their rearing became the topic. This was an area in which Gus and Beth had previously found they had little in common.

Beth's mother was committed to rearing her daughter with every skill required to be a successful wife, mother and homemaker. Beth would summarize that she could cook like a chef, clean like a housewife, be the homeroom mother the other women envied, and oh yes, screw your husband at least three times a week, if you can't provide that frequency then when you do it, you'd better be able to make his eyeballs roll around their sockets until they ring like a slot machine.

Beth knew the truth was she really didn't mind any of the task as much as she resented being told that she had to do them.

Gus did want to understand what Beth had been attempting to share but his father had been preoccupied with his businesses and his mother was preoccupied with her "social responsibilities". When it came right down to it, both were inept. Gus always described their parenting style as being emotionally distant.

But his Uncle Bob and Aunt Elizabeth were superior pseudo-parents. He could have asked for no better examples and received no better guidance.

Then, a cancer unexpectedly took his mother when he was away in the Pacific during World War II. His father had experienced a prolonged grieving but had returned to his obsessive involvement in the family retail stores by the time Gus received his discharge.

As a boy, Gus worked in the dry goods store doing everything from sweeping out the store to working the sales floor on Saturdays. His father taught him much about business but little about the personal or intimate side of life.

His dad would say, "A man is defined by the quality and success of his work."

From a practical perspective, his Uncle Bob and Aunt Elizabeth reared him. As he looked back upon them, Gus knew his uncle and aunt had a most functional emotional and romantic relationship despite the wounds his uncle sustained in World War I. His Aunt Elizabeth simply refused to allow her husband not to love her as unconditionally as she loved him.

Gus would carry one element of her council throughout his life, "Unconditional love breeds unconditional love. Gussie, you really are what you give. I'm not saying everything is equal because it isn't. It is simple. Sometimes will be great, other times not so much. You can decide to enjoy it all."

Gus could still see his aunt sitting at her kitchen table with him. Her face giving little clue as to her thoughts. She was always quite straightforward about the qualities it took to sustain a solid marital relationship, honesty at the forefront.

She taught Gus her refrain. At any given time, relationship demands were seldom 50-50. But one party had to always be ready and willing to carry them both.

"Gussie, a man may never have as much to give as woman. But a man should always give everything he can. He does that and he'll receive everything a woman has to give in return," Elizabeth shared this wisdom one night as they sat by the fireplace listening to the radio. Uncle Bob, dozed in his chair, no longer tuned into the radio.

Gus had always been grateful to his Uncle Bob and Aunt Elizabeth.

Beth said, "Gus, I know that my mom cares for me. I'd say she loved me if I was prone to say such things."

Gus' eyes made it clear he was making a sincere effort at understanding. Beth was trying to explain the nuances one of the most complex of human relationships, that between mother and daughter.

"I truly believe mom wants me to be happy. But happy as she defines it. Happiness involves a husband and two and half babies."

"Beth, I wish I could tell you I completely understood." Gus stopped, shrugged his shoulders while he shook his head sideways. Gus felt any man profited by knowing when the emotional context of a conversation had reached a depth beyond his ability to appreciate and comprehend.

He recalled his Uncle Bob saying, "Silence is golden, 'specially when you're talkin' feelings with a woman."

Beth confided, "Babies are easy to make, even downright fun, but raising both a child and a husband is another matter. Mother assured me I'd grow to love him, not a particular him just any old him," Beth said hoping the fog would lift from Gus' eyes.

"Well, don't look at me", Gus observed. "I'm the guy whose interesting uncle had the sex talk with him. But I'll say this, I think my Uncle Bob has a wife, his high school sweetheart, who has guided him to as rich an intimate life as anyone might ever aspire to."

Beth cackled, "Just what wisdom did your wise but eccentric uncle give you?"

"Well, it's the kind that has mostly kept me safe from the wiles of women."

"Poo bah. You just can't risk your frail male ego in a relationship."

"Life's biggest disappointment will be the first time you have intercourse. That was the first thing Uncle Bob told me about intimacy and the ladies."

"And?"

"There are circumstances and expectations. He wasn't completely wrong. And he did go on to highly recommend that second and third time," Gus paused and then continued, "My Uncle Bob was special."

Gus laughed but the fog still didn't lift from his eyes.

The walk home, despite the raw wind shoving the again snow filled air, was almost pleasant. They dashed into the lobby, laughter filled and bodies thrashing. Only the substantial rug line preventing them from sliding on the marble floor.

The apartment smelled of fresh coffee. It was a smell in which both found comfort.

Coffee cups warming their hands, they stood next to the radiator. There was considerable to be said for steam heat on a cold, snowy Chicago New Year's Eve.

"More Coffee?" Beth offered, "I'm going to have some."

Uncle Bob would have had a comment about her serving him in his apartment. Gus made a note of how easily Beth had taken the role. He thought it just wasn't like her.

"Yes, Ma'am. Please."

Beth knew that his eyes were following her as she moved toward the kitchen. The thought that he might find her appealing pleased her.

She smiled as she imagined him trying to sort out the physical and the emotional intricacies of their friendship.

She wished she was taller than five feet, five inches and wished she weighted fifteen pounds less. She had this thing about remembering in multiples of five. It kept her life orderly. She loved her auburn hair, abundant without being coarse. She fretted that the angle of her shoulders, descending to rather narrow hips gave her boyish appearance. It didn't.

If it had, her breasts were adequate to belie her assumption.

Beth found self-analysis to be obstinate and awkward. She suspected the whole process appealed more to women than to men, but then again Gus's writing had now and again reflected a superior insight into the female psyche.

Of course, Gus would deny such insights existed. He professed women left him in a state of profound befuddlement. But he was a keener observer of both genders than he would willingly acknowledge.

"Just black", Gus instructed as if she hadn't gotten his coffee at more times and in more places than either of them could recall. This left her considering that perhaps Gus was not as evolved as she thought.

This whole mental exercise left her amused.

The electricity was out as far as they could detect in every direction. The street lights were out so there was no backdrop to illuminate the falling flakes.

"Thank God steam will always warm up your pipes," Gus said as he warmed his hands over the radiator.

"And the fuel gets in the boiler."

As the damp heat rose from the core of the radiator, Gus continued, "Dang, that feels good,"

Beth was momentarily lost in her thoughts. As reality retrieved her, she observed, "Steam heat and large candles. This was once the good life on a harsh winter's night."

"I wish I'd been smart enough to have a kerosene lamp of two." He thought further and added, "You know, my Uncle Bob and Aunt Elizabeth still use kerosene lamps in our family fishing cabin back home."

Beth looked at Gus and smiled.

Gus and Beth scooted the couch closer to the radiator and sat down. They each rolled up in a blanket, and talked. They were looking out the window as if they could actually see the wind driven snow beyond the window. The sounds of the storm suggested it was intensifying.

Gus wound his watch and said, "It is almost 1969." Then, he wrapped up snugger in his blanket.

"Gussie, 1968 was a hell of a year. I'm happy to see it flushed down the toilet of life."

"Oh, Sweet Jesus, I agree. '68 left me with some really ugly memories hanging out there. I think, most years, just a couple of memorable things happen. This year, Old Man Time is leaving carrying a heavy sack of bad stuff, a big heavy sack full of evil, unpleasant and immoral happenings."

Beth laughed. Gus liked hearing her laugh. It was exceedingly feminine. Beyond any gender boundary, Beth's laugh could be downright sensual.

"How about vile, abhorrent, and loathsome? Depraved? Come on, you are alleged to be a man of letters, use your big boy words."

"A challenge for you, Lady McBeth. A lot has happened in 1968. Let's rank-order them given their ultimate importance to history."

"Well, Gussie just who is going to judge said contest?"

"We are. We will use words and logic to defend our choice."

"Oh, I've got it. We will write this down and in twenty-five years we will determine the winner. Now how does that sound." Beth sounded a bit excited.

"You going to be the secretary?"

"Screw you."

Gus smiled broadly stating, "Ah, who could not be excited by the proposal of an intellectual joust?"

He added a question, "The prize?"

"A quarter century from tonight, a dinner with the identical menu as we ate tonight."

"And a bottle of Johnnie Walker Blue if I win. A jug of Dom Perignon if you win."

"Accepted. You go first."

They relocated their limbs just enough that eye-contact was easy to maintain. Then, Gus got up.

"You have no idea how reluctant I am to get up but I think we both need a pencil and a pad," Gus said as he moved toward his writing space.

Beth said, "I've already got you retreating to the security of a Laddie Pencil and a Big Chief tablet."

Gus had told her of WK's writing concept. They both enjoyed the intellectual foray of regressing into designing a creative piece with a Laddie Pencil and a Big Chief Tablet. They liked the visual image.

She laughed as Gus responded with a familiar hand gesture.

Beth's gave brief consideration to the options, brief but adequately thoughtful

"My number one is LBJ not seeking reelection. His decision opened the door for Nixon's election, forced the war in Viet Nam in a different direction and fueled the environment for the Convention down the street to become a disaster."

Gus was ready and said, "I'll take what to me is the obvious number one. The murder of Martin Luther King, Jr. It has reinvigorated the more peaceful movement Dr. King promoted. Also, the gentleman was an orator. He gave his movement words that will provide the emotional fuel to get the Civil Rights Movement across the finish line."

"Well, give us a little blood and we will give it a full page in our history text." Beth again blended her sense of humor with her genuine skepticism about our species preoccupation with violence.

"There she is, the woman who adored *In Cold Blood* and *Bonnie and Clyde.*"

"So, says the old curmudgeon who loves *The Lion in Winter,*"

"We have seen some good movies together this year, The *Graduate* and *Cool Hand Luke.*" Gus countered.

"And we saw *Funny Girl* and *Rosemary's Baby.*" Continuing, Beth added, "We do still need to settle up on *2001: A Space Odyssey.*"

Gus smiled. If he had to get stranded in a snow storm with someone Beth would have been his choice.

He chuckled and added. "Let's not forget *Hang'em High.*"

The Last Dance in Delta

"Hell Gussie, that's because we do see a lot of movies together. Especially for people who aren't dating or married."

Beth's observation gave him pause.

"Real good friends and no reason overthink it."

"Right. What do you have in mind for number two?"

"Okay, number two. The election of Richard Millhouse Nixon to the presidency. I'm not a Nixon fan, but just his election has convinced the South Vietnamese government it is time to join the party in Paris. The odds are that he will be President for eight years. Surely he'll do something worthy of notice to merit the number two spot."

"My second pick is the Apollo 8 Mission. It orbited the Moon. Tees up landing on the Moon We'll be on Mars in twenty-five years. Well ahead of the Soviets."

"Hell fire, those boys are hardly back on the ground. But then you're still buying into all that Buck Rogers manure, aren't you?" Beth's voice carried a derision tone.

"Of course, I am. After all Captain Kirk kissed Uhura, first interracial kiss, this season. Civil Rights Movement on the Enterprise. All true progress is in space." Gus countered. "Number Three?"

Beth answered, "The assassination of Bobby Kennedy. He could have been President."

"Maybe."

"Your turn." She still found this murder saddening and didn't want to discuss it any further.

Gus nodded, reflected and said, "Nixon wins the Presidency because George Wallace carries five southern states. The solid south isn't solid anymore."

"Well, I thought I took Nixon winning. I'm not at all certain those southern states wouldn't have voted for Nixon. HHH doesn't really appeal to your typical southerner." Beth felt she needed to add this qualifier.

"You took Nixon winning. I took George Wallace running."

"Oh, Pish, posh! Only a man could come up with a pile of crap like that." Beth shook her head and then went on, "Okay, my turn. Number four."

"The Black Panthers v. Mayor Daly v. Jerry Rubin and the Great Unwashed at the Democratic National Convention. It was right up there with professional wrestling."

Gus scoffed. Not really, he just wanted her to think he did.

"My number four. I'm going with the war. More specifically the Tet Offensive. As much as I hate to acknowledge it, I think history will clearly demonstrate we got our ass kicked all the way to Thursday."

"You know this is going to go on for a while?"

"Yes. Isn't it great?"

The friends smiled warm smiles.

"Lordy, number ten."

Gus feigned exasperation.

Beth face became soft and knowing. She adored her dear friend. She reached beneath his blanket and secured his hand. Their fingers interlocked. She liked the ever so slight indication of callousing. His hands felt strong yet mellow, filled with energy and promise. She squeezed his hand ever so tenderly and for a few moments held on.

Beth offered, "Number ten. I say that people will be singing the Beatles *Hey Jude* in fifty years."

"Beatles, smedeles."

In a quite decent alto, she began to sing:

> *Hey Jude, don't make it bad.*
> *Take a sad song and make it better.*
> *Remember to let her into your heart*
> *Then you can start to make it better.*

"I'm betting people if people remember those lyrics at all it will be the, Na Na, nana na part." He sang the rhyme in his timid baritone.

Beth said, "Alright, your ten."

"UCLA losing to Houston by two in the NCAA championship game. Hayes outplayed the entire UCLA team.

The Last Dance in Delta

UCLA streak is broken and the big guy, Alcindor, will change the game."

"Well, I don't know about any of that."

Beth yawned.

Gus lifted his glass and offered final toast to 1968 and challenged 1969 to be better.

"Nineteen-sixty-eight, Tis' the devil with whom you had a date. Nineteen-sixty-nine, you're gonna be fine! Just hurry! Please don't be late." He smiled.

"That's just pathetic." Beth giggled. "Accurate but pathetic."

Gus took her arm and directed her to the hallway door.

"See the mistletoe?" He pointed to empty space.

"No."

"Pretend."

She did.

Gus kissed her.

Beth yielded and kissed her friend back.

CHAPTER 31:
New Year's Day 1969

"I'VE PUT FRESH SHEETS ON THE GUEST ROOM BED and set out towels and a wash cloth for you. I still just have one bathroom, so knock, hold and your nose but I suspect you remember the drill."

Beth answered, "I am telling you Augustus Kelly, I have no intention of sleeping alone in a cold barren bed on a snowy night in Chicago." As Beth stood bordered by the door to the bath and backlit by two rather large candles, she placed her hands on her hips and stiffened her stance. She was aware her physical assets were well framed.

Regardless of her gender preference, Gus believed her to be a truly lovely and quite desirable woman. He reached for the word he had recently heard and found it, doable. He left it unspoken.

Gus shook his head and quipped, "Just my luck, snowed in and sharing my bed with a breath-taking woman and – well, Sweet Jesus, won't you know it, she's a lesbian."

"Well, you silver tongued devil you, feel blessed you've had my company for dinner and conversation. I think you've already been awfully lucky don't you think?", Beth asked. Then, she pivoted and moved toward the bath.

"So, you're telling me my night is done and I've already been as lucky as I'm going to get?"

"Maybe I am."

"I'm smart enough to know there is only one opinion that matters in such affairs."

The Last Dance in Delta

Then, she stopped. She glanced back over her shoulder at Gus. She felt like a starlet in a movie, a film she was directing.

Beth smiled.

Gus smiled.

Beth giggled to herself as she made her way down the hall to secure the fresh towels from the spare bedroom. She very much liked being a woman.

In his bedroom, Gus laughed at himself. He enjoyed their shtick.

He lit the candle beside the bed. The flame flickered, then blossomed. He extinguished the match. He thought about how to describe the candle light. Such a description could have a place in a western. Candle light could make any scene suggestive.

As was his ritual, Gus sat on the edge of his bed and removed his shoes and socks, then slid the shoes under the edge of the bed. His socks sailed into the clothes basket. He hung his shirt and pants on hangers. He tossed his underwear into the dirty clothes hamper. His briefs hung on the side. He checked the follow-thru on his shot.

Gus changed into his pajama bottoms. Even on a night this cold, the tops remained unused and still folded in the top dresser draw. Beth had always joked she wanted to be first in line to buy his used pajama tops.

He sat on the edge of the bed and watched the light flicker from beneath the bathroom door.

He crawled between his flannel sheets, pulling layers of blankets over him. Turning on his side, he listened to the tranquil sounds of a woman's nighttime rituals, swishes and splashes, a lid being unscrewed and set upon the tile, coming from his bathroom. The most peaceful of reverberations.

Her long flannel nightgown struck just above her ankles as she hustled across the rug to the bed. She stepped from her house shoes into the bed with single fluid motion.

"Damn! It is cold."

"Feel free to come snuggle to my backside."

She rustled the covers over near him. Her arm draped over him, her fingers coming to rest on his chest. Her history with men told her that despite his very best efforts he would not be able to ignore her. She snuggled against him well-aware of the fashion in which her curves were contacting his body. She smiled and settled in. She was very pleased.

His tussles, toils and troubles began.

"Oh, here, let's turn over and see if that makes you more comfortable." Beth had forgotten how much fun it was to tantalize a man. Her sister referred to it as tormenting. But her sister, Inez, did it with no intention of bestowing on her husband the releases she seemed to be promising. Inez saw it as her husband's just reward for going to work each day and leaving her with their four children who were mired in varying stages of early childhood development.

While her motives might not be pure, Beth's seduction strategy involved no such pattern of withholding. Withholding was the last thing on her mind.

She began turning beneath the covers without waiting for his answer. He carefully positioned his hand just below her breasts. He held her close. She nestled closer.

She stretched her legs, repositioning her posterior.

He tried to ignore her turnings. It was challenging. It was impossible.

She felt him firm behind her. She thought, "Well, where have you been stranger?"

"Beth, I'd better." Feeling he should turn away from her.

Not allowing him to complete his sentence, Beth said, "Don't you dare!"

As she reached down, retrieving her gown tail, she inadvertently pushed harder against him. He uttered some uniquely male sound and inched away. She stifled a laugh.

Her gown now bunched at her hip line, she pulled him nearer.
"Beth?"

Again, not allowing him to complete the sentence and trying to add a degree of urgency to her voice, she said, "Yes! Yes, I'm certain."

Gus began to turn toward his bedside table.

Beth said, "It's okay, I've got mine in."

She added, "And we don't have to rush."

They didn't.

Awakening in the early morning hours, Beth found that the stranger had returned and was prepared for another visit.

She turned on her back and stretched beneath the blankets. A lazy quality draped itself over her. She started to tell him he would need something from the drawer of his bedside table. His hand was smooth yet slightly calloused. He touched her inner thigh. Strong, the uneven roughness almost faded, his hand found her and remained. It began with the tingle of arousal and concluded in a state of breathlessness.

"Oh, Sweet Mother of God, Gus." Her exhale was audible. "Oh my God."

She put her hand on his and held it close. She pressed against it.

A binging and dinging from the steam radiator as it sporadically functioned deep in the nights was more of a comforting companion. When on the third night the electricity returned, lights and radio came on, Gus sat upright. Beth moaned.

Gus got up. He cursed the power company and the cold. He turned off the radio on his bedside and wondered how in the world he left it on so loud. Then, he turned off the random lights throughout the house.

Finding himself standing in the living room in the dark, he cursed himself for not turning on the light on the bedside table.

He bumped his shin on the coffee table. He cursed aloud as he took two hops.

Shin still stinging, he settled back beneath the covers. She snuggled tightly to him.

His body warming, he said, "I'm almost sorry it's over."

"Me too. But we will have better coffee in the morning." She referenced his electric coffee pot.

They dozed, actually snoozing rather soundly.

Gus was savoring his morning coffee. With the writer's eye, he studied the fashion in which her hair fell carelessly across her cheek. He did enjoy her company.

"Well?" Beth asked. She knew he had been looking at her. Her eyes were actively involved in her inquiry.

Gus felt uneasy and wondered if there was going to be a correct answer. He took another sip of his coffee.

"If I didn't know you so well, you'd have completely fooled me," Gus eyed her trying to get a read on the situation. Of all things, he did not want to hurt his friend.

"And?"

Gus didn't believe he was greatest of conversationalists when the topic was sex regardless of the gender of his fellow conversant. This dialogue would be even trickier than typical. Upon consideration, he opted for candor.

"Alright Miss Beth, these three days and nights have been wonderful. Beyond the sex, the intimacy has been magnificent. A lady of words such as yourself might describe it as delicious."

Deciding against humor, he regrouped. He spoke in a more paced fashion in which each word took on meaning, "Beth, the sex was incredible. The intimacy far better. I have absolutely loved sleeping with you, waking up beside you. Hell, getting to crawl back in bed with you made the getting up in the middle of the night in the freezing cold to go pee worth it."

He reminded himself about his no humor decree.

Continuing, "The talking, the eating, the laughing. And I never once felt like there was some place you'd rather be."

She swatted his hand with the Time Magazine she had been twisting and rolling since their conversation began.

"Beth, do you want to tell me what's up?"

"The rest of my life, my future life. I want children. I want what my mother called a traditional family for my children. I do not want to raise my children on any societal edges."

She checked Gus to be sure he was with her and then continued, "Gus, I want children. Children with a father." Beth studied him, then added, "If the price of that is a husband, I'm okay with that."

She more intensely measured him. Then, she sought to reassure him, "Don't worry. It isn't you. It's not anyone right now, but it is someone."

"Beth, I'd be lying if I said at my age, I wouldn't consider it. Sweet Jesus, I'd be flattered."

"But?"

"But I'd know."

"But you'd know." Her voice reflected her agreement. And her fear. She restated her concept, "Gus, I'm willing to commit my entire heart and soul to this."

"You'd damn well better be."

"Gus, when I find the guy, I promise I'll make him the happiest man in Cook County." Beth paused and then a more tranquil expression consumed her face. "I know it is about a lot more than screwing his brains out once a week."

She read him and continued, "I'm okay with the wife thing."

"Your career? Your writing?"

"I'll figure it out. I was reared a 50's girl and in a lot of ways I still am."

Some way, somehow, despite all logic to contrary, Gus believed her.

"Beth, don't ask some guy to make you happy, to marry you, and then cut him off at the knees."

"I promise."

"Happy 1969."

CHAPTER 32:
A Storm of Opportunity

THE 1967 HURRICANE SEASON in the Atlantic had been mild until mid-September. Then, Hurricane Beulah organized herself and took dead aim on northern Mexico. By September 18 a sudden intensification raised the storm to a Category 5 hurricane and it started a move north. On September 20 Beulah howled into South Texas as a Category 4 storm, the eye making landfall near the mouth of the Rio Grande River.

South Padre Island, with its newer hotels and older beach houses, lay on the north side of the eye. Many of the newer structures, though not intact, survived. Most of the remaining buildings splintered and collapsed. The debris scattered anywhere the water and wind wished to take it. Some remnants washed into the bay, Laguna Madre. Other vestiges of the storm were carried out into the Gulf of Mexico. Seemingly most of the remains had been randomly dispersed about the island, inanimate objects with no sense of where they came from or where they might be going.

After Beulah, in Port Isabel, the fishermen and shrimpers regained their business footings. On the island, some people had rebuilt, others had simply posted for sale signs and left. By Summer of 1969, where beach houses once stood, lots that appeared to be little more than sand dunes were for sale cheap.

Richard Nixon was President. The war in Viet Nam lingered. Anti-war protesters continued to be a pain in Gus Kelly's backside. Reasoning that there had to be fewer protesters in extreme south Texas than in Chicago, Gus decided to go have a look.

The aging Texas International DC-3 had puddle-jumped its way from Dallas to Austin to San Antonio finally bouncing to a landing in Brownsville. Gus was pleased he had taken an evening flight. A moderate scotch-induced buzz was known to smooth bumpy flights through the washboard skies of south Texas. It did.
After a night at the Fort Brown Hotel and a breakfast of Tex-Mex eggs, he cranked over his Hertz Ford and headed northeast toward the island.
The landscape between Padre and Brownsville was interesting but not appealing. Scrub trees, rows of sorghum and cotton fields lined the roadway. Occasional commercial development spotted the navigation channel that bordered the hiway to the south.
Port Isabel was a fishing community. Visual and olfactory stimulations provided ready confirmation. An ancient wooden causeway the only link between Port Isabel and the island. The causeway appeared to be made of railroad ties and thick hand-hewed planks. Waves seemed to lap just below the level of wooden bridge.
The causeway exited on the north edge of Isla Blanca Park. Gus rolled down his window. The smell of gulf air filled his lungs. He wished he'd thought of lowering the windows before he drove across the causeway. The morning air smelled right.
He turned north up the island.

Don Grimes was a Chicago native. While attending Northwestern, he met a vocal music major, Jane Marie Bass, a rancher's daughter from extreme South Texas.
Falling in love, they mated then married.
Constance Anne "Connie" Grimes was born in October of 1951 in Northwestern Memorial Hospital in Chicago.
Early on, Jane and Don discovered a pair of untidy facts they neglected to share with each other. As a rancher's daughter and unable to become a world-class entertainer, Jane viewed her only acceptable fallback position as rancher's wife.

Beyond knowing there was a stockyard on Chicago's southside, Don knew nothing of the cattle industry.

Oh, he liked the concept of buying and selling cattle well enough. He enjoyed the wardrobe. It was the animals he didn't like. He didn't like horses and he liked cattle even less.

But he gave it a try and discovered he was of little to no value on an operating cattle ranch. It was embarrassing.

Don Grimes found his father-in-law, Jon T. Bass, more sympathetic to his plight than he anticipated. What Jon T. knew was that he detested city life. Beyond a periodic gambling excursion to Las Vegas, Jon T. Bass had no desire to ever leave South Texas.

Further, he had no desire for his son-in-law to leave Texas with his daughter and his grandson.

On August 12, 1956, Jane Marie Bass Grimes had given birth to second child, their son, Jon Bass Grimes, at the family ranch house north of Harlingen. Now, Jon T. adored Connie. But in a different fashion from the manner in which he viewed young Bass.

To commemorate the boy's first steps, Jon T. gave the toddler a pair of hand-crafted boots with the Winding River B brand on the side and with riding heels.

There are those boys said to be able to ride before they could walk. Bass might have been one of them. Bass had been sharing his grandfather's saddle for longer than anyone had accurate memory. Bass slept in his boots until it was pointed out that his grandfather didn't.

Jon T. had no doubt that Bass would be the fourth generation of his family to operate the Wandering River B Ranch.

Don Grimes had tried a couple of businesses with marginal success until he stumbled into real estate. When he entered the real estate business in the Rio Grande valley, Don found his niche.

He acquired some valuable land at distressed prices for the Wandering River B. Jon T. approved.

Jane Marie, with considerable input of her mother Mary Clyde, and her sister, Susan, the Grimes built a home about one hundred yards from the main ranch house.

Grimes & Bass Real Estate established a headquarters just south of the ranch in Raymondville. By the mid-1960's, their branch offices dotted the Rio Grande Valley. After the hurricane, seeing opportunity in the disaster, the business opened a branch office on South Padre Island.

Jon T. was the embodiment of the prevailing vision of the western cattle rancher. He firmly believed he roped and rode better than any hand he ever hired. Perhaps he did.

There was no task on the ranch John T. couldn't do. His ancestors were said to have populated the ranch by putting their brand on any cow that found its way onto his property. Jon T. was no different.

Despite wrapping himself in the cloth of the family, Jon T. had no intention of following the path of his father, Lemuel "Lem" Bass. Lem was an excruciating rigid man who relentlessly pursued land. Lem died land and cattle rich but cash poor. Jon T. inherited an empire and a ton of debt. Jon T. saw it as his mission to fill in the void.

Now, Jon T. found himself with a son-in-law who never sat a horse well nor could he use a hammer without endangering his fingers, but he was convinced the same business principles applied to all businesses. Don quickly found this philosophy compatible with his own conclusions.

Grimes & Bass Real Estate formed Grimes & Bass Construction Company. They built and sold residential developments and commercial properties. They always kept the best of the land for themselves.

Don Grimes kept a desk in every Grimes and Bass Real Estate Office. He regularly if briefly occupied them all in the course of a week. Today He sat behind his desk on South Padre Island. He appeared physically oversized for the space, with his eel skin cowboy boots propped upon the desktop. He admired his boots and kept them shined to high gloss. They were not practical on a sandy barrier island but taking considerable pride in them, he worn them everywhere.

He enjoyed watching the cars move up and down the island. He sipped his coffee and snacked on a maple bar from Rovans. His preference for such passive pleasures had added considerable meat to Don's bones over recent years.

He contemplated the impact that the new causeway just coming off the drawing board might have on the rather lazy island life.

Don's brother, a Chicago literary agent, had referred one of his clients to him. Some well-known western writer or some such person. Having met a few of his brother's clients, he had yet to be impressed. In fairness, they weren't impressed by him either.

Gus Kelly pulled into the parking lot. Don Grimes peered through the window and watched him exit the car. He expected authors to act in some predictable fashion but he couldn't define it.

This man wore Levi's and starched white shirt nicely fitted his slender frame. Don thought to himself, "Our humidity going to take the starch outa' your shorts pretty quick."

Just a few years ago, Don would have judged Gus in bad need of a haircut, but his longish brownish, reddish hair, graying at the temples, now seemed quite middle of road. He wasn't fresh from the military but he wasn't a hippie.

So, Don categorized Gus as scrubbed and skinny, maybe a bit too tidy for his taste. It was a totally erroneous first impression.

Don stood, pulled his pants up, adjusted the large belt buckle so that it wasn't concealed by the roll of his stomach. He pulled on his camel linen sport coat, another effort to minimize the bulge.

Don was gregarious and Gus wasn't. But they enjoyed doing business with each other. Gus was realistic and direct. He did not leave Bob guessing or wasting time. Bob listened and guided. After a couple of hours of driving and walking around dunes, they agreed to meet again the next day.

The Last Dance in Delta

He spent the night in the Ramada Inn on Padre Boulevard. The next morning, he walked the beach to the north.

His Chuck Taylor's draped over his shoulder; Gus walked. The surf was soft, a couple of feet at the best, rushed the cool water over his feet. When he paused, his feet sank easily into the sand.

He was working for words. The sound and sand seemed to embrace him. He liked them. He sat down and looked out at the Gulf of Mexico. He picked up a half-dollar shaped piece of black tar. He tossed it back into the gulf. He thought maybe he shouldn't have.

A jellyfish puffed itself up in the surf seeking a ride out. Jellyfish. In a recent conversation with Beth in Chicago, she said, "Beware the Jellyfish."

"But if you do get stung, first pull out the stinger and then use a white vinegar on it. Don't, don't pee on it! That is just silliness you guys fall for and girls say huh!"

Gus responded, "Cause a guy can visualize hitting the target, a woman, not so much."

Gus smiled and gave the jellyfish some distance.

During the walk, Gus had decided to build a beach house and he wasn't fond of overly close neighbors. Gus thought the hurricane might extinguish folk's enthusiasm for island property for a while. It did and it didn't.

Gus returned to the Grimes & Bass office just before lunch, met Don and purchased seven adjoining gulf side lots. He intended to build on one.

Deals struck, Don said, "I understand your family is in the cattle business in Oklahoma."

Gus acknowledged that they were and told Don a bit about the family operation in eastern Oklahoma.

"You know I once had a baseball glove made in Delta, Oklahoma. Heck of a glove!" Don mused for moment and continued, "I loved that glove."

"Me too," Gus said, "Me too."

"They still make them?"

"They do," Without hesitation Gus added, "Do you want one?"

"Hell yes. And I think we should sell them some place in the valley."

Gus laughed. "Every boy needs a ball glove as well as some of old boys too."

"I played baseball at Northwestern."

Gus picked up and said, "I knocked around the minor leagues for a few years right after the war."

"Greatest game ever made."

Gus nodded a smiling agreement.

"Gus, let me get on working all these details out. Tell you what, if it works for you let's meet for lunch to tomorrow. There is an open-air place on the beach called Wanna-Wanna. Great burgers and beer," Don said. He wavered, then snuck in, "My daughter, Connie, sings there on summer evenings."

"You sound like the proud papa."

Don nodded, smiled and said, "See you for lunch tomorrow."

So, the fraudulent cowboy from the Printers Row neighborhood of Chicago and the Irish Choctaw writer from rural Delta, Oklahoma, parted.

Gus nestled into an Adirondack chair, took a glimpse toward the surf, and settled in. There were comfortable times, there were prickly times. Gus reflected and sorted.

His retreat from the city to the sand and surf had been more fruitful than he could have imagined. There had not been a single protester outside his home. He wrote, an effort to bring the reality of *The Darkest Night* into a western set in the Texas panhandle during the 1880, was due to be released soon. Gus was optimistic about its success, both critically and financially. Most importantly, Gus liked the story. I believed W.K. would.

A half-dozen close friendships had evolved. He sought no more.

His long nights endured. Perhaps less volatile, less explosive but they remained disruptive and unsettling. He now applied a South Texas term to describe them to himself, tolerable. He knew term had a self-delusional property to it but he accepted the improvement.

The Last Dance in Delta

Gus paused for reflection. When his troubles weren't bothering him, he felt better.

Gus Kelly had mustered out of the Marines emotionally frail and without direction. After a three-year adventure-filled foray into minor league baseball and with the assistance of the GI Bill, Gus went to college.

Beginning as an English and History major, he stumbled forward. In fulfilling a requirement, he found himself covering the university baseball team. He embraced his love of words. He read his favorite Zane Grey novels. He discovered his knack for writing. Organizing words to reflect his thoughts was quite gratifying.

His first two works, both westerns, garnered him something of a small but loyal fan base but little financial support. Holiday visits to his parents' home in Delta and several lengthy conversations with his Uncle Bob and Aunt Elizabeth, he guilt-free took his substantial quarterly check from Kelly Holding Company.

During those times in Delta, he would occasionally see Mary Helen, now a wife and mother, on the street or across the sanctuary at Mass. Gus found he liked his church and found special comfort attending Mass at St. Joseph's Church in Delta.

For him these encounters with Mary Helen were tender aching reminders of the girl he once knew. Clear cues to the life that once had been but no longer was. He carried the notion that the most tender of affections might endure were they not so raw, their loss so excruciating to recall.

They avoided each other. When avoidance was impossible, they were gracious. Both ached but tried to prevent the other from knowing it.

His skill at writing reality based western novels and historical fiction grew. He was personable. The demand for him in book sellers and libraries multiplied.

Gus thought long and often about the role Lookout's suicide had on his life. Ultimately, it was there in Tulsa that his literary life changed. He wrote *The Darkest Night*.

Although it was taken as a novel by many, this memoir on World War II spoke from the prospective of a marine rifleman fighting on Peleliu and Okinawa. This memoir experienced considerable financial success during the mid-1960's. Critical acclaim, film rights and prizes all followed.

This novel had been both a blessing and a curse. For near twenty years Gus had unsuccessfully tried to forget the war. Most nights served as reminders of his failed efforts. It was as he recorded his memories in *The Darkest Night* Gus begin to find a degree of relief. He possessed memories that stubbornly refused to leave him alone. His unrelenting experiences had a mercilessly buried their talons deep into his essence and they refused let go. They would make a stealthy return during the chilling fragment of some random night. An emotional seizure would emerge from deep in his unconscious and rip into the very fabric of his sleep. Reluctantly, Gus elected to allow clarity and detail to creep into these nocturnal retellings of his stories. In writing, he allowed his emotions to bleed out on to the pages.

Perhaps it was little more than a marginally successful effort at self-directed therapy but it helped. Some nights now, Gus slept almost peacefully.

Following the release of his memoir, an unexpected and undesired celebrity came Gus's way. After the initial blush waned, Gus felt it burdensome, undesired and downright undeserved.

It was only after the fact that Gus knew he had written about the collective horrors of his generation. Nonetheless, he didn't believe his experiences were any different from every Marine rifleman in the Pacific Theatre. It was the fashion in which he had captured the commonality of their experiences that fueled his recognition. Wives read *Darkness*. Between its pages they found an uncommunicative husband they believed they has lost forever and couldn't understand. Parents found their emotionally missing child they believed they had lost forever. Children would read his recollections and discover their fathers.

It was not that he didn't enjoy people and conversations because he did. Discussions were a human activity that stimulated his creative processes. However, it was only in an uninterrupted quiet that his creative thoughts would begin to gather and organize themselves into a cohesive form that could be transcribed to paper.

He had unlimited time for fellow combat veterans, regardless of their war. There was a uniqueness to talking about his writing with men who understood the fear that filled his pages, the craziness, the sheer raw horror. He learned about them, he learned about himself.

Once sitting on the banks of the Mountain Fork Creek near Delta, fishing with his Uncle Bob he was trying to justify being corrected in his classroom for excessive talking.

His Uncle Bob told him, "If you're doing the talking, you only learn what you already know. Listening is the royal road to learning."

So, as much as humanly possible, Gus listened to the veterans and try to understand the un-understandable.

It didn't matter which island, the emotional carnage always seemed to be similar. It seemed a foxhole as the rain fell and socks rotted was no different on Guadalcanal or Peleliu, the stench of rotting bodies only covered by inches of soil was the same on Iwo Jima or Okinawa. Just as it was different, every island was the same.

Even islands designated as rest and recreation sites, mounted a similar but distinct assault upon the senses. This war created a bond between large groups of men that few generations would ever know.

Because he visited with Viet Nam veterans just as any other vet, he got painted even broader with the "War Monger" brush. He had painted himself into the corner of having to talk about the events he least wanted to talk about.

Gus had followed his Uncle Bob's advice about listening. He needed to learn there were times to keep your mouth shut.

Still, despite his history with islands, Gus found a respite on this island. He was grateful. He thanked God in his prayers.

CHAPTER 33:
Life on the Island

THE EXTERIOR OF THE STILTED BEACH HOUSE appeared worn although the structure was only four years old. Depending on the eye of the viewer, it might appear as little more than a beach front shack. It was elevated in such a fashion that it seemed to fit precisely among the dunes.

Appearing to simply be an extension of the stairs that descended from the porch, a plank boardwalk made its way across the sand toward the beach. At a point where the boardwalk melted into the dunes, there was a wooden sign. The hand painted sign, professionally lettered, said <u>Beware Splinters</u>. Three years of exposure to sand and saltwater carried in on the sea breeze had weathered the lettering.

Gus frankly didn't care. Father Joe Sesek, the pastor of Our Lady of the Sea Catholic Church across the causeway in Port Isabel, had erected the sign when the boardwalk was new and thorny. Gus' friends knew the planks were unkempt. As for the individual who came up his walk way uninvited and bare footed, well, Gus believed a sliver of wood might be deserved. Splinters were only a minor annoyance unless you allowed the site to become infected.

Fr. Joe might be considered the exception. He ambled up the boardwalk, returning from the beach quite proud of the new sandals he had purchased during a recent visit to Progresso. The soles of the sandals were cut from recycled automobile tires. The sandals traction was not what he had imagined it to be. He slipped. A splinter made its way into his exposed heel.

Fr. Joe cursed without evoking the name of the Lord. From his chair, Gus laughed. Fr. Joe did not see the humor which made Gus laugh all the more. Joe hopped and splashed into the other Adirondack chair. Placing his leg on his thigh, he examined his wound.

Gus said, "Sit still".

He went into the house and returned with a pair of tweezers and antibiotic ointment. He extracted the sizable shard of wood, quickly poured a little scotch whiskey on the puncture.

"Son of a bitch!" The words escaped before the unsuspecting Fr. Joe could restrain them.

Regardless of the quality of the scotch, it stung when poured into an fresh wound.

Gus wasn't certain that it would help but he knew that it would produce a burning sensation. Gus took a wicked pleasure in exasperating his friend.

He applied the ointment and handed Fr. Joe a band-aid.

Three days later the sign appeared. Shortly, its post leaned toward the walk. Fr. Joe had it set in concrete but kept the lean.

Gus had always felt that the red wooden Adirondack chairs fit his porch. Ordered from LL Bean, the finish on the wood managed the gulf side environment better than the paint that been applied to his house. The wooden chairs reflected his simple resistance to plastic furniture.

He liked them so much that he ordered two more. However, by the time they arrived he had realized that he rarely had more than one visitor at a time. So, he hadn't assembled them yet. He always told himself that if the need arose, he would.

Finished writing for the time being, he would turn off his IBM Selectric, covering it as best he could with a plastic cover. He kept his Royal manual close by. A practical decision given the unpredictable nature of the island's electric supply. A good wind would take down a number of lines. There was also the variable of the corrosive nature of the salt water.

Gus would then commence to enjoy his chair, the sounds of the surf and about three fingers of Johnnie Walker Black.

The southeast breeze blowing in off the Gulf of Mexico was warm and salty. The flavor of sip of Black label seemed unaffected by the content of the air. Prior to coming to the island, he drank his whiskey with ice three cubes of ice. Here on the island, the ice melted so rapidly that it diluted the whiskey, thinning its flavor. Gus adjusted.

He didn't know if each geographic environment gave whiskey its own unique taste, but he found his island palate had come to favor a good scotch whiskey. Previously, he would blend in some Maker's Mark or a Bacardi and Coke, depending on the day. Initially, he attempted to acquire the local affinity for tequila. Assuming taste and smell where related, tequila reminded him of coal oil. But given the durability of island ice, he became a single beverage consumer, Johnnie Walker Black.

His writing day done, Gus sprawled out in his chair, ate peanuts from the shell and drank his Johnnie Walker Black. It was off-season, so he recognized most of the folks who made their way up and down the beach.

During these winter months, the mean population of the island aged. Most of the couples now strolling the beach appeared to be older than him. He was grateful because a summer could leave a guy believing the whole world was younger than him.

It seemed the whole world was paired off and he wasn't. Whatever the reason, the island existence had made him more aware of his marital status.

Today, he wondered if the woman, the newcomer in the white coverup, would walk his way again. He had first noticed her a couple of days ago.

He knew that women possessed a flexibility to which men could only aspire. The female form, just up the beach seemed to bend itself into the configuration of a hairpin, erect to the waist and bent forward until her hands appeared to comfortably retrieve shells from the edge of the surf.

The wordsmith in his soul worked to describe what he saw. He picked up the ballpoint and the tablet and wrote.

She bent at the waist, knees unbent, as her hand plucked a sea shell from the surf. She was straight up from her feet, bent at her waist, her hands filtering the sand.

When she walked into view, he was delighted. The extent of his gratification surprised him. He stopped, looked, measured her with his mind's eye and then repeated the process.

Gus was intrigued by the fashion in which her body simply bent at the waist as if it were the only moving part she had, straight upright from her sandy feet and her hands reaching down for the sand. Her hands caressed her ankles. He judged that no more an inch ultimately separated her ascending thighs and her descending arms. Her lithe and agile movements seemed to be effortless.

Her body performed in a ballet with which he was not familiar.

She wore what he took to be a white linen cover up with sleeves that struck her just below her elbow and adequate fabric below the waist that nothing embarrassing was ever revealed.

As he studied it more, the garment appeared to be elegantly draped across her until it reached a flowing conclusion about mid-thigh, emphasizing her long slender legs as they protruded from beneath the fabric. The limber brim of her floppy straw hat would blow upright, as accurately as a telltale weather vane pointing out the direction of the wind. The movement of wide pale blue ribbon surrounding the hat delicately reinforced the course of the breeze.

She seemed to wander along the beach near the tide line, moving as if the sand was as familiar with her and she was with it.

There was the hint of a swimsuit beneath the cover but the fabric was such he wasn't certain. Gus didn't have a great eye for fashion but he had an eye for what pleased him. This pleased him.

Fr. Sesek, cautious not to spill the steaming coffee, sat down in the unoccupied Adirondack chair.

"Gus, it beats the heck out of me why we drink hot coffee in this climate. Can't tell the coffee steam from the air."

Gus fell back on one of Fr. Joe's priestly responses, "It's a miracle!"

Before Fr. Sesek could answer, Gus interrupted, "There she is, the beach walker I was telling you about."

Father tried focused, adjusting the bill on his Isla cap to better look into the morning sun. Then, Father smiled and said, "I know her. She is a new parishioner. From Houston, I think. Grace something or the other."

Father further adjusted his cap and said, "Grace something Irish. No. Grace Wojcik."

Gus laughed, almost spewing his coffee.

Father continued, "Wojcik is her married name. I'm helping with her annulment papers. She has been divorced a few years now but former husband's new bride wants to get married in the church. She is taking her maiden-name back, Murphy I think."

"I haven't seen her at the eight o'clock Mass."

"She is an eleven o'clocker."

"Fr. Joe, I want to meet this woman."

"And so, you shall, my son. And so, you shall."

Gus extended the peanut bowl to Fr. Joe.

"How do you eat peanuts with coffee?"

Gus relaxed back into his chair and watched Grace Murphy extract a shell from the surf.

CHAPTER 34:
My Oldest Friend

AFTER SEEING MEN MANGLED BEYOND RECOGNITION on the beaches of the Pacific, Gus no longer judged the timeliness of death. But he did believe a scarce few died before their time. Those we just can't imagine a world without.

Gus and Mary Helen were born weeks apart. They were childhood playmates. They had been next door neighbors. As the first of many bouts with developmental curiosity struck, they became each other's confidants. Confidants they would remain. The adventurous and perpetually curious Mary Helen Ellsworth and the pragmatic and reasonable Gus Kelly were never far apart.

As they aged, they dated and then they didn't. Gus went away to war and Mary Helen stayed home. She married and Gus didn't.

When a telephone rings in the very early hours of the morning, there is rarely good news on the other end of the line. Gus answered the phone but was still trying to shake the cobwebs of sleep from his head.

"Gus, Finnegan here. Mary Helen is dead," The caller paused. Gus could hear him choke a bit but stayed quiet. Tate Finnegan continued, "She had a few drinks at the club, got into an argument with Sissy and stormed out. Hell, you've seen her do it."

Gus had seen Mary Helen do a lot of things in a lot of places, from under her parents' front porch to a carnival tent to beneath their special tree. So yes, he had seen her throw what his mother called "a Mary Helen". He had never found them to be anything that a little space and a firm hand could not resolve.

But he reminded himself it had been years since he had seen her in any fashion that he did not judge to be superficial.

Gus thought of his mother. His mother adored Mary Helen. Until her death, his mother felt that if it hadn't been for the war Mary Helen and Gus would have married. Without ever consciously acknowledging it, Gus felt much the same way at times. Gus also felt you just can't spend too much time second guessing life.

Tate pushed back what sounded to be a sob and said, "She had the best heart of all of us".

"Damn it, Tate!" Gus snapped, "Tell me what happened?"

With each word clipped, he replied, "She hit a truck head on." "Going over ninety.' "Crossed the center line and hit a coal truck head on."

"Ah!" It was the involuntary guttural sound of pain escaping. Gus' soul shrunk. Gus surrendered to another loss.

"Took'em over two hours to pry her out." Tate's sobbing overwhelmed his efforts to speak.

Gus was silent.

Both men were quiet.

"Gus, the services are tomorrow. I know you can't get up here but." Tate stopped mid-sentence. "Well, anyway I knew you'd want to know."

Again, the men went stone silent.

"I know how close you two were."

Gus remained silent. He knew the timing of Tate's call was designed to prohibit his attendance at his wife's service.

Tate bristled as if Gus' silence had brought to mind the many nights, he believed he was sharing his wife with "the great Gus Kelly". He had been forced to share her life. He refused to share her death.

How emotions can make their way over a thousand miles of telephone line Gus didn't know but they did. Gus didn't like Tate. Tate jealously hated Gus. Gus felt sorry for Tate.

Gus said, "Thanks for the call. We'll talk soon."

"Yes".

Both men knew they would never speak again.

The telephone ringing on night stand and wakened him. Fr. Sesek wondered why he allowed his Parishioners to convince him that having a telephone beside his bed was a good idea. When he had to walk to the living room to answer the infernal machine, he was at least awake by the time he answered.

Then, he remembered. He complained about being awakened and stumbling toward the sound of the ringing phone only to have the caller hang up just one ring before he answered the phone. He conceded some Parishioners had a valid need to speak with him at odd hours. After all he was a priest.

"Fr. Joe."

The good father only responded with an unresponsive grunt acknowledgement.

"Padre. Gus. I need your ear."

"What's up?"

"I've lost --." His voice trailed to silence, then he found his voice again. His pressured words would not come out.

Fr. Sesek was now more awake. Knowing his friend was not prone to histrionic overstatement, he said, "Your place?"

"Yes. Thanks Father."

"See you in a minute."

Gus drew in a deep breath, audible enough that Fr. Joe heard the sound.

Gus poured the dregs of last night's coffee into his cup. He set a fresh pot to perking in the percolator.

Opening the shutters, he looked for the Gulf through the water that collected on the glass overnight. He took a beach towel from the peg and wiped the moisture that had collected overnight from his Adirondack chair and sat down.

He knew the Gulf was out there. He could hear it. Sunrise would come.

He lifted the mug of hot coffee to his lips. It was foul-tasting but he really didn't care. It was hot and tasted something like coffee. He had given a passing thought to pouring a touch of

Black Label into the cup but he just hadn't acquired the taste for consuming alcohol in the morning.

He would miss Mary Helen. They had come of age together. They had shared the deepest and most private secrets of childhood and adolescence. She was a grand fantasy that filled many an uncomfortable night. He could think of her and feel less alone. He could not recall life without her.

Mary Helen had watched her older sisters and determined that femininity was fun. Observationally, she learned about the manipulative power of femininity. She tested her emerging powers on Gus. She came to believe little boys would jump through hoops for what she had. She didn't know what she had but she was glad she had it and she was determined to find out more about it.

Her mother had stoically delivered a sanitized explanation of the birds and the bees. Mary Helen had already concluded otherwise.

The sea breeze blew moist and salty, it saturated him back into the moment.

In the moment, Gus missed the illusion of Mary Helen. He smiled. His memories softened. His thoughts again drifted back.

"Why do guys always seem to be in such a hurry?" Mary Helen asked. Then, she realized the intensity of what she intended to be a casual question.

Gus answered, "I don't know." Gus thought. "I suppose boys rush on because they are afraid a girl is going to change her mind."

"You should take your time." With a soft laugh, Mary Helen concluded, "It sounds like the advice our parents should be giving us but can't."

"Do you mind that your parents screw?" Mary Helen both ask her question and experimented with the stronger word. She was coming to believe people were just too polite when discussing sex.

"Sweet Jesus, Mary Helen! I don't even like to think about it."

He gave a shaking motion with his shoulders and added, "Gives me the chills."

"Well, if they didn't think about doin' it, you wouldn't be bouncing around on this earth." She paused and finished, "Oh, they had to be more than just thinkin' about it, didn't they?"

"Sweet Jesus! Enough already!"

He knew Mary Helen enjoyed making him uncomfortable.

He wondered if he ever truly knew Mary Helen as an adult. He had no ready answer.

Gus looked at the Gulf. He asked God to look fondly on his friend.

Fr. Joe opened the sliding glass door, stopped when he saw his friend, facing the gulf and kneeling at the deck rail in prayer. Father waited.

CHAPTER 35:
A Night at the Wannie

CONNIE GRIMES WAS A PERFECTLY DELIGHTFUL YOUNG LADY. This summer, after her third year in the University of Texas music program, Connie was spending her summer, guitar across her lap, playing country and folk music in Gus' favorite beach haunt, The Wanna-Wanna.

Gus considered her a quite lovely young woman both in appearance and personality. He viewed her as being possessed of a soft and promising way. Her look was not yet that of an adult but her appearance had lost its childishness. She owned the effervesce of youth.

From somewhere back in her gene pool she had been given beautiful amber hair which she grew to where it rested on her frequently bare shoulders. Her style of dress enhanced her physical attractiveness. Most evenings, she wore long loose-fitting dresses of various prints made for her by the seamstress that had sewn for her since she was a girl. She shunned the popular hippie fashions except when she wore a tie dye with her Levi's.

Her vocal range and texture fit the folk music of the day. Her genetic lineage did her no harm. She enjoyed being a Bass.

She wore her grandfather's bluster with her mother's ranch house elegance and she wore them well. She was the granddaughter of a south Texas legend.

Gus considered her special. Her parents, Don and Jane Marie Grimes, were his friends. Her grandfather, Jon T. Bass, was his favorite valley character. Gus swore he would someday write a story with a major character based on Jon T. Bass. Gus truly liked the man.

The Wanna-Wanna, known locally as the Wannie, was an open-air bar and grill setting on area between the beach and Gulf Boulevard, an easy walk from Gus' home.

At its core, The Wannie was an open-air establishment with a large wood plank deck raised four steps above the dunes at the east entry and level with the side walk on the west. The seating area was covered with a blue and white striped canvas roof that hung over a frame of wooden beams. A more permanent roof covered the bar and kitchen area which was elevated three steps above the dining deck. On that level there was a more traditional bar where conversation with the bartender could be conducted.

A small performance area has been squeezed into the southeast corner of the main floor. The main dining area was furnished with white plastic furniture, a table and four chairs to the set.

Lights and ceiling fans hung from the beams. The wiring snaked it way across the room clinging to the aged wooden structure.

Gus would look at the slowly rotating fans and visualize Sidney Greenstreet and Peter Lorre in some tropical bar plotting evil deeds in *The Maltase Falcon*. He had seen that movie with Mary Helen just before he left for the Marine Corps. Like many things Mary Helen, it occupied a tender place in his memory bank.

On this late July evening, the air hung thick, only lightly stirred by the gulf breeze. Gus sat alone at the dining room rail looking out toward the Gulf. He was still seeking a word to improve the closing line of an otherwise non-descript chapter.

He had come to listen to Connie sing. He was two drinks and fine cheeseburger steak into his evening.

Gus became more attentive as Connie shifted from the *Desert Pete* into *Stewball*. Connie's voice came to the song like a woodland sprite to a racing stream. She gloried in *Stewball*. It was just fun. Whatever dance she had in her that evening would find her feet as she sang it. She twirled old Stewball right through the finish line.

The applause was generous. Connie smiled.

Gus scooted his chair back around and looked out toward the gulf. He sipped the Johnnie Walker Black and watched the phantom forms that inched their way along the edge of the surf. He could envision them carrying their shoes and holding hands as the saltwater lapped at their feet. He drifted a little.

Gus was unclear as to how the altercation started.

He later heard a half-dozen or so young men, all looking to be of college age, full of beer and themselves, floated into the Wannie. They had finished watching the fireworks at Louie's and now were coming to hear the cute girl they had heard about sing. Their behavior was on the rude and raucous side as they made their entrance. They brought attention to themselves.

They attempted to scoot a table around to get a better view of Connie and the stage, only to find it secured to the floor. Some folks nearby laughed. The boys scowled.

One young man, University of Texas cap reversed, snatched two chairs and moved them closer to the stage, bumping into a seated older couple in the process. A plastic plate slid off their table and bounced along the floor, leaving catsup and fries in its wake.

Words were exchanged. Connie joined in. One boisterous young man, far too full of beer and testosterone, objected to Connie's intervention. A word led to words, push led to a shove, Connie landed on the floor, skirt flying. The bartender grabbed his two by four bat and rushed toward the scuffle. A member of the now unruly group tripped him, sending his bat spinning across the planks.

A cook was making fruitless and frustrating attempts to exit the kitchen area only to find himself blocked by a milling collection of increasingly interested onlookers.

A boy, perceiving himself to be a budding comedian, placed his hands on his knees and positioned himself as if securing a better view beneath Connie's fluttered skirt, barked, "My God, she ain't wearin' no panties."

The rowdies laughed.

The Last Dance in Delta

The boy's humor eluded Gus. He didn't know just when he picked up the chair. But he did. He was unaware of bringing it full force onto the back of the hooting comedian who had held his pose too long, driving him forward to floor at Connie's feet. She doubled up both fist and hit him in the back of the head, driving his face into the planks.

The academic in a Houston Football tee shirt tackled Gus. The force of Gus' swing had carried him to a knee and he was trying to get up. They scooted under a table.

A beer bottle was thrown.

Gus saw a bayonet graze past his head.

The fetid smell of rot and stale mothballs rose from the mud overwhelmed him. Gus smelled the rank mud. He felt its ooze and tried to shake it away. He reared to be loose of it, bumping his head against the underside of a table.

He tasted blood, real enough. He spit it into the mud. His mouth filled with the aftertastes of zinc and copper. He swung a fist through the driving rain. He hit something.

He reached for his K-Bar only to find it gone. He swung wildly, reaching up and grabbing a Jap by the helmet and began beating his enemy's head into the ground.

He was attacked from behind. He rolled and ripped his knee upward. The knee found solid contact. He heard the air escape from his assailant.

He snatched a stone from the ground with the intention of smashing it into the Jap's head. The rain got bitter cold and intensified. Through the haze, Gus saw a woman floating over him. He sat up. Ice cubes rolled along the back of his shirt while a few seeped beneath his shirt collar.

Two boys fled the Wannie leaving their companions to deal with the daft man.

Another scooted along the floor, trying to simultaneously get up and flee, screeched, "This son-of-a-bitch is crazy."

Connie re-entered the skirmish. A once frosted mug in hand, she wound up and threw from the floor. She hit a rotating fan.

She threw a punch that can only be described as a cowboy's round house right, hitting the collegiate square in the ear, peeling him from Gus' back.

A Caucasian version of Fat Albert lost his balance and fell into her and taking both of them to the floor. She kneed herself free of him, leaving him squirming across the planks.

Approaching sirens could be heard. At a distance, coming closer. The scholars searched for a way out.

The older couple had remained seated throughout the brawl. The lady rose, lifted a half full pitcher of beer and poured it on the pants of the scholar wearing the UT cap. She displayed the downward horns, took her husband's arm, helped him with his cane and they left.

Connie made no effort to rise, she sat in the floor cradling Gus' head. Gus started to get up. She held him down. She sat on his chest.

"Calm down Marine."

A voice behind her said, "Your nameplate might say Grimes but you fight like a Bass."

Connie laughed, greatly pleased with the observation, and began to hum the last verse of *Stewball*. She was oddly happy.

She knew J.T. would be quite proud of her.

Don and Jane Marie Grimes came in to hear their daughter sing. They brought along a friend from the Saturday Vigil Mass. As they arrived several panicked young men, fleeing the establishment, forced them to step off the sidewalk and into the sand and stub grass.

"Assholes!" Jane Marie's vile tongue lashed out.

They walked inside to find their daughter sitting on the plank floor and supporting the anguished head of their friend. Closer visual examination revealed Connie had a large rosy blotch on her cheek and blood trickled from her right elbow.

Both combatants, looking the worse for wear, seemed inexplicably satisfied with their circumstances.

Jane Marie, hands at her hips, demanded of her daughter, "Just what the hell is going on?"

Behind her, Don could no longer stifle his laughter. His wife turned and glared at him.

He smiled and stepped up beside her.

"Well, daughter, I come to listen to you sing and look what I find." Her father's mischievous smile coated his face and he continued, "Been in a bar room brawl and laying in the floor with some doddering old fool."

Her mother still flustered but beginning to waver between amusement and embarrassment. She reached down and pulled Connie's dress tail down, returning it to a more modest length. Just making the effort seemed to make Jane Marie feel better.

Connie leaned down and whispered into Gus' ear, "You do know Loch Lomond."

"I do." Gus raised himself and sat up beside her.

"Then, follow me."

Pure joy covered her face.

"Be yon bonnie banks and by yon bonnie braes,
Where the sun shines bright on Loch Lomond,
Where me and my true love were ever wont to gae
On the bonnie, bonnie banks o' Loch Lomond.

They hit the chorus in full throat. Connie thought Gus' baritone was good, good not great. And fun.

O ye'll tak' the high road and I'll tak' the low road
An' I'll be in Scotland afore ye,
But me and my love will never meet again
On the bonnie, bonnie banks of Loch Lomond.

Connie tightened her grip on his hand, she went on solo.

Mo mo leannan bhoidheach
Mo mo Leannan bhoidheach
Mo mo Leannan bhoidheach

"What is she singing?"

"Oh, Gaelic, our daughter took some class at UT."

Gus joined her on a final refrain.

My, my beautiful darling.
My, my beautiful sweetheart
My, my beautiful darling.

They finished. They laughed. Gus kissed Connie on the forehead as he straightened himself. She hugged his neck. They stood up.

A collection, now forming an irregular circle around them, clapped and laughed.

Gus stood, stretched himself erect. He looked up square into the eyes of the woman from the beach, the seashell collector. He sputtered.

As Gus bumbled, Don introduced the woman to his daughter. Then turned to Gus.

"Grace, I'd like you to meet Gus Kelly."

"Gus, my friend, Grace Murphy."

Grace nodded. Her smile was hesitant, enigmatic. She didn't know quite what to make this glorious mess of a man who had just arisen from the Wannie floor. His blue eyes still ablaze from the exhilaration of the brawl. Though his age wasn't immediately clear, she judged him to be of adequate age that he should have known better. His short hair, soaking wet and styled in a fashion he could have cut it himself and greying at the temples, belied his age.

"Grace." He acknowledged her then subliminally cursed the almost adolescent stammer that invaded his voice. He was flustered by his situation and totally smitten with the woman.

Grace, for her part, had been hearing about this man from both her parish priest and from her friend, Jane Marie, for over a month now. She was becoming rather amused at what felt like a plot had been formed to have her meet this man. On a more divine plane, over the past month, their paths had comedically failed to cross.

For her own part, she was rather interested in the man she had labeled "her personal voyeur." It seemed that many mornings during her walk, she was conscious of him sitting on his deck and looking her way. Acting oblivious to his existence, sometimes she stretched for interesting seashells. Other times her movements were designed to make a not-so-subtle effort to attract his attention. She was curious and she had wished he was.

She had thought it might be nothing but it might be something. She chastised herself for embracing such whimsies, fantasies that moved her no closer to her goal, whatever that was. She considered just boldly walking up and introducing herself to him. She was uncertain. Maybe someday soon.

Tonight, she had accompanied her friends willing to meet this man. If nothing else, Jane Marie would be happy. And she was interested in hearing the Grimes girl sing.

She searched for feelings. Where did she place this man who rose from a wood plank saloon floor to a wonderful height, all scraped with budding bruises from what can only be described as a barroom brawl and a concluding sing-a-long with a pretty girl half his age.

She recognized the man from the deck. Unable to contain her laughter at this incredible irony, she laughed.

Her eyes filled with the mischief of a Leprechaun, Grace said to Jane Marie, "If you think this is the man of my dreams, what must you think of me?"

Jane Marie surveyed the pair, evaluated her available replies and responded from her Bass side, "Isn't he?"

"Maybe."

Grace extended her hand and steadied him. He wobbled, awkwardly leaning toward her. She firmed her grip. He steadied. Grace looked at Gus, shook her head and whispered "Well, you're just a fuckin' mess."

"Yes, I am," he replied. His head hurt. He was dizzy.

"I'm driving you home." Her voice was firm.

"Yes, you are." He offered no resistance. "And thank you."

The Grimes walked slightly behind Grace and Gus as they left the Wannie.

Jane Marie asked, "Do you believe in 'Love at First Sight'?"

"Not really."

"I might be ready to change my mind on the subject." A transcendent grin showed itself. Jane Marie gave a head bob to the couple.

"If they don't now, they will soon."

The story of the old Marine, the bartender, the little girl singer and the fight at the Wannie became a thing of legend. The number of intoxicated scholars grows exponentially with the passing seasons.

CHAPTER 36:
The Mating Game

THE SMELLS OF BACON FRYING AND COFFEE BREWING awakened Gus. He hurt some but not horribly. After a stop in the bathroom, he opened the bedroom door. There in his favorite sea-foam green Isla tee shirt was the lady formerly in white.

"Good morning. Coffee's ready."

Stiff and still unsteady, Gus inched toward the kitchen table.

"How do you feel?"

Gus extended his hand and waved it up and down in an attempt to express the profound iffiness of his situation.

"Well said and you earned every ache and pain of it." Grace giggled to herself. She turned the bacon.

He saw the blankets and pillows on the couch.

"Scrambled or fried?"

"Soft boiled."

"Scrambled or fried?" Her smile broadened.

"Scrambled."

"Good choice."

It had been a lifetime since she felt this contented. It made no sense yet it made perfect sense.

Gus was smitten. In white or in sea-foam, she was the most beautiful woman he had ever seen. Every graceful move possessed a genuineness that left him captivated. Even removing bacon from a frying pan with a fork, she was extraordinary.

"Oh, do you know a Beth Inman? She telephoned."

Puzzled, he answered, "Yes. A good friend from Chicago. She writes for the Tribune."

"Does she now? I'm quite impressed."

"And?"

"And she said to tell you she had found the man and she was marrying him."

"Well, I'll be damned."

"She said you'd say that." Grace was somehow quite pleased.

"And I suppose she was curious as to exactly who you were?"

"Of course, she was. Who, what, when and where?"

"And?"

"I told her I was the woman who had driven you home after a drunken brawl."

"And?"

"She said alright, wished me good luck and invited me to her wedding too."

"Of course, she did."

Grace and Gus sat quietly and closely in the Adirondack chairs. The surf and breeze were doing their morning cleanse. Comfortable with the silence, they spoke little and were not distracted from their thoughts.

He knew he should tell her about his night terrors but he feared frightening her away. He thought of the cartoon reflecting a man in the throes of a great moral dilemma illustrating a petite angel on one shoulder and a small devil on his other shoulder. Both moral miniatures were fervently advocating their positions.

Before the little devil could take another turn, Gus spoke, "Grace, there is something about me you need to know. About me and the war."

Grace took another sip of coffee, looked at him said, "Gus, I've read your book."

"Oh." He didn't know why it surprised him.

"That and I heard you fall in the floor last night."

"Yeah, that was me."

Grace felt the door was open and this was the time to address more questions. She said, "Gus, I've been here three days. Your injuries are healing. I need to go home."

Gus was unsure why panic struck but it did. He barely thought the words and they were spoken.

"Fine. But only so long as it is just to gather up what you need to stay a bit longer. I don't want you to leave. It isn't time."

"Gus, I don't know."

"I do. I waited a lifetime. I know."

"You know I'm divorced. What you don't know is he divorced me because I can't have children."

"The asshole."

"Yes, he is." Not yet reassured but feeling better, Grace smiled.

He kissed the back of her neck. She felt different, transformed, rehabilitated, a mental form and shape that lacked clear definition.

"I've waited a lifetime." He spoke to her hairline.

Somehow oddly embarrassed, she stammered, then her voice became breathy, "We need to do this and get on with it. I need us to get this over with before you start to think it is more than what it is."

Grace stepped just behind the glass door, the outside all covered with the mist and water droplets deposited by the morning air. She stopped and waited for him.

"My Uncle Bob once told me that the first time with a woman would be one of life's greatest disappointment."

"Well, maybe your uncle is right but I'll do my very best." The most enigmatic and flirtatious smile appeared. The robe puddled around her feet, leaving her in the sea-foam Isla tee shirt and a pair of Gus' ill-fitting slippers. She was beautiful.

"Let's go straighten up your bed." She extended her hand. He reached and took it.

Uncle Bob wasn't always right.

CHAPTER 37:
It's a Fine Time for a Dance

GRACE STEPPED OUT ONTO THE DECK. She sighted Gus sitting in his wooden framed blue canvas chair, the surf lapping up and over his outstretched legs. His right hand stirred the sand below the water. He allowed the sand to filter between his fingers as if searching for the perfect shell for no reason other than to briefly gaze at it and then toss it back into the surf. A fleeting pleasure but nonetheless a pleasure.

Gus was holding his sunglasses up in his left hand, protecting them from a passing wave. Using his right hand, he removed his cap and held it by the bill in the surf as if he were capturing the water. Then, he returned the cap to his head. The cool surf water escaped from the cap in relaxing rivulets. The water dripped from his cap. The surf became more placid so he put his sunglasses back on.

She couldn't help the smile that crept across her face. She was fond of the boy in the man who captivated her. As she increasingly understood the boy, she proportionally grasped the intricacies of the man.

She knew that at his core he was the boy. The boy's being was wholesome, effortless and authentic. She now understood he was happy with his own company but that he was happier when she was there.

Now in the bedroom, Grace laid out her swimsuit and cover-up. She hung her dress and folded her half-slip laying it on the bed, then her panties and bra on top it. She looked at the stack of clothing and shook her head. She knew when Gus came in that he would notice. He might not notice what she considered to be the most beautiful of dresses neatly spread on the bed but he would always comment on appealing lingerie. Such was the nature of the man. In a moment of candor, she smiled, knowing it pleased her. After all, going to the doctor today she had worn the good stuff. She laughed at herself.

As with most women possessing a modicum of attractiveness, she was accustomed to men's gazes lingering on her. While on occasion a look would make her uneasy, most often she now thought little of it.

Grace's face softened and a faint smile appeared as she recalled her mother's awareness of such behaviors. On a day of enduring the pain of swimsuit shopping, she and her mother locked eyes.

Her mother took a deep breath and her face reflected a profound resignation. Then, she said, "You know, when a girl dresses to be looked at she forfeits the right to complain when the boys look."

Grace objected.

She turned to the full-length mirror and her fingers outlined her tummy. She smiled an inquisitive smile. She glanced at her tan lines. Some doubt again started to spread. She wondered what Gus was going to think. She discarded this worry as ludicrous. Her Gus was, if nothing else, a man, unadulterated man.

She was concerned about how Gus would take her doctor's report. She was still trying to absorb the message herself. It was so contrary to the image that had evolved over recent years, the belief that motherhood would never be hers. She had accepted that this uniquely female experience would always lie just beyond her reach.

Motherhood. She dabbed away the tears.

She walked up behind him and tossed some water on him. Then, she reached around him hugging both Gus and his chair. She kissed his cheek.

Gus stood up and with a quick snap he broke his chair loose from where it had sunk into the sand. He turned the chair so that it faced Grace and the descending sun. She sat on the firm sand at water's edge so that the water only found her feet.

"Woman, you might think you're going to keep that swimsuit dry but you're not", Gus said.

She placed her hand beneath her chin and in good Italian style flipped him off.

"Did Doc say you were the healthiest woman he'd ever seen?"

Grace smiled a complicated smile. She faltered as an unfounded doubt snatched her breath. Her hesitancy betrayed her.

"Grace, are you alright?" he blurted out. The concern had shifted to him and his voice gave it away.

"Gus, I'm pregnant."

"Sweet Jesus, Grace," Gus stammered, "How?"

Grace's smile broadened. She gave mischievous shrug.

He corrected himself, "Oh, I know how! It is just I thought you couldn't – you know that you – couldn't have any babies."

"So, did I. But it seems that I can. I am. We are."

Gus shook his head in incredulous incredulity. Downright joy was beginning to cover his face. He wanted to jump up and down. He could not believe his good fortune.

Then, the question he believed he should have asked at the beginning was asked. He steadied them both in surf, made certain Grace's eyes met his and he asked, "Grace, are you good with this?"

"Oh, Gus, yes, of course I am. I was worried about you."

Gus stood up in the water and started moving around aimlessly, almost chanting, "Well I'll be damn, I'll be damn."

In seconds, he moved from the surf and reached down taking Grace by both hands, pulling her to him. He hugged her so tightly she wasn't sure she could breathe.

"Oh God, I love you, Grace Murphy."

He couldn't stay still.

He began to spin in the surf with her, the water trickled over their sun warmed skin as it splashed upon them. Their primordial dance appeared to be liberating an exultation of life, a delight too long encapsulated.

Gus hadn't said anything but Grace knew ecstasy when she was in its presence. Gus was joyous. Joy is contagious. Laughter flowed from Gus and then from Grace.

The sand fled from around their feet, they stumbled and fell into the waist deep water. Soaked they regained their balance and crawled onto the firm sand edge just beyond the surf.

It was unclear as to who kissed who but the gloriously salty kiss seemed eternal. All of Grace's concerns flowed away with the outgoing surf.

Gus said, "I guess you're going to have to marry me and make an honest man out of me."

"We can talk about it." Grace's voice sounded of a coy flirtation she wasn't certain still existed in her being until this moment.

This time there was no question, Grace kissed Gus until all that remained was an almighty passionate commitment to each other. All conscious awareness evaporated into the pure enchantment of the kiss.

Gus carried the chair over his left shoulder as they walked hand in hand toward the beach house. Everything was spontaneous. Gus couldn't control his eruptions of laughter. Grace pulled him closer until their hips bumped. They wobbled in the loose sand.

Life took on an emotion with which they were unacquainted, an intimate elation. It was exciting and filled with an anticipation of the unknown. They liked it.

They were still giggling as they stumbled behind the screen of the large outside shower. They bathed under the luxury of four shower heads. Gus thought the intense water pressure was worth every dime it had cost him to make it happen.

"Grace, I love you. I want to marry you. I am absolutely thrilled."

Grace melted.

"I'd better call Aunt Elizabeth. She will be as excited as we are."

There was no concealing Gus' eagerness to share their news with his recently widowed aunt.

"And you know she is going to want to talk to you."

Gus poured two fingers of Johnnie Walker Black and settled into his chair. He watched and listened as Grace laughed, smiled, whispered, spoke loudly so he could hear her and more than once blushed.

To Gus' astonishment, Elizabeth Kelly and Grace, soon to be Kelly, talked for over forty-five minutes.

"Gus, she wants to talk to you." She handed him the telephone.

"Auntie, --."

Elizabeth interrupted him, saying, "Gus, you are one lucky s-o-b."

She stopped, "Your uncle would just be overjoyed." Her voice hitched, then she said, "In his eyes you could do no wrong."

"Fr. Joe, how do you feel about weddings?"
"Why do you ask?"
"Oh, the usual reason, I knocked her up."
Grace mouthed a profanity to Gus.
"Remind him my first marriage was annulled."
"He knows. He's been giving you Communion."
"There are some things a lady just feels needs to be said."
Gus made a swing at her behind and missed.

Two weeks to the day later, Grace and Gus married in Our Lady, Star of the Sea Church across the causeway in Port Isabel, Texas. Father Joseph Sesek, OSA, presided.

The newlyweds honeymooned in Delta, Oklahoma. The groom's aunt, Mrs. Elizabeth Kelly, hosted a family gathering at Delta Country Club. Mrs. Elizabeth Kelly was reported to have been in all her glory. There were extensive introductions to his family, now mostly a wide collection of nieces and nephews, and friends. It was reported in the local newspaper that the couple's first dance was something to behold.

Two months later, Elizabeth Kelly died peacefully in her sleep. She had experienced no illness. She went to bed and did not awaken. She was buried beside her husband, Robert, in the Kelly Family Cemetery.

Gus was his aunt and uncle's sole heir. Settling the estate and cleaning out their home fell to Gus and Grace.
"Gus, did you know your Aunt Elizabeth kept diaries?"
"I never had a hint", Gus answered. He looked over his wife's shoulder, clearly excited at the prospect of reading his Aunt Elizabeth's words.
After a few seconds of consideration he added, "And I don't think Uncle Bob had a hint!"
"Maybe not, you know how sneaky we women can be", Grace mused.
"Well, if a guy doesn't know, he should", Gus smiled then ask, "Where on earth did you find it?"
"Oh, it is not an it, it is a them and a lot of them." With the book she held, Grace pointed to a considerable stack of Journal style books on top of the kitchen cabinet. "I found them at the very back of the bottom shelf behind all the pots and pans."
"Well, for certain that is place Uncle Bob would never have been prowling around", Gus said. He approved of his aunt's choice of hiding places.
Gus picked up a couple of the books and said, "I'm about ready for an iced tea on the front porch and a little reading. I'm certainly curious."
With an exaggerated deference to her and to the fact she was six months into her pregnancy, Gus said, "I'll bring you something. What will you have, Milady?"
"Just say it. You're afraid if I pick up one too many books, I'll go tilt."
"Oh, Fair Lady that never crossed my mind."
"Gus, you know you can go to Hell for lying?"
Gus responded, "Then, ice tea it is."
Grace smiled and reached up to kiss him on the cheek. Grace felt a wave of contentment wash over her.

Gus looked at Grace and said, "I'd be lying if I said you didn't look lush. Sweet, you just look – well I can't find just the right word for it but a luxuriously sensual look will do for now."

As she was prone to do, Grace replied with a none too subtle extension of her middle finger and then took an awkward flop back into the Adirondack chair.

"Anyone who believes an expectant lady loses her look should think again."

"Gus, just go get the damn tea."

She leaned back in the Adirondack chair. She had long dreamed of the time when a child would be growing inside her. Despite the discomfort, it was perfect. Life was perfect.

Gus placed a napkin on the table and sat the tea glass on the side table beside her.

Gus scooted his chair over beside her, adjusted his end table and sat down. He opened a diary and his aunt's script words just poured from the page into his mind. The graceful immaculate script seemed to have meticulously captured each word and each thought as if it were a work of art. Every sentence appeared to have been structured in the most unhurried of fashions.

Gus and Grace found the thoughts and descriptions so irresistible that there was a flow of words being read back and forth to each other. Elizabeth had recorded her emotions so precisely that the written words transmitted the feeling to the reader intact.

"God, it is hard to grasp how much your aunt loved your uncle."

"It seems so complete. I'm astounded at her intuitive grasp of the rest of my family. You know I just don't know what to say," Gus acknowledged then continued, "At least not yet."

Grace took advantage of the pause to ask, "Gussie, who do think she was recording these for?"

Gus pressed his right index finger over his lips and offered, "I don't know but I'm guessing for herself."

Gus thought more and added, "I don't think she intended to share some of these things with anyone."

Gus recognized a contradiction, "But she recorded everything so neatly, so legibly. Do you do that with something you don't intend others to read?"

Grace mused, "Maybe she needed to hope someone, at some future time – I don't know. I do know she saved them and didn't destroy them."

Gus felt that his answer was incomplete. He went on, "Maybe the very first volumes were for her children. But she continued well past the time she hoped for children."

"Maybe it's my hormones bouncing all over the place, but I think she ultimately wrote – and kept –these stories for the romantics in her family," Grace suggested.

Grace felt her conclusion was so hokey she thought the author and critic in Gus might josh her a bit but such censure never came. To the contrary, he nodded, his expression suggested he was giving her interpretation much consideration.

"I think you might be right. It took enormous love to write some of these passages. What she writes about war, mercy's sake. She was brutally honest." Gus' finger returned to his lips, thoughtfully sealing them so that speech could not interrupt his thoughts.

"Look, this is the first one", an obviously enthusiastic Grace said. "Cost four cents and it was a gift. Inscription says "Preserve your thoughts"."

"Gosh, does it have a date?"

"June 7, 1910. Maybe her tenth birthday?" As she said it, Grace began to read the early entries.

Then, she observed, "Can you imagine writing from the time she was a pre-teen girl until she was a woman in her seventies?"

Gus acknowledged he could not.

As Gus opened a randomly selected journal and letters spilled out. He lifted the opened flap of one and saw it was letter from his Uncle Bob to his Aunt Elizabeth during their war, World War I. Even at this time in his life, Bob conserved words. His messages were crisp and clear. His descriptions of trenches were glossy, but it was easy to see from the notes Elizabeth made in the margins that she was adept at reading between the lines.

As it can be with men and women, Gus and Grace interpreted Elizabeth's words in a somewhat different fashion. Still, each concluded that Elizabeth treasured Bob and Bob was completely smitten with Elizabeth.

Over the next week, as they read the journals together, it became undeniable Elizabeth had left them a comprehensive accounting of the evolution of her life. As if unencumbered by correctness, she had recorded both factual detail and raw emotion.

Despite knowing how the story ended, they couldn't stop reading.

Morning broke. Grace was awakened to the sound of an IBM Selectric clicking away in the spare bedroom. She sighed and settled back into the bed. Catching a hint of Gus' scent that remained on his pillow, Grace held the pillow nearby. A smile began somewhere deep inside and then crept across her face.

She said quietly to herself, "Damn, that Gussie knows how to mark a pillow."

Grace was now accustomed to the erratic tempo of Gus playing the typewriter keys. In fact, she now found a comforting rhythm in the sounds. She smiled.

She heard the ball stroke, a moment of reflective silence followed by a staccato "Shit!".

Gus didn't like something he had just written. The wheel turned. She could visualize the red wax pencil marking through the line.

Gus knocked out several more lines before he noticed Grace, her white cotton grown and robe draped over her giving the illusion of a polished marble Roman statue and beautifully framed in the doorway as the morning light poured through. It was as if the morning dew itself had nourished her skin. She glowed.

Gus slid his chair back and gazed at her with an appreciative artistic eye before he said, "Gracie, you are without a doubt the most beautiful woman I have ever seen."

He studied her. "Pregnancy becomes you."

There are times when words are simply well intended flattery. This was not such a time. Grace, outlined in the fresh morning light and deep into her pregnancy, took his breath. The camera of his mind snapped an image he would carry the balance of his years.

To say Grace was pleased with her husband's attention would be the classic understatement. She turned away, gently placing her hand on her abdomen, cradling their child.

"You are going to write Bob and Elizabeth's story, aren't you?"

"Yes."

"You know how pleased Elizabeth will be."

Gus nodded.

"And I'm pleased."

Again, Gus nodded, "She left volumes of fertile ground from which a story can grow."

Grace turned toward him and said, "I believe she wrote those for you." She tried to measure the effectiveness of her hypothesis.

"I think somehow she knew you before there was a you."

Gus's mental wheels screeched and turned at the suggestion. He knew there had to be something there. He knew it but he didn't understand it.

Satisfied, she then said, "Well, I'm going to go scramble us some eggs."

"Soft boiled."

"Scrambled it is."

Gus said, "Now you don't think you're going to come out here and stir up this mess and then go stir eggs?" He scooted the chair back and stood.

Grace contemplated his state of arousal and smiled. It would have been a lie for her to say that she was not pleased. There are times a lady needs to feel desirable. Gus left her without a doubt.

She took a step back toward their room, stopped and said, "Well, scrambled can wait."

The screech of the chair legs told her Gus would quickly be following her.

Grace was happy.

The central heat and air system had not yet been installed. On an impulse, Grace had purchased an oscillating fan from Delta Hardware. Most nights Grace had found the fan gave a pleasant assist to the efficiency of the aging window unit in their bedroom. With each pass the breeze from the fan rustled the sheet that covered them. The sheet moving over her bare skin produced the most pleasant of sensations.

She considered making her customary dash to the bathroom but she just didn't want to, she tried to lay closer to him only to find that it was impossible to be any closer.

She relaxed and lingered in indulgence. Uncharacteristically, she reached for him again and found him.

Her bathroom dash could wait no longer.

It was an hour before Gus made his way to the kitchen. He put the coffee on and had just cracked the eggs for scrambling when Grace made her way into the kitchen.

She could not describe how luxurious she felt. Motherhood lay just over the horizon, every element of her world seemed to be in its place.

Gus pulled out her chair and seated her. Standing behind her chair, he lifted her hair to one side and placed a lingering kiss on her neck.

"God, I love you," he said. He took a deep breath, exhaled and reluctantly moved on about his breakfast business.

"Coffee?" he asked.

"Yes, please." Her voice had a husky quality that surprised her.

He sat the mug in front of her and announced, "Genuine decaffeinated coffee. Folgers direct from a green can."

He teasingly chuckled. She slapped at his hand. Her smile felt so large that it made its way to the tips of her toes.

Both would admit to a stout yearning for stronger post-conception coffee. But they denied themselves.

Eggs scrambled and eaten, coffee and conversation consumed, dishes washed, dried and returned to their place in the cabinet, Gus returned to the Selectric.

Grace wasn't certain what she was seeking but she searched for it among Elizabeth's words. Words that were inconceivably intimate in their detail. She knew Elizabeth better. The warm, friendly intimate side as well as her harsh, protective side. From her own words, Grace felt she increasingly knew an expansive Elizabeth. She was making Bob's acquaintance.

As she read, she became increasingly pleased that Gus was diligently working to tell their story. Grace adored her husband.

Gus heard Grace stirring. He hailed her, "Going somewhere?"

"Yes. I'm going to St. Joseph's to get acquainted with Elizabeth's pew. Pray a bit."

"Okay, Sweet. Love you."

An announcement in Delta Tribune dated September 9, 1976 read:

Grace and Gus Kelly of Delta, Oklahoma announce the birth of their son, Robert Augustus Kelly on September 6, 1976. Robert Augustus "Bob" weighted 7 lbs., 7 oz. The Kelly family resides on the Kelly Ranch, just northwest of town.

Eighteen months later, the following announcement appeared in the Delta Tribune.

Grace and Gus Kelly of Delta, Oklahoma announce the birth of their daughter, Kinta Elizabeth Kelly on April 17, 1978. Kinta Elizabeth weighted in at 6 lbs., 12 oz.

Five months later the first galleys of My Uncle's Wife were read. The early reviews were quite positive.

THE END.